# A YEAR WITH THE MILLIONAIRE NEXT DOOR

## BARBARA WALLACE

# THE MARINE'S ROAD HOME

## BRENDA HARLEN

## MILLS & BOON

First Published in Great Britain 2020
by Mills & Boon, an imprint of HarperCollinsPublishers,
1 London Bridge Street, London, SE1 9GF

*A Year with the Millionaire Next Door* © 2020 Barbara Wallace
*The Marine's Road Home* © 2020 Brenda Harlen

ISBN: 978-0-263-27892-7

0820

**MIX**
Paper from
responsible sources
**FSC** C007454

www.fsc.org

This book is produced from independently certified FSC™
paper to ensure responsible forest management.

For more information visit: www.harpercollins.co.uk/green

Printed and bound in Spain
by CPI, Barcelona

# A YEAR WITH THE MILLIONAIRE NEXT DOOR

## BARBARA WALLACE

# PROLOGUE

*Actress Leaves Fortune to Pet!*

*Dame Agnes Moreland, who passed away last month, left her entire estate, solicitors have revealed, to Etonia Toffee Pudding—a ten-year-old pedigreed Turkish Angora.*

*The cat was listed as the sole recipient of Ms. Moreland's £11.2 million fortune. The funds are to be placed in an independently managed trust for the feline's care.*

*According to the terms of her will, Ms. Moreland's only living relative, her nephew, Theodore Moreland, of London, England, will inherit the remainder of the estate upon the cat's death.*

*Considered by many to be a grand dame of English theater, Agnes Moreland first gained recognition for her performance as Adelaide in* Come the Night *in 1951.*

*During her career she received countless honors and awards, leading to her receiving a DBE in 2012. In her later years she was known for her eccentricity, which included traveling with her pet.*

*An outside estate manager has been hired to care for the cat and manage the property.*

# CHAPTER ONE

*Summer*

STELLA STOOD ON the rooftop terrace and breathed in the warm summer air. Before her lay Belgravia, the London neighborhood whose stucco mansions and crescent-shaped streets once played home to Neville Chamberlain and Ian Fleming. Now she would walk in their footsteps.

She allowed herself a satisfied sigh. "Congratulations, Stella. You finally made it to the penthouse." And it only took a nervous breakdown to make it happen.

Her parents would say she was being overly dramatic. They preferred the term *burnout*, or better yet, no term at all, as if her freezing in midtown traffic had never happened.

Whatever the term—or lack thereof—she was here, in London, living in a luxury penthouse for the next twelve months. A pretty decent perk if she said so herself.

"What do you say, boss? Should we continue unpacking?" she asked.

Etonia Toffee Pudding lay across the top of a bespoke velvet sofa as if she owned it—which she did. Until this morning, the Angora had been bunking with Peter Singh, the estate's attorney, and upon returning home, she had wasted no time reclaiming her space. She blanked her mismatched eyes in response to Stella's question.

"I'll take that as a yes." Stella adjusted the band that was keeping her hair out of her face. The chin-length bob was supposed to be low maintenance. Unfortunately, no one told her bangs were not.

Across the room, a portrait of Dame Agnes Moreland looked down from over the mantel, a sleepy-eyed smile playing on the late actress's lips as though she was laughing at a bunch of humans kowtowing to her pet.

"I may talk to her, but if you think I'm going to start carrying the animal around like you did, you're crazy," Stella said. Taking care of the cat was part of the job, same as managing the estate's property and investments. The cat wasn't a pet. "Right, kitty?"

A knock on the door interrupted the conversation. Sharp, loud raps that made Stella jump. "What the...?" The apartment occupied one half of the top floor and was accessible only by private elevator. The only other person up here would be her neighbor from across the hall.

The knocking continued. Etonia Toffee Pudding disappeared under the sofa fringe.

"I'm coming!" Stella called. If this was how the person planned to introduce themselves, it was going to be a long year.

Looking through the peephole, she saw a man in a tweed jacket. He had thinning gray hair and blotchy skin, the kind of complexion that came from spending too much time indoors. He didn't look like the kind of neighbor who popped in for a cup of coffee. If he even *was* her neighbor. To play things safe, she slid the door chain in place before opening it.

The man's eyes looked her up and down through the opening, clearly unimpressed with her cutoff shorts and Big Apple T-shirt. "My name is Theodore Moreland," he announced, the words reaching Stella on a waft of pungent mint. "Is the estate manager available?"

So, not the neighbor, but Dame Agnes's nephew. Peter had warned her about him.

"I'm the estate manager," she answered. "Stella Russo."

Moreland scowled. Stella tamped down the flutter of insecurity that always bothered her when facing disapproval.

*His opinion doesn't mean anything, Stella. You're the one in charge.*

Lessons from her childhood kicked in—when in doubt, act as if you don't care—and she lifted her chin. "What can I do for you, Mr. Moreland?"

"To begin, you can open the door and let me inside," he said.

No, Stella didn't think so. At least not until she talked to Peter Singh. According to all accounts, Theodore Moreland had taken the terms of his aunt's will very poorly and was actively working to have the will declared invalid. Letting him inside would only invite disaster.

"I'm not really prepared to receive guests today," she told him. "I'm still unpacking and getting acquainted with my new boss."

"Are you refusing to let me enter my aunt's home?"

"You mean Etonia Toffee Pudding's home," she said, "and yes, I am."

Moreland's jowls flapped as he worked his jaw up and down. "How dare you. You have no right—"

"Actually, as the estate manager, I do. I'm in charge of all comings and goings, in fact." She made a mental note to talk to the downstairs security guard about calling before sending visitors upstairs. "Perhaps in a day or two, when I'm settled in, you and Peter can come by and we can talk."

Stella had never actually heard a man harrumph before. His mottled skin turned cranberry, calling attention to the veins crisscrossing his nose. The color reminded Stella of the drunks that used to sleep on the benches in central London. For that matter, so did the sheen in his eyes.

"Well, I never," he said in a minty huff. "I insist you let me in in this instance."

"I've already said no. You're going to have to come back next week." No longer feeling polite, she went to shut the door in his face, only to have him jam his foot between the door and frame.

*Shoot.*

"Is there a problem?" a voice asked.

"No," she and Moreland replied together.

A face appeared behind Moreland's shoulder. This one was far more attractive, with eyes the color of the Atlantic Ocean. The newcomer looked back and forth between them. "Causing trouble, Teddy?"

"This is none of your concern, Collier," Moreland replied.

"Mr. Moreland was just leaving," Stella added. "Weren't you, Mr. Moreland?"

"Is that why his foot's in the door?" the stranger asked.

"Agnes Moreland was my aunt. As her only living relative, it's my responsibility to make sure her property is managed soundly."

"Funny. I thought she asked that an estate manager be hired for that job. In fact, I distinctly remember that you weren't named caretaker."

Moreland's face grew redder. "This is none of your business."

"Au contraire, Teddy. I own half of this floor, which means you're causing a row on my property. That makes it very much my business. Now, Ms....?"

Stella smiled. "Russo. Stella Russo."

"Pleasure to meet you, Ms. Russo. Would you like Teddy, I mean, Mr. Moreland, to leave?"

"Yes, I would."

"There you have it, then. We would both like you to leave. Hopefully you will do so without further fuss.

Otherwise, I might have to call security, and I don't think any of us want the unnecessary attention. Do we, Teddy?"

Moreland's caterpillar eyebrows merged together as he glared at the two of them. For a moment, Stella thought he might argue. In the end, however, common sense won out. "I'll be back," he said.

Stella couldn't wait.

Linus pretended to fiddle with his keys until Moreland stepped on the elevator. He would be back soon enough, asserting his rights as Agnes's nephew. "My nephew is nothing if not predictable," Dame Agnes used to say. That poor estate manager was going to have her hands full.

When the news first reported that she'd left her money to her cat, Linus was probably the only person in all of London who wasn't surprised. Dame Agnes spent her life being strong willed and eccentric. Why would anyone expect her to be different in death? When it came to finding someone to actually carry out Agnes's wishes, Linus assumed the law firm would hire some kind of professional cat lady. Someone older, who wore cardigan sweaters and pearls.

Shame on him, because from what he could see of his new neighbor, she wasn't old, and she definitely didn't wear cardigans. She had better legs than he'd imagined, too. He caught a glimpse of them—all right, he took a good look—before she shut the door. Those cutoff shorts were splendidly short. God bless current fashion.

Toeing his shoes off by the front door—Mrs. Paracha hated it when he walked on her clean floors in his dirty shoes—he picked them up and headed to his bedroom. He was halfway up the stairs when his phone began to chirp like a cricket.

He let it ring several times before answering. "Linus Collier speaking."

From the other end of the line came a loud sigh. "Why do you insist on doing that?" his sister, Susan, asked.

"Doing what?"

"Answering so formally. We both know I'm the only person you have programmed to ring as a bloody cricket."

"Because." You could fill in the blank with a number of answers. Because it annoyed her. Because that was what big brothers did. Because he was supposed to be the quirky middle child and so it was expected. "Why are you calling me on a Friday night? Shouldn't you be out with your boyfriend?" he asked.

His sister was dating Lewis Montoya, the ex-footballer. The two of them made a rather odd couple, his prickly baby sister and the reformed Casanova, but they seemed to be making it work. Lewis's turnaround gave him hope that zebras could change their stripes.

"Movie night," Susan replied. "We're going to watch that rock-'n'-roll documentary everyone's talking about. Interested in joining us?"

A romantic Friday night playing third wheel? Sounded peachy.

Walking into his bedroom, he loosened his tie before lying down on the bed. "Thanks for the offer, but I've got plans."

"Really? What?"

*Anything else*, he almost answered.

"Nothing fancy. Dinner. Paperwork. A couple of pints."

"In other words, nothing."

And what was wrong with that? "I'll have you know Mrs. Paracha made her lamb stew. One doesn't walk away from such culinary perfection."

Another sigh. "Linus…"

"Susan…"

"I'm serious. What is going on?"

"I don't know what you're talking about."

"Yes, you do. You've been preoccupied and living like a monk for months. It's not like you."

Ah, but that was precisely the point. He was an outrageous flirt who hurt people without thinking. He wanted to be someone different. Someone better. "Maybe I'm on a journey of self-discovery," he told her.

"Are you? Or are you punishing yourself?"

"Must you attempt to ascribe a motive to everything?" He wasn't in the mood for her armchair psychology, especially when it cut close to the truth. "Maybe I've had a long day and feel like staying in. Is that so unbelievable a concept?"

Her silence spoke volumes.

"By the way, I met the new neighbor today," he said, changing the subject.

"The million-pound pet sitter? What are they like?"

"Antisocial. Teddy Moreland was on her doorstep."

"I'd be antisocial, too, under those circumstances. Did you see her? You did say she was female."

"Yes, she's female. American, from the sound of her accent."

"Huh," his sister said. "I wonder what would make someone cross the Atlantic to become a pet sitter."

"Giving a guess, I'd say it was because she likes cats and wants to live in London. There are worse ways to make a living."

Rather than answer, his sister let out an uncharacteristic half giggle, half squeal that left him rolling his eyes. Only one person made his sister giggle, and that was her boyfriend.

"Sorry," she said. "Lewis surprised me coming out of the shower."

"Is that what the kids are calling it these days?" In the background he could hear mumbling, followed by another giggle.

And they wondered why he didn't want to join them for movie night.

Seizing the opportunity, he wished his sister a good time and ended the call.

It was nice, he thought, as he stared at the ceiling, to see his siblings find happiness. Both Susan and their brother, Thomas, deserved it.

Someday maybe he'd again believe he did, too.

He continued to stare at the ceiling, but in his mind he saw his nightstand and the cream-colored envelope tucked inside. The letter had been neatly written, the lines painstakingly straight, each cursive loop the same height and width. Perfect penmanship to deliver a harsh truth.

It wasn't the first swipe at his behavior. Just the first one to hit home. The first one to make him truly understand the consequences of being Linus Collier, playboy.

Better to live like a monk until he learned to be someone else.

He lay on his bed until nature called too loudly to be ignored. Struggling to his feet, he made his way to the bathroom, barely registering the way the sun filtered through the terrace plants to cast shadows on the floor.

Until he heard the meow, that is. Forgetting all about nature, he looked out the terrace door and then down.

A large white cat with mismatched eyes looked back.

Stella stared at the stacks of cans in the pantry. Thirty of them, organized in groups of two by flavor. Chicken. Chicken and liver. Chicken and salmon. Chicken and tuna. Flavors were to rotate daily with no flavor repeating two days in a row. Apparently Etonia Toffee Pudding didn't like repetition. She did like chicken, though, because she was also to receive one chicken tender roasted fresh at midday. A note on the instruction file said that the housekeeper would take care of the cooking. The woman wouldn't be returning from leave, however, until tomorrow.

From down the hall, the grandfather clock chimed six times. Stella plucked a can at random and hoped it wasn't a duplicate.

"Dinnertime, kitty!" she called. *Etonia Toffee Pudding* was way too much of a mouthful.

Odd, but she assumed the cat would come running as soon as she peeled back the lid. Wasn't the sound supposed to be some kind of universal feline signal? Maybe British cats weren't as needy as American cats. She set the bowl on the floor.

Where was the cat? "Kitty?"

She headed down the glass-lined corridor, back to the living room. The velvet sofa and matching chairs were empty. No one was hiding underneath, either. "Here, kitty, kitty," Stella called. Where the dickens was she hiding?

Just then, the doorbell rang, causing her to jump. Again. So help her, if that was Theodore Moreland, she was going to slam the door on his foot.

It wasn't Teddy. It was her neighbor, the handsome one with twinkling eyes. He smiled and lifted a furry white face up to the space in the door. "Lose something?" he asked.

Stella stared at the animal in his arms. "Etonia?"

"She prefers Toffee," he replied.

Whatever. What was he doing with her?

"Found her meowing at my terrace door, asking to come in."

"But that's impossible. You're on the other side of the building." Except the terraces wrapped around the corners and she'd been standing in the opening when Teddy knocked. Stella looked over her shoulder at the terrace door.

"Dammit. I left the slider open when I went to let Mr.

Moreland in. She must have run outside while we were talking."

"Smart cat. If only we could all escape from Teddy's visit."

"I'd rather she did her escaping under a bed," Stella said as she unlatched the door. "Come here, you naughty kitty." The cat let out an indignant meow at being transferred, but she settled down once Stella cradled her. "Thank you for bringing her back. I would have had a heart attack when I discovered her missing. You and I are going to have a long talk about house rules, missy," she said.

"She doesn't look too worried."

"Probably because she knows who's the boss in this house. Come on inside. It's time for her supper, and I don't want to put her down while the door is open."

While her neighbor did as he was told, she set Etonia— or rather, Toffee—on the floor. The cat, having understood the word *supper*, immediately trotted toward the kitchen. "I wanted to..."

The words caught in her throat. For the first time, she got an unobscured view of her neighbor. Originally, she'd pegged him has handsome, but now that she had a better view, she realized that description was inadequate. Linus Collier was capital-*H* handsome. Tall and slender, he was built to wear his custom-made suit. His sandy-brown hair was stylishly cut and he had sharp features that gave him an aristocratic air. All and all, he looked exceedingly sophisticated and very British—if that was a thing. Standing there wearing a training camp T-shirt and tattered sneakers, Stella felt extremely common.

She coughed and started again. "I wanted to thank you for earlier. With Mr. Moreland."

"No need to thank me," he said, waving a hand. "You looked to have the situation well under control."

She liked to think she did, too. However, confirmation

was nice to hear. "Even so, I appreciated the gesture. It was very gallant."

His laugh was sharp. Self-deprecating. "You give me far too much credit. I was simply there for the entertainment value. Teddy's been making himself at home up here for as long as I can remember. He visited Agnes pretty much every week."

"Really?" And yet Dame Agnes had cut him from the will. Since she'd taken the job, Stella had been trying to ascertain why someone would skip over a relative in favor of a pet.

"I know what you're thinking," Linus said. "Do not mistake frequency with quality." Hands in his pockets, he strolled toward the glass wall. The late-afternoon sun caught the highlights in his hair, turning them golden. "Agnes left Teddy out of the will for good reason."

"Which was?"

"She liked the cat better," he said, turning and tossing a grin over his shoulder.

Stella grinned and looked away. The man had to know how attractive he looked doing that. If he didn't, then he was either clueless or his apartment lacked mirrors. "Did you know Dame Agnes well?"

"Well enough. Her last few years she began inviting me over for dinner, and we developed a friendship. She once made me read Othello to her Desdemona. Said practicing lines kept her mind sharp."

And having a handsome dinner companion probably kept her spirits up.

Just then, a sated Toffee came strolling down the hall. In a demonstration of superiority, she plopped herself down against Linus's leg and began washing her paw, completely unconcerned with whether she was getting hair on his pants or not.

"Do you think she knows she's worth the cost of a Van Gogh?" Stella asked.

"Oh, I'm fairly certain she thought herself priceless before Agnes passed. Isn't that right, you little diva?" Bending on one knee, he buried his fingers in the fur at the back of Toffee's head. The cat immediately began purring like a small engine. "Are you at loose ends now that Agnes is gone? Is that why you came hopping across to my balcony?"

He looked up, and Stella saw softness in his gaze that hadn't been there before. His eyes had become muted, shifting into a blue gray that reminded her of the sky right before the dawn. The change suggested there were layers to the man. That if you peeled back the charm and the good looks, you would discover something even better.

Of course, she wasn't looking to discover anything, but it was nice to think her neighbor seemed decent. She coughed away the thought, and said, "Nothing personal, but I'm planning on her escape being a onetime event. I prefer not to think of her taking that leap more than once."

"Can't say that I blame you." Giving the cat one last rub behind the ears, her neighbor stood up and tucked his hands back into his pockets. "Now that the fugitive has been returned to custody, I should let you get back to your unpacking. It was a pleasure meeting you, Ms. Russo. I hope…" The sentence drifted off, as if he thought better of whatever it was he intended to say. "I'm sure we'll run into one another again."

Stella was sure they would, too. Hard to avoid when they lived across the hall from one another. She walked him to the door, thanked him again for bringing home Toffee and said good-night. It wasn't until she locked the door that she wondered about the sentence he didn't finish.

# CHAPTER TWO

A FEW DAYS LATER, Stella found herself working outside, the penthouse terrace being nothing like her tiny balcony in New York. The wraparound exterior had been designed with both sunrise and sunset views in mind, depending upon your location. The sunrise seats were off the dining room, while sunset was a few feet from the master bedroom. Agnes—or someone—had designed the space to flow accordingly. A breakfast table and a chaise lounge led to an outdoor seating area, which in turn led to a cozy love seat from which to enjoy the day's end. Like the apartment itself, the furnishings had a vintage elegance. Given her taste, Stella wondered why Dame Agnes had chosen such a contemporary apartment in the first place instead of one of the mansions a few streets over. Unless she liked being a study in opposites.

The lives of other people, their quirks and personal histories, had always intrigued Stella. When she was younger, before she focused on more practical subjects like finance and economics, she used to love to devour biographies of the important and famous, fascinated by the way their lives had played out against world history. Dame Agnes was precisely the type of person she found interesting.

On the chair beside her, Toffee stretched and rolled onto her back, a paw bent across her eyes. The cat had fought the leash and harness at first, but it appeared she was getting used to the idea. Beat being stuck inside or plunging to her death jumping off the terrace wall.

The thought of Toffee falling caused Stella to look next door. Her breakfast nook faced Linus Collier's sunset side. Only a few feet separated their terraces. When Stella first noticed, she could see how an enterprising cat might be tempted to make the jump. The thought made her nauseous. She wondered if Toffee hadn't seen a bird or something, and that was the reason she'd leaped. Linus had a trio of potted trees arranged in the corner. The plants partially obscured her view of what looked like more potted plants. He had a mile-high arboretum. For a cat, it would be temptation extraordinaire.

To Stella, the unexpected garden proved people were multifaceted.

She hadn't seen her neighbor since the day he brought Toffee home. Not that she was disappointed. She'd expected as much. People had lives. Jobs. Linus Collier probably had a very rich social life.

"What do you think he does for a living?" she asked Toffee. "Professor? Investment banker?" Both seemed too stodgy. "Member of the royal family?" He did give off an old-money kind of vibe. Plus, she could see him playing an old-money sport like polo.

"I know, I know," she said to Toffee's uninterested face. "Speculating about the neighbor isn't going to get my work done."

She turned her attention to the file in front of her. It contained a listing of the various properties and items of value that made up Agnes's—that was, Toffee's—estate. Her task over the next few days was to account for every piece of memorabilia and jewelry listed. Hardly high-level finance, but part of the job. Judging from the thickness of the file, there was a lot of memorabilia and jewelry.

She opened the first page and shook her head. Turned

out Dame Agnes had included not only photos but background information. The top page read, "Sterling silver salt dishes from India, given by the Sultan of Brunei in 1959. We had dinner in his suite, and I complained that the curry was bland." The anecdote continued for several paragraphs.

"Oh, my," she said to Toffee. "This is going to be fun."

Before she could read any farther, however, the alarm on her cell phone rang, letting her know it was midmorning in the States, the time when her father usually took a quick coffee break.

Kevin Russo answered on the second ring. "Hey, Dad," Stella greeted.

"Stella? Is that you? What are you calling for?"

His questions always sounded like she'd made a mistake. Stella did her best to not let the tone get to her. It was just his way, she always told herself. He didn't mean to sound accusatory. "You weren't home when I called the other night. I thought I'd call back to say hi."

"You're going to have to speak up. Wherever you are has horrible service."

"Hold on." She gave Toffee a quick glance before walking over to the front railing. "Is this better?" she asked, raising her voice a little.

"A little. Where are you?"

"On my terrace. Getting a little fresh air. It's a gorgeous day."

"Sounds nice," her father replied. "We got a delivery of oranges this afternoon. Whole place smells like Florida. You arrived in London okay, then?"

"Yeah. I'm all settled in."

"Well, that's good." Her father didn't hide the fact he disapproved of her taking a leave of absence, or "running off to Europe," as he put it. The Russos had left Europe so they could make something of themselves, he reminded her. Stella would lose career momentum. "You don't see your brother or sister needing a break from their stress, do you?" he'd said.

Back in the present, he remained awkwardly silent on the other end of the line.

"I started work this morning," Stella said. She started explaining about Dame Agnes's descriptions.

"Doesn't sound like finance," her father said.

"Can't manage an estate until I know what's included."

"I don't know. Sounds more like they're taking advantage of you. First making you watch that foolish cat, and now counting spoons or some nonsense?"

"I told you before, Dad, that foolish cat is my client. Watching her is part of the job. Did Mom tell you I'm living in a penthouse?"

"She told me," her father replied. "Sounds fancy."

"It is. I've got a housekeeper, too." Mrs. Churchill, who had worked for Dame Agnes, was in the house dusting.

"That's all great, but I doubt Mitchum, Baker is going to care much about your living arrangements. They're going to want you to have done more than pet sit for a year. If you want to catch up with your colleagues."

Stella closed her eyes. *It's just his way.* She wanted to tell him that Mitchum, Baker only cared that she did not freak out on their time. What she did on her leave was her business. But she didn't. For all his harshness, Kevin Russo wanted the best for his children. Wanted them to have success in a way that he hadn't. It wasn't his fault that Stella couldn't keep up with her siblings.

Nor was it his fault he couldn't understand Stella's decision, since she didn't completely understand it herself. All she knew was that her parents' option—that she spend a few weeks in Boston and then head back to work—made her struggle to breathe. It was like the very words *Boston*, *New York* and *Mitchum, Baker* squeezed the air from her lungs. The job posting in London was the first idea that didn't make her feel like she was having a heart attack.

"I'm résumé stacking," she told her father. Her voice sounded more defensive than she wanted. "When I return, I'll be one of the few risk-assessment managers with international estate-management experience. In today's job market, it's all about being unique."

"If you say so."

For a second, she might as well have been in Boston, with her father eyeballing her with his trademark doubt. Or was it her trademark doubt? He never looked at Camilla or Joseph with anything less than beaming pride. But then, she'd always been the less-than child. The one in the background. The one who wasn't quite as smart or as talented or as lauded as Camilla and Joe.

Pushing her hair back from her face, she changed the subject. "What's going on back home? Anything interesting?"

"Your brother won his case the other day. They're starting to talk about making him a partner. He'd be the youngest in firm history."

No surprise there. She leaned back against the wall and looked toward the apartment. Toffee was awake and had jumped on the breakfast table. Her little pink nose was sniffing the glass surface.

"And I haven't had a chance to talk with your sister yet. You know what it's like being a resident. Well, you can imagine."

Yes, thought Stella, she could. She could also imagine her sister sailing through the experience. Camilla was unflappable.

"She said she may present her latest study at a conference in Spain. I was telling Marjorie Bowman the other day that when Camilla's done with school, I'm going to have her work on my brain. See if she can make me smarter."

It was an old joke, one she'd heard before. Her father told either it or a variation to just about everyone he ran into. Camilla would make him smarter. Joseph would get him out of trouble. And Stella would count his money. At least that was the joke before London. He probably didn't say anything about her now.

When she returned, though... She would kick ass when she returned and show him—show the world, that is—that she was a force to be reckoned with at Mitchum, Baker.

She forced a smile into her voice. "I'm sure Mrs...."

"Oh, for crying out loud. Don't stack them like that. You trying to bruise every orange in the crate? I've got to go," her father said. "I'm sorry, Stella, I've got to go. I'll talk to you later."

"All right," Stella said. "Love you."

Her father had already disconnected the call.

Stella set the phone on the ledge and let out a frustrated scream.

Linus loved his terrace. Over the last couple of years, he'd turned the balcony into a mini potted garden. His own high-rise nature retreat. If he was going to be alone with his thoughts, he might as well do so surrounded by flamingo trees and Australian bottlebrush.

This afternoon, having decided to work at home, he was lingering over a second cup of tea—one of the benefits of being part owner of the company. He had his bare legs stretched out in the sun while he caught up on Parliament's latest drama.

"Arrrgh!"

The cry cut through the city noise, making him start and nearly spill tea on his robe. There could only be one source at this altitude. Forgetting Parliament, he headed toward the western end of the terrace, where he spied his neighbor. She was only partially visible through the foliage, but it looked like she was pushing against the wall, her arms stiff and her hands wrapped around the metal guardrail. Unlike the other day, she was dressed for business in a purple sleeveless dress and, he hoped, high heels. Her hair wasn't pulled back today, either. It hung like a dark brown curtain in front of her cheeks.

In the old days of last year, he would have gone on an all-out charm offensive, hoping—planning, actually—to establish more than a neighborly friendship. After all, she had everything he liked in a woman: great legs and two X chromosomes. When it came to women, he didn't believe in being discriminatory.

"So long as they sleep with you, right?" his last ex-girlfriend had said.

She'd chosen to storm off before he could answer. Otherwise, he might have told her it was the challenge, not the sex, that mattered.

All that was before the letter. His new neighbor didn't realize it, but she was safe from his disreputable behavior.

Except here he was, watching her through the bushes like a voyeur. He stepped around the trees and into the open. "Are you trying to make the terrace wider?" he asked.

The question made her turn quickly. Her wide-eyed expression was made sensual by the parting of her lips. That the sensuality was unintentional made it that much more arousing. Linus willed himself to think dampening thoughts as he watched her recover. First straightening her back, then brushing the hair from her face.

"Didn't mean to startle you," he said, once she was finished. "I was reading the paper when I heard you scream. Is everything all right?"

"Oh, that." He could practically hear the blush creeping into her cheeks. "Frustrating phone call."

"I know how those go. Don't tell me work is already getting to you?"

"Not work."

Something else, then. He wondered what, but didn't ask. If his neighbor wanted him to know more, she would have said. "How is your charge doing today? No more flying leaps, I noticed." Leaning forward, he spied Toffee stretched out on a table. "Is that a harness?" he asked.

"We came to a compromise. She stays on the leash; I let her sleep outside while I work."

"Impressive. I'm surprised your arms aren't covered in cat scratches."

"She's surprisingly cooperative for a cat."

"Agnes did take her everywhere," Linus said. "She must have learned it was best not to put up a fight."

He studied the space between their respective ends of the terrace. The distance was no more than a few feet. Why had he never noticed how close the two balconies were to one another? Most likely because he seldom sat on this side. If he wanted to see the sunset, he repositioned the double chaise near the living room; the seat was far better for relaxing with company.

"I take it this is where she made her escape," he said, looking downward. Below he saw a small patch of green shrubbery.

"I still can't believe she did," Stella replied. "Something must have caught her attention in your garden. That's quite a display you've got going."

"Thank you. It's my way of bringing nature to central London."

"You mean other than the parks?" She pointed toward the Belgrave Square Garden grounds, which could be seen in the distance.

"Last time I checked, public parks frowned on you having tea in your pajamas. This way I can enjoy nature on my terms. Not to mention that I find the different foliage inspiring."

"How so? Are you an artist?"

"I like to think there's artistry involved, but my brother would disagree."

She drew closer to her side of the wall. As she walked, Linus watched the way her hips rolled into her steps. Definitely high heels. Linus tightened the belt on his robe to keep his body from reacting.

"I'm a chemist," he said. "I'm head of research and development for Colliers of London."

"Oh, I've seen their products. They sell them at some of the high-end boutiques on Fifth Avenue. Sounds like a fun job."

"It has its moments." She hadn't made the connection yet. "At the moment I'm working on a new idea—scented oils and candles based on our botanical products. What do you think of a lavender-heather combination?"

"I don't know. I've never smelled heather."

"It's surprisingly floral. The problem is I can't decide on a top note. I want something clean but not too overpowering. Mint would be my first instinct, but there's also basil and...you're smiling." A tiny, amused smile. "Sorry," he said, rubbing the back of his neck. "I take the science of scents very seriously."

"Don't apologize. You love your job. That's nice."

"It's just that there are so many possibilities and combinations, I have trouble not getting carried away. My brother and sister are forever giving me a hard time."

"But isn't that what a scientist is supposed to do? See all the possibilities?"

"Will you do me a favor and explain that to my brother the next time he tries to rein in my research budget?"

"Sure. What is it about siblings that they feel the need to…"

The words died on her tongue. *Connection made.*

Stella cringed. Talk about clueless. He wasn't just the head of R & D. "Your family owns the company."

"Guilty as charged," he replied. "Although in fairness, Colliers is really my brother's company. I'm more of what you would call an active shareholder."

Six of one, half dozen of another. He still owned a stake in the company. Explained the penthouse, and the fact he was lounging about in his bathrobe on a weekday. "I can't believe I didn't make the connection," she said.

"Why should you?"

"Oh, I don't know, maybe because *your last name is Collier.*"

He laughed at her emphasis. "Personally, I'm glad you didn't. It was nice to meet someone who didn't know my history straight off. Meant we could get acquainted without pesky assumptions."

"Why would I assume anything?" Other than his being rich, which was fairly obvious seeing as how he lived in a penthouse apartment.

"When you have a famous name, people gossip. You never know what people may have heard. You know, rumors, preconceived notions and the like."

"I see." She didn't, not really, but the shadow that flickered across his face told her not to keep asking. She understood what it was like to be saddled with people's expectations, and their disappointment when you failed to measure up. "For what it's worth, the only assumption I had was that you could afford to live next door. Unless you're squatting and about to get tossed out."

"No squatting. At least not yet." It cheered Stella to see the light return to his eyes. Without their sparkle, his eyes—all of him, actually—lacked vitality. Like how a passing cloud marred a sunny day. She didn't know Linus Collier well, but he struck her as a man with a lot of life inside him.

Huh. Looked like she had made a few other assumptions.

"Speaking of jobs," he was saying, "we got sidetracked from our discussion. How is your job going? Beyond keeping Toffee in line."

"Haven't done a lot yet," she said. "At the moment, I'm conducting an inventory of the estate. Cross-checking items listed in the records, then listing what's appropriate for donation or auction, what should be saved for historical preservation, etc."

"A challenge, considering everything Agnes did in her career. Every once in a while, when I visited, she would trot out a photograph of her and some icon. Made me think she had boxes and boxes of memorabilia hidden away in one of the upstairs rooms."

"Based on the file Toffee is currently sleeping on, I think you may be right. I'm also going to be double-checking all the financial investments. Toffee has a very diversified portfolio. Between investments and properties…"

"Did you say *properties*, with an *S*?"

Sounded strange, Stella had to admit, especially when discussing a cat. "She owns two. This apartment and a country cottage in Berkshire."

"Really? Our family had a place in Berkshire. We had to sell it when my father died."

"I'm sorry." The apology was a reflex, born out of a lifetime of etiquette lessons. Whenever someone mentioned death, you offered regrets.

Linus waved her off. "No need. None of us wanted to take the property on. Now that you mention it, though,

Agnes often talked about going to the country. Your job will be to manage everything?"

"Yes and no. There's actually a team. My job is to take care of the day-to-day management, make recommendations regarding investments and, of course, make sure the heir is comfortable." When said like that, the job didn't sound all that awesome. "It's more challenging than it sounds."

"I'm sure it is," Linus replied. He leaned against the railing, causing the front of his paisley robe to gape. "May I ask you a personal question?" he asked.

"What?" She was busy trying not to stare at the freshly revealed patch of chest hair.

"What makes a person from America come all the way to London to take care of a cat's estate? Don't get me wrong—it's lovely to have you—but don't they have estates in your country?"

"They do." How did she explain her running across the ocean in a way that didn't make her sound unstable or weak? "But this job sounded interesting. I've never worked for a cat before or on an estate with such renown. And since I was looking to get away from New York for the next year—"

"Get away?"

Bad choice of words. "Travel bug. I never got my semester abroad, so I decided to come to London for the next twelve months."

"Your plan for seeing Europe. Smart."

"Oh, I won't be traveling. I'll be too busy working to see anything outside London proper. Except the summer house."

He was looking at her, confused. "I thought you said you had the travel bug."

"I meant to see London, not the rest of Europe. I figured I'd come, spend a year seeing the city, gain some invaluable experience in British finance and then head back to New York."

She could tell Linus didn't quite buy the story, despite it being true, minus the part about wanting to see London. Whatever. She wasn't about to explain. She didn't have time, even if she wanted to. A quick look at her phone said as much.

"Sorry to run on you," she said, "but I better get Toffee inside and brushed. Teddy Moreland wasn't kidding about contacting the law firm. He'll be here in fifteen minutes to provide me with some 'historical perspective' regarding my job."

"Lucky you. If he drones on too much, close your eyes and think of England."

Stella snorted. "I think that phrase is supposed to mean something else, but thank you for the advice. I'm planning to detox with a nice long run this afternoon."

"I had a feeling you were a runner. Your legs," he added. "You have runner's calves."

"Oh. Thank you." She guessed. Compliment or not, the idea Linus had checked out her legs closely enough to notice made her warm from the inside out. "I was going to pace out a route this afternoon when I was finished work."

"I usually go around 4:00 p.m. myself. There's a very nice route around the gardens in the park."

"Is there? I'll check it out."

"I tell you what," he said. "Why don't we head out together when you're done with your meeting and I'll show you."

"You... You want to go running together?"

"Why not? I'm going to run anyway. Unless you're one of those antisocial runners who only cares about besting her time. Are you?"

"Not usually." Running was something she did for health and vanity purposes only. Keeping track of times would only depress her, as they would invariably be less than her runner siblings.

"Then why not join me? I'll show you the best route, so you'll have the lay of the land for when you go the next time. Consider it a runner's courtesy."

"Sure," Stella replied. Why not, indeed? Wasn't as though the man was asking her on a date. Back home she joined male running friends all the time. Running with Linus would be no different.

Well, almost no different. Back home, when the guys invited her to run, she didn't get butterflies in her stomach.

# CHAPTER THREE

WHAT WAS HE THINKING? Runner's courtesy, his behind. She was a grown woman, perfectly capable of using an online map. There was zero reason to volunteer to play tour guide. Except…

Something about the way she talked about herself made the nerves tingle. The self-deprecating comments—self-defeating, really—that she dropped into conversation. Her certainty she was about to be fired. When he spoke to her on the terrace, it was because he heard tears in her eyes. Over a bloody cat. Then there was a tension that emanated off her in waves.

Victoria had been uptight and self-deprecating, too. He thought it part of her charm. Considered it part of the challenge.

He'd missed the signs once. He'd be damned if he missed the signs a second time. And so, he was extending a friendly hand to his neighbor.

That's all. Just a friendly hand.

Idiot that he was, he should have thought about his ankle first. He knew when he rolled the damn thing the other day that he'd tweaked it, but he figured that between tape and adrenaline he would be fine.

Wrong. His foot throbbed, and they had another half kilometer before they reached Belgrave Square.

That'd teach him to be nice.

He looked sideways at his running partner. Stella wore earbuds, blocking any attempt at conversation. That didn't mean he couldn't treat himself to a look now and then. After all, he was embracing monkhood, not death. Her tank top and running shorts showed off her toned body to perfection.

It was funny. She had the body of an athlete, but she didn't move like one. He'd expected long, graceful strides that matched her legs. Instead, she was stiff jointed and awkward. She was someone who ran because it was good for her, but she was not a runner.

He tapped her on the arm. "Three more blocks and then turn left," he said. As though voicing the distance would make it feel shorter.

She nodded. All business.

That was another thing that bothered him. There were a few details missing from her answer about getting the job. Like why she decided to take a leave of absence from her usual job to become what was basically a glorified pet sitter. She said she needed to "get away." Why? Had something—

The dip in the sidewalk came out of nowhere, causing his leg to collapse beneath him. He pitched forward, his hands and knees skidding across the concrete.

"Oh my God, are you all right?" Stella spun around the moment he went down. "What happened?"

"Bloody dip in the pavement." He rolled over onto his rear end. The entire situation was embarrassing. People were staring at him.

"Are you all right, mate?" one man stopped and asked. "Need a hand?"

Of course he wasn't all right. His palms were bruised and scratched, his knee had a raw red patch that would be stiff in the morning and his ankle was throbbing.

"I'm fine," he told the man. "No need to worry."

"Are you sure?" Stella asked. She crouched down to eye level, her eyes wide and very brown. Like melted chocolate. For a minute he lost himself in them.

"Linus?"

"Sorry. I'm all right. Nothing a stiff drink and an ice bag won't solve. Help me up?"

He didn't want a hand from the stranger, but he would take one from her. Her palm was moist from the heat. Oddly enough, he liked the feel. Gripping her fingers tightly, he slowly made his way upright.

Only to come within inches of her concerned eyes again.

One of the things he'd learned over the years was that people had different body chemistries resulting in very different, very unique scents. Stella's scent, even with the musky undertones of exertion, was sweet. His body reacted with enthusiasm, arousal stirring deep inside.

"Thanks." He stepped back quickly, stumbling from the abruptness as well as the pain stabbing his ankle. "Dammit," he rasped.

"Is it your knee?"

"My ankle. I twisted it." So much for running. The last time he hurt his ankle, he didn't run for weeks. "I'm afraid I'm done for the day. You can go on, if you'd like. Three more blocks and turn left. You can't miss the park. It's large and very green." He took a step and winced on the word, killing his attempt at lightness.

"Nonsense," she said. "If I go on, how will you get home?" Before he could stop her, she had grabbed his arm to steady him. "We'll try walking back, and if that doesn't work, we'll flag a taxi."

"It's only a mild sprain, not a broken bone. I'll be fine. You don't need to hold me up."

"Are you sure?"

"Definitely." Besides, he didn't want to spend the next kilometer with her holding him. It felt too nice.

Slowly, the two of them made their way along the street. "I have to admit," Stella said. "Truncated run or not, the exercise felt good. Thank you for insisting I go."

"To be honest in return, you looked as though you could use the stress relief."

She laughed. "Whatever gave you that idea?"

"Your aggravated scream for starters." He'd practically wanted to hug her when she was berating herself. "Although I can't entirely blame you. I'd scream, too, if I had to spend a day with Teddy. How was it, by the way?"

"As you would expect. He made it very clear that he knew the house backward and forward. I got a complete tour. Then he made himself at home and proceeded to tell me how Dame Agnes changed her will when they had a spat, and that she had changed her mind since then."

"Couldn't have changed it too much since she kept the terms of the will."

"Oh, he knows. He claims Agnes had grown very forgetful in her later years. Not that he minds, according to him. He said his initial reaction was one of surprise, not anger. That he doesn't need the money, and it's not as if he won't inherit Agnes's estate after Toffee dies. Not that he wishes any harm to come to the poor sweet dear, of course."

Linus could hear Teddy droning every word. "Then he insisted on inspecting every room in the house to make sure everything was shipshape. This was after the tour, mind you. By the time he left, I was jonesing for a run like you wouldn't believe."

"I'm assuming 'jonesing' means you wanted one," Linus said. He liked the Americanism.

"Try dying for one," she replied. "Toffee had the best

idea. She hid under the bed for the visit. Does he always drone on that way?"

"Do you mean like a pompous windbag? Usually. I do my best to avoid him. Was he drunk?"

"I'm not sure. His breath smelled like he'd swallowed a tube of toothpaste, so he's either got incredible dental hygiene or he was trying to mask something. Did I mention how much he loves Etonia Toffee Pudding? He insisted on using her full name every time. Says he's always adored her. I think he may be planning to challenge the will."

They stopped at a corner to wait for a traffic light. Linus lifted his foot to let his good leg bear the weight a moment. "What makes you think that?" he asked.

"Nothing specific. The way he kept talking about how much he loved Toffee made me think he was up to something. I don't know him very well, though. I could be mistaken."

Was she kidding? She'd captured him perfectly. "I wouldn't be surprised if he did mount a challenge. I was at the reading of the will. What he calls surprise certainly looked like outrage to me."

"What this meeting told me is that I need to be extra careful to have all my records in order so as to not give him any ammunition. I'm going to be the best feline caretaker in Europe."

"I'm sure Toffee will appreciate the dedication." Ahead, he saw a familiar blue and red sign and smiled. "Would you mind if we stopped at that restaurant?" he asked, pointing. "Mrs. Paracha doesn't work on Mondays, so I need to pick up some curry for supper." And give his foot a chance to rest. With the adrenaline having worn off, it was throbbing more than before.

Stella checked her watch. "If we hurry," she said. "Mrs. Churchill can only stay until 6:00 p.m."

Toffee was a cat, not a child; she'd survive a few minutes unsupervised. Linus kept the thought to himself. The comment wouldn't be well received. Not after her speech about being the "best feline caretaker in Europe."

"My stomach thanks you," he said instead.

They both bought takeout. Stella couldn't resist the aromas of turmeric and fresh-baked naan hanging in the air. Exercise always brought out the eater in her.

She watched Linus hobble the last few blocks. A bad ankle did nothing to take away from his gracefulness. He even limped elegantly. When they were running, it had taken all her effort not to keep watching him move. He ran with such fluid motion, like a natural athlete. Personally, she hated running, and only did so because she liked carbs.

She also liked how easy it was to talk with Linus. As they killed time waiting by sharing their days, she tried to remember the last time she had had such a relaxed conversation. Usually her brain ran amok, critiquing everything she said and did, but not with Linus. He made her feel comfortable with herself, at least in the present.

Maybe that was why, when they reached their homes, she invited him inside.

"I just thought it seemed silly to take our food into different houses to eat alone when we could eat together," she said when he hesitated.

For the first time in an hour, she second-guessed herself. Maybe he didn't find her company as relaxing as she found his. Or maybe he feared she was misinterpreting his kindness for something else. "But if you'd rather go home, that's fine. It's no skin off my nose either way."

"No," he replied. "It would be nice to eat across from a real person instead of my television set. Lead the way."

Toffee was in the entryway meowing when she opened the door. Seeing the big fur ball safe and sound made her feel less guilty about being home five minutes late. There was a note from Mrs. Churchill on the entryway table.

"I hope she doesn't think I'm neglecting my job," she said while walking into the kitchen. The note said Toffee had had dinner, although you wouldn't know it. The crystal bowl was licked so clean it looked like it hadn't held food in the first place.

"Who? Mrs. Churchill? Why would she think that? Because you didn't arrive home when the clock struck six? I doubt she cares. Don't forget, the woman worked for Dame Agnes. I'm sure she's seen everything."

"Maybe, but I'm not Dame Agnes. Part of my job is to take care of the heiress here. Blowing off dinner doesn't look good."

"First of all, you didn't blow off dinner. You missed feeding time by..." He checked his watch. "Seven minutes. While I realize seven minutes is an eternity in cat time, it's not that huge a deal. If anything, after working for Agnes, Mrs. Churchill's probably relieved to see someone treating Toffee like a cat."

"You don't understand," she said, handing him a plate from the cupboard.

"Try me."

Maybe she was being overly conscientious, but she didn't want another failure on her résumé. What would people think—what would her family think—if she couldn't ace something as easy as taking care of a cat? "It's important I do this job right."

"Right or perfect?"

"Is there a difference?"

An odd look crossed Linus's face. Serious and intense, like he was seeing her for the first time. The expression left her feeling exposed. "You're thinking I'm an uptight nutjob, aren't you?"

"Did I say you were a nutjob? Oh good, we're in luck."

Reaching over her head, he took a bottle from the wine rack. "I was hoping she had a bottle of Viognier left."

"Before you grab a corkscrew, let me check my inventory list." There were several collectible bottles listed. Her head would be on the block if they drank one.

"Doubt you'll find this label. I bought it around the corner myself for thirty quid. A wine snob Agnes was not. When push came to shove, the old broad stayed true to her coal-mining roots."

Without waiting for a yes or no, he took out the corkscrew. Stella watched as he handled the bottle with strong, capable hands. Everything he did, from running to scratching Toffee to changing the subject, he did deftly. She could see why Agnes had wanted his company.

"You and Dame Agnes were a lot closer than simply sharing dinners once in a while, weren't you?" she asked once her glass was poured.

"I told you, she liked my company. I flirted with her. Who doesn't like being flirted with?"

By a man who looked like Linus? No one. "It was kind of you to give her the time."

He shrugged. "She was a national icon. Hardly a sacrifice. Besides, it wasn't all one-sided. She listened to me a time or two as well."

"I'm surprised she didn't ask you to be Toffee's guardian."

"We discussed it, but I don't think she thought my lifestyle was cat friendly enough."

"Why is that? Did you own a dog?"

"No, I ..." His features drew together as though he were weighing his next words. "Let's say I had an active social life until recently."

Meaning he didn't now? What happened? Something serious, she suspected, because his eyes had grown grayer. The color didn't suit.

"Does this mean I shouldn't worry about you throwing loud parties?" she asked.

"Not even a quiet party," he replied. "I'm on what you'd call a social sabbatical."

Stella assumed that was Brit-speak for sticking close to home. Again, she wondered why. Not that it was any of her business, but why would someone as handsome and charming as Linus need a break from his social life?

Afraid any further questions would look nosy, she sampled the wine instead. The label might not be expensive, but the dry taste went down smoothly. She took a large sip, savoring the metallic apricot flavor on her tongue, and let the remaining tension from the day ebb away.

"This is delicious. You have good taste."

"Thank you. I pride myself on being able to buy the best inexpensive wines in the city. I leave the high-end buying to my siblings. Scotch whiskey, on the other hand, is a different story. Give me a couple hours and I'll tell you everything you need to know."

"My father is all about buying expensive wine. The higher the price tag, the better. He and my mother took some kind of class, too, so they can use words like *bouquet* and *finish*."

"I had a stepmother who did that. Always sounded like too much work to me. Dining room or living room?"

"Living room. You can elevate your ankle. And that's a bold statement coming from a man who makes his living evaluating different scents."

"Different animal," he replied as he limped toward the sofa. "Chemistry is my job. Wine is a drink. I don't need to work that hard for my beverages."

"What about Scotch?" Didn't he say he'd talk her ear off on the subject?

"My dear girl, Scotch is nothing like wine. It's art in a glass."

"I stand corrected." The conversation was completely nonsensical, which only made her relax more.

Once Linus was seated, she set one of the pillows on the coffee table and insisted he rest his foot. Then, after making sure he didn't need an ice bag, she settled next to him. Toffee immediately jumped between them. With her head resting against Stella's thigh and her tail draped across Linus's, she began purring.

"Someone feels at home," Linus remarked.

Stella swallowed her mouthful of wine. "Maybe your company reminds her of the old routine."

"Maybe. Or she's accepted you."

"Or she decided this was the most comfortable spot in the room. Never underestimate a cat's ability to know the best place to sit." She raised her glass. "To cats and their uncanny knack for putting their comfort first."

Linus tapped his glass to hers. "And to neighbors who help you limp home," he said. "Appreciate the helping hand."

"Don't sweat it. That's what friends are for, right?"

His eyes widened. "You consider me a friend?"

"Shouldn't I?"

He looked into his glass for a moment before looking back at her and smiling. "Yes, you should." As she met his gaze with a smile of her own, Stella felt a ribbon of satisfaction winding through her. The feeling reminded her of how she felt those times when—if—she did something right and made her parents proud. At the same time, the feeling was different, too. Her parents' pride never made her insides turn upside down. Suddenly she realized why.

This sensation wasn't satisfaction—it was pleasure.

"Do you find it difficult, being the spare?" Dinner was over and they were enjoying the last of the wine. Comfortably full and fuzzy headed, Stella was relaxed enough to ask the question.

"Spare what?" Linus asked.

"Collier. You said your older brother ran the company."

"Oh, that. For a moment, I thought you were referring to royal lineage. I never gave it much thought one way or the other."

"You didn't?"

"No need," he said with a shrug. "It was always assumed Thomas would take over. My grandfather all but named him heir apparent when we were children."

"Because he was the oldest," Stella commented.

"Probably, and he was the only one who paid attention when we visited the company museum."

"You have a company museum?"

"Doesn't every family?"

Stella shook her head. "Mine doesn't."

She leaned forward and reached for the wine bottle. Sometime during the evening, she'd taken off her running shoes and curled her legs beneath her. Toffee was long gone, having moved to her favorite chair, allowing the space between Stella and Linus to shrink.

"Damn," she declared, holding the bottle upside down. Her glass was close to empty, too. First time all night. "Should we open another bottle?"

"In my experience," Linus replied, "whenever you ask yourself if you should have another drink, the answer is always no."

"Good answer." She would have said yes and regretted it in the morning. Especially since she suspected she'd drunk most of this bottle. She definitely filled her glass more often than Linus had.

"What's it like, your company museum?"

"Your typical celebration of a four-hundred-year-old company. Yes, really," he added when she gasped. "Sounds old to Americans, but it's barely a blip in British history. Like your revolution."

He grinned. She smacked his shoulder.

"There's one section where children can mix different scents to see how they blend. I spent most of my time there while my grandfather dragged Thomas around and lectured him on duty and legacy. Susan usually spent the visits asking if we could go for ice cream."

Silently, Stella agreed with Susan's thinking. Leaning her head back, she studied Linus's chiseled features, trying to imagine him as a little boy. "Did it ever bother you? That Thomas got all your grandfather's attention?"

"What makes you think he did? Oh, because he was Grandfather's choice to carry on?" He shook his head. "If anything, I was grateful. My brother carried a lot of weight on his shoulders, and it nearly ruined his life, while I was free to pursue my own interests. Besides, Grandfather wasn't stupid. It was obvious we were on different paths."

His smile grew nostalgic. "If the museum didn't convince him, my propensity for kitchen experiments did. By the way, never light flour on fire."

"Why not?"

"Trust me—just don't."

He punctuated his advice with a stretch, his arm reaching across the back of the sofa. Stella pulled her legs tighter, saving the feeling of security currently enveloping them. "Sounds like you were a natural-born chemist."

"And Thomas was a natural-born CEO, bossy git that he is. Made the division of labor quite easy."

"What about your sister?"

"Susan? Took her a little longer to find her place, but that had nothing to do with Thomas being in charge. All and all, I'd say we all mesh rather nicely."

"You're lucky." A smart person would come back with a clever answer like how a lot of family businesses had conflicts or some other response that deflected the conversation back to Linus. The smart answer, however, didn't want to come off her tongue. "You knew what you wanted to do."

"Are you saying a life of corporate finance wasn't your life's calling? No stories about little ten-year-old Stella Russo sitting in the kitchen playing with the calculator?"

She rolled her eyes. "Hardly." Ten-year-old Stella Russo was reading juvenile historical fiction and being told to stop daydreaming. "I didn't choose my career path until I was in college."

"What made you decide on finance?" He shifted his position so he was looking at her straight on, the genuine interest in his eyes catching her by surprise. Between the wine and his sincerity, she found herself answering honestly. "Because it wasn't law or medicine."

She'd never said the words out loud before. Having done so, she rushed to explain. "My sister is a neurosurgeon, and my brother is a criminal defense attorney."

"So rather than copy one of them, you chose a path to call your own."

"Something like that." More like she took a path unlikely to invite comparison.

"Your parents must be very proud."

"Of Camilla and Joe? Very."

"I meant of all three of you."

She shrugged and looked down at her glass.

Only a few swallows of golden liquid remained. She was more relaxed than she had been in years. Whether it was from too much wine or the security of Linus's company, she couldn't be sure, but thoughts she usually kept buried were suddenly comfortable bubbling to the surface. "I think I'm like your sister, still finding my way."

"No crime in that," Linus said.

"You're not a Russo," she replied. "My father has very high expectations." She tipped back the rest of her glass before continuing. "My grandfather died when my father was in high school. He had to quit school and take over Grandpa's fruit and vegetable market to support the family. Turned it in to a regional corporation. Biggest distributor in New England."

"Quite an accomplishment."

"It is." But it wasn't enough for Kevin Russo. "My dad hates that he didn't go to college. Didn't even graduate high school. Meanwhile, my uncle went to Yale and so did all his kids. Uncle Donny's always bragging about them. So, Dad has made it his mission to make sure we are bragworthy, too. Camilla and Joe are fulfilling the mission admirably."

"You don't include yourself in the list?"

"Oh, sure. I'm doing peachy." Reaching for the bottle, she turned it upside down again and watched as a trickle dripped into her glass. Barely enough to count as a swallow but better than nothing. She drained her glass.

"Did you know I finished in the top five percent of my glass at graduate school?" she asked.

"Congratulations."

"Thank you. Camilla and Joe finished first."

"I'm pretty sure a potential employer would call that splitting hairs."

Says the man who worked for his family. "I got hired by the top consulting firm in Manhattan."

"See?"

"Yep. Lasted a whole five months before I blew it."

The room wobbled when she set her glass down. She sat up and pressed her hands to her knees to still the movement, shivering slightly as her body mourned losing Linus's body heat. This wasn't the kind of confession that deserved coziness.

"I'd been doing great," she told him. "Working a ton—seventy, seventy-five hours a week—but that wasn't new. I've always had to work more than others to keep ahead.

Plus, I was working on this project that had huge potential. The kind of project that can turn an employee into a rock star."

She remembered how the night before, she and her father had talked about the project's make-or-break potential. *You need to make them notice you*, her father had said.

"Then one morning I was on my way to work, and I froze. Right in the middle of Fifty-Second Street. Couldn't move forward or backward."

As she expected, when she looked over her shoulder, Linus wore a frown. "Eventually, I managed to cross the street, but that's as far as I got. Standing on the sidewalk, shaking. I couldn't talk. I could barely breathe."

The moment was etched in her memory forever. The way the building seemed to stretch and grow larger. The rush of white noise in her ears. And the fear. The paralyzing fear that if she went inside, it would kill her.

"A coworker took me to the emergency room. Severe burnout is what the doctor said. I just knew that I couldn't go back to work. I wanted to, but I didn't want to. If that makes sense."

"What did you do then?"

"What could I do?" she replied. "Went home and told my parents I'd messed up."

"I wouldn't say you—"

Stella was on too much of a confession roll to hear him. "Do you have any idea how humiliating that was? There were Camilla and Joe racking up the accolades, and here I was, pulling up the rear. Again. So, I ran away. Couldn't face the idea of running into someone I knew and having to explain. Figured England was far enough to get my act together."

She flung herself back against the sofa, back to the security of Linus's proximity. "Now you know why I need to do the best job possible while I'm here. I need to show them that what happened in New York was an anomaly. To prove I'm not a disappointment." Her voice cracked on the last part. Damn alcohol.

A reassuring hand cupped her shoulder. Stella found herself pulled toward Linus in a semihug. She rested her head on his shoulder and drank in the comfort. "I don't think you're a disappointment," he said.

"No offense, but how would you know?"

"Your story. You may have crashed, but you picked yourself up and came to England. If you ask me, that shows resilience. Disappointments aren't resilient."

Stella pulled back far enough to look into his face. What she saw was a friendly smile. No mocking or sign of insincerity. "That might be the nicest thing anyone has ever said to me," she said.

"Then you're clearly not receiving enough compliments."

Stella met his smile.

Suddenly, the room grew small. Reduced to the sofa and the air around them. A lazy heat started low in Stella's belly, a longing for closeness. She wanted to feel a man's hands on her skin. To feel desirable. She looked into Linus's eyes and saw a beautiful gray sky. Scrambling to her knees, she let herself fall into them. Deeper. Closer. Until her lips met his…

# CHAPTER FOUR

"Stella…" He breathed her name into her mouth like it was a prayer. She felt his fingers sliding along her cheeks until they cradled her face. He combed back her hair and pulled away.

"Stella," he repeated. "You've had too much to drink."

He was rejecting her.

"Well, isn't this humiliating," she said, backing away. "I…"

Linus backed away, too. The tenderness she imagined in his gaze had morphed into embarrassment. "I should go," he said.

"Yeah, I think that's a good idea."

She kept her attention glued to the coffee table while Linus got up and limped toward the front door. "I'm sorry," he said when he reached the landing. "But I don't think either of us wants to do something we'll regret."

Not trusting herself to speak, Stella only thanked God for that. She'd rambled on about her failings and made a fool out of herself, but at least she hadn't done something she'd regret.

Linus closed his front door and collapsed against it. That might have been one of most difficult things he had ever done. *Give yourself a pat on the back, old boy. You behaved like a gentleman.* Eighteen months ago, if a beautiful woman threw herself in his arms, he would have kissed the daylights out of her. Lips that soft and delicious? How could he resist?

But he did resist. Had to. It was clear his neighbor needed a friend far more than she needed sex.

*I need to prove I'm not a disappointment.*

How could the woman with whom he'd spent the evening disappoint anyone? It was inconceivable. She was funny. Beautiful. Smart.

His rejection probably hadn't helped her self-esteem issues. Still, he'd done the right thing. Maybe that meant he was evolving into a better person. Because for once he cared more about helping a woman than seducing her.

Now if he could only stop thinking about how amazing Stella's lips tasted, he'd be fine.

When she woke up, Stella decided the best recourse was to pretend the night before never happened. Easier said than done, since she woke with a pounding headache, but she pretended that was the result of stress.

"A believable excuse, right?" she asked Toffee. The cat had spent the night at the foot of Stella's bed, her imported silk cat bed apparently not comfortable enough.

Toffee yawned and rolled on her side.

Didn't matter what the cat thought. Burying the humiliating experience was far preferable to recalling what an ass she'd made of herself. Between telling Linus about New York and kissing him…

Yeah, pretending it never happened was definitely the best idea.

Instead, she spent the morning taking inventory. One of her assigned tasks was to catalog Dame Agnes's personal belongings. After six decades of performing, the woman had amassed large collections of memorabilia, objets d'art, jewelry and other items. According to Peter, some pieces were bequeathed to friends and colleagues, but the majority were to be inventoried and then either sold or donated as part of a historical collection. Stella's job was to track down as many of the known items as possible, especially the theater souvenirs, many of which were quite rare and valuable. The task was surprisingly interesting, and burying herself in a spreadsheet was exactly what she needed. If she were focused on hunting objects, she wouldn't have time to think about the feel of Linus's hands on her skin. Or how comfortable and at ease he'd made her feel.

"Have you seen a gold-and-enamel cigarette holder, Mrs. Churchill?" she asked later that morning.

The housekeeper looked up from the desk she was polishing. "A gold-and-enamel what?"

"Cigarette holder. It says on this spreadsheet that Dame Agnes had one from the show *Suite Envy*, but it doesn't seem to be in the media room with the rest of the items."

"And you think I know where it is?"

"I was hoping," Stella replied.

The older woman swatted the desk with her dust cloth. "It could be anywhere. Mrs. Moreland was always taking those things out to show people. Once I found a crown in the bathroom."

Great. Another item unaccounted for. Circling the item on the spreadsheet, Stella made a mental note to ask Peter when the list was last updated. So far three of the first six items were a bust.

"Thanks anyway," she said to Mrs. Churchill. "Oh, and thank you for watching Toffee while I went for my run yesterday. Sorry I was late getting back."

"That reminds me," Mrs. Churchill replied. "Did you take one of the wine bottles from the rack? Not that it's any of my business, but I noticed you were one short."

There went her plan to erase last night. "Mr. Collier came over after our run for dinner and he opened the bottle," Stella said as she pretended to study the spreadsheet. The eleven-by-seventeen paper made a perfect screen to hide her warm cheeks. "He said he'd buy a replacement bottle."

Meaning she would see him again. If anything could be worse than last night's rejection, it would be seeing pity in Linus's eyes.

The sad thing was that she didn't know what she'd been thinking. She had zero interest in a relationship, casual or otherwise. But then she'd lost herself in those blue-gray eyes, and kissing him felt…natural.

Was there some kind of self-help group for people who self-sabotaged? Screwing up was a common thread lately. Mess up her job. Nearly mess up another job. Get drunk and kiss the only friend she had in London.

You'd think she didn't want to be successful.

Oblivious to her mental turmoil, Mrs. Churchill shrugged. "Don't matter to me either way. Most likely he bought the bottle in the first place. He was always bringing one when Mrs. Moreland invited him for dinner."

Stella recalled how capable Linus had looked opening the wine. The conversation had opened a floodgate of images that made her stomach turn over. She kept her gaze on the spreadsheet. "So he said."

Mrs. Churchill continued. "Mrs. Moreland loved to have him over, that's for sure. Said he prettied up the place. Can't disagree. Man wears a suit well. Her highness liked him, too." She nodded at Toffee, who was on her perch looking out the terrace door.

"He's a hard man not to like," Stella replied. Suddenly she needed some air. Excusing herself, she stepped onto the terrace, taking a moment to scratch Toffee's chin on the way by. "I'll be right back, Toff. Then I'll give you your daily brushing."

Whereas yesterday's weather had been perfect, today's was merely nice. A collection of cumulus clouds made the sunshine inconsistent. A good thing, actually, since the air was humid. Wishing it was long enough to pull into a ponytail, Stella brushed the hair from her face.

There was music coming from next door. At first, she tried to ignore the noise, but then a woman's laugh rang out.

Stella's stomach sank. Social sabbatical, her ass. He could have simply told her he wasn't interested. To further rub salt in her wound, they sounded like they were seated by his bedroom. What had he done? Left her and immediately called someone else?

Intending to move inside, where she could ignore the distraction, Stella stepped toward the terrace door. That's when the woman laughed again.

What was she like? The woman Linus preferred. He probably liked them blonde and sophisticated. Or did he prefer brunette and sophisticated? Assuming he preferred this woman at all. She could be a business associate.

Because women giggled uproariously all the time during business meetings.

She needed to check this woman out. Not because she was jealous, but to satisfy her curiosity. If she stood in the corner of the terrace, near Linus's clump of trees, she could peer through the branches without being seen.

*You're going to regret this*, the voice in her head said. *He's going to be in the paisley robe looking sexy as ever and you're going to regret spying. Just go inside.*

She looked through the branches.

No robe, thank goodness. Linus had his back to her, but she could see he wore a pale blue shirt, the cotton stretched across his broad shoulders a taunting reminder of what it felt like be nestled beside him. The woman, meanwhile, wasn't at all what Stella expected. She was short, with large breasts and a thick waist, and she wore a giant, soppy smile.

This was a foolish idea. Stella started to back away.

"Oh, hello!"

*Damn.*

At the woman's greeting, Linus swiveled in his seat. Stella stepped out of the shadows. "Hello," she greeted.

"Can we help you with something?" the woman asked.

"I...I didn't realize you had company," Stella replied. "I had a question for Linus, but it can wait. Sorry to interrupt."

"Nonsense, you're not interrupting anything. Is she, Linus?"

"Um, no. Not at all." Stella couldn't decide if the awkwardness in his reply was real or her imagination. Same went for the color in his cheeks. "What was it you wanted to ask?"

Good question. What did she want to ask? "The wine. Do you remember the brand? Mrs. Churchill said she'd buy a replacement bottle."

"Mrs. Churchill doesn't have to go out of her way. I told you I would replace it."

"She doesn't mind. It's on her way home. And this way you won't have to make a special trip over here."

"I don't mind." He stood up to face her. That's when Stella saw the reason for the woman's soppy smile. A baby sat cradled in the crook of Linus's arm.

"Oh," he replied, noting her open mouth, "this is my nephew. I'm babysitting while his parents attend parents' day at my niece's summer camp."

"He's adorable," Stella replied. Even from a distance she could see the baby's plump cheeks.

"He is a handsome fellow, isn't he? Takes after his uncle, don't you, Noel?"

Still in her chair, the woman cleared her throat. "As usual, it looks like I'm going to have to introduce myself. I'm Susan Collier."

The baby sister Linus mentioned. She was jealous of Linus's sister. *Curious*, she corrected. And she was relieved because she hadn't interrupted a date. "Stella Russo," she replied.

"The pet sitter."

"Estate manager," Linus corrected. "She's also helping to catalog Dame Agnes's property."

"Sounds interesting."

"It is," Stella replied. Susan Collier had a very sharp stare to go with her sharp tongue that made Stella wonder if the pet-sitter comment had been meant as an insult or a test.

"Ignore her," Linus said. "She came out of the womb sarcastic."

"Only way I could survive in this family. It's a pleasure to meet you, Stella. Would you care to join us?"

"Thank you, but I have to get to back to work. I really only wanted to check on Linus's ankle."

"Ankle? I thought you wanted to ask about wine," Susan said.

"Yes. That, too. Wine and his ankle. How is it, Linus?"

"Better. I taped it this morning for stability. With any luck, I'll be running in a few weeks."

"I hope so. I'd feel terrible if being my running guide caused you problems."

"No problems. It was my own stupidity."

They could have been apologizing for the kiss. In fact, part of Stella wondered if, behind the words, they were. Certainly felt awkward enough.

The rustling of leaves filled the silence between them. Stella was about to end the moment with a goodbye, but Noel beat her to the punch. He squirmed and made tiny noises of discomfort.

"I think someone is getting hungry. Rosalind packed a bottle of mother's milk. Hand him over, Linus, and I'll feed him. You two can…" She gestured between them. "Talk."

Easier said than done. The words Stella needed wouldn't form. They sat there in a giant tangle, clogging her throat.

"Look, about last night," Linus started. "If I gave you the wrong impression…"

"It was the wine," she immediately shot back. "I had way too much and acted stupidly. I didn't mean to put you in such an awkward position."

"It's not that I don't find you attractive…" She held up a hand. No need for false compliments.

"You made it clear you're not looking for anything beyond friendship right now, and truthfully neither am I. In fact, until I get my career back on track, relationships are totally on the back burner. And a one-night stand would have made things super awkward, so I appreciate you being a gentleman."

"*Gentleman* is a bit generous." He smiled as he said it, but she spied a cloud crossing his features. It wasn't the first time he'd drawn back when she complimented his kindness. Why?

"I hope what happened won't ruin our friendship," she told him.

"I'm all right if you are," he replied.

"Right as rain." She was relieved. That's why her insides felt buoyant. She could use a friend, and she enjoyed Linus's company. He was the first person she'd met in a long time who made her feel comfortable.

*Or do you mean special?*

No, she meant comfortable. Special was what she'd felt when she had looked in his eyes last night. And she was not going to repeat that mistake. She would just have to tuck *special* as far back in her brain as possible.

"So that's the pet sitter," Susan said, once Stella disappeared behind her wall. "She's pretty."

Linus hadn't moved since Stella said goodbye. "Estate

manager, and yes, she is pretty. But no, I'm not interested in her."

"Did I say anything?"

His sister didn't have to. After twenty-eight years together, Linus knew her thoughts. "We're friends, nothing more."

"If you say so." She sat down, baby Noel draped over her shoulder.

"I know that voice," Linus replied.

"What are you talking about?"

"You're using your 'I don't believe you' voice. You're playing armchair psychiatrist, looking for things that aren't there. I'm not romantically interested in Stella. We're friends and that's all."

"Fine. I'm not trying to read into anything. You're allowed to have female friends."

"Thank you."

"However, if I were to offer an opinion…"

*Here we go.* "Go ahead." He sat down. Susan's opinions could get long-winded. "What's your opinion?" As if he didn't know what she was about to say.

"You can't spend the rest of your life feeling guilty. What happened with Victoria wasn't your fault."

"I didn't help matters." A more sensitive man, a more empathetic man, would have recognized Victoria's troubles. But no, he'd been focused on conquest, and once he succeeded, he'd moved on. "I should have realized how unhappy she was."

"How? No one realized, Linus. Not even her family."

So everyone continued to tell him, but he had been Victoria's lover. The role demanded an intimacy that he'd failed to achieve.

What Susan and the rest of the world failed to realize was that his guilt ran far deeper than Victoria. For years, he'd treated women as objects to pursue, writing off their post-breakup insults as brokenhearted rants. They were the problem, he told himself. After all, he never pretended the relationships were anything but physical and casual.

Ultimately, it didn't matter if he was the direct or an indirect factor in her death. He was still a bloody ass.

"One would think you'd be happy for me," he said to her. "I'm in a platonic relationship with a woman."

"Break out the champagne. Hell hath frozen over."

"Damn straight." He needed this friendship with Stella, if not to help her, then to help himself. To teach himself how to be a decent human being.

"And, before you ask, the lady is not interested, either," he added. At least, not when sober. "She's one hundred percent about the job. Makes Thomas look rational."

Susan let out a whistle. Their brother tended to commit in the extreme, including managing the company. "Sounds hard-core for a pet sitter."

She wasn't a pet sitter, but Linus didn't feel like arguing the point. Besides, after their conversation last night, he wondered if Stella's drive to succeed wasn't powered by something deeper. All her talk about coming up short in comparison to her siblings. "Her family is very accomplished," he said. "Her parents, her siblings all have successful careers. Lawyers, surgeons."

"And she feels like the family outlier. I understand."

Yes, she did, better than most. "But you carved your own space."

"Wasn't easy, what with Mother always criticizing and living with you two Greek gods." Linus laughed at her description. "Honestly, it wasn't until I found Lewis and realized I was lovable on my own merits that I finally grew comfortable in my own skin."

Another reason why he placed such value in maintaining a platonic relationship with Stella. She needed someone to prove she mattered regardless of what she did for a living, and that could only happen if she trusted him. For once, the woman's needs mattered more than his.

Maybe he was evolving.

He and his sister spent the afternoon cooing over Noel's cuteness until the baby fell asleep. "I'm not sure who is more tired," he told Thomas. "Smiling at a baby all day is a lot of work."

His brother just laughed and picked up the collection of toys and snacks left strewn around Linus's living room. "He is deceptively charming, isn't he? Must be the Collier in him."

"Which version? You, me or Dad?"

"Right now, I'd say he's leaning toward you. The other day, we were out for tea and some random woman gave him a treat simply because he smiled at her."

"Better watch it," Linus said, "or he'll be trying to steal kisses on the schoolyard before you realize it."

"Well, at this rate he won't have to try too hard, will he? Another one of his uncle's qualities it looks like he inherited."

*Hopefully not*, thought Linus.

"Noticed you're limping. Don't tell me, you tripped over my boy?"

"Nah. Rolled it while out for a run." Briefly, while Thomas buckled Noel into his carrier, Linus relayed what happened with Toffee and how that had led to him going for a run with his new neighbor.

"Can't say I blame her," Thomas said, regarding Stella's stress about her meeting with Teddy. "Although next time you want to calm someone down, I'd take it easier. You're lucky you didn't break your bloody leg. You must really like this woman."

"We're friends. Nothing more," Linus replied. "Neither of us is interested in anything more."

"Well, friends are nice, too." Thomas looked like he was about to say something more, but thankfully he changed his mind. Linus was not in the mood to have a second conversation about his friendship with Stella. Honestly, was it so difficult to believe he had a platonic relationship with her? How much of a playboy had he been for both his siblings to jump straight to the same conclusion?

A few moments passed in silence, Thomas chewing his lip as he finished his last-minute gathering. "You know you can talk to me if you need to," he said once his arms were full. "About anything. Lord knows you were there for me when Rosalind and I had our problems."

"Because you and Rosalind were meant to be together. Anyone with two heads could see how much you loved one another. Trust me, this isn't the same thing. Not by a long shot."

Thomas wasn't like their sister, thank goodness, and didn't press. Inside, Linus let out a grateful sigh of relief. He wasn't in the mood to explain things again.

Seriously, how many times could he explain that he was not romantically interested in Stella?

Even if he had dreamed of her kiss all evening long.

Having declined Thomas's invitation for dinner, Linus poured himself a glass of stout and limped back to the garden. Not that he didn't love his family, but he wasn't in the mood to play fifth wheel.

The air had grown thicker over the past few hours. Looking up, he saw the beginnings of dark clouds. Rain was coming. Usually, he liked the fresh, musky smell that permeated the air just before a storm. It was the smell of anticipation.

Tonight, the scent left him with a hollow feeling. If he didn't know better, he'd say it felt like loneliness. Felt lonely.

More likely, he was simply unsettled after all the talk about Victoria. And Stella.

He wondered what his neighbor was up to. Was she, like him, planning on a night of paperwork and television?

There was only one way to tell. Setting down his drink, he limped over to his favorite rock. Stella's garden was empty. The terrace doors and windows were locked tight. Crickets chirped in the emptiness. How they made it to the top of his building, he hadn't a clue, but their noise could be heard along with the steady hum of an air-conditioning unit. He imagined Stella sitting at her dining room table, carefully balancing a plate of whatever Mrs. Churchill made so she didn't spill on the paperwork spread before her. Occasionally talking to Toffee who, no doubt, wanted whatever was on the plate.

Last night's conversation bothered him in ways he couldn't describe. The way she talked about not measuring up, as though life were a competition for a prize. She was a beautiful, intelligent woman. How was it that he could see her laudability within five minutes of meeting her, yet she couldn't?

Why did it matter to him?

*Because you like her.*

Of course he did. They were friends, and friends cared about one another. Granted, his feelings were a bit intense for someone he'd just met, but he blamed the intensity on his issues. Bottom line was that two years from now, he didn't want to hear that sweet, tightly wound Stella had had another breakdown. Or worse. The girl needed to know her worth, and he, as a friend, needed to help her unwind and believe in herself.

An idea started to form.

# CHAPTER FIVE

STELLA WAS FLUMMOXED. She'd spent the last week gathering and organizing the items on Dame Agnes's inventory list, and, by her count, at least a dozen items were missing. Things like a silver cigarette lighter. A pair of garnet earrings. A topaz brooch. All small to midsize, and all things that Dame Agnes could have given away. Or that could have been removed from the house unnoticed.

For fun, she searched the online auction houses for Agnes Moreland memorabilia, but the only items were Playbills and autographed photos.

"I don't suppose you know," she asked Toffee.

If she did, the cat wasn't talking.

Tired of staring at pages with no answers, Stella tossed her pen on the table. "How about I get my apron and give you a brushing, Toff?"

Brushing Toffee's white coat was one of her daily duties. The first time, Stella found her skirt covered with white fur. Since then, she'd made a point of wearing a protective apron.

As soon as she saw the brush, Toffee jumped on the sofa and flopped on her side. "You are so spoiled. In my next life, I'm coming back as a cat so someone will stroke my fur every afternoon."

Not that she'd tell Toffee, but the ritual was one of her favorite parts of the day. The slow, methodical strokes were like meditation. Her shoulder muscles would relax and she'd finish in a calmer mood. Maybe, when she went home, she'd get a cat, too. So engrossed was she in her task that when the doorbell rang, she didn't hear it. Only when she heard Mrs. Churchill talking to someone did she realize there was a visitor.

*Please don't let it be Teddy Moreland.*

It was Linus. "Hello, stranger," he greeted. A grin broke across her face. He was dressed for work, in a gray suit similar to the one he'd worn when they first met, only instead of the glasses in his breast pocket, they were perched on the bridge of his nose. He gave off a very sexy professor vibe as a result.

"Hello to you, too. I haven't seen you all week." She'd kept an ear out for noise every time she stepped outside, but his backyard had been quiet, and his house was dark whenever she looked over from her balcony.

"Sorry for that. Been burning the midnight oil for a bit. Joint meeting with sales and marketing. How goes the battle?"

"If you mean the daily quest to make Toffee's life as easy as possible? Look for yourself." She leaned against the back of the sofa so he could see the cat sprawled across her lap.

"Looks to be going well. I'm sure she has complaints, though."

"She's a cat. Of course, she has complaints. I see you're still limping."

"Only at the end of the day," he said as he took a seat across from her. Across from, not next to.

"I guess that means you're not here to see about a run."

"No. Actually I'm here for another reason. Would you stay, Mrs. Churchill? It involves you as well."

"Me?" The woman's confused face matched Stella's. "What do you need me for?"

"I need a favor," Linus replied. He looked back at Stella. "Have you seen any of London since you've arrived?"

"Sure, I have." The other morning she'd run a few errands and seen Piccadilly Circus.

"I mean, really seen it? Buckingham Palace, Trafalgar Square, the Eye... You do know what the London Eye is?"

"Don't be ridiculous. Everyone's heard of the Eye." It was the big Ferris wheel thing on the other side of the Thames. "But I'm not here on vacation. Sightseeing isn't part of the agenda."

"It is tonight," he announced. "I refuse to let you spend a year in London without seeing everything our city has to offer."

He wanted to take her sightseeing? Memories of what happened the last time they went out together flashed before her eyes. "I don't think... I have a lot of work to do."

"All work and no play makes Stella a very dull girl."

"Are you calling me dull?" The words came out louder than expected, startling Toffee off her lap. "I have a job to do. I'm still trying to sort out the inventory inaccuracies."

"Which will still be there in the morning."

"And what about Toffee?" She'd already explained why she didn't treat the animal like a regular pet.

"I don't think Toffee would like sightseeing." He responded to her glare with a smirk. "Toffee is precisely why I asked Mrs. Churchill to stay. Would you be willing to watch the cat for a few hours while I show Stella Tower Bridge?"

Dear Lord, not only was he asking Mrs. Churchill to stay and cat sit, but he was making puppy-dog eyes. "Mrs. Churchill shouldn't be expected to—"

The housekeeper cut her off. "You know I could never say no to you."

Who could? Those eyes were impossible to resist, all big and steel blue.

"I'd be glad to stay a few hours," Mrs. Churchill continued. "It'll do you some good to get out of the house, Ms. Russo."

With a sigh, Stella looked at the dining room table and the spreadsheets strewn across the surface. If she were serious about doing the job right, she'd stay home and begin grouping items into lots. That's what Camilla or Joseph would do. They'd buckle down and focus on the task at hand.

She turned back to Linus. There was something anxious beneath his plaintive expression, as though he needed her to say yes. Her imagination, she decided, although her stomach fluttered anyway.

This was her first time in London. And honestly, she doubted even her driven siblings would be able to resist Linus Collier's plaintive expression.

"All right," she said. "Let me get my walking shoes."

"It's at least two hundred years old. There's a note in the paperwork saying the count sent it to her with a marriage proposal after watching her onstage. I mean, who does that?"

"Very rich men with very little common sense," Linus replied.

They were on their way to dinner on the South Bank of the Thames. Linus had promised her a dinner with a view that he said would take her breath away.

On the way, Linus asked about her day, which he probably regretted, because she'd been chatting his ear off ever since. She couldn't help it. Dame Agnes Moreland had been an amazing woman. Every item she inventoried had a spectacular origin story. More than once, Stella had stopped what she was doing to investigate a source online. That's how she learned the backstory behind the bracelet Count Domenici gave Agnes.

"What's more," she continued, "she kept these things in her jewelry box like they were something she bought at a local jeweler. Clearly the woman didn't worry about theft."

"You mean the woman whose cat is wearing a diamond collar? Definitely not."

She matched his grin. "I know Peter was talking about selling the pieces, but I'm hoping he'll reconsider."

"In favor of what?"

"A collection of some sort, maybe?" She didn't know. "I just think it would be a shame to sell them off at auction when people might enjoy learning about Dame Agnes's life. You know she left diaries, too?" Stella had lost another few hours to reading them in the name of research.

"What?"

Linus was studying her with an odd expression. She couldn't tell if it was amusement or appreciation. There was definitely a sparkle in his eyes. "Your expression," he said. "It's obvious how much you're enjoying yourself."

"I've always been fascinated by artifacts and antiques," she said. "There's something almost magical about holding a piece of someone's history in the palm of your hand."

"I'm surprised you didn't go into the field, then."

"Business was more practical." And a fascination didn't make a career. At least not one of note. *The world is full of baristas who majored in history*, her father liked to say. "Anyway, I sent a long email to Peter this morning with my suggestion and letting him know I've made notes on the pieces. Hopefully, he'll consider it. If not, the expanded backstories might drive up prices."

"If you believe that strongly, why not offer to stay and curate the collection yourself?"

She liked how he thought she was capable enough to do the job. "First of all, I'm not an experienced curator, and besides, I already have a plan, remember? I'm heading back to New York." Didn't matter how much she enjoyed her current task. She had things to prove.

The London Eye came into view. The giant wheel, with its oval passenger pods was already lit for evening. A pale pink circle in the blue sky.

"Best way to see as much of London as possible in one shot," Linus said.

Stella looked up at the top car, hovering over four hundred feet above the city. Small wonder there was a long line waiting to board. Her stomach rumbled in protest at having to wait.

"I know you suggested dinner and a ride, but do you suppose we could do dinner first?" she asked. "I'm starving."

A sparkle appeared in his twilight-colored eyes. "Or we could dine and ride. The two aren't mutually exclusive."

"Fine with me." A hot dog and a soft drink while standing in line worked for her.

To her surprise, however, Linus took her elbow and, bypassing the crowd, walked straight to the entrance.

"Right on time, Mr. Collier," the woman at the ticket wicket replied when he introduced himself. "Your car will be arriving any moment."

Stella looked at him through her fallen bangs. "You reserved a car?"

"I did more than that," he replied.

Since the wheel moved slowly, there was no need to wait until it stopped moving to board. Passengers could walk on and off the cars with ease. As they strolled down the ramp, Stella noticed the car approaching contained a table set for two. It had a white tablecloth and a pair of artificial candles—real ones being too much of a fire hazard. There were two plates, two large goblets and an ice bucket positioned on the floor nearby.

Stella's insides swooped. "A private dinner?" For her?

"Knowing how you hate leaving Toffee with a sitter, I was afraid you might grow impatient taking time for both dinner and sightseeing. Therefore, I decided to multitask. Of course, if you're feeling awkward, we can tell them to let on a few more passengers."

A worker hurried past them to place a large square box in the center before hurrying off again. Pizza. That's when she noticed the ice bucket didn't contain champagne, but rather a growler of British brown ale. "I'm not sure we have enough food for guests," she said. The pizza only had eight slices.

"I was trying to stay low-key. The gesture felt romantic enough as it was."

And heaven forbid she get the wrong idea. "Pizza and beer are perfect," she replied.

The pod doors slid closed, leaving them to begin their ascent. The Plexiglas space was purposely designed to hold multiple passengers. Despite this, it felt very small and crowded. Linus was the kind of man whose presence took up a lot of space, no matter what size the room. She could feel his energy all around them.

While he busied himself with pouring the beer, Stella took a slice of pizza and walked to the window. Linus was right. London was a beautiful city. Although sunset was still a few hours away, Big Ben blocked the late-day glare, allowing them a perfect view of Westminster Abbey and Westminster Bridge. Across the way tour boats drifted up and down the river. They ate standing up, and as they moved higher, she spotted Tower Bridge in the distance. She could also see Trafalgar Square with its columned tribute to Admiral Nelson in the center.

"It's amazing," she told Linus.

He took a sip from his beer. "The best time for a ride is right at sunset, but this isn't bad. Look off in the distance. You should be able to just see Buckingham Palace through the trees."

For the next several minutes, Linus played tour guide, pointing out landmarks and providing amusing anecdotes. Buildings he didn't know, he cheekily made up. Stella guessed this when he described one building as the Ministry of Monkey Business.

"You've done this before, haven't you?" she remarked. His patter was too smooth and polished to be the first time.

He ducked his head, pink streaking his cheekbones. "Once or twice. Never served them pizza and beer, though."

More like champagne and truffles, she bet. Knowing he put in the extra effort to do something different made her feel special. Respected.

"Which building is your company?" she asked.

"Hold on." Setting his beer on the window ledge, he stepped behind her and grasped her shoulders, gently angling her body eastward. "Do you see that high-rise tower with the gray slanted roof? Next to what looks like a greenway? Colliers is about two blocks northeast."

"I'll take your word for it." All Stella could see were rooftops. Linus remained behind her with his hands resting on her shoulders. The half embrace was warm and soothing, like being draped in a blanket. He'd long since shed his jacket in favor of rolled shirtsleeves. Stella swore she could feel his shirt buttons brushing the zipper of her dress. If she relaxed her neck, her head would rest on his shoulder.

"Are you having a good time?" he asked, the timbre of his voice running through them both.

"Very." Hearing the way her voice sounded—like a breathy whisper—startled her back to reality. She pulled away, clearing an imaginary frog as she did so. "Very," she repeated. "I wish we had something like this in New York. We have the Empire State Building and the Freedom Tower, but…well, I guess they offer the same thing except you're not moving." She was babbling. Where was her beer?

"Here." Coming to her rescue, as usual, Linus appeared with her glass. "Need more?"

"Please." Her cheeks were still warm.

He lifted the growler from the bucket and filled both their glasses. "Speaking of New York. You never said what it is you did there, or rather, what it is you hope to return to."

"Didn't I?"

"Only that you worked for a consulting firm," he replied, handing over her glass.

"Not a consulting firm. The top international consulting firm in the city." Every time she said that, a bundle of nerves went off in her stomach. "It's incredibly competitive to get hired. They only take the top candidates."

"Congratulations, then."

"Thank you." But the good wishes felt undeserved. Was that why she was doing such a hard sales job?

"They must think very highly of you if they were willing to grant you a leave of absence."

"Either that or they're afraid of a lawsuit." It was a joke, but it fell awkwardly. Maybe because it wasn't out of the realm of possibility. "Anyway, I was hired to do risk assessment. Analyze companies' plans for expansion and so on."

"Sounds interesting."

She hoped so. "It's definitely a field with room for growth, that's for sure." Sipping her drink, she strolled to the other side of the pod, where St. Paul's dome could be seen shining in the sunlight.

"Which is important," Linus remarked. "Growth potential."

"Of course. Not much of a career if you can't move up the ladder."

"Number one or nothing."

"What?" He'd spoken softly, almost as if talking to himself.

"I said, number one or nothing. You gave me the impression that it's your family motto."

Right. She remembered her embarrassing behavior that night. "In case you forgot, I was a little drunk. I said and did a lot of stupid things."

"No, you didn't." Said in a gentle voice, the words took Stella aback. Linus closed the distance between them. "Haven't you ever heard the phrase *in vino veritas*?"

In wine, truth. She rolled her eyes. "Wine also brings on pity parties."

"Is that what happened?"

Which time? When she bemoaned being the family loser or when she kissed him? The kiss was…a moment of weakness. A foolish overreaction to someone making her feel special.

"I have a lot of regret over what happened in New York. I spent my entire life working my tail off only to blow it by freezing up while on the job. If you were in my shoes, wouldn't you indulge in a pity party or two?"

"I suppose I would."

*But…* The unspoken word hung there between them. Stella resisted rubbing her shoulders. Sometimes it felt as though Linus didn't believe her answers. He had this way of looking at her as though he were looking beyond her surface and trying to read her thoughts.

She studied him back, taking in the way he leaned against the window rail and drank his beer. The relaxed posture was deceptive. She could tell from the way his index finger tapped the railing that he was mulling over his next comment.

"Go ahead," she said. "You obviously have something you want to add."

"Not really. I was thinking, is all."

"About what?"

His attention dropped to his glass. "I couldn't help but notice that when you were talking about cataloging Agnes's memorabilia, you were so excited you were practically bouncing. Yet, when it came time to talking about the job that you call your life's goal, you had far less enthusiasm. Hardly any, to be honest."

"Because cataloging Agnes's belongings is my current job. New York is still a year away. Doesn't it make sense that I would be more enthusiastic about the work I'm actually doing? I'm sure when next spring arrives, I'll sound equally bouncy. More so."

"You're right," he said.

"I know I am." Even as she defended herself, an uneasiness twisted in her stomach. Dammit, he was making her doubt herself.

Linus again contemplating his beer didn't help. "May I ask one more question?' he asked her.

"What?" Why ask for permission? He was going to ask whether she said yes or no.

"Your plan is to climb as high up the corporate ladder as possible, right? What are you going to do if you can't move up? If you aren't able to take the risk-assessment world by storm?"

Failure wasn't an option. "This isn't like your family company where everyone stays for hundreds of years. If there isn't a promotion available at one company, I'll move to one where there is one."

"Building a career is that important?"

"Building a career that matters is that important. You wouldn't understand," she told him. "You're already successful."

"I was under the impression success was a personal definition."

"Says the man whose role in the family legacy is already

secure." She slapped her drink on the table and stomped to the opposite window. The conversation left her irritated. Who was he to judge her plans?

"I'm sorry," he said from his side of the observation pod. "I didn't mean to spoil the evening. I shouldn't have said anything."

No, he shouldn't have. Why did he? "What does it matter to you what my life plans are, anyway?"

There was silence, followed by the sound of footsteps. When he spoke, his voice was close to her shoulder. "Because you're my friend," he said, "and I'm concerned about you."

"Concerned?" Stella nearly laughed, except she could tell by the tone of his voice that he was serious. A fact confirmed by the look in his eyes when she turned around. "Why?"

"You remind me of someone I used to know. Her name was Victoria. She also took things—life—very seriously. Too seriously, some might say."

"Let me guess, the two of you dated."

His expression grew somber. "We had a short relationship, yes."

"All right, I remind you of an ex-girlfriend." One, if she were to guess from his expression, that didn't leave him with fond memories. "I don't understand why that has you concerned. We aren't dating, so there's not going to be any kind of messy breakup. If anything…"

"She died."

Stella stopped talking. She hadn't stopped to think the relationship might have ended tragically.

"Apparently she had a prescription for sleeping pills."

Oh God. Stella felt sick to her stomach. She waited for Linus to say it was an accident, but there was no such reassurance. Her irritation disappeared, replaced by an ache over the regret in his voice. This was the reason for his "social sabbatical." The reason he wasn't dating.

Instinct told her there was also more to the story. Setting aside, for the time being, what he was implying about her, Stella sat down at the table. "Tell me everything," she said.

Linus ignored her invitation to sit down. He hadn't intended to talk about Victoria, hadn't planned on mentioning her at all, but listening to Stella go on about needing to prove herself triggered something. She'd looked so happy talking about curating Agnes's collection. Her face lit up. Unlike the desperation that simmered beneath the surface whenever she talked about New York. Suddenly, he'd needed to make her see the difference. Make her question if going back to New York would really make her happy.

Instead, she was asking him to confess the depths of his insensitivity. How the tables did turn.

Then again, he'd opened the door, hadn't he? Spying his half-empty glass on the table, he grabbed it and headed to the window, standing with his back to Stella and the Lambeth landscape. "She was a graphic designer. Colliers hired her when we were redesigning our packaging. She was very, very good. Took her job very seriously." Like she took everything. "The two of us hit it off."

"You had a workplace fling," Stella supplied.

"In a word? Yes. Generally I avoid them—having seen the mess my father made by marrying his secretary, I knew better. But I broke my rule with Victoria."

"She was special."

"She was a challenge." He turned so Stella could see his face, not wanting her to mistake guilt for grief. "She was adamantly opposed to an affair, but eventually I wore her down. I can be quite persuasive when I want to be."

A smile teased the ends of her mouth. "So I've noticed," she replied. "How long were you, um, together?"

"A few months. Project ended and that was it. She took the news poorly. Like I said, she took things seriously, including our relationship."

A right awful scene it had been, too. "I knew she was tightly wound, but I should have realized there were deeper issues. If I'd paid better attention… If I were a better person…" But no. He'd behaved as he always did. "Instead, I saw she was getting ideas, and I ended things. Because I didn't do serious. Two years later…"

"Wait," Stella interrupted. "Two years? You're not blaming yourself, then, are you?"

Linus sighed. She wasn't thinking anything he hadn't thought himself. Only someone with an ego the size of Europe would think a woman was so in love with him that she'd be mourning the breakup two years later.

Thinking of the letter tucked in his nightstand drawer, he shook his head.

"Only in the sense that I was a contributing factor—one of many contributing factors, I'm sure." And it didn't negate the fact that he had behaved poorly.

"But you're talking about two years. Anything could have happened in that time. You don't know what was going on in her head."

"I got a letter."

Once again, he left Stella speechless. She sat still as a rock, with her eyes focused on her clasped hands. In a way, he was grateful she wasn't looking at him. He wasn't sure he wanted to see her expression. "I never told anyone, but it arrived the day after I heard the news. She apologized for not living up to my expectations. As if she was the problem, and not me. Victoria's sister said she'd written dozens of those letters."

"Sounds like she had a lot of demons," Stella said.

"Making my behavior all the more deplorable." Damn, but he wished people would stop letting him off the hook.

"My entire life, I've been a playboy. Women were for pursuing, not for commitment. If I had taken time to see Victoria—to really see her—I would have realized she was more than tightly wound. Maybe I could have helped. Or at the very least left her alone."

After being trapped in his head for months, the words came out in a rush, eager to be free. When he finished, he felt his shoulders sag under their weight. "The whole situation made me realize I needed to rethink my behavior," he said. "How I treat women."

"So you stopped dating."

He looked down at his glass. "Better I spend the time working on myself, right?"

"Oh, Linus."

"Don't," he said. "I didn't tell you to make you feel sorry for me. It was so you'd understand why I'm worried."

Stella didn't respond. Chancing a look, Linus saw her staring at her hands, which were tightly clasped in front of her. "Do you really think me that unstable?" she asked finally.

"No. I don't think you're unstable at all. But the way you take your position, that is, the way you're so hard on yourself when you make mistakes. I don't want someone I…" The explanation stuck in his throat, forcing him to cough. "I worry. Isn't that what friends do?"

Stella continued staring at her hands. The wheel was nearing the end of its rotation. He'd paid for a second trip, but he wouldn't be surprised if Stella insisted on leaving.

"I suppose they do. I've never really had a friend close enough to pay attention before. I was always too busy working or studying or whatever."

Proving his point, Linus wanted to say, but he didn't. Instead, he gave a soft laugh. "Then it's a first for both of us."

That earned him a look. "Are you trying to tell me you don't have friends?"

"No, I've plenty. Just not women." Sisters and sisters-in-law didn't count.

"Lucky me, then."

Their car reached the landing platform. Stella glanced at the doorway, then stood up. To his surprise, however, she walked away from the door, toward him, stopping inches away. Her eyes were dark and serious as she searched his face. "I'm not Victoria," she said.

"I know." Despite their similarities, there was no confusing the two. Everything about Victoria had radiated delicacy and fragility, whereas Stella was strong and capable, more so than even she knew.

"I was burned out that day in New York. Burned out and exhausted." Reaching out to cradle his face, she forced his eyes to stay locked with hers. "And you're not a bastard. At least not to me."

"Don't get too confident. There's still time."

She didn't rise to the bait. "Don't sell yourself short."

Suddenly, her arms were wrapping around his shoulders, throwing his entire body into alert. Muscles stiffening, he tried to back away. "Stella."

"Relax," she replied. "It's only a hug. Friends can hug one another, can't they?" Without waiting for a response, she pressed herself closer, her chin coming to rest on his shoulder. "I'm honored to be your first," she whispered.

How did this happen, Linus wondered. How did his precautionary tale switch into his receiving comfort? As he slowly returned the embrace, Linus felt something shift in his chest. Something large and swooping, as though it was his insides and not the Ferris wheel resuming the ascent. It was a foreign, heady feeling that he wanted to hold on to and never let go.

What was he going to do when things began to descend?

# CHAPTER SIX

*Autumn*

"WHAT ARE YOU doing this weekend?" Stella asked.

"Same as last weekend," Linus replied.

In other words, nothing.

The two of them were preparing for a run around St. James's Park. Since Linus's ankle had healed in mid-August, they'd made running together an afternoon habit. At first it was around the neighborhood, but as his ankle grew stronger, Linus began taking her on longer routes past historic landmarks. Sometimes they even took the Tube to run other sections of the city. It was all part of his insistence that she see more of London than one aerial tour.

Things had changed following their spin on the Eye. There was a connection between them, a closeness. Linus's confession touched her in a way she couldn't explain. The look she saw in his eyes struck her square in the chest and squeezed until she wanted nothing more than to hug away his pain. Ironic, since he began the conversation by suggesting she was the one in crisis. It wasn't until after the ride ended and they were on their way home that it occurred to her she should be angry about his presumption. But by then she couldn't work up the energy. Besides, she couldn't remember the last time someone had expressed concern about her well-being without the conversation leaving Stella feeling like she was the one messing up. Since the day they met, Linus had had her back. The least she could do was have his.

"Why are you interested in my plans for the weekend?" Linus asked.

"I, um…" His leg muscles flexed as he stretched his thigh, momentarily distracting her. He was the only person she knew who could wear neon-green Lycra and look masculine.

"I have to go to Berkshire. I need to inventory Agnes's country house."

"Looking for a cat sitter, are you? I'd be glad to keep an eye on Miss Toffee for you."

"Actually, I'm taking Toffee with me. It's her house, after all." Not to mention, she'd miss the little fur ball sleeping at the foot of her bed. Over the past few weeks, she'd come to think of Toffee more as a pet than a responsibility. She made for terrific company. The perfect distraction for when late-night dreams conflated friendly hugs with more intimate acts.

"I was wondering if you would come with me," she said.

"Away with you for the weekend?"

The way he said the words made her insides squirrelly. "You don't have to come with me. Toffee and I can rent a car. I just thought it might be nice to have the company. Especially someone who knew the area. Didn't you say you used to live near there?"

"What you're really asking is if I want to be your chauffeur for the weekend."

"Not at all. I just thought it would be nice to have company. I brought up the area thing because you're always tells me to see more of the UK, and I figured you could play tour guide."

"Relax, luv. I was teasing. I think it's a splendid idea."

"You do?" Stella didn't realize how anxious she'd been about his response until her insides relaxed.

"Absolutely. I'd love to go away with you for the weekend." He was teasing again. The smirk at the end of his sentence said so.

Now, if only her squirrelly stomach would get the message.

It was cold and raw when the three of them departed Saturday morning. A typical English fall day. Linus and Stella sat in the front of his sports car, while in the back seat, Toffee sat in her travel carrier, blinking at them with annoyance. For the first part of the ninety-minute drive, Stella entertained herself by watching the passing landscape. It was a beautiful mix of suburban and pastoral. The foliage was a mosaic of red, brown and yellow interrupted every so often by a service station or steeple. Occasionally she would see a stretch of farmland in the distance. The farther out of the city they drove, the more frequent the stretches. "Oh my God, is that a thatched roof?" she exclaimed as they drove by a stone cottage.

"Probably," Linus replied. "They're popular again, I hear."

"Seriously?"

"Don't knock it. A good one will last you a few decades."

She admired the UK for maintaining its quaintness, something she rarely saw in the city. "We have a Berkshire County in Massachusetts, too," she told him. "My parents took us once so we could see the BSO at Tanglewood."

"BSO?"

"Sorry. Boston Symphony Orchestra. Tanglewood is their summer home. I remember thinking how rural the place was. Clearly I didn't understand rural."

Linus chuckled, the vibration filling the small space. "I

hope you're not expecting an orchestra in this Berkshire. You'll be disappointed."

"I'll survive. I'm not much of a music person, anyway. We only went because my sister was performing in the student chorus." Stella had auditioned a few years later but only made alternate.

"Me, either. We had to take piano lessons when we were children," Linus said. "Chopin hasn't recovered."

"From the playing?" Somehow, she suspected Chopin had survived their efforts quite nicely.

"No, from our whining about having to play. Susan was particularly dramatic about it. Then again, her mother was an actress, so she has the drama gene. Oh, sorry," he said when she frowned. "I should have explained. Susan's my half sister."

"I thought you said your father married his secretary."

"That was his third marriage. Susan was a product of marriage number two. Father was what you would call a serial committer."

Interesting. "How many times was he married?"

"Three, but only because he passed away young. If he'd been healthier, I'm sure there would have been at least one or two more." While he spoke breezily, the tone sounded practiced, like a precomposed interview answer.

"No wonder you don't believe in commitment," she replied.

"You sound like Susan when she's playing armchair psychiatrist."

One didn't need to be a psychiatrist to make a connection. Linus's imposed solitude was a third rail that, up until now, Stella had avoided. Partly because she feared if she talked about it, Linus would then bring up New York again. And partly because she didn't like the heavy feeling she got in her stomach whenever she thought of Linus dating.

However, hearing about his father made her curious.

"What do you think about Susan's theory?"

"I don't think. That's my problem."

"And yet you had deep enough thoughts to stop dating. Seems to me, if you were a bastard, you'd have shrugged off what happened to Victoria and carried on."

She watched as he worked through her logic, only to shake his head. "You're basing your thoughts on the new and improved me. Proof that I was right to back off and enter monkdom. Prior to my evolvement, there is no way you and I would be taking a friendly trip to the country. At least not sleeping in separate beds."

"Aren't I the lucky one," she replied.

*Are you?* a voice asked in her head. His comment had her fighting not to squirm in her seat. Ever since she'd kissed him, her late-night mind had been playing what-if, imagining what might have happened if Linus hadn't pulled away. Inappropriate as the thoughts were, the fantasy—full of tangled limbs and heated kisses—was a tempting one.

Before the image could invade her mind again, she turned her attention to the window. They'd left the highway and were driving deeper into the country. Occasionally the rock walls and hedges were broken up by the appearance of a village. Tiny clusters of Tudor-style buildings with modern window displays. "What do you think? Anything look familiar?" she asked Toffee.

Head resting on her front paw, the cat blinked and went back to sleep.

"Is that a yes or a no?" Linus asked.

"I think it's more an 'I don't care.' She looks quite comfortable, I have to say. Must be used to the trip."

"Agnes did bring her everywhere."

"I can see why. She and I chat all day long."

"You do? About what?"

Stella blushed. Admitting you held long conversations with a cat was akin to saying you had an imaginary friend.

"Oh, you know. The weather. Her food. Agnes's inventory." Linus. "The usual."

Linus nodded. "Everyone needs a good sounding board. How is the inventory going?"

Ah, the inventory. "Pretty good. I'm eager to dig into the country house to see what I can't find. I still can't get over how interesting a life Agnes led." In addition to her love life, she bore witness to some major moments in history. "She crossed paths with just about everyone who was anyone, and I swear half of those people gave her gifts."

"She wasn't the queen of British theater for nothing," Linus remarked.

It was funny. Based on the still photographs, Agnes Moreland wasn't a traditionally beautiful woman. Her nose was too long, and she had an overly prominent jaw. There was something about her, though, that captivated.

"I saw one of her movies the other night," she said. *Sixpence Sunday.*

"Is that the one where she jumps off Tower Bridge?"

"That's the one." Though her role as the suicidal prostitute wasn't the lead, she managed to overshadow everyone every time she was on-screen. "You can see how she became a star."

"Definitely had charisma, she did, even in her eighties."

Explained why Linus had taken a shine to her. They were two of a kind, he and Agnes. He, too, made a room light up when he entered.

"Any more missing objects?" he asked, oblivious to her thoughts. She'd filled him in on her mystery a few weeks ago.

"Nothing so far that I've noticed. Of course, Agnes owned a lot of bric-a-brac she didn't consider valuable enough to list in the addendum. Who knows if any of that's missing?"

"What does Mrs. Churchill think?"

"She doesn't know, either," Stella replied, recalling that awkward conversation. "Neither does Teddy."

"Hmm…"

"What? You think one of them is lying?"

Linus raised and lowered his right shoulder. "Let's just say I wouldn't necessarily trust one of them."

Stella had an idea which one, too. Thing was, why would Teddy steal such minor objects when he had access to the more valuable ones?

"The less expensive ones are easier to sell," Linus replied when she voiced the question out loud.

"Maybe so, but it's not as though he needs the money." As the man had tersely pointed out multiple times during his visit last summer.

Linus didn't look convinced. "What does Peter say?"

"I haven't mentioned it yet," Stella replied. She didn't want to make him think the situation was anything less than one hundred percent under control. "Not until I have a good theory." She didn't want to chance any bad news, or less-than-awesome news for that matter, leaking out. The weekly status updates her parents demanded were difficult enough. The last time Stella brought up her inventory project, the conversation somehow ended up about the best way to leverage the task on her résumé. The actual details of her job didn't really matter.

Except that Stella was really, really enjoying the details.

"Don't worry. You'll figure out an answer before you leave," Linus said.

At first, Stella didn't quite understand, and then she realized she must have sighed out loud. "Thanks for the vote of confidence."

He looked across the seat at her. "I have plenty of confidence in you." The gentleness in his voice wrapped around her insides. When he said things like that, in that voice, her midnight fantasies developed another layer. Unable to stop her face from warming, she turned her head back to the scenery.

Linus tried not to enjoy the blush Stella was trying to hide, but it was difficult. He wasn't so evolved that he didn't enjoy having an effect on a woman.

There was a moment a few miles back when he feared he'd crossed a line. When he said he'd have seduced her in the old days. It was clear from the way her body tensed that the comment made her uncomfortable. Thankfully, he'd reassured her quickly and changed the subject. The last thing he wanted was to cast an awkward pall over the weekend, especially considering how much he valued the invitation.

Stella had no idea, either. No idea what it meant for her to trust his friendship that much. All the more reason not to muck things up with mention of seduction and sharing a bed. If only...

Ever since the night on the Eye, when she'd hugged him—hugged him!—he couldn't stop thinking about the way she felt in his arms. The moment wasn't supposed to be romantic or tender, but dammit, having her pressed against him, her scent clinging to his clothes afterward, had made an impact. Here it was weeks later, and he could still feel the moment. Definitely a test of his resolve.

He stole a look across the car. Stella had her chin propped on her hand as she studied the landscape, her expression contemplative. So serious. Even in jeans and a sweater, she looked all business.

A familiar tightness gripped him. Sometimes, when he looked at her, he couldn't breathe. Too many emotions clogged his chest. Concern, of course. Desire—he'd be lying if he didn't admit to finding her attractive—and others he couldn't name. Or didn't want to.

The GPS told them their street was the next left. "Almost there," he said. "What do you know about the property?"

"Very little," Stella replied. "I meant to go online to see if I could find a photo, but I didn't get the chance. On one document, it's referred to as a country manor and on another, a cottage. In my head I'm picturing a little carriage house kind of thing."

"Maybe." He thought of the sprawling property thirty or so kilometers east that his family used to call their country home. "*Cottage* could mean a variety of things."

Whatever the house was, it certainly had privacy. The property was hidden behind an ancient stone wall and acres of woodland. To gain access, they drove along a narrow road. "Good thing Toffee's over her explorer phase," he remarked. "Lose her in here and you'd never find her. The tree line is ahead. The house should be right over this bend."

As they rounded the corner, the trees broke to reveal a sprawling nineteenth-century hunting lodge.

Stella gasped. "Holy cow. Toffee owns Downton Abbey."

Not quite. By estate standards, the house was small—certainly smaller than the Collier estate—but it was definitely a luxury home. The stone building boasted large arched windows and an intricately carved wooden door. There were multiple chimneys attached, no doubt, to multiple fireplaces. One, in the middle of the house, was happily puffing smoke.

A dark sedan was parked in the drive. "Were you expected?" he asked Stella.

She shook her head. "The estate pays for a cleaning company, but I don't know why they'd light a fire. Can't be that cold in the house."

"Last time I checked, maid services didn't use rental cars," he said, noting the tag on the license plate. There was only one person he could think of who would be using the house.

From the look on Stella's face, she had come to the same conclusion. "Teddy has his own house. Why would he come here?"

"If I were to venture a guess, I would say he fancied a weekend in the country. Does he have visiting privileges?"

"None that I know of," Stella replied. She undid her seat belt. "Would you mind getting Toffee? I'm going to see what's going on."

If Stella had any doubt they'd entered the wrong house, it disappeared as soon as she crossed the threshold. A giant portrait of a younger Agnes greeted them in the entrance-way. The house itself was cozy and rustic with its faded floral wallpaper and antique furniture.

"Bit like walking into a grandma's house," Linus remarked, "if your grandma was a dowager duchess." He set the carrier on a nearby bench and let Toffee free. The cat stretched and began sniffing her surroundings.

"What do you think, Toffee? Smell like home?" he asked.

Leaving them to their conversation, Stella walked a little deeper into the house. Soft music was coming from the room behind the staircase. "Hello," she called out.

"I beg your pardon, but this is private... Oh!" With a tumbler in one hand, and a newspaper tucked under his arm, Teddy Moreland rounded the corner and stopped. He looked dressed for the weekend, a maroon sweater-vest buttoned over his stomach. The color matched the blotches on his cheeks.

He looked at her with wide eyes. "Miss Russo, what a surprise."

"I could say the same, Mr. Moreland. Toffee and I are here to check out the property."

"You brought Etonia Toffee Pudding? All the way from London?"

"Why not? It is her house." They'd had this conversation before.

As if on cue, Toffee jumped off the bench and began weaving between her legs. Stella scooped the cat up to cuddle her. "Besides, I couldn't very well leave her unattended for the weekend, could I?" she added.

"You're staying for the weekend? All of you?"

Teddy's second question was directed at Linus, who had appeared at her shoulder. The insinuation was clear.

"I had the car," Linus answered, without missing a beat. "Since Stella isn't familiar with directions or driving on the left side of the road yet, I offered to play chauffeur."

A slight rearranging of facts, but Stella wasn't about to correct him, especially as the truth only added fuel to Teddy's fire. "I'm here to start an inventory of the property," she said. "Might I ask what you're doing here?"

"Keeping an eye on the property," Teddy replied. As if the answer was obvious. He was using the same tone he used during their initial meeting. Imperious and condescending. "I made a habit of coming by on weekends as a favor to Aunt Agnes after she became ill. Now that she's gone, it's the least I can do to make sure her estate remains cared for."

"That's very kind of you." Her gaze slid to the drink in his hand. "I'm guessing you spend the night as well. To make sure the house looks occupied."

"Naturally. We wouldn't want people thinking it's vacant. Between the memorabilia hounds and common thieves, not to mention vandals..."

She and Linus shared a look. Squatter though he may be, Teddy raised a good point. The house did benefit from being occupied.

She wasn't in the mood to get into a protracted argument, either. "Looks like the three of us will be spending the weekend together, then," she said. "Maybe you can help me locate some of the items on the inventory sheet."

"Splendid. Anything I can do to help." Teddy's smile looked as forced as Stella's felt. "In fact, why don't I take Etonia Toffee Pudding into the study while the two of you bring your bags upstairs. Come here, my lovely." Before Stella could object, he had the white cat tucked in the crook of his elbow. To Toffee's credit, she didn't object. She looked as indifferent as ever. "I'll just bring her into the library to sit on the sofa with me," he said.

"Well, that certainly showed him who's boss, didn't it?" Stella let out a sigh after Teddy and Toffee disappeared around the corner. "I might as well have asked for permission to stay."

"Don't be so hard on yourself," Linus said, placing a hand on her shoulder. "What were you supposed to do, toss him out? He wouldn't have gone quietly."

"I know, and I wasn't in the mood for a scene." That didn't change the fact she felt as though she'd messed up.

"Look, you let him know that you're on to him. Chances are, he'll be less inclined to make himself at home in the future. Especially if you drop a few a hints about returning."

While she'd been talking with Teddy, Linus had brought in their luggage, along with Toffee's travel bag. "Are you sure she's staying only for the weekend?" he asked as they headed upstairs.

"I wasn't sure what was here, and I wanted her to be comfortable."

"You know she's going to just sleep on the furniture."

"Well, now she has choices." Sue her for wanting her cat to have choices. Agnes's cat. Toffee.

"You know what irks me the most about the Teddy situation," she said when they reached the second-floor landing.

"He's not wrong. It is safer to have someone here once in a while. Not that I buy for a second that's the reason he's hanging out here." More likely he figured Toffee wouldn't be visiting the place.

She tried to put herself in Teddy's shoes. Annoying as the man was, she felt a little sympathy. Knowing you were second in someone's eyes hurt. Losing out to a cat had to be infuriating.

"Does that mean you're going to let him spend weekends here?" Linus asked.

"Depends. Toffee and I will be traveling this way for a good chunk of the fall. He might decide our company isn't worth the effort. Where do you want to sleep?"

She meant which bedroom, as it was clear Teddy had moved into the master suite. Linus, however, arched his brow, causing her to look away.

"I'll take door number two," he replied with a chuckle.

Leaving her with door number one. The blue room. Everything in the room was a shade of the color, from the sapphire brocade bedspread to the blue toile drapes. Tossing her bag on the bed, she opened what she thought was a closet, only to discover the door connected to Linus's room.

"Sorry."

He was in the middle of peeling off his sweater. The sport shirt underneath had ridden up halfway, exposing his torso. She knew he was well built, but this was the first time she'd seen his bare skin. Her eyes followed the dusting of blond hair running from below his navel to where it disappeared beneath his belt.

"I thought this was a closet. I'll…um…give you your privacy."

He freed his head, his hair mussed with static electricity. Seeing her, he smiled. "No worries. I was getting warm, is all. Thought I'd change into a T-shirt. You can leave the door open. That is, unless you want privacy yourself to…"

"No. That is, I'm going to stay dressed. In these clothes."

"Suit yourself. These old houses can get very dusty." With that, he removed his shirt as well.

Stella always thought it a cliché when people said their mouths ran dry, but the sight of a shirtless Linus Collier had her swallowing several times to moisten her throat.

*Focus on work, Stella.*

"What?" He tipped his head. "Did you say something?"

Damn. "I said I'm going to get to work. Unpacking can wait until later." Much later.

# CHAPTER SEVEN

AFTER CHECKING ON TOFFEE, who, to her surprise, was happily stretched out on the back of the sofa behind Teddy, Stella hid herself in the attic. Steamer trunks and boxes made for the perfect distraction, or so she hoped. Stella had a suspicion she'd be haunted by that strip of skin for quite a while.

Why, though? She was never the kind of woman who craved sex. Liked it, sure, but she never ached for physical connection. Now, here she was having fantasies and getting flushed over the sight of a man's treasure trail.

Not any man's. Linus's. Her insides went end over end.

Wasn't this just like her? It really was as though she had a subconscious need for self-sabotage. Why else would she develop a thing for the one man in England who wasn't interested in dating. To top it off, she shouldn't be developing a thing, period.

"Save me, Agnes," she said as she flipped the latch of a footlocker. "Distract me with your memorabilia."

Agnes obliged. Sort of. The footlocker turned out to be a stash of journals and photographs. Not the Limoges pieces Stella was supposed to find, but far more interesting.

Two hours went by before she realized.

"I come with tea."

The voice came out of nowhere. Dropping the stack of photographs she held, Stella clutched her hand to her chest and turned around. Linus stood in the attic doorway, his silhouette backlit by the stairway light.

"Sorry," he said. "Didn't mean to make you jump. I thought you could do with something warm. These old attics can be drafty."

"I hadn't noticed," she replied, her heart rate slowing to normal, "but now that you mention it, I do feel a chill. Thank you."

He came all the way into the room and handed her one of the two earthenware mugs he was carrying. Steam and the aroma of black tea drifted into Stella's face. She inhaled deeply before taking a sip.

"So what is it that has you so engrossed that you didn't notice the temperature?" Linus arranged himself atop the steamer trunk a few feet from her, using a smaller box as a footrest, and cradled his mug. The sloping roof and small space made his presence seem even larger. He was wearing a T-shirt. A gray cotton reminder of earlier.

Suddenly, Stella didn't need the tea for warmth. She sipped it anyway, for something to do. "I found another collection of old photographs. Personal ones this time." The pile she'd dropped lay scattered at her feet. Bending over, she sorted through until she found the one she was looking for. "This looks like it was taken on someone's yacht. Check it out."

Linus whistled. "Is this who I think it is?"

"Read the back. There are journals, too," she added when he arched his brow. "I couldn't stop reading. It's like a giant Pandora's box of awesomeness. The more I read, the more amazed I am." A woman who carved out her life on her terms, that's who Agnes Moreland was. Stella was inadequate in comparison.

Before the dissatisfaction could ruin her mood, she switched topics. "How was your afternoon?

"Quite pleasant. I watched rugby and read a few lab reports and Teddy fell asleep reading the paper. He snores, by the way."

"And Toffee?"

"When I last left her, the owner of the house was batting a piece of uncooked pasta around the kitchen. Do not ask me where she got it."

From the mischievous glint in his eye, Stella could guess. "Thank you for entertaining her," she said.

It dawned on her that while she'd packed for Toffee, she'd invited Linus along without a single thought as to his entertainment. "I'm a terrible hostess," she said. "I've been ignoring you all afternoon."

"I knew what I was getting into."

And he said yes anyway? A little piece of her melted. "You're a good friend," she said. A reminder for them both. Mostly her, though, since she was also thinking how amazing he was at the moment and how nicely he filled out his T-shirt.

He smiled in response, causing her to smile back, and for several minutes the two of them just sat there smiling.

Linus was the one to break the mood. "That reminds me," he said. "The other reason I came upstairs. Teddy has volunteered to watch Toffee so we could go out to dinner."

"He did?" A frisson of suspicion passed through her. "Why?" Teddy didn't seem the type to make magnanimous gestures.

"We were talking about the Rose and Badger, and I mentioned that I hadn't been there in years but that you don't like to leave Toffee home alone, so he offered. My guess is he wants to win your favor, since you caught him staying here," he added before raising his mug.

"And what is the Rose and Badger?"

"A pub a few kilometers north of here, near the henge.

Serves the most amazing roast beef and pudding. My grandfather used to bring us when I was a little boy."

"Did you say *henge*?"

"I did. There's a large one in Avebury. Not as famous as Stonehenge, but very popular with the pagan community. Are you interested? In dinner, I mean."

Dinner with Linus in an authentic English pub across from a pagan henge? Sounded…romantic.

"I had planned to work most of the night." Soon as she answered, she realized how rude that sounded. "I'm also filthy. I've been digging through these dusty papers."

"You look fine. We're talking about a pub, not a five-star restaurant."

"But I packed dinner. Mrs. Churchill made a giant casserole. I put it in the cooler."

He frowned. "What cooler?"

"Sorry. The hamper."

"I know what a cooler is. I was asking what cooler."

"The blue one. I set it next to Toffee's bag."

Linus shook his head. "I unpacked everything from the car. There was no cooler, or whatever you want to call it."

"Sure there is. I distinctly remember putting the casserole in it. Don't tell me we forgot to pack it?"

"Sorry, luv." He offered her a contrite smile. "Sure you don't want to change your mind about the pub? Least you can do after ignoring me all afternoon."

"You…" He was joking. Nevertheless, his teasing hit a nerve. Stella sighed. She'd hoped to use tonight to make up the time she wasted this afternoon. On the other hand, it was only dinner, and she did owe Linus something for driving.

As for the night sounding romantic…? Romance was ninety-nine percent mental. Linus by candlelight didn't have to be any different than the Linus she saw every day.

"Sure," she replied. "Dinner it is."

* * *

The relief Linus felt at Stella's acceptance surprised him, although not nearly as much as the tremor of excitement accompanying it. Taking Stella to dinner wasn't something he'd considered until Teddy mentioned the pub in passing. As soon as he did, though, Linus seized on the opportunity. It would be a complete waste for Stella to work the entire weekend—and she would, too, using Toffee as the excuse. Therefore he immediately began dropping hints until Teddy found himself "volunteering" his cat-sitting services. Linus told himself the night out was for Stella's sake, and he played off his excitement as satisfaction that his plan worked.

At least he did until dinner. He was in the front entranceway talking with Teddy when he heard Stella descending the stairs.

"I didn't keep you waiting, did I?" she asked.

Dear Lord. All that talk about stopping a room with her entrance... Linus glanced at the portrait on the wall and mentally shook his head. Not even close.

How could Stella not see her own charisma? She'd changed clothes, switching her turtleneck to a V-neck sweater that reflected pink onto her skin. Wide and boxy, the soft-looking knit ended above her waist. Long enough to cover her, but square enough that there was space between sweater and skin. A man could easily slide his hand underneath. The thought affected Linus's ability to breathe.

"Aren't women supposed to make men wait? Aunt Agnes took forever when I was simply visiting for tea."

Thank God for Teddy. Gave him time to clear his throat. "It was worth the wait," he replied. "You look lovely."

She smiled and tucked the hair behind her ear. "I know you said I didn't have to, but after an afternoon in the attic, I needed a shower. Are you sure you don't mind watching Toffee?" she asked, turning to Teddy.

"My dear girl, Etonia Toffee Pudding is like family. I've spent many hours with her sitting near me. Tonight won't be any different."

"We'll only be gone a couple hours," Linus told him.

"Or less," Stella quickly added.

He hated how she was already shortchanging her enjoyment by planning to hurry back.

The Rose and Badger stood on the outskirts of town, on a road leading to Avebury proper. Linus had never given it much thought before, but once upon a time, the pub must have been an inn for Travelers. The building itself was white stucco with thick brown shutters. Above the faded white lettering on the sign was a painting of a badger, a rose trapped beneath its front paws. Sometime during the afternoon, the clouds had receded, leaving behind a full moon. It cast a silvery glow on the parking lot.

"Do you know how pubs got their odd names?" he asked as they stepped out onto the gravel. "The pictures were for illiterate travelers. If you were meeting someone and couldn't read, you could locate an establishment by describing the picture. 'Meet me at the Rose and Badger pub.'"

"Interesting."

Linus winced. He sounded more like a tour guide than a dinner companion. He was out of his element. Normally he took his dates out in the city, where he could charm them with witty anecdotes. This was the first time he'd taken a woman to a place from his childhood.

It also wasn't a date, he reminded himself as he opened the front door.

"I'm going to go out on a limb and say not many pubs were named after their owners then. Unless they knew a professional artist," Stella said, still on his original comment.

"No, but there are a few Slaughtered Lambs and what not."

"Sounds appetizing. Oh, this is lovely."

Not as lovely as her enchanted expression. The pub's interior hadn't changed much since he was a boy, or in the last four hundred years, for that matter. The room was still dark, the light limited to a handful of hanging lanterns and candles on the tables. The same antique farm implements from around the area hung on the exposed beams. At this point Linus almost suspected they were original furnishings, like the pagan symbols interspersed among them.

The air around them smelled of wood smoke, fennel and onion. As they walked to a table near the fireplace, he breathed in the aroma and decided his ruse definitely was worth it. "Admit it," he said. "This is better than reheated casserole."

"Out of respect for Mrs. Churchill, I refuse to comment until I've actually tasted the food. However, I'll admit the atmosphere is impressive."

Why, then, wasn't she relaxed? He could see the tension in her shoulders. Come to think of it, she'd been tense when he first made the suggestion of dinner as well. "If you're worried about staying out too long..." he started.

"It still seems odd that Teddy would volunteer to cat sit. When he came to the apartment, he was all about being served."

"That was before, though. Like I said earlier, maybe he feels the need to get on your good side." Stella shrugged, not quite convinced.

"If you're worried, we can go back."

She looked about to speak, only to stop and shake her head. "No. We're here. And I'm being overprotective, or under-trusting or whatever. I'm sure Toffee will be fine."

Linus let out the breath he hadn't realized he'd been holding. "I fed her before we left. She'll probably spend the night bathing and sleeping by the fire. In fact, I imagine both of them will. Sleep by the fire, that is. I'd rather not picture Teddy licking himself."

"Oh my," Stella said, pressing a hand to her mouth. "Me neither."

They shared a mutual shudder. In the candlelight, Stella's eyes took on a golden sheen. Linus had never paid close attention to a woman's eye color before. He limited himself to three basic descriptors: brown, hazel and blue. Stella's eyes, however, were multidimensional. Multiple shades of brown blended together. A man could stare into them for hours and not be able to pick out all the different colors.

She looked away, and he felt her gaze's absence. "How old did you say this restaurant is?" she asked as she studied the fireplace mantel.

He wanted to catch her chin and turn her face back to his. "Four hundred years. Give or take a few decades."

"Wow. Can you imagine? Four centuries ago, another pair of travelers ate in this very spot."

A fanciful thought. He liked the dreamlike expression it brought to her face. "Maybe. Bet they didn't have as good a wine list, though." He winked at her over the menu.

*Get a grip on yourself, Russo.* Stella raised the menu in front of her face so Linus couldn't see the blush on her cheeks. What was with her? You'd think she was a nervous teenager on her first date. All day long, her insides had been fluttering and tumbling like someone replaced her organs with a giant swarm of butterflies. It was embarrassing. Right up there with how she took thirty minutes to change her sweater. At least showering and redoing her makeup made sense after being in the attic all day. Blushing at every little thing her friend said did not.

Gosh, but he looked good in candlelight. The flame brought out the blue in his eyes. Thank goodness for the menu or she'd lose herself in them.

The meal passed in a blur of conversation. Linus entertained her with stories of his childhood. So different from hers. Linus and his brother were clearly close, as evidenced by the antics they got into. Even Susan, the so-called outsider, was involved in some of the adventures.

One obvious thing was the role tradition played in their upbringing. Colliers was more than a family business. It was the family identity.

"Did it ever occur to you to do something different? Work someplace else?"

"Of course. We all did. Thomas even went north and played carpenter for a few years. Grandfather may have talked our ear off about legacy, but we were always free to go someplace else if that's what we wanted. It's only by sheer luck that I happened to love chemistry."

"Your family wouldn't have cared if you decided to design women's shoes or become a barista instead?"

He thought for a moment before answering. "Hard to say. Father was devastated when Thomas didn't join the company straight off, but he was the heir apparent. But Susan and me? I don't think so. Not if that's what I really wanted to do."

"You're lucky," Stella replied. He was free to be himself.

"Let's talk about something else." She pushed her Cabernet aside. Once again, she'd let the alcohol go to her head and started saying stupid things. "Is there really a henge nearby?"

A look passed over Linus's face, but if he thought her behavior abrupt, he didn't say so. "Across the street. Been here longer than the pub."

"I remember watching a cable show about Stonehenge when I was a kid. About all the mysticism and supernatural theories surrounding it, like how it'd been built by aliens."

He laughed. "We were all about those stories when we were kids as well. Some of the locals still believe them, at least the mysticism part. Why do you think there are herbs everywhere?"

Sitting in the middle of their table was a bud vase with a sprig of dried flowers. Linus reached across and gave the stem a gentle touch with his finger. "Did you know that some people believe lavender can be used to attract love and happiness?"

"Really?" What a nice thought. "You don't?"

"I think the plant has a very pleasant scent and that your olfactory sense reacts in very specific ways to different smells."

"Spoken like a true scientist."

"If the shoe fits," he replied with a smile. "My siblings are the fanciful ones."

"Really?"

"Oh yeah. Thomas and his wife are convinced they were touched by some kind of magical influence." For the next few minutes, he told her about their miraculous reunion following his sister-in-law's accident.

"Your brother really didn't know she was alive?"

"And Rosalind really had amnesia," Linus replied. "Talk to the two of them, and they'll insist Christmas magic was at play. For that matter, my sister, Susan, will tell you the same thing about her romance."

"While you have no magic at all. Poor baby." She was only half joking. While she didn't believe in magic any more than Linus did, it bothered her that he was the odd man out.

"I'll survive," he said with a wave of his hand. "I don't need to turn basic coincidence into anything deeper."

Maybe not, but what about feelings in general? While his siblings were falling in love, he was swearing off the emotion. The thought left her with an empty feeling. He deserved love as much as anyone. Without giving it a second thought, Stella covered his hand with hers—the way any friend comforting another friend would.

"You might not need to, but you deserve the chance anyway," she said.

Linus stared at their hands for a second before rotating his so that their palms touched and gently closed his fingers around hers.

When his thumb rubbed the outside of her little finger, Stella felt the touch all the way to her toes. If he were to lean across and kiss her right now, she would...

"Hey, come with me." His voice broke her thought. "I want to show you something outside."

They left the restaurant and went across the street. The night was quiet. With each step they took deeper into the field, the farther the sounds from the pub receded until eventually the only noises they could hear were their footsteps in the grass and the occasional snap of an animal in the brush. The full moon was like a giant silver lantern making it easy to see the outlines of the ancient stone rocks that formed the circle. What the moon couldn't illuminate, the flashlight on Linus's phone did. He kept the light trained on the ground so they wouldn't lose their footing.

As she walked along, Stella could see why people found the site special. The air definitely felt charged with something. Like a sense of anticipation.

"Where are we were going?" she asked. "You're not offering me up as a sacrifice, are you?"

"Depends. Are you a virgin?" He gave her hand a squeeze.

They had been holding hands since the restaurant. Linus claimed it was to keep her from stumbling. Stella didn't care. Jokes about sacrifice aside, she found his grip reassuring.

"Seriously?" she asked. "We've passed at least a half dozen of those large rocks. What is it we're looking for?"

"It's a surprise. At least I hope it will be. Hopefully it still exists."

Again, Stella didn't care. The wine, the air, the hand in hers were enough.

They walked awhile longer in comfortable silence. Then suddenly, Linus spoke. "Ah, here we are. Watch your step."

It was a large tree in a nearby gully. Although they were buried by leaves, Stella could see bits and pieces of the root system as it spread across the ground like giant tentacles. Considering the roots' size and range, the tree had to be ancient. "It's a beech tree," Linus said. "There are only a handful of them around. Supposed to have mystical properties. At least particular ones."

Letting go of her hand, he stepped behind her and shone the light upward. Stella gasped. Ribbons of every color and size adorned the branches. Some were old and tattered, others new.

"What are the ribbons for?" she asked.

"Wishes and desires."

"Like a wishing well, only with branches and ribbons."

"Precisely. I'd forgotten about it until you mentioned magic."

Stella watched the ribbons moved in the breeze. With the moon overhead and the silhouettes of monoliths behind them, the branches looked almost otherworldly.

She tilted her head farther back, even though it strained her neck. Linus was gazing upward, too. "Did you ever make a wish and tie a ribbon?"

"Once, when we were kids."

"Do you remember what you wished for?"

"Probably a chemistry set or to be a starter on the football team. Something that seemed very important at the time, I'm sure."

The wishes of children. Stella tried to imagine Linus

as a little boy with little-boy dreams. "I'm sure I'd have wished for something equally earth-shattering." She thought of all the times she'd tossed pennies into fountains with the hopes she'd be as good as her siblings at some endeavor.

"I'm sorry I don't have any ribbons or we could leave a wish right now."

"That's all right." The pennies never worked; why would a ribbon? Although she was curious. "What would you wish for if we did have ribbons?"

"Me?" She felt him shrug. "A new chemistry set?"

"Seriously," she replied. Even if she didn't believe in wishes, the surroundings called for honesty. She knew what she'd wish for, for him.

His ensuing silence lasted for so long, she was afraid he wasn't going to answer. Finally, in a soft voice, he said, "I would wish to be better. A better brother. A better person. Just better."

Oh, Linus. What he should wish for was the ability to forgive himself. As far as Stella was concerned, he was good enough is as.

"What about you?" he asked. "What is your heart's desire?"

*To know my heart's desire.*

The thought sounded clear and loud in her head. Stella pushed it aside. The thought didn't even make sense. "To be happy," she said instead. Again, the thought came out of nowhere. What she should have said was "to become a major player in the world financial market." Something concrete and in keeping with her goals. Wishing for happiness was as nebulous as wishing for peace on earth.

She started to clarify herself when Linus's hand settled on the back of her neck. Cold skin met cold skin, sending warm shivers down her back. Her knees very nearly buckled. "I hope you get your wish," he said. "I want you to be happy, too."

And then he kissed the top of her head.

They walked back in silence. Linus didn't hold her hand this time. He wanted to, but after their interlude under the tree, signs of affection felt presumptuous. Especially since his initial answer to Stella's question had been "you." He would wish for Stella, in his arms. Exactly the kind of wish he had no business making for a number of reasons. Starting with the fact that she needed a friend, not an affair. And so he wished to be better, because better was what he needed to be.

Even though what he wanted was to kiss her until she couldn't breathe. He licked his lips and imagined the taste of her. Imagination: the price of being better.

Stella finally broke the silence in the car, a half kilometer from home. Until then, she'd stared out the window with a faraway look on her face.

"Thank you for a wonderful evening," she said. "I'm glad you talked me into going."

"I'm glad you enjoyed yourself." It struck him just how much satisfaction he gotten out of the evening. Making Stella smile gave him a rush, not dissimilar to the thrill he used to get from the chase, only he wasn't looking to gain anything further from the outcome.

"Don't tell Mrs. Churchill, but I'm glad we forgot her casserole in London."

The casserole. He'd pushed that part of the evening out of his head. Did he want to ruin such a good evening? "About that…" Might as well tear the bandage off now. She was going to find out regardless. "I'm afraid I might have fibbed a bit."

"Fibbed how?" she asked. Her eyes narrowed.

"The cooler. It might be in the kitchen back at the house."

"You lied?"

He preferred to think he misrepresented the truth for a greater good. "Only when it was obvious you weren't going to say yes otherwise. And I really wanted to take you out this evening."

Stella huffed and folded her arms. "I don't like being lied to."

"I'm sorry, but I meant what I said. I only lied when I realized you weren't going to say yes unless backed into a corner. If I hadn't, you'd have spent the night up in the attic and left me to hang with Teddy."

"Don't try to guilt me," she said.

"I wasn't trying to make you feel anything." Perhaps he was trying for a little guilt, but she couldn't say he wasn't speaking the truth. She would have worked all night. "I lied because I wanted to spend some time with you, pure and simple."

"You could have just told me. You didn't have to play games."

"Would that have changed your mind?"

Stella didn't answer. In the dark, it was impossible to see her expression, but Linus imagined her jaw to be tensed.

*Way to go, Collier.* First real female friendship he'd ever had, and he'd mucked it all up. Why didn't he come out and say he wanted to spend time with her?

Because then it would feel too much like asking her on a date, that's why. He didn't want her to feel that kind of pressure.

Or was he simply afraid she'd say no?

# CHAPTER EIGHT

THE FRONT OF the house was dark when he parked the car, including the exterior lights. Only a glow coming through from the rear of the house indicated anyone was home.

The car engine had barely stopped when Stella threw open the passenger door. "I'm going to get Toffee and head to bed."

"Stella, wait..."

She shut the door on his sentence.

Fortunately, the front door was unlocked. They let themselves in, and Linus felt along the wall until he found the switch. "Teddy? We're back."

There was no answer.

"Looks like someone fell asleep in front of the telly," he said. Or passed out. A daylong diet of gin and tonics could do that to a person.

Still bent on ignoring him, Stella marched off in the direction of the library. Linus headed toward the stairway. No sense trying to talk tonight. He'd wait until she got a good night's sleep, as well as a few hours' work under her belt, and then he'd talk to her. Maybe—hopefully—by the end of their drive home, things would be back to normal. If not... His stomach grew heavy.

He had one foot on the stair when Stella's voice cut through the house.

"What the hell do you think you're doing?"

* * *

Stella entered the library in time to see Teddy crouched in front of an open French door. At the sound of her voice, he jumped up, Toffee clutched to his chest. The cat reacted to the sudden movement by scrambling up and over his shoulder, landing on the sofa before running full speed out of the room.

"That was almost a disaster," Teddy said. "Thank goodness she ran down the hall. You should know better than to holler like a banshee, Miss Russo."

"Excuse me?" *She* should know better? He was the one she'd caught standing in front of the open door.

Linus came running down the hall. "What's going on? I heard Stella yell, and then the cat nearly tripped me trying to run upstairs."

"I caught Teddy here trying to put Toffee outside," Stella told him.

Teddy's nostrils flared. "I did nothing of the sort."

"I saw you crouching in the doorway. What was the plan?" she asked as she shut the door. "Put her out in the woods and hope she got lost for good? Maybe get eaten by a badger?" With Toffee lost in the woods, he would be the heir.

She knew she should have stayed home.

"How dare you! What kind of man do you think I am?"

"A person who stands to inherit eleven million pounds if Toffee disappears," Linus said.

"I don't need your help," Stella said. It was partly his fault Teddy was alone with Toffee in the first place. If having dinner with him hadn't sounded so appealing…

"For your information, I was protecting Etonia Toffee Pudding. She very nearly got outside," Teddy said.

"And why was the door open in the first place?" Stella asked. He couldn't fool her. The man was trying to shoo

Toffee outside hoping she'd get lost in the woods. One lost cat would mean payday for him.

"Earlier in the evening, there was an issue with the fire, and the room became smoky. I opened the door a crack to air the room out. You remember, Collier. You were with me."

Stella looked at Linus. He gave her a sheepish nod. "He's right. There was a backdraft."

"Unfortunately, the door must not have latched tightly when I closed it, and it blew open with the wind. Thankfully, I was coming in to turn out the lights when I saw Etonia Toffee Pudding sniffing the ground outside. I had just managed to lure her in when you screamed like a banshee, scaring us all."

When he finished, Teddy stood and waited for her apology, arms folded across his midsection. There was a pull in his sweater from where Toffee had climbed over his shoulder. Stella was willing to bet there was a good long scratch on the skin beneath as well.

"What was Toffee doing in a room with an open door?" she asked.

"Well, it certainly wasn't my fault. She was sleeping on the sofa when I started my rounds." Should she believe him? She'd already been lied to once this evening, and quite believably. Teddy could be lying to her as well.

On the other hand, Teddy's story made sense. And, Toffee had a history of sneaking outside when no one was looking. Witness her visit to Linus's house this summer. And even if Teddy was lying, Stella had no proof other than her gut.

"I'm sorry, Teddy. Forgive me." As much as it galled her to apologize, she had to coexist with the man for the rest of her tenure. She couldn't afford to get on his bad side. "I'm extremely protective of Toffee, as you can see, and that sometimes leads me to jump to the worst-case scenario. Thank you for making sure Toffee was safe."

"Well…" The older man made a production out of checking his cuffs. "It is important that the cat be protected at all costs. I should be grateful that you're taking your job as seriously as you are. Therefore, I accept your apology."

"Thank you," Stella replied. "Now if you'll excuse me, I'm going to find Toffee and get some sleep."

"Do you think he's telling the truth?" Linus asked when they were on their way upstairs.

"You tell me. I'm not very good at sussing out lies these days." She was still annoyed at him, too.

Part of her felt like she was overreacting to the whole thing with the cooler. A casserole was hardly life or death. But it wasn't what he'd lied about that had her angry; it was that he'd played her, like she imagined he'd played countless other women. She'd thought she was different.

She wanted to be different.

And there was the real source of her annoyance. She was upset because she'd allowed herself to fall under the night's spell. To think that what they were sharing in Avebury was special.

She didn't bother waiting to hear Linus's answer about Teddy. When they reached the top of the stairs, she went straight to the master bedroom to look under the bed, figuring Toffee would hide in a familiar place. She was wrong. After checking the room thoroughly—if Teddy whined about invasion of privacy, he could stuff it—she headed to her own room.

Linus sat on the bed, fluffy white cat in his lap. "Peace offering," he said. "Found her sitting next to my pillow. She doesn't seem too traumatized."

"Well, that's good." She stroked the cat's head. "Sorry I scared you, sweetie."

"I'm sorry, too," Linus said. "For the bit about the cooler. I should have straight-out said I wanted to take you to dinner. Truth is, I was afraid."

"That I would take it the wrong way."

He looked her in the eye. "That you would say no."

*Oh.*

"In case you haven't guessed, I like your company," he continued. "I like…spending time with you."

"I like…spending time with you, too." More than she should, really. "In fact, you're the only person who's ever been able to drag me away from a project."

"Really?"

"Don't let it go to your head." She sat down on the bed next to him. "I'm glad we went out tonight. It was really…" *Special*, she wanted to say. "Nice."

"Yeah, it was. I meant what I said, too, in Avebury. I want you to be happy."

Stella's breath caught in her throat. Linus's gaze was dark and unshuttered, revealing the vulnerability within. When was the last time a man had looked at her with such sincerity? Ever? The emotion set off a heavy heat deep inside her. She felt special. Wanted.

They were friends. Good friends. But suddenly friendship wasn't enough. Her body wanted more. Needed more.

She began to lean forward, then caught herself. The last time she'd kissed him, he'd pushed her away. She wouldn't repeat the mistake.

"I should leave," Linus said. "Before I do something we regret."

"Would we?" Stella asked. "Regret it?"

"We're friends."

"Friends can have benefits."

She waited, watching as his eyes dropped to her mouth. The ache inside her had intensified. *Please*, she pleaded silently. *Please.*

"I don't want to…"

"You won't," she said. "I know what I'm asking. This won't change anything."

Something flickered in his expression, but it moved too quickly for her to catch. There was no time to think about it anyway, because a moment later he was kissing her. Slowly. Deeply. His fingers tangling in her hair.

There was a soft thud that she realized was Toffee jumping to the floor. It was the last she thought of the cat as she sank into the mattress, Linus's body atop hers.

"Does this mean I'm forgiven?"

Linus laughed and tightened his embrace as Stella gave him a playful shove in the shoulder. This, pressed chest to chest in the sheets of Stella's bed, was the last place he imagined he'd be when he left London this morning. Hell, it was the last place he'd imagined an hour ago.

What an hour, though.

*"This won't change anything."*

Stella's words drifted into his post-lovemaking haze. Her attempt at reassurance. That they would still be friends. Friends with benefits. No expectations. No misreading of intentions.

Why did that bother him?

"Hey. Where'd you go?" Stella's gentle voice lured him back to the present.

"Nowhere important." He brushed the bangs from her face. Her skin still bore a hint of flush. Stella pink. His new favorite color.

"Was thinking how nice this feels. Never expected to end up here."

"Mmm…" Giving a little purr, she began to nuzzle closer only to pause and pull back. "It's good, though?"

The doubt in her voice broke his heart. How on earth

could she think otherwise? "Very." He pressed his lips to her shoulder to emphasize the point.

"Good." This time she tucked her head under his chin without pause.

They lay that way for a while, Linus's fingers tracing a lazy trail up and down Stella's spine. There was a soft meow, and a few seconds later a weight landed on the bed and began to purr.

"Why yes, Toffee, we'd love if you'd join us," he said.

Stella giggled. "As far as she's concerned, you're the interloper. Her house, remember?"

"True. Although in fairness, she would assume she owned any house she was in as a matter of feline privilege. Isn't that right, Toffee?" Proving his point, the cat plopped down against his leg.

"Do you think Teddy was telling the truth?" He'd prefer not to think of Teddy at all under the circumstances.

"I don't know. Like I said, it's a plausible story. We have no way of proving he isn't telling the truth."

"You're right. I suppose even if he was lying, there's not much we can do now. We'll be back to London tomorrow, and I'll make sure he's never alone with Toffee again."

"So much for late-night walks in Avebury," he muttered.

"Not unless we bring her along."

"Wouldn't that make an interesting picture. The two of us hauling a pet carrier in the moonlight." He smiled at the image.

Closing his eyes, he listened to the synchronized rhythm of their breaths. Each rise and fall reminding him of waves crashing against the shore. Little by little, he felt himself being pulled toward sleep.

"I meant what I said," Stella said suddenly.

"About what?" In his dreamlike state, his brain was slow to comprehend. Was she talking about Toffee still?

"About this not having to change anything."

He was awake now, a heaviness filling his stomach. "It won't?"

"No, so you don't have to worry about my freaking out or wonder if you're hurting me. Because I don't have any expectations. I promise."

"That's… Okay." Of course she didn't have expectations, as she'd made it clear time and again that any kind of emotional entanglement wasn't part of her plan. And as someone who'd vowed the same, he should be relieved.

Why, then, was he disappointed?

# CHAPTER NINE

*Winter*

LINUS STARED AT the brightly wrapped package in his hand. Inside was a gold chain with a tiny gold charm shaped like a ribbon. He knew because he'd spent an afternoon debating whether he should buy the bloody thing. A week later, he still wasn't sure.

"You're wasting your time, Linus, old man."

Linus stashed the box in his jacket pocket just before his brother, Thomas, clapped him on the shoulder. The normally staid executive was wearing the most garish Christmas sweater known to man and was munching on a Christmas cookie.

"Christmas Eve was last night," he said. "You're going to have to wait a whole three hundred and sixty-five days if you want to catch Santa."

Linus forced a smile. "Figured it was worth a try. Seeing as how you all have a special Christmas connection. Kids asleep?"

"Just about. Maddie crashed before I finished reading her first bedtime story. Rosalind's tucking in Noel. Who's the present for?"

"What present?"

"The one you just hid in your pocket," Thomas replied.

"Oh, that present. It's nothing. Just something I bought for a friend."

His brother took a bite of cookie. "This friend wouldn't be your pet-sitting neighbor, by any chance?"

"Estate manager." The correction was automatic. Linus swore his siblings purposely used the wrong title to bother him. Turning from the fireplace—and his brother—he headed to the other side of the living room, where Thomas had placed the bar.

"I'll take that as a yes," Thomas replied. "Hardly a surprise. She's the only person you socialize with outside of family. Why all the fuss?"

"Because I haven't decided if I want to give it to her," Linus replied. "Are you out of Scotch?"

"Bottom shelf, and why not?"

For a host of reasons, starting with whether Stella would consider the gift too extravagant—or worse, too sentimental. So uncertain was he that he'd even bought a backup present.

"I'm not sure, is all. We didn't talk about exchanging gifts. I don't want to put her on the spot."

In the past, if he was dating someone at Christmastime, he bought her something sparkly. But Stella wasn't the "something sparkly" type. Nor were they dating. They were "without expectations."

Stella had been right about one thing. When they returned from the country, things didn't change. They continued much as they had before, except that Linus slept over once or twice a week. She didn't ask where their relationship was going or talk about the future. She didn't ask him to share anything but her bed. If the two of them stopped sleeping together tomorrow, they would probably carry on. It was the perfect no-guilt affair. And yet, for the past six weeks, he'd been growing more and more unsettled.

He poured two glasses and handed one to Thomas. "The ice is melted. You'll have to drink it neat."

"I didn't realize I was drinking," he replied.

"I don't feel like drinking alone." Linus let the alcohol slide down his throat, savoring its warm burn. "That's how good Scotch should taste. Merry Christmas," he said.

"Merry Christmas." Thomas mirrored his action before setting the glass down on the bar. "You've been spending a lot of time with your neighbor these days."

"So?"

"So nothing. Glad to see you're getting out again after that whole Victoria nightmare. Susan said the woman seems very nice."

"Yeah, she's fantastic," Linus replied. The warmth inside him spread up and out, causing him to break out in a smile. "I've never met anyone like her."

Thomas gave him a long look.

"It's not what you think. We're friends. Good friends." He washed the words down with another swallow.

His brother continued to look at him, skepticism evident, so Linus added, "Lady's choice. She wants to keep things casual."

"Ah. Suddenly the present debate makes sense. Never thought I'd see the day when you were more serious than the woman."

"I'm not serious, either," Linus replied. "It's a mutual arrangement."

"Is that why you didn't bring her to Christmas? Whatever your status, I'd hate to think she's alone for the holidays."

"She's not. Her parents are visiting from Boston."

Stella had been high hover about the visit all week. Everything had to be perfect. The gifts, the decorations, the menu. One thing not on the list was her neighbor-slash-lover. She'd insisted he spend the holiday with his family like he always did.

Because she didn't want him feeling obligated, he told himself.

Problem was, he really wanted to see her. It'd been days since they'd spent time together, and he missed her smile.

"I'm debating stopping by on my way home to say merry Christmas. I don't want to intrude. On the other hand, it's the holiday."

Listen to him. He sounded like a lovesick idiot. Was this what it was like for the women he'd dated? This continual vacillating of uncertainty? Clearly, he owed them all apologies.

"Are you sure this is casual, Linus?" Thomas asked. "Because you're not acting like you normally do."

Because Linus didn't feel like he normally did. He didn't want to put a name to the emotions squeezing his chest because then he'd be in real trouble, but his refusal didn't stop the sensation. "Positive. She's out of here in six months. Plans to go back and take the international consulting world by storm."

"Plans can change," his brother replied. "Look at me. Couple years ago I was ready to leave the company for good, remember?"

"Different situation." Thomas had been trying to save his marriage. Stella's goals were about winning her father's pride. "Besides, there's no reason for her plans to change. We're simply having fun in the moment. If anything, it's refreshing to be on the same page with a woman. Much less stress."

"Except for the Christmas gift," Thomas said.

"Except for the Christmas gift." Having finished his drink, he debated pouring a second. Two Scotches felt too much like wallowing in alcohol.

"What did you get her?"

"A reminder of a very special night we shared, and before you say a word, get your mind out of the gutter. I'm referring to the tree in Avebury."

"I have zero idea what you're talking about, but I say go for it. If I've learned anything from being married, it's that women appreciate thoughtful gestures. If you bought something that has meaning, she'll like it." He gave Linus another look, this one using his glass to mask a grin. "Keeping it casual and fun, eh?"

Linus started to rethink that second Scotch.

Stella's sister's face filled half the divided computer screen. She wore a scrub top and a white lab coat.

"I wish I could be there with all of you," she said. "Cafeteria turkey is not the same as Mom's."

"We miss you, too, honey," Kevin Russo said, "but we understand. There'll be plenty of time for you to get away one you're established."

"In the meantime, I'll overnight you a container of stuffing as soon as we get back to Boston," Rose Russo added.

"What about me?" Her brother's face filled the other half of the screen. "I like your stuffing, too."

"I'll send you both stuffing. And apple pie."

Stella watched the conversation from the ottoman behind her parents. Toffee sat on her lap, the Angora doing her best to mark Stella's skirt with fur. Behind her, Agnes's china was neatly stacked on the dining room table, next to her silverware and glasses. They'd washed everything by hand since her mother was uncomfortable washing borrowed dishes in the dishwasher.

The Russo family video chat had become a tradition as neither Joe nor Camilla could spare time from work to travel. Both her parents took their continued absences in stride. They liked being able to tell people their oh-so-successful children were too important to spare.

This was the year she was supposed to be too important to spare as well.

"How's London?" Camilla was asking.

"Very nice," her mother replied. "Stella's been a wonderful tour guide."

"Guess when your boss is a cat, it's easy to get time off, hey, sis? Just throw a little extra food in the bowl and you're good to go?"

"Catnip," Stella replied. Her smile was tight, but Joe wouldn't notice. "Works every time."

"I thought maybe you had to bring her everywhere like those crazy cat ladies," Camilla said.

"I'm surprised she doesn't," her father said. "You should see the routine this cat has. Food. Brushing. She lives like a queen."

"Guess you should have gone to grooming school instead of studying finance, sis."

"You know, I do more than pet sit," Stella replied. Why did everyone treat her job like it was a joke? "I manage the estate. I'll have you know this cat has a sizable investment portfolio—"

"Which an outside investment company handles," her father cut in.

Yes, but Stella worked closely with them.

Working wasn't the same as doing, her father had been saying all weekend. He'd been saying a lot of things, like how she shouldn't have spent the money on plane tickets, about how she should push for more substantial work. How she shouldn't have signed a one-year agreement. Same script she'd been listening to—and would continue hearing until she returned to Mitchum, Baker.

She would return, though, and next Christmas, she'd be video calling home, too.

"Hey! I almost forgot! Guess who is presenting at the Association of Trial Lawyers midwinter meeting?"

Rose clapped her hands. "Joseph, that's wonderful! Congratulations. Where is the meeting?"

"Miami."

"No way! That's where I'm presenting my paper on odontoid synchondrosis fractures in toddlers. Wouldn't it be a riot if we were there at the same time?"

"You're presenting a paper, too?" Kevin said. "I told you all that work would pay off."

Stella edged away from the conversation. They would be talking about papers and Florida for a while, so no one would notice if she wasn't participating. She looked around her living room. There was a tree in the center, lit with tiny white lights and plastic decorations. Stella thought it odd until she realized Agnes must had purchased decorations with Toffee in mind. She found a box of vintage decorations tucked away in the attic along with a note signed by Larry and Vivien. Every item was another piece in the Dame Agnes Moreland story.

Stella hadn't told anyone, but she'd begun writing Agnes's story using the information in Agnes's letters and journals. Her parents didn't understand the fascination. Every time she tried to tell them, her father would wave off the topic. And Linus...

Without meaning to, she sighed. Linus would encourage her. Like he always did. There was no reason not to tell him. No reason to tell him, either. They didn't have to share everything because they shared a bed.

The best part of her week, the nights with Linus. Took all her restraint not to invite him to stay every night. She was determined to keep her promise and keep things between them casual. The guilt over Victoria was still there; Stella saw it in the shadow that crossed his face whenever he didn't think she was looking. He feared hurting her, and so she worked extra hard to make sure he knew that wouldn't happen. That she didn't expect anything from him beyond what they had.

The job would be a lot easier if she didn't miss him desperately on the nights he wasn't here. All she'd wanted these past couple days was to see his smile over morning coffee.

Sometimes, when they were having breakfast, Stella would look across the table at him, and her chest would feel like it was about to explode with fullness. So much of her life had been spent working toward a goal, on chasing some form of better or more that she could never quite reach. In those moments, though, when she looked at Linus, she didn't need to chase anything. The feeling was addictive and terrifying.

That's why she said no to spending Christmas together. It was clear to her that she was getting a little too attached to Linus. To see him smiling at her from across a family dinner table... God knew what effect that would have on her.

In the other room, she could hear the video chat wrapping up. Not wanting to be rude, she pasted on a smile and went back to say merry Christmas.

"Well, this makes a very merry Christmas indeed," her father said upon ending the call. "Always enjoy hearing the kids' good news. I can't wait to tell Donny. Maybe now he'll stop yapping about Dougie's pediatrics practice."

"Janice will be beside herself," Rose added. "Her daughter has always had a crush on Joe."

"Joe's always had a crush on Joe."

"Did you say something, Stella?"

"No, Mom."

"Those two are really making a mark in this world. I couldn't be prouder. You know what it is? It's because they're focused. They know what they want, and they don't stop until they've achieved it. They don't let a little adversity slow them down."

"No, they don't," Stella said. She added her father's speech to the list of things she'd heard before. Best to simply agree. Anything less would sound defensive, and as her parents were quick to point out, praising her older siblings didn't mean they were slighting her. Except they were.

"Are you expecting someone?" her mother asked when the doorbell rang.

"Not really." Hoping, but not expecting. She could kick herself for the way her pulse quickened. Couldn't she get through a week without needing to see the man?

She could give herself a double kick for the butterflies taking flight in her stomach when she looked through the peephole.

She flung open the door. "Merry Christmas," he greeted.

"Mer—" Before she could finish, he had pulled her into the hall and was kissing her. He tasted like fresh air and peppermint. Needing more, she pressed herself against him, her leg hooking around his in a quest to get closer. They were putting on an indecent show, but she didn't care.

"Merry Christmas yourself," she whispered when they finally parted. "Do you greet everyone who answers their door like that?"

He brushed the hair from her cheek. "Only the really gorgeous ones," he replied. "Can be a bit awkward if their spouse is home."

"Or their parents," she said, untangling herself. Her body protested at losing his warmth. "They're going to wonder what I'm doing outside. This is a very nice surprise. I wasn't expecting you to come by tonight."

"I…" There was that shadow again. The concern she wanted more. "I wanted to wish you a happy Christmas. Doesn't pack quite the same result on December 26."

"No, it does not." It was a struggle not to grab him by the lapels and start kissing again. Stella had no idea how badly she'd missed him—that is, she knew she'd missed him a lot, but she'd had no idea how much a lot really was. It was like a switch inside her had been turned off and his arrival turned it back on.

Not good. Not good at all. She was going to have to do something about her attachment.

"Did you want to come in?" she asked, before quickly adding, "You don't have to stay long. I know it's late, but my parents—well, my mother, really—will want to know who rang the doorbell, so it might help if you stuck your head in and said hello. Nothing big. I'm not expecting you to stay." The last thing she wanted was for him to feel forced into a "meet the parents" scenario.

"Because it's late," he said.

"Exactly, and I'm sure you're tired after chasing your niece around all day."

"Not so tired that I can't step inside for a moment."

"Really?" Could she sound any more eager? "I mean, great."

The two of them stepped inside to discover her parents standing in the center of the living room. Her mother was holding Toffee. Her father was frowning.

"Everything all right, Stella?" he asked.

When did time revert back to high school? Her parents were staring at her like she'd missed curfew, and her heart was racing like a girl on her first date.

Stella took a deep breath. "Everything is fine. This is my…" She stumbled for the right word. "Neighbor, Linus Collier. He stopped by to say merry Christmas. Linus, these are my parents, Kevin and Rose Russo."

Linus had never met a woman's parents before. Family introductions carried implications. They were a benchmark that implied you were no longer dating, but rather a couple. He and Stella were neither, and yet, he had to wipe his palm on his pants before shaking Stella's father's hand.

Kevin Russo was tall and barrel-chested, with a thick head of silver hair. He had the calloused handshake of a man who worked hard and the cashmere sweater of one who was reaping the benefits. His wife, Rose, looked like an older version of Stella, only with salt-and-pepper hair.

"Merry Christmas," she greeted. "It's nice to meet you. Stella didn't tell us she was friendly with her neighbor."

He didn't even warrant a mention. Linus tried not to let his disappointment show. "Well, we are the only two people on the floor."

"Linus and I are running partners," Stella explained. "That's how I know my way around London. He's been running me all over the city."

"Bit of a rabbit, she is. I've taken more than a few seconds off my time keeping up."

"Liar," Stella said. "I'm the one working to keep up with him."

They took seats in the living room, Stella's father taking the large chair by the tree. Linus drank in Stella's appearance. She looked magnificent tonight in a black turtleneck and watch plaid skirt. The hem was short enough he could see a glimpse of thigh when she crossed her legs.

"My children are all athletes," Kevin was saying. "Our eldest, Camilla, ran track in college. The four-forty."

"Four hundred meters," Stella supplied.

"Impressive. Good for her." Stella had already told him, along with the fact that she—unlike her sister—didn't run in college.

Meanwhile, Stella caught him checking out her thighs and winked. He wondered what her father would say if he knew that while he was singing his eldest daughter's praises, Linus was thinking about running his hands along the inside of the man's youngest daughter's legs.

"Are you enjoying your trip to London?" he asked. "I'm guessing Stella has shown you all the highlights."

"Couldn't ask for a better tour guide," Rose replied. No surprise there. Stella had spent the week before their arrival staying awake late into the night, searching for tourist tips. "Of course, Kevin and I have been to London several times, but we liked getting her perspective. It's been nice seeing how she's getting along after... I mean, over here."

"From the looks of things, I'd say she'd doing quite well," Linus said. "At least she seems put together when I see her getting the mail. Are you failing at anything we don't know about?"

"If I am, my lips are sealed." She grinned, and damned if his insides didn't get turned around. He had to cross his legs to keep his arousal at bay.

"Has Stella told you about Dame Agnes's vast collection of memorabilia? The woman was quite a character."

"We guessed that when she left all the money to that one." Rose tipped her head toward Toffee, who was sniffing the Christmas tree branches.

"Creative types. They don't think like the rest of us, do they?" Kevin said. "I always told my kids, make sure you go into something practical like law or medicine."

"Or business," Linus interjected.

"Or business. I never met anyone who made money majoring in history or the arts."

"What do you do for a living, Mr. Collier?" Rose asked.

Linus wanted to tell her a job that involved history or the arts, especially after the way Stella looked down at her hands at her father's comment, but he didn't want to cause an argument. "I'm a chemist."

"See? Science. A good practical major. Camilla, that's Stella's sister, majored in biology. She's a neurosurgeon now."

He went on for several minutes about Stella's siblings and their careers. Good, practical careers. Linus nodded and showed the appropriate appreciation, all the while waiting for the man to get to his youngest.

Across the way he could see Stella folding in on herself, the weight of her father's obliviousness bearing down on her. Her mother was no better. Her attention to her daughter focused on Stella playing the proper hostess. Twice she interrupted to suggest Stella get him coffee or a cocktail.

He wasn't sure he liked the Russos. He didn't care how big the chip on Kevin Russo's shoulder over dropping out of school was.

"Sounds as though you've raised three successful children," he said.

"That's always been my goal," Kevin told him. "To make sure my kids had the chance to accomplish everything I never had the chance to do. Of course," Kevin continued, "Stella's real career is in New York. Corporate finance. She won't be doing this job forever. Isn't that right, sweetheart?"

Stella's smile looked strained as she nodded. At least he didn't call her a pet sitter. He might have been tempted to consider Russo's words a warning about getting serious with his daughter, but he doubted the man thought him a threat. He was too secure in his knowledge that Stella would be returning to New York. To "have the chance" to do everything he hadn't accomplished.

And why shouldn't he be confident? Stella bloody flew them here to impress them.

Meanwhile the man was busy bragging about everyone but her. The man had a beautiful, smart, amazing daughter sitting five feet away, and he couldn't see her. Took all of Linus's willpower not to strangle Kevin Russo's thick neck. Or, at the very least, to tell him to take his aspirations and stuff them.

"Toffee, no!" Stella clapped her hands, startling everyone in the room. She was answered by an annoyed-sounding meow and the tinkling of glass.

"Sorry," she said. "Toffee's obsessed with one of the bird ornaments on the tree. I caught her trying to climb the branches the other day."

It was the break in the conversation he needed. Linus stood up. "On that note, I think I'll say good-night."

"Do you have to go?" Stella asked.

He both loved and hated the disappointment in her voice. "I'm afraid so. Maddie ran me ragged. My niece," he added for her parents' benefit. "It was a pleasure meeting you both."

Stella walked him to the door. When they were far enough from the living room, she slipped in between him and the door. "Are you too tired for a visitor later?" she asked. "I was hoping to bring by a little Christmas present."

God, but he loved when her voice turned husky. He dropped his gaze to her lips. "I could be persuaded to stay awake for a bit."

"Good. I'll be by as soon as I can."

As she spoke, she ran her finger down his stomach to his belt and crooked a finger into his waistband. Linus sucked in his breath, his head suddenly filled with what he might do under his Christmas tree.

"I'll leave the door unlocked," he whispered.

Tiny Tim could bless everyone if he wanted; Stella blessed jet lag. It meant she only received a short inquest following Linus's departure. Her mother wanted to know why she hadn't mentioned Linus before while her father treated her to another lecture on focus. Finally, they declared themselves exhausted and, after thanking her for a wonderful Christmas dinner, headed to bed.

Stella waited until the light underneath their door disappeared before tiptoeing to the living room in her bare feet. Sneaking out of the apartment made her feel like a teenager, the illicitness adding an extra layer of excitement. She paused long enough to grab a small box from beneath the tree and then slipped out the door.

Just as Linus had promised, the door was unlocked. Linus's apartment was a mirror image of hers, only decorated with a more masculine taste. She stepped inside to find the apartment dark, except for the Christmas tree. The evergreen bathed the grays and blacks in red light. A fire crackled in the gas fireplace.

"Linus?"

"Merry Christmas, love."

His voice wrapped around her like a warm caress. Turning around, she saw him in the easy chair by the fire, his clothes shed in favor of his paisley robe. His bare chest looked pink by the light. Her fingers itched to comb through the exposed hair.

"Brought you something to unwrap," she said, holding up the package in her hand.

"Lucky me. I love unwrapping things."

"What a coincidence. So do I." Smiling, she swayed toward him, and climbed on the chair, one knee at a time. Reaching down, she gave the belt of the robe a tug. The silk half knot fell loose easily. "See?"

"I thought I was supposed to be doing the unwrapping?" Linus's voice was thick and heavy with promise. Stella melted a little more. Her breathing quickened as Linus slipped his hands beneath her skirt and brushed her skin. Slowly, lightly, his fingers skimmed upward. When he reached the apex, his eyes widened.

"Silly me," Stella said, leaning forward. "Looks like I forgot the wrapping paper."

They didn't talk after that.

# CHAPTER TEN

LATER, THEY LAY beneath the Christmas tree, Stella resting on top of him, Linus's robe draped over her back like a blanket. She kissed the hollow of his throat, the taste of salt coming away on her lips. When she was in his arms, her parents, their expectations, the shadow of her insecurity, all faded away. In these moments she felt competent.

No, she felt special. Lucky.

Was this how his other lovers felt? Did he make the world disappear for them as well? The power he possessed frightened and amazed her.

"Penny for your thoughts?" Linus's voice vibrated in his chest.

"I'm thinking every Christmas should end this way."

"Naked and under a tree?"

"Mmm…" With limbs too boneless to move.

"I'll make a note for the future."

Only Stella wouldn't be here. She'd be in New York while he lay with someone else. She pushed the thought away. Thoughts of the future made her chest squeeze.

"I should go back soon," she said instead. "My parents will expect me in the apartment when they wake up."

"We still have time. There's no rush."

"If I stay here too long, I'll fall asleep."

"So?"

"So…" She lifted her head. "Your floor isn't as comfortable as a bed."

"Then we'll switch to my bed."

"Then I'll never leave."

"Damn, you've discovered my evil plan."

Stella yelped as he suddenly flipped their positions. Their bodies aligned naturally, her legs parting as he settled between them.

"I guess a few more minutes won't hurt," she managed to say, just before his mouth claimed hers. As always happened, she lost herself in the kiss.

Linus was in the process of kissing his way down her sternum when a flash of red caught her eye. Largely because her back was arched. It was enough, however, to bring her back to the present. "Your present. I forgot all about it."

"I thought I already opened my present. In fact, I was thinking of opening it again." He tried to resume his kissing.

Stella gave him a playful shove. "Your real present, silly. I dropped the box by the chair when we were otherwise occupied. I want you to open it before I leave."

Ignoring his exaggerated sigh, she scrambled out of his arms to retrieve the package. As she turned around, she caught him staring at her. "What?"

"You're beautiful," he said.

"I'm a mess." Her hair was tussled. Her makeup had to be smudged. And, she was kneeling bare-ass naked, her skin bathed in red Christmas lights.

"I happen to love messes," he said.

She looked at the box in her hands. A figure of speech. He didn't actually mean the words. They weren't… Well, they just weren't.

"Here." She held the box. "I know we didn't discuss getting presents, but…"

"Wouldn't feel right not to exchange gifts on Christmas," he finished.

"Precisely. Go ahead. Open it." She held her breath as he peeled off the paper. It had taken hours of web surfing and inner debate before she found what she hoped was an appropriate gift. Something of substance. Not too personal. Not too impersonal.

"A Swiss watch."

"A scientist's watch. At least that's what the ad said. It's antimagnetic. Durable, too. We'll have to see, since I dropped the box on the carpet."

Linus took the watch from the box and ran his fingers across the face. The shadows made his face unreadable.

"Do you like it?" she asked.

"It's…lovely."

"I'm glad." Her shoulders relaxed. "There's a note, too. At the bottom of the box."

Writing the note had been more agonizing than picking out the gift. She'd wanted to write something poignant like "certain memories last forever" or "you are timeless," but everything she came up with sounded too intimate or trite. She'd finally settled on simple.

"'To the best friend and neighbor a girl could have. Merry Christmas, Stella and Toffee.'" Linus looked up.

"Figured it was only appropriate her name be included."

"Of course. Wouldn't be right to exclude the cause of our friendship."

Stella got an uneasy feeling. Linus was saying all the right words. His response, though, felt off. Like she'd messed up somehow.

She'd spent too much time with her parents. They always exacerbated her insecurity.

"I believe I promised you a present, too." Linus set the watch aside and reached under the tree, the light dancing off his skin. And he thought her beautiful? He took her breath away.

She watched as he picked up a narrow gold box only to pause and set it aside in favor of a brightly wrapped square. "I hope you like it."

It was a silver bracelet with a tiny silver cat charm. Stella held up the charm so she could watch it sparkle. "Was Toffee involved in this gift, too?" she teased.

"I thought it the appropriate choice."

"I love it."

"I'm glad."

Again, he said the right words, but she swore his eyes weren't sparkling as brightly as before. There was a serious edge to his expression as he searched her face. Before she could ask why however, his hands were cradling her face. Her eyes fluttered shut, and once more, she lost herself in his kiss.

The day after New Year's, Teddy showed for what had become his monthly oversight meeting. Having officially challenged the will, he was now mandating them. Stella made a point of staying out of the matter. As she told Linus, while she loved Toffee and her job, she considered the inheritance battle a family matter. On the plus side, the situation served as a good reminder that the apartment and her position were only temporary. There were times when she felt entirely too at home.

"I understand there was an auction planned. That the estate was planning to liquidate some of Aunt Agnes's belongings," Teddy said when Mrs. Churchill answered the door. Since the incident in Berkshire, he'd dispensed with congenialities.

"Happy New Year to you as well," Stella replied. "How was your holiday?"

Teddy shed his overcoat and handed it over to the housekeeper, along with a request for tea. "My holiday was fine. I see you embraced the Christmas spirit," he said, taking in the greenery.

"Toffee and I did indeed. We had a wonderful holiday." If you called four days of trying to impress her parents and failing wonderful. She was beginning to wonder if she'd ever win their approval. There were bright spots, though. Like Christmas night. She fingered the silver charm dangling from her wrist. That weird moment under the tree, she'd decided, was simply leftover neuroses from being with her parents.

Teddy helped himself to a seat on the sofa, his arms stretched along the back as far as they could reach.

"I want to know about this auction. What were you planning to sell?"

Nothing anymore, thanks to his lawsuit. "The plan was to liquidate some unnecessary assets such as the wine collection and the art and furniture Agnes had in storage. The proceeds would have been reinvested and the interest added to the funds for Toffee's care. Obviously, the plan has been put on hold." Along with every other major financial decision.

"I should hope so," Teddy said. "That you would even consider selling assets without consulting me is appalling."

Stella settled in the chair across from him and dug her nails into the ends of the armrest. "It's the trust's job to decide what assets are sold. The only reason you are being given courtesy now is because of the lawsuit."

Apparently, she'd given up congenialities as well. "But if it makes you feel better, I can assure you we weren't selecting items willy-nilly."

"Now you aren't selecting items at all, are you?" Teddy replied.

"No. We are not." In football, they would call that a blocked kick.

Satisfied he'd gotten the last word on the subject, Teddy smiled. "Peter also tells me there's to be a museum exhibit. A retrospective of my aunt's career."

Peter had been chatty. "Yes. I've been talking to the V&A about it. Dame Agnes was an English institution. I have a meeting with the museum director next week."

"I would like to attend as well," Teddy told her.

"You would?" She didn't know why she was surprised, what with Teddy's increased scrutiny.

"My aunt had a lot of idiosyncrasies. As her only living relative, it's my duty to ensure that the narrative surrounding her life is told in a manner equating to her stature."

Bull. This was another ploy for control. Stella suppressed an eye roll. If only Linus were here. She could picture him giving Teddy the side eye. He had this way of arching his brow just so. Never failed to make her giggle. The man made everything more enjoyable.

Even something like New Year's dinner with his sister and her fiancé. A smile threatened as she recalled the mischief they'd gotten into hiding in the coatroom. Happy New Year indeed.

She'd hated sending him to work this morning. Forty-eight straight hours together and there she was practically begging for him to come back tonight.

She was definitely getting too comfortable.

"What is that?" Teddy interrupted her thoughts by pointing to the dining room table behind her where stacks of paper littered the surface. A disorganized outline of her novel. The past week had found her working on the novel more and more. Something about the project called to her. Jotting down notes and cross-referencing anecdotes with history reminded her of when she was young. She was ten years old and daydreaming again.

She doubted Teddy would approve, though. He'd want to review the narrative. No way.

"Here's your tea, Mr. Moreland." With exquisite timing, Mrs. Churchill came down the hall carrying a cup and saucer. "Black rooibos, two sugars, no milk. Just the way you like it," she said. "Oh, and I found this in the kitchen."

Using her free hand, she held up a gold-and-silver egg. "Looks like someone's been poking around the library desk again," Mrs. Churchill said.

Stella sighed. "Put it on the mantel, please. She hasn't been able to get up there since I moved the chairs."

"Is that Aunt Agnes's kaleidoscope?" Teddy snatched the egg from the housekeeper's hand, teacup rattling from the motion. "Are you telling me you let the cat bat this around like a common cat toy?"

"I didn't let Toffee do anything. She's was being a cat. They get into things and cause mischief."

"Not if they're being properly watched."

This time she did roll her eyes. "Clearly you've never owned a pet."

"If I did, I wouldn't let it crawl all over the furniture messing with valuable items. I'd pay closer attention."

How dare he? The man comes in and starts throwing his weight around, doesn't bother to ask about Toffee—doesn't even say her name—and now suggests she wasn't keeping a close enough eye on her cat? "I keep a very close eye on Toffee, thank you very much." Rising from her seat, she crossed the room and snatched the kaleidoscope from Teddy's hand. "I know everything there is to know about that cat. Where she sleeps, what cat food flavors she likes best. I even know what kind of brush she prefers. Don't tell me I'm not paying attention." She ended by gently setting the egg on the mantel, beneath Agnes's portrait. The gold's shine looked brighter behind the evergreen needles.

"Obviously you weren't paying attention when she decided to play with the kaleidoscope."

"In Miss Russo's defense," Mrs. Churchill said, "the creature causes most of her trouble in the middle of the night. Hard to watch her at two in the mornin'."

"Then she should be crated overnight," Teddy replied. "I'm not going to see a valuable object broken because of a cat's curiosity."

Stella's eyes widened. "Did you seriously suggest I put my cat in a crate? No wonder Agnes didn't make you Toffee's guardian."

"She's not your cat," Teddy replied. "You are the cat's caretaker, and to be honest, I'm not sure you're doing as good a job as you should be."

He joined her at the mantel. Picking up the kaleidoscope, he turned the egg back and forth in his fingers. "First you left her unattended in Berkshire, and now this."

"I left her with you."

Teddy ignored her. "Who knows what's been broken or lost on your watch."

"Nothing," she replied, snatching the kaleidoscope back.

"All the same, I would like to see that inventory you were working on. To ascertain for myself."

Stella's stomach dropped. There were still a large number of items unaccounted for. The trust had hired an investigator to look into the situation, but so far, no luck. While the disappearances predated her arrival, Teddy would still take issue.

"Of course," she said. "I'll need a few days to pull together all the information. There are a number of files to be merged." She also needed to talk with the trust advisers before handing over anything.

"Next week will be fine. I'm nothing if not flexible.

Although I'm warning you. If I detect any kind of subter-fuge or an attempt to delay hoping I'll forget the request, I'll have your job. Do I make myself clear?"

The threat came on a cloud of tea and peppermint so strong it made her want to gag.

"Crystal," she replied.

And to think, when she first met the man, she'd thought him a pompous buffoon. The thought that he could ruin her reputation—and being sacked for mismanaging the es-tate would definitely ruin her reputation—made her stom-ach churn more.

She needed to call Linus. She needed his levelheaded way of telling her everything would be all right.

She needed him.

"It's going to be fine, you know," Linus said when they went to bed that night. "You have done an amazing job of taking care of Toffee."

"I think you're a wee bit biased, but thank you anyway." She kissed his cheek. Just as she knew he would, he spoke to her common sense. The missing items weren't her fault. In fact, talking with Teddy might actually answer some of her questions.

The man beside her yawned. "Sorry," he said. "I'm get-ting old. Can't stay up the way I used to."

"Then go to sleep. We'll talk in the morning."

"Mmm… Sounds perfect." Rolling onto his side, he pulled her close. Big spoon to her little one. "G'night, love," he slurred.

"Good night, old man." She smiled to herself before scooting backward until the space between them disap-peared completely. His arms were the perfect cocoons. She closed her eyes and listened to Linus's breathing. He made her feel so safe and secure. Special.

What would she do without him?

*You'd better learn. You're out of here in six months.*

Stella's eyes flew open, her heart suddenly racing. The antsy sensation she'd felt at Christmas returned, only tenfold. She understood why now. She was getting way too attached. Her casual affair was playing much too large a role in her life. Everything she did, everything she thought revolved around this man.

At least a half dozen times a day she had to stop herself from texting about some random idea or occurrence, and when he texted her? It was like sunshine wrapped in the ding of her phone. And on the few nights he didn't sleep over, she would toss and turn all night for the emptiness in her bed and wonder if the separation caused his chest to ache, too.

No wonder her heart was racing. She was digging herself a hole she did not need.

There was only one solution—expand her world beyond Linus. Of course he played a central role in her life. How often did she see anyone else? Maybe if she saw other people, Linus's presence wouldn't have such a pull.

There was a man at the auction house with whom she'd had several meetings. Niles Brown. He'd invited her to dinner at their last meeting, but she'd said no because she had to get home to feed Toffee. Tomorrow, she would give Niles a call, see if he wanted to grab coffee.

She tamped down the guilt in her stomach. It was just coffee. She was increasing her circle of friends. And even if it was more than coffee, she and Linus weren't in a committed relationship. What they had was casual, fun and noncommittal. Linus knew that, same as he knew he was free to go out for coffee with a friend, too. It was no big deal.

She continued arguing the point with herself for the rest of the sleepless night.

* * *

"You're going out to dinner," Linus said. "With another man."

"You say it like I'm planning to commit murder," Stella replied. "We were originally going to have coffee, but Niles's schedule got messed up, so we decided to do dinner instead."

"I see."

He looked her up and down. She was dressed in a black dress and pointy heels. Pretty fancy.

Oh, but what did he know? They were only friends and neighbors, right?

The phrase had been eating at him since Christmas night. And now she was going out with some bloke from an auction house he'd never heard her mention before.

The worst part was he couldn't say anything, not really, because he'd arrived at the same time as Teddy Moreland. The older man was standing by the fireplace waiting on Stella's inventory report.

He leaned against a sideboard, attempting a casual veneer. "I didn't realize you'd become friends with anyone at the auction house."

"Yes, well…" She smoothed her beaded necklace against her throat. "I thought it a good idea to expand my social circle. I mean, I've been monopolizing your time since I arrived."

"Did I say I minded?"

"No, but that doesn't mean it's fair. Especially since we're not, well, you know."

*In a real relationship.* "So you're doing this for my benefit? Is that what you're saying?"

"Yes. I mean, no." She began fiddling with her necklace again. "I just think it would be a good idea if I spent time with more people than just you and your family."

"Right. Where is he taking you?"

"A restaurant in Soho. He didn't say." That explained the dress.

"Soho has some lovely places." He'd been planning to take her to one of his favorites for Valentine's Day.

"You're okay with my going, then?"

No, he wasn't okay, but what good would saying so do? "Are you asking my permission?"

"Of course not. I… Never mind."

"Excuse me for interrupting such an important conversation." His expression anything but sorry, Teddy strolled toward them, hands stuffed in the pockets of his overcoat. "I don't have all evening. You called and said the inventory list was ready?"

"On the dining room table," Stella said. "Hold on."

While Stella went to retrieve the paperwork, the old man smirked at Linus. "Trouble in paradise, Collier?"

Linus would be damned before admitting anything to Moreland. "How are things, Teddy? Still fighting to prove you're better than a cat?"

"I don't have to prove anything. I'm confident things will work out in my favor."

"You know what they say about overconfidence, Teddy. It often clashes with reality."

"We'll have to wait and see about that, won't we," Teddy replied, his smirk widening. His cocksureness set the hair on the back of Linus's neck on edge. The man was up to something.

"Here you go, Teddy." Stella returned carrying a thick manila envelope. "If you have any questions, call."

"Don't worry, I will," Teddy replied. "Have questions, that is. Nice to see you again, Collier."

"Still upset about what happened in Berkshire, isn't he?" Linus remarked, once Teddy closed the door. "Man knows how to hold a grudge."

"I'm still not one hundred percent certain he was telling the truth about what happened that night," Stella said. "You can't tell me he wouldn't have been happy if Toffee disappeared into those woods."

Linus was prone to agree. While he figured Agnes had her reasons for disinheriting Teddy, he largely thought the man was a harmless, drunken blowhard. Then again, eleven million could turn even a harmless blowhard nasty.

"I still don't think you have anything to worry about as far as your job is concerned. Teddy's interested in the money, not being a guardian."

"Maybe, but a guardian controls the money and Toffee's life span." She looked over to the terrace door, where Toffee lay on her side. Seeing the worry in Stella's profile, the lines that deepened by her mouth, the forlornness that clouded her eyes, Linus's first instinct was to wrap her in his arms. He couldn't, though. If he did, he would end up kissing her senseless, and he was no longer sure that's what she wanted. From him, anyway.

"I should be leaving," he said. "Your company will be here soon."

"You don't have to leave," Stella said.

"Don't you think having your FWB around might make things awkward for your date?"

FWB. Friend with benefits. The term sounded sour on his tongue.

"Will I see you tomorrow?"

He had his hand on the doorknob when she asked. "I don't know," he said, keeping his eyes on the brass knob. "Thomas wants to start discussing our summer product line. There's a good chance I'll be tied up all week."

"Oh."

She sounded disappointed. "These things happen."

"I know. I... It'll be strange not seeing you, is all."

"I'm sure if you get bored, your friend Niles can entertain you." Immediately, he regretted the childish remark. To make amends, he turned and offered her a half smile. "Have a nice time at dinner."

# CHAPTER ELEVEN

"KEEPING IT CASUAL. Nothing will change. I'm going to dinner with some bloke from work." Scotch splashed the sides of his glass as he waved his arms widely. He was on his second Scotch and probably his second mile of pacing the living room.

How could Stella go on a date with someone else? Sorry, dinner. It was ludicrous. They were sleeping together, for God's sake. Had been for months. Didn't that mean anything?

Not for friends with benefits, it didn't. The two of them were neighbors. They were keeping things casual.

Casual, casual, casual. He was going to strangle the next person who said the word.

He should have kissed her like he wanted to. Grabbed her and kissed her until she forgot all about what's his name.

He should have told her he didn't want her seeing anyone else, because… Because…

Suddenly the emotion that had been squeezing his chest for months had a name. "I love you," he whispered, the words loud in the silence. He loved her. The more he repeated the words, the more certain he became. He, Linus Collier, had fallen in love with the American next door.

And she didn't love him back.

Christ. He plopped down on his sofa. When irony hit, it hit hard, didn't it?

Appeared he'd finally learned what it was like to be just another shag. Was this how his former lovers felt? As if someone had plunged a knife in the center of their chests? He owed them all apologies, because damn, it hurt like hell.

"You made your point, universe. You finally doled out your punishment." He emptied his glass. That was the universe's ultimate punishment.

Just then he heard the elevator doors. Leaping up, Linus hurried to the front door. This was what his life had become. Standing with his ear pressed to a door trying to eavesdrop. On the other side were muffled voices. Stella and her date. He heard Stella's keys. Imagined her opening the door, then leaning in for a good-night kiss. Linus squeezed the tumbler. That should be his good-night kiss. He should be leaning against her door frame waiting for an invitation to come inside.

So help him, if she invited what's his name inside...

She didn't. The elevator doors dinged, telling him as much. Linus breathed a sigh of relief, because he wasn't sure how he would have ended the thought.

What did he do now?

*Talk to her, you idiot. Tell her how you feel.*

If she knew how important she was to him—that he bloody loved her—then she'd realize this whole "casual lovers" thing was ridiculous.

In the back of his mind, he wondered if he should wait until he had a clear head, but he pushed the thought aside and headed outside. He needed to talk with her tonight. Otherwise, it would eat at him all night long. Besides, he was declaring his love, not picking a fight.

Now that he'd had a moment to get used to the idea, he was gobsmacked. Never in his life had he expected that he, Linus Collier, would fall in love and want to commit to a woman. Guess there was more of his father in him than he realized.

Stella answered the door in her stocking feet. Since the summer, her hair had grown so that the bob skimmed the center of her neck. Tonight she wore her hair pulled back in a hairband to better show off her heart-shaped face. As happened whenever he saw her, she took his breath away.

"Linus, what are you…?"

He didn't let her finish. Cradling her cheeks, he kissed her deeply. Instead of smiling her hands clutched at his shirt as she kissed him back.

"Bet you didn't kiss him like that," he rasped when the kiss ended.

Her brows drew together as she stood a step back and stared at him. "Were you spying on us?"

"Don't be sound so surprised. I live next door. Did you think I wouldn't notice when you came home?"

"That is possessive and creepy."

"Are you serious? After I let you go out with another man?"

Stella glared at him. "You didn't let me do anything."

"You asked for my permission."

"Hardly. I was keeping you informed out of courtesy. You didn't have a say in it one way or another."

The conversation wasn't going how he planned. Stella stomped away from him, into the living room, where she stopped in front of the fireplace. Toffee's portrait stared down on them while the original wove around his legs. At least someone in the house was glad to see him. Linus obliged the cat and gathered her in his arms.

"I'm sorry," he said. "You're right. I don't own you and I shouldn't have implied that I did."

"Thank you," she said. "Now, why are you here?"

"Because I…" *I love you.* Suddenly he was afraid to say

the words. "I wanted to see how the evening went. Did you have a good time?"

"Seriously?"

"Yes, I want to know. I'm curious." She continued giving him a skeptical look. "All right," he said after a few moments. "I'm jealous."

Stella blinked. "You are?"

"Does that surprise you? We *are* sleeping together. I'm not one for sharing."

"Is that so?"

Terrific. She thought him possessive again. Closing his eyes, he out a long breath. Everything was coming out wrong. They shouldn't be fighting.

Still holding Toffee, he turned and put some space between them. There was a cat perch near the terrace doors. He placed Toffee on the top level, then stared at their reflection in the glass. Behind him, Stella could be seen playing with the armchair piping.

If this was going to work, he needed stop dancing around the words and tell her how he felt. "I know that night in Avebury, we said we would keep things light and noncommittal." He refused to say that horrid word. "But I don't think I can. I hated thinking of you being out with someone else tonight. Absolutely hated it."

As he spoke, he watched her reflection. Thus far, she hadn't stopped studying the chair. "What are you saying?" she asked.

"I don't want us to see other people. What we're doing isn't a low-key thing for me anymore." He spun around. It was important she see his face. See his sincerity when he bared his soul. "I love you."

"Wh-what?"

He smiled at her stunned expression. "I don't blame you for being shocked. I was shocked too when I realized it."

"You're drunk."

"No. I'm completely clearheaded right now, and I mean every word. I love you and I want us to be together."

Unable to stay separated a moment longer, he took her in his arms. "You're trembling." Like a leaf in a cold wind. He tightened his embrace.

"I…I can't believe it," she said. "You can't be in love with me."

"But I am."

"You don't understand." She pulled away, leaving his arms empty. "I mean you can't be in love with me."

Linus looked like she'd slapped him. "What the bloody hell is that supposed to mean?"

"It means we had an agreement. We were going to keep this—us—casual." For some reason, he grimaced when she said the word. "I have plans," she said. "In New York."

"You're not in New York now. You're in London."

"I know where I am," she snapped. What mattered wasn't where she was, but where she was going. "My point is that I'm leaving in a few months."

"So?"

"So, I don't have time to fall in love." Unable to face him and continue this argument, she headed to the mantel. "When I return home, I need to give one hundred percent of my attention to building a career in finance."

"Right. Just like your father wants. So he can brag about you to the relatives."

"I'm not doing it so he can brag." It was a good thing she'd turned her back to him. Kept her from snarling in his face. "This is about me, and proving that I'm—"

"As good as your siblings. You shouldn't have to prove anything."

Stella shook her head. He didn't understand. Not really. How could he? He'd spent his life accepted. The born scientist, his role in the family predetermined, what did he have to prove?

Linus's hands came to rest on her shoulders. Without looking, she knew his expression was marked by softness, his eyes compassionate and heavy lidded. "I don't care what you do or who you are," he said. "I just want to love you."

And she wanted his love. Oh, but she wanted it. She closed her eyes. Her limbs were shaking. Just like that day on Fifty-Second Street, she was afraid to move. It was like she was holding on to a ledge by her fingertips. If she let go…

*You'll be happy.*

*You'll forever be a disappointment.*

Her heart twisted in her chest. "I can't…"

"There's nothing more to be said, then, is there?"

His hands slipped away, leaving her standing by the fire, cold and alone, listening to his footsteps grow fainter.

"Linus, wait!"

She turned just as he reached the door. "I…" The words wouldn't come. Not the ones he wanted to hear. They remained trapped in her chest, blocked by fear. "I'm sorry."

She could see the disappointment in his eyes from across the room. The sorrow reached across the distance and pierced her heart, where, she suspected, it would stay for a long time. "So am I," he said. "I'd hoped… Never mind. Doesn't matter now. Goodbye, Stella."

Goodbye? Was this it? She stumbled a few steps forward, only to stop and collapse on the sofa. From out of nowhere, Toffee leaped on the cushion beside her, meowing softly. "It's for the best," Stella told her. "We were getting too attached."

Forty-eight hours later, there was still a persistent lump in Stella's throat that had her constantly feeling on the verge of tears.

Thing was, crying would be welcome. Only she couldn't.

God knew she'd wanted to since Linus walked out the door, but tears refused to come. It was as if her body wanted to hold on to the sadness.

*I'll be fine in a few more days.*

That had become her new mantra. She'd been repeating the words all morning. When she woke up in her empty bed. When she found Linus's T-shirt in her laundry hamper. When she heard the elevator door sound as Linus left for work.

*I'll be fine in a few days.*

This heavy, pervasive sadness was a normal reaction to the ending of a friendship. And that's all it was—a friendship. A friendship with good sex.

Make that great sex. Not to mention being the best friendship she'd ever had.

Dammit! Why did Linus have to spoil everything by saying he loved her? Didn't he realize that if she let her feelings go beyond casual she would be forced to rethink…?

No, she wasn't going down that road. She had to return to New York and focus on her career as expected. That was what she wanted.

"You understand, don't you, Toffee? I have to prove myself."

Toffee didn't answer. The Angora had her back to Stella and was bathing. She hadn't slept on the bed the past two nights, either. A paranoid person would think the cat was trying to punish her.

She'd come around. Eventually the cat would need her chin scratched and Stella would once again be her best friend. In the meantime, she had a meeting to prepare for. The accountant was coming by to discuss the yearly expense budget.

Numbers work was exactly what Stella needed. Forty-five minutes later, she was properly immersed in figures when there was a knock on the door. Stella's breath caught. He'd come back.

"I'll get it, Mrs. Churchill!"

She hurried to the foyer, pausing to check her reflection in the mirror. Her face was peaked and her hair flat, but otherwise, she was presentable. She brushed the bangs from her face and, taking a deep breath, opened the door.

It was Teddy Moreland.

He wasn't alone, either. Peter Singh was with him as well as another man she didn't recognize. "Hello, Stella," Peter said. His dour expression clashed with his red cashmere scarf.

Seeing the three men together set Stella's nerves on edge. She and Peter always met at his office. "Is something wrong?"

"I'll say there is." Teddy pushed the door wider and barged inside. "I need you out of my apartment."

"Your apartment?" Stella squinted at the man in confusion.

Peter took a deep breath. "Teddy. We agreed that I would handle the situation."

"What situation?" Stella asked.

"Let's sit down, shall we?" Peter said. He and the other man stepped into the living room. Teddy was already there, still wearing his overcoat and pacing in front of the fireplace. The other men shed their overcoats and draped them over the back of the sofa before making themselves comfortable.

Stella opted to stand. She had a very bad feeling. "Would someone please tell me what's going on?" she asked.

Peter started. "Stella, this is Montgomery Armstrong."

"My attorney," Teddy stated.

"Nice to meet you." It wasn't really, but she didn't know what else to say.

"I'm afraid this isn't a social call," Armstrong replied. "My client has come to me with some very disturbing concerns about the estate and your management."

"What do you mean?" Stella asked.

"It means you're a thief," Teddy said.

"Teddy, we agreed."

"Well, she is."

A thief? Stella decided to sit down after all. "I don't understand. Is this about the discrepancies in the inventory I gave Teddy? I've already told Peter about that. We've asked an investigator to look into the matter."

"Yes, I know," Armstrong said.

"Then what is the issue? Did the investigator find something?" And if so, what did his finding have to do with her?

"Stella, it appears—"

"What are you tiptoeing around for?" Teddy stopped his pacing to glare at her. "The truth is that those items were never missing. You only said they were so you could sell them online."

"What?" He was drunk; he had to be. "That's ridiculous."

"Is it? I first got suspicious when I discovered a crystal figurine missing following your visit to the country house. At the time I thought I was imagining things, but then I read your inventory report and saw how many items you claimed couldn't be accounted for, so out of curiosity, I decided to do a little investigating on the internet. Lo and behold, I found the very same crystal figurine being offered on an auction site."

Upon finishing, he smirked like a detective having announced the killer in the drawing room mystery.

Feeling very much like an accused killer, Stella glared daggers at him. "I didn't steal anything," she said. If anyone was guilty of helping themselves at Agnes's country house, it was him, the miserable liar. He was the one spending his weekends there.

She turned her attention to Peter. "Are you certain it's the same figurine?"

"Yes." Reaching into the briefcase he'd brought with him, the lawyer removed a tablet. "The same account was auctioning off several other items that have been listed as missing as well."

"And you think I'm the one responsible?"

She wasn't sure if she should scream or be sick to her stomach. How could they possibly think she would do something so blatantly dishonest? Teddy seemed awfully confident, though. Taking the tablet from Peter's hand, she studied the contents. Sure enough, there were Agnes's belongings, on a page registered to a user named Expat92.

"I had my tech people track the account," Armstrong said. "It's registered in your name."

"But that's impossible! I didn't open any account. I didn't steal anything." Stunned, she looked at the tablet screen again. The auction page listed a dozen items, all objects she'd listed as missing, including the crystal cat figurine. All posed in front of a backdrop of gray linen and described as having been owned by the late Dame Agnes Moreland.

This was a nightmare. "I didn't do this," she said.

"Then how do you explain the site being registered in your name?"

"I...I don't know." Teddy had set her up somehow. Paid a hacker or something. Why, she wasn't sure. Yet. "But it's not my account. Why would I be so stupid as to sell items from the very estate I'm managing, and such benign items at that? A figurine? Garnet earrings?"

"Obviously you figured the smaller objects wouldn't attract attention," Teddy said.

"He's right," Peter said. "A few trinkets in an estate this size wouldn't be missed."

Panic started rising in her throat. Her innocence wasn't going to be enough to acquit her; she needed proof.

If only Linus were here with her. His faith in her would have given her confidence. He always believed in her.

Linus wasn't here, though, so she had to go it alone. She looked down at the tablet screen. The first item for bidding was Agnes's monogrammed lighter, which, Stella knew from reading, she had bought herself after getting her first acting paycheck. The auction had both the dates and the history incorrect.

"Here," she said, showing the tablet to Peter. "Read the description. It's incorrect. Wouldn't I list the correct anecdote?"

"Not if you were looking to deflect?" Teddy was smirking again, like the cat who had eaten the canary. Stella did her best to ignore him.

"And where would I take the photos or store the objects? They aren't here in the apartment. Go ahead and search— you won't find them."

"Of course we won't. You're not that foolish," Teddy said.

*Thanks for the credit.* Apparently, she was only slightly foolish—enough to post the items in the first place. "You won't find photos on my computer or phone, either."

"Photos can be deleted," Armstrong said. "I'm sure if we had an expert check, we would find—"

"Nothing," Stella snapped. "You would find nothing." If they thought she was taking this lying down, they were sorely mistaken. This was her reputation they were defaming. She would fight them tooth and nail.

Her phone lay on dining room table where she'd been working. "Here," she said, practically throwing it at Teddy's attorney. "Let your experts have at it. They only thing they'll find are photos of London and Etonia Toffee Pudding." And a few photos of Linus. If they deleted any of those, there would be hell to pay.

"Do you think us so naive that we don't realize you could have used a second phone?"

Stella let out a frustrated scream.

"Is everything all right?" Mrs. Churchill came running down the hall from the kitchen. "It sounded like someone stepped on the cat."

"Everything is fine," Stella replied.

"Speaking of Etonia Toffee Pudding, where is she?" Armstrong asked.

"Sleeping in the guest bedroom, like she has the past two days," Stella replied. "Why? Are you afraid I tried to sell her, too?"

"No, but Mr. Moreland has also voiced concerns about her level of care."

"What? Her care is fine."

The doorbell rang. Probably the police, arriving at Teddy's helpful suggestion, since he seemed determined to have her carted away.

"I've got it," Mrs. Churchill told her.

Meanwhile, Stella attempted to stare down Teddy's attorney despite the man's unimpressed demeanor. "I treat that cat as if she were my own pet. No, better than my own pet. I treat her like a bloody masterpiece."

"Exactly the way Dame Agnes would have wanted," a familiar voice added. Stella's insides swooped at the sound. What was he doing here?

Linus stood next to Mrs. Churchill, looking gorgeous in a navy blue suit. In a gathering of four men, his vitality dominated the room. Stella's insides ached with the desire to disappear into the safety of his embrace.

"I heard you scream and was concerned," he said. "What's this about Toffee's care?"

"Who are you?" Armstrong asked.

"Linus Collier. I own the apartment next door. Dame Agnes was a very good friend of mine, and I can vouch that Miss Russo here has taken extraordinary care of Toffee." Stella gave him a grateful smile.

"Is that so?" Tilting his head, Teddy's lawyer fixed his attention on Linus. There was a hint of satisfaction to his expression. Her brother used to make the same face when they were younger, at awards ceremonies. It was the look of a person who believed they had a win in their pocket. What had Teddy told him?

"My client has mentioned a pair of incidents that has left him concerned," the man said as he pulled a notebook from his briefcase. "He believes Miss Russo isn't paying close enough attention to Etonia Toffee Pudding. There was an incident in Berkshire where the cat nearly escaped into the woods."

"Because he didn't latch the terrace door properly! I wasn't even there."

"Exactly my point," Teddy replied. "I watched her the entire day. You were clearly too busy looking for objects you could steal."

"I did not…"

"Stealing? What are you talking about?" Linus looked back and forth among Armstrong, Teddy and her. "And I was with Toffee as well that afternoon. We spent time with her together, at least when you were awake and not sleeping off the gin and tonics. Miss Russo is correct," he told Armstrong. "The cat escaped because after the backdraft, the terrace door failed to latch. If anyone failed to keep a close eye on Toffee, it was Teddy here. I asked him to watch the cat while Miss Russo and I took a dinner break."

"Proving my point," Teddy said. "You were neglecting her."

"Oh, come on. If I wanted to neglect the cat, would I

have brought her with me to Berkshire? She was with me precisely because I didn't want to leave her alone." What next? Stella wondered. Suggesting she left the terrace door open on purpose?

Meanwhile, confusion continued to mark Linus's features. "What was all this about stealing?" he asked.

"Teddy thinks I'm selling Dame Agnes's belongings online," Stella told him.

His face went from confused to appalled before she could blink. "That's ridiculous. Those items were missing before you even arrived."

Stella very nearly cried. Even after she rejected him, he still believed in her. What had she done to deserve him in her life? "I've been trying to tell them, but apparently the online account is in my name."

"Accounts can be falsified. May I see?" She handed him the tablet.

"We've had experts verify the account," Armstrong said. Peter nodded in confirmation.

While Linus looked at the tablet, Stella returned to the more recent questions. "You said there were a pair of incidents."

"Mr. Moreland found the cat playing with a valuable heirloom."

"You did no such thing, you big blowhard." At Mrs. Churchill's retort, the group leaned back in surprise. Apparently, after years of waiting on him, the housekeeper had decided not to hold back any punches.

"I'm the one who found the 'heirloom' on the floor in the kitchen. I also found a pen cap, a pencil and a pair of ear swabs from the jar in the guest bathroom. Quite the little devil at night, that one is. We were always finding things in strange places. Once Miss Moreland and I caught her batting around a diamond drop earring after Miss Moreland left them on the dresser."

"Come to think of it, she was fond of my son's bouncy balls when we had her at our house," Peter said.

"Proving my point that the cat should be secured at night, so that she doesn't hurt herself or break something of great value."

"You mean stick Toffee in a crate," Stella said. "She owns the freaking house!"

Teddy looked down his nose. "For the time being. The courts may decide differently, and if that's the case, I don't want to risk losing something of import because the cat is running amok."

"As far as I'm concerned," Armstrong added, "Mr. Moreland has raised a number of adequate concerns, not the least of which is the evidence of criminal activity. Therefore, we request that Miss Russo be removed as manager of this estate."

# CHAPTER TWELVE

STELLA SANK INTO a seat. She wished she could say she was surprised, but she'd been expecting the request since they sat down. She'd failed. At a job simple enough to do in her sleep. When the numbness wore off, she was going to be sick to her stomach. What did she do now?

Armstrong wasn't finished. "It's clear the cat should be watched by someone with a vested interest in her health and welfare as well as the future of the estate. We're going to petition that Mr. Moreland be named temporary guardian until a ruling on his lawsuit is issued."

There it was. Stella had been wondering about Teddy's endgame. It was control over the estate. If she was named unfit, and he got temporary guardianship, he could then try to maneuver his way into a permanent guardianship if he lost his case. Either way, he had control over Agnes's money. The bastard.

Poor Toffee. She would be locked in a crate at bedtime and/or ignored for the remainder of her life. This would be as good a time as any to muster up the ability to cry.

"I have a couple questions," Linus said. His face was still focused on the tablet. "Did you track the IP location for the user?"

"We did. It led to the coffee shop around the corner," Armstrong told him.

"Did you check the security tapes?"

The lawyer smiled. "This isn't *CSI*, Mr. Collier. Not every business in London has security cameras."

"Too bad. The time stamp says the photos were unloaded around forty-eight hours ago. Stella wasn't home."

"No kidding," Teddy said. "She was—"

Linus cut him off. Seemed everyone was done with Teddy. "No, I meant she was out for the evening on a... date. Look." He showed Stella the first auction item. "Unless I'm mistaken, you were out for dinner at that time."

Sure enough; the auction was listed as starting at 7:00 p.m. "Teddy must have heard me talking about meeting Niles for coffee." Clearly missing the section of the conversation where they'd switched to dinner.

"I'm sure he'll be able to vouch for you, and you know I will." His smile was tinged with sadness.

"No one said she did the posting on her own. She could have easily hired someone." Being as close as he was to his payday, Teddy wasn't giving up.

"Who would I hire?" Stella asked. She knew, maybe, a half dozen people in the city.

Teddy pointed to Linus. "Him. The two of you are sleeping together, aren't you?"

Stella watched as Linus drew himself up to his full height. With slow, even strides he crossed the room to the mantel where Teddy stood. The older man's body shrank in on itself in the face of Linus's towering presence.

"Did you just accuse a member of one of London's wealthiest and most established families of selling stolen items over the internet? My family was doing business with the royal family before your first ancestor wielded his first coal shovel. We have never, ever been associated with illegal activity. If you're going to toss out those kinds of accusations, you better be ready to back them up in court."

"Men have done worse for the woman they're sleeping with."

If looks could kill, Teddy would be dead on the spot. Linus's voice, however, remained calm and controlled. "Hate to break it to you, old boy, but Stella and I are nothing more than friends."

One at a time, his words landed hard in her stomach. How she wished she could cry.

Since she couldn't, she channeled her energy into one last question. One she wanted to hear Teddy try to answer. "Why would I sell Agnes's belongings so blatantly anyway and risk being fired? Over what amounts to a few trinkets. I need this job and Peter's good reference for when I return to New York. Getting fired would ruin my life."

"She's right," Linus said. "If anyone has anything to gain from all this it's you, Moreland. Have you searched his property?" he asked Armstrong. "Checked his computer?"

"How dare you!" Teddy said, glaring. "I would never steal Aunt Agnes's belongings. She was precious to me."

"Little defensive, aren't we, Teddy? And let's be honest. Agnes disliked you intensely."

If it weren't such a dire situation, Stella would have laughed out loud. The sparkle in Linus's eyes reminded her of the day they met. Seeing it eased the tightness in her chest. He made even bad situations tolerable. "Mr. Collier makes a good point."

For the first time in a while, Peter Singh made himself known. He stood up and smoothed the front of his suit coat. "I think, in the spirit of due diligence, we should investigate Mr. Moreland's computer and phone along with Miss Russo's. After all, we don't want to make any false assumptions."

"Feel free to investigate mine as well."

"We appreciate the cooperation, Mr. Collier."

Teddy looked about to have a spasm of some kind. His

eyes were huge and his spine rigid with tension. When Peter made his request, he'd blanched and clenched his fists.

"This is an outrage," he said. "I refuse to be a victim of a witch hunt."

"You started the witch hunt," Stella said. "If they're going to search my belongings, then they are damn well going to search yours as well."

"What's the matter Teddy? You don't have something to hide, do you?" Linus asked.

"My client will be happy to cooperate," Armstrong said. "He has nothing to hide."

Based on the rattled look in Teddy's eyes, Stella wasn't so sure. It was clear he'd counted on her being so shaken by the evidence that she wouldn't put up a fight.

The meeting ended with her agreeing they could take her laptop and phone for examination. Linus insisted on having his company lawyer present for when they examined both his and her electronics. To protect their interests, he explained.

"Thank you," she said once the trio had left. Armstrong had made a point of saying she would be closely monitored until the issue was resolved. Mrs. Churchill had gone as well.

"Silly to have separate lawyers when one will suffice, and he's on retainer," Linus replied.

"I meant for defending me." That he believed in her innocence unconditionally meant a lot. "Especially after the other day."

He shrugged. "Our personal issues don't change the truth. You're an honest, good person. What shocks me is that I had no idea the lengths Teddy would go to, to get control of the money. He must have been planning this for a while. Since before Agnes died."

"Money makes people do crazy things. Agnes must

have told him the terms of the will and he figured he needed a backup plan. Or two. Makes you wonder what he'll try to do next."

"With luck, nothing. They'll trace this little scheme back to him and that'll be the end."

"What if they don't? What if he's covered his ass?" Granted, he looked terrified at having his electronics searched, but Stella had already made the mistake of underestimating the man once. She didn't want to make the mistake again.

"They'll find something. His witch-hunt bluster was the last stand of a man who knew he was in trouble."

"I hope you're right."

"I am, and if I'm not, my lawyer will make his life such a living hell that Teddy will wish he'd never thought of the idea." His smile came and went in a flash. "Don't worry. You'll head back to New York with your glowing reference as planned."

"You needn't sound sarcastic."

"My apologies. I'll keep the bitterness at bay next time."

"Linus…"

"I'm sorry," he said, gaze dropping to the floor. "I'm being childish. You're right. There's no need for sarcasm, especially when your livelihood is at stake."

"Thank you." She dropped onto the sofa next to him. Now that the immediate threat was gone, exhaustion replaced the adrenaline in her system, and all the feelings she'd been keeping at bay washed over her. Once more she longed to fall into his arms.

"I've missed you," she said.

"I've missed you, too."

What she really wanted to say was that she'd had a giant hole inside her since he walked out, that without him she'd been empty and alone, but she was too afraid to say the words. She let her body do the talking instead, her fingers shaking as they touched the back of his hand.

A soft sigh escaped Linus's lips. "Stella." Longing laced his whisper. "Don't."

"Why not?" she asked. Why ignore the need they felt for one another? Their bodies were made to be together. She kissed the corner of his mouth, then kissed the other corner. Over and over, butterfly kisses that moved to the middle until his lips parted. "Why should we be lonely when we work so well together?" she whispered against his lips.

As much as it killed him, Linus pulled away from her. "Because I want more," he said. "I want more than sex and passion in the moment. I want you."

"You have me," Stella said.

"Do I?" He had her body, yes, but he wanted all of her. Her heart and soul. "I want your love."

"I already told you, I can't love you."

"You keep saying that word. I can't love you. You can't love me. Like we would be breaking some kind of rule by having feelings for one another." He wasn't asking if she could love him; he wanted to know if she did.

"Oh, Linus." She flung herself backward, her head falling back against the sofa, and covered her eyes with her hands. "What good would saying *I love you* do? It wouldn't change anything. I would still have to go to New York."

Slowly, she let her palms slide down her face. When she lifted her head, he saw pleading in her eyes. "Can't we just leave things the way they are rather than invite a whole lot of pain?"

But he was already in pain. Payback for Victoria and every other heart he ever broke. That he was getting what he deserved didn't make the pain easier to swallow. Neither did the desperation in Stella's eyes. "What good would it do?" he replied. "How about the fact that we could be happy? We could build a life together. One that you actually want instead of a career to appease your father's ego."

"My father's ego has nothing to do this." Even as she argued, Linus could see she didn't believe what she was saying. "This is about me going back and proving I'm not a delicate, anxiety-ridden flower who can't handle the pressure."

"Bull." The word came out harshly, but Linus didn't care. He was angry now. Two minutes earlier, Stella had all but admitted she loved him, only to run away. "At least be honest with yourself. You want your father's approval. You want him to tell you that you're as good your brother and sister."

"Is that so wrong?"

"It is if it's never going to happen." Her father's approval might as well be a cat toy on a string. "There will always be another goal, another sibling accomplishment to best. You're going to be spending your entire life running a race you can't win."

Stella stared at him, eyes shining. "Are you saying I'm not good enough, too?"

"Of course not!" He kicked himself. "I think you're bloody marvelous. I'm saying no matter what you do, it won't be good enough for your father."

"You don't know that."

"Yes, I do!" Knew it in his gut and she did, too. Problem was, she blamed herself rather than the man truly at fault.

Washing a hand over his features, he paused and looked her in the eye. "It's not your job to fulfill your father's dreams."

Stella shook her head. "You don't understand."

"Yes, I do. I watched my sister, Susan, beat herself

up for years because she didn't think she measured up. I watched Victoria—"

"I'm not Victoria," she snapped.

"I know," he snapped back. Their stories weren't remotely the same—he realized that now. The dissimilarities didn't stop him from fearing she would fall into a dark abyss, though.

Their argument was going off the rails. He could argue with Stella until he lost his voice, but she had already made up her mind.

The most maddening part? He would give up everything and go to New York with her if he thought that was what would make her happy.

"Do you even want to work in finance? At Mitchum, Baker?" he asked.

As he expected, she scowled in response. "Of course I do. I worked my ass off to get that job." The ends of her hair moved back and forth as she shook her head. "I don't understand why you're doing this. You know how badly I need to go back and prove myself."

"There you go again. You *need* to go back. You *can't stay* in London. What do you want, Stella? Do you really want a lifetime of seventy-hour weeks and working Christmas? Or do you want to be happy?"

"What makes you think I won't be happy?"

"Because you bloody froze in the street going to work, that's why. Happy people don't freak out on the way to work."

He'd gone too far. Anger flashed in her eyes. "I think you should leave," she said. "Check that. I *want* you to leave. Who do you think you are telling me what I want and don't want? What I do with my life is my business. I choose my path. Not you. Not my father. Me."

And the choice she made didn't include Linus. "Fine." He wasn't about to beg any further. "Go ahead and choose.

But ask yourself this. Why did you freeze in the street that day? Was it really burnout or were you trying to get off the path?"

For the second time in forty-eight hours, he walked away.

Luck was on Stella's side—in terms of work, that was. The outside expert was able to prove her computer was not the computer used to create the auction account. Linus's lawyers delivered the news a few days after Teddy's visit. Apparently that was how they were going to communicate from now on—through third parties. The lawyer also told her that the expert traced the account back to a bartender who worked at a pub near Teddy's house. He also revealed that Teddy paid him to set up the account, citing technical ineptitude. Poor guy had no idea Teddy was scheming to get custody of Toffee.

When confronted with the evidence, Teddy naturally proclaimed his innocence and blamed Stella. At least he did until they found the crystal cat figurine wrapped in a swath of gray linen in his flat. Then he proclaimed righteous indignation over being cheated out of what he considered his rightful inheritance. In the end, to avoid scandal, he agreed to withdraw his challenge. Whether he would succeed Toffee as the heir, Stella didn't know. Since the cat would survive for years after Stella left town, it didn't really matter.

She hadn't seen Linus since he walked out of her apartment the month before. Nor had she cried. At least the lump in her throat felt smaller, and she wasn't chanting "this will pass" as often. Probably because she was furious. As badly as she missed him, she wanted to spit in his face. How dared he presume what she wanted or judge her rationale? If he cared at all, he'd support her decisions, not tell her to chuck everything so she could stay in London and work on Agnes's biography.

"You understand, don't you, Agnes?"

From her spot over the mantel, the actress gave her an imperious stare. Stella had discovered an old journal of Agnes's at the bottom of a box of books. Reading it gave deeper resonance to all the artifacts she'd collected. Dame Agnes had been as ambitious as she'd been beautiful, and as such, she'd ruthlessly pursued her career. The men she knew were divided into two groups: Casual Lovers and Men Who Could Aid Her Career. Stella added a third category, which she called Unfulfilled Suitors. They were men who showered Dame Agnes with gifts but got nowhere. Dame Agnes didn't have room for foolish romantics.

Dame Agnes spent the last years of her life with a cat for a best friend.

Stella didn't want to think about that.

Instead, she decided to go for a run. The weather outside was rainy and cold, but she didn't care. The fresh air would clear her head so she could work.

She got as far as the elevator when Linus's door opened. Holding her breath, she turned expecting to see his blue-gray eyes.

"Sorry." Susan Collier gave a wave. "Just me. Linus is in Scotland for a few weeks. He asked me to water his plants."

"Oh," Stella replied. "I didn't realize."

"I figured."

The two of them shuffled from foot to foot while waiting for the elevator to arrive.

"Started wedding planning yet?" Stella asked after a moment. She thought about mentioning her breakup—*was* it a breakup if you weren't dating?—but if Susan was watering the plants, she probably already knew.

"A little," Susan replied. "We're thinking of a Christmas wedding. The holidays are a bit of a thing in our family."

"So Linus said. That sounds nice. You can do a lot with a holiday theme."

"I think so. Lewis doesn't really care. He said he'd be happy eloping, but I want the wedding. Call me vain, but I like showing off my handsome fiancé."

"At least he's willing to indulge you. Means he respects your choices."

"More like he knows how good he looks in a tuxedo," Susan said. "I'm not the only one who likes showing Lewis off. Lewis likes showing off Lewis, too."

The elevator bell dinged, and the doors parted. As they boarded, Stella suppressed a smile. Susan and Lewis were forever teasing one another. Reminded her of how she and Linus would banter back and forth.

Her stomach grew heavy. Seemed to grow heavy a lot lately. Such as whenever she thought of Linus. The night before she'd been watching a movie when the actor playing the lead turned his profile to the camera. The man's nose and cheekbones looked so much like Linus's she had to turn off the television.

Susan was staring at her. Linus's sister had a way of looking at a person and reading their thoughts. She had to be getting a hell of a reading right now.

"You must hate me," Stella said.

Susan shook her head. "Don't be ridiculous. I understand where you're coming from. I think you're wrong, but I understand."

There were days when Stella wasn't sure she understood herself. "May I ask you a question?" she asked.

"Sure," the youngest Collier replied. "Can't guarantee I'll have an answer, though. What do you want to know?"

"Well…" She hoped the question wasn't too prying. "Linus mentioned that when you were growing up, you struggled with being different from Thomas and him."

"Not exactly. More like I struggled with not being as

perfect. I don't know if you've noticed, but Linus looks like an underwear model. Thomas is worse."

Stella blushed. She had noticed. "Must have been hard growing up in their shadows."

"Try impossible," Susan told her. "I spent the better part of my teens and twenties feeling like the dumpy, ugly stepsister."

"I'm sorry." Stella took a long look at the woman. Linus's sister was on the thick side, but she carried herself with such confidence and pride, it was impossible to see her as anything but beautiful. What had changed?

"Simple," Susan replied, when Stella asked. "I met Lewis." The doors opened to the lobby. "He made me realize that I was special in my own unique way, and that it was okay if I wasn't tall, dark and handsome like the other two. Why do you ask?"

"No reason." The awkwardness of the lie was made worse by Susan's knowing look. "I was curious is all."

"It also helped that my mother moved to Australia to be part of a reality show. She was the chief reason I felt inferior. But you know all about that."

"What do you mean?"

"Your dad," Susan said. "Linus told me how you're under pressure to be successful. Relax," she added when Stella's shoulders went back. "He only mentioned it because he thought I might have insights. I didn't, by the way."

Having reached the first floor, they stepped out into the lobby. "I told Linus everyone needs to work out their issues at their own pace. You can't force someone to change their behavior just because you want them to."

"Thank you. I appreciate the vote of confidence," Stella said. A little too late to bring her and Linus back together, but it was nice to know she had an ally.

"No problem," Susan replied. "According to my brothers,

sharing my opinion is one of my strong suits." Flashing a grin, she headed toward the front door. Stella followed and was heading down the building steps when Susan turned around.

"One more thing," she said, "because that's who I am. Something I learned from Lewis this past year. When you feel like you can't compete, you can either stay in the race and struggle, or you can find a race you like better."

A taxi pulled up and she slid inside, leaving Stella alone to ponder her comment.

# CHAPTER THIRTEEN

*Spring*

"WHAT IS GOING on with you?" Thomas asked. Seated at the head of the conference room table, his brother stared at him over the frames of his new reading glasses. "Florence tells me you forgot the Paris teleconference?"

"I didn't forget," Linus said. "I wrote down the wrong date. There's a difference."

"Barely. I had to spend twenty minutes explaining to Philippe d'Usay that we weren't purposely wasting his time."

"I'm sorry. I'll send him an email and apologize."

As he typed a reminder note in his phone, Linus could feel his brother's eyes on him. "I don't understand," Thomas said. "You've always been slightly on your own planet, but you've been more distracted than ever these past few months. Half the time, I don't know where your head is at."

"People confuse dates all the time. It's hardly a major crime," Linus replied.

"I know what's bothering him." The comment came from Susan, who sat at the table across from him. Thomas's version of a family intervention. "Stella's leaving in a few weeks. I take it the two of you still aren't talking?"

"Stella broke up with me, remember?" Not that it

stopped him from staring at her door every day debating whether he should knock.

"I'm sorry. I really hoped after she and I talked in the elevator that Stella would come around."

"I know you did," Linus said, "but I'm learning some baggage is simply too heavy to throw off." She loved her father; she was afraid to admit she loved Linus. It was too big a hill to surmount. He simply had to accept that she was leaving.

"Just so we're clear, this is Stella your neighbor we're talking about. The one we helped out this winter." Thomas looked between the two of them. "Is she the woman you were talking about at Christmas? The one who wanted to keep things casual?"

"One and the same," Linus replied.

"Only Linus didn't want to keep things casual," Susan said, "so they broke up."

"I'll be. Where the hell was I during all this?"

"Running a company and raising a family," Linus said. "I figured you had enough on your plate."

The comment earned him a serious glare. "You should know better than that. We're family. I always have time for you."

"Maybe I wasn't in the mood to share. The only reason Susan knows is because she's nosy."

It was a testament to how miserable he must look that Susan didn't protest.

The seriousness of Thomas's expression softened into one of brotherly affection. "I'm sorry. I wondered when we talked at Christmastime, but I hadn't realized how serious your feelings were."

"Surprise!" Linus faked a smile. "They crept up on me as well. Doesn't matter, though. The lady has commitment issues." Along with daddy issues and self-worth issues.

And now she was leaving in a few weeks, and he was

wondering if he hadn't made a mistake by insisting that Stella declare her feelings.

"For what it's worth, I think she feels the same way you do," Susan said. "The expression on her face when I ran into the other day? She was crushed I wasn't you."

"She does feel the same way," Linus told her. He may be new at love, but he could see the emotion in Stella's eyes.

Her Christmas present, the real one, was in his nightstand, the package unopened, a new reminder of his past mistakes. Wasn't that always the way? He finally made peace with his guilt and remorse over Victoria, only to have new guilt and remorse.

"You know, she's not leaving just yet," Susan was saying. "There's still time to fix things. At the very least you can steal a few more weeks."

"I don't want just a few more weeks," Linus said. "I want forever. What?" Thomas and Susan were looking at him like he'd sprung a second head.

"Sorry," his brother said. "I'm still getting used to the idea of you wanting to settle down."

"You've got plenty of time. In case you weren't listening, the lady's moving back to New York."

"So?"

"So," Linus told him, "she'll be on the other side of the Atlantic."

"Last time I checked, we're a global economy. There's this thing called an airplane that will take you across the ocean. Our company owns one, as a matter of fact. There's no reason you can't continue long-distance or relocate yourself."

"If only it were that simple." Briefly, he explained what happened to Stella in New York and her need to win her father's approval. "I tried to convince her that it was a waste of time, but she wouldn't listen."

Again with the staring. "What now?" he asked them.

"Let me see if I understand," Thomas said. "You tried to undo a lifetime of insecurities with one conversation, and when she didn't listen, you walked away?"

"What was I supposed to do?"

"Stick it out, you idiot," his brother said. "If you love her, it shouldn't matter if she's off chasing her father's dream or not. What matters is being there to support her and being there if she stumbles again."

Linus stared at his phone. Thomas was right. He'd been focused on making Stella love him on his terms and hadn't stopped to think how it would be for Stella to untangle her complicated family relationships. If he loved her, he needed to be willing to fight for her heart. "If I went to Manhattan, I would be leaving Colliers," he said.

"Most likely," Thomas said, "but I think we'll survive. What matters to Susan and me is that you're happy."

Stella made him happy. All he wanted in return was for her to find happiness, too, like she wished for in Avebury. If her happiness lay in New York City working seventy hours a week for Mitchum, Baker, then that's where he'd go, too.

Only question now was, would she let him?

"Did you talk to Mitchum, Baker and give them a return date?" Kevin Russo boomed over the phone in an effort to talk louder than the static. "You've only got a month."

"Yes," Stella replied, "and I know." To be precise, she had twenty-nine days.

She also had a headache. Nothing severe, but enough to leave her distracted and fuzzy headed. Talking to her father was the last thing she needed.

At least the weather was turning. Today was the first day of sun in weeks. Opening the terrace door, she stepped outside to see if reception would improve. After months of being trapped inside, it felt good to feel the sun on her skin. Below her, Belgravia waved hello. She was going to miss this view when she went home. She was going to miss a lot of things.

*Stop thinking about him.* Nearly four months and thoughts of Linus still plagued her.

*Maybe if you told him you loved him, he'd still be around.*

What good would it have done, though? Admitting her feelings would have only made saying goodbye harder.

Stella had long given up trying to figure out when she went from burying her feelings to admitting she loved the man. The words bubbled up one day and refused to be denied. Too bad she hadn't been able to say the words when they counted.

"Stella? Can you hear me?"

"Sorry, Dad. I went outside for a better signal. I was saying that they're installing the exhibit on Dame Agnes's life at the end of the month as well. I think I might stay an extra day to make sure everything goes all right."

"It's a museum exhibit. What could go wrong? You hang a picture in the wrong place?"

"It's a lot more complicated. You want the exhibit to—"

"Stella, honey, you finish the job on the thirty-first. You don't need to work for free, especially for a bunch of stuff from some actress's career."

"Dame Agnes wasn't just some actress, Dad."

"Regardless. You've had your leave of absence. Now it's time to come home and build something you can be proud of."

"I'm proud of this exhibit," she said. In fact, she was proud of everything she'd accomplished over the past eleven months. Maybe it wasn't a job at the top consulting firm in the world, but she'd tackled some pretty interesting projects and done a good job.

"Did I tell you that Joe is going to be lead counsel on

this double murder trial in Chicago? City councilman's wife killed him and his mistress. It's going to be super high profile."

Good for Joe. Another legal feather in his cap full of feathers. The change of subject annoyed her more than usual. "Did you hear what I said, Dad?" she asked. "I said I was proud of this exhibit."

"I heard you. You're proud."

"Very," she said.

"I'm glad. You should be proud of a job well done, no matter how small it may be."

God, did he have to diminish everything? Her head throbbed in response. Slowly, she began to pace the terrace perimeter, using the click of her heels on the concrete as a kind of meditation metronome. With each step eastward, she tried to steady her breathing.

*You'll be chasing forever.* Linus's voice floated into her head. Was he right? Was she chasing something unobtainable? Ever since Linus said it, she'd been listening to her father's voice more carefully. Little by little she saw the pattern. No matter what she accomplished, her father wasn't impressed. Maybe it was because he disapproved of her having gone to London, and once she was back in New York, the negativity would ease up.

Would it?

There was one way to find out. She took a deep breath. "Can I ask you something, Dad?"

"Sure," he said. "What do you need?"

"Nothing. I was wondering what you'd think if I decided to write a book. About Dame Agnes."

She could tell from the silence on the other end of the line that he didn't think much of the idea at all. "Why do you want to write a book about her?"

"Because she lived a fascinating life. You know how I've always liked history."

"Hey, you want to write a book on this woman, have at it. Personally, I would write a thriller or something that people might read. Always surprised me your brother didn't do something along those lines. You might decide the same thing once you're back in America."

"Actually…" Time for the test. "I was thinking of taking another year off. Peter Singh said I was welcome to stay here and keep an eye on Toffee in exchange for rent."

She wasn't really thinking of time off. Sure, she'd felt a thrill when Peter made his offer—her first thought being that she could rekindle her relationship with Linus—but she'd already made her plans. The only reason she was floating the idea now was to gauge her father's reaction.

There was more silence on her father's end of the line, followed by a loud, boisterous laugh. "That was a good one," he said. "You really had me until you got to pet sitting."

"It's not a joke, Dad. Peter really did offer me the penthouse so I could work on the novel."

"Yeah, but you're not seriously considering it, right? You already lost a year on this pet-sitting thing."

"Estate management, Dad." Did it really matter at this point? "And it's a tempting offer."

"I didn't spend all that money on your education so you could run away to Europe and pretend to be a novelist. It's embarrassing enough that you couldn't hack the pressure and had to take this leave of absence."

She didn't burn out to embarrass him. In fact, the opposite. She'd burned out trying not to embarrass him.

Interesting how either way it was about him. The fact she'd actually had a nervous breakdown didn't seem to matter.

Linus was right. "I'm never going to win with you, am I, Dad?" Not unless she was perfect, something she would never be. Eventually she'd stumble or fall short. It was inevitable.

"What are you talking about?"

"You're not going to be happy unless I'm a superstar like Camilla and Joe."

"Don't knock your siblings. Your sister and brother worked very hard to get where they are."

"Yeah, and I worked hard, too. I busted my ass in grad school and at Mitchum, Baker, and all you did was tell me how Camilla and Joe were doing better."

"That's because you needed the motivation. You always needed that extra push."

"No, Dad, I didn't. I was doing the best I could."

"You can always do better. I tell the same thing to Joe and Camilla. Never settle. That's always been your problem. You were willing to settle."

Stella shook her head. Her father couldn't see it, couldn't see the effort she put into trying to make him proud. That was because effort wasn't a tangible outcome. You couldn't brag about effort the way you could an award or accolade. Her father couldn't hold up effort as evidence of his success.

The question then was, did she really want to keep chasing what she could never catch, or did she want to chase something—and someone—that mattered?

Did she even still have someone to chase?

All this questioning was making her headache worse. She needed to lie down.

"I've got to go, Dad. I'll talk to you later."

Her father was in midsentence, but she didn't care. She hung up and headed back to the western end of the terrace.

"Hey, Toffee," she announced on her way inside. "You want to lie on the bed with me? I'll rub your belly."

The sofa where Toffee had been sleeping was empty. "Toffee?"

Suddenly, a horrible sense of déjà vu gripped her. She'd left the terrace door open. Rushing outside, she searched under every piece of furniture and anything else a cat might find interesting.

There was no sign of Toffee.

She was afraid to look down. From this far up, Toffee would look no different than a speck of garbage. A big, furry, flat speck of garbage.

*Think positive, Stella.* She hurried inside and across the hall.

Thankfully, Linus was home, and he answered the door. Stella didn't have time to register how surprised he looked, or how good. She rushed past him into his living room. "Toffee got out," she said. "I need to check your terrace."

Linus followed her outside, and together they searched the entire length. No Toffee.

Stella was going to be sick.

"Don't panic yet," Linus said. His hand rubbed gentle circles between her shoulder blades. How was it after all these weeks and all her rejection, he was still comforting her? "Did you check everywhere in the apartment?"

The apartment? "No. I saw the open door and assumed Toffee escaped." Stressed out as she was, she didn't think to look around the apartment.

There was gentleness to his smile that made her heart skip. "Then maybe we should check there before we assume the worst," he said.

He said *we*. "Thank you. I didn't mean to make you drop everything to help me."

"Don't apologize. I'll always be here if you need me."

If only he knew how wonderful those words made her feel. "I don't know what I'd do without you," she said. "Truly."

She didn't have time to examine the emotion that crossed

his face before he'd taken her hand and led her back to her front door. "Let's go check your apartment," he said.

On the way, Stella crossed the fingers on her free hand and said a little prayer that her little Toffee Pudding had decided to hide in a bedroom instead of going outside.

Her prayer was answered sooner than she expected. As they walked into the apartment, they saw Mrs. Churchill standing in the living room holding a furry white bundle.

"Toffee!" Stella rushed to take the cat from the house-keeper's arms.

"Caught the little demon batting the bloody kaleido-scope around again," Mrs. Churchill said.

"Naughty kitty. You scared the daylights out of me." Ignoring the cat's struggle to escape, she buried her face in Toffee's fur.

Free from her charge, Mrs. Churchill closed the terrace door. "Can I ask you to keep the door closed? The breeze kicks up the dust."

Because dust. Stella couldn't help but smile at the re-quest. "Absolutely, Mrs. Churchill. My apologies. Would you mind getting this little mischief maker a chicken treat? It's almost her snack time."

"Oh, sure. She causes trouble and we give her a treat. It's like Dame Agnes never left. Come on, you. Let's get you a chicken tender."

Once the housekeeper was down the hall, Stella turned to Linus. He looked so right standing in her living room, it hurt.

"Thank you," she said. "Seems like whenever I've got a problem, you show up to help me solve it."

"Everyone needs a wingman," he said with a grin. "I'm glad I was home."

"So am I."

Now that he was here, she didn't want him to leave. There was so much she wanted to say. Where did she begin?

Maybe with three simple words. Would that be enough? A lump rose in her throat.

"Linus, I…"

"Hold that thought."

He disappeared out the door, only to reappear holding a small package. "I'd planned to come by and give you this as soon as I worked up the nerve."

Taking the box from him, she studied the gold foil wrapping paper. The box looked vaguely familiar, but she wasn't sure why. "What is it?"

"Something for New York. Open it and I'll explain."

Her hands shook as she peeled off the paper. Inside lay a gold necklace with a charm in the shape of a ribbon.

"It's to remind you of our night in Avebury. You wished for happiness."

"I remember." The lump in her throat had tripled, making the words hard to get out.

"I meant what I said that night. All I want is for you to be happy. And if going back to New York so you can prove yourself is what makes you happy, then I'll support you every step of the way." Lifting the necklace from the box, he stepped behind her to fasten it around her neck. "I love you, Stella," he whispered. "I'd rather support you in New York than live in London without you."

Had he said what she thought he said? Needing to see his expression, Stella whirled around. Eyes filled with love met hers.

"Do you mean it?" she asked.

"Every word."

The logjam in her chest broke open. Stella burst into tears. Deep, sobbing tears that wouldn't stop.

"Shh, it's okay, love," she heard Linus whisper.

The arms she'd been missing desperately wrapped around her. She collapsed against his chest and cried like she'd never cried before.

Linus loved her. He supported her, no matter what her choice. She didn't deserve him, and he loved her anyway.

How did she get so lucky?

When she could breathe again, she kissed him. Passion wasn't enough, though. She needed to speak the words.

And so, when they finally broke apart, she wiped the tears from her cheeks and began. "I lied," she said, earning a confused frown. "That night in Avebury. I didn't really wish for happiness. I my real wish was to know my heart's desire. I was afraid to admit it at the time, but I didn't know what I wanted to do with my life."

"All right."

"Don't back away. Let me finish." She gripped his hands to keep him close. "I still don't know what it is I want to do with my life. Part of me wants to go to New York, and part of me wants to stay here in London with you and Toffee. But as confused as I am, there is one thing I know for certain, and that's what you mean to me. I love you, Linus Collier. You are my heart's desire. Without you, nothing else matters."

"You have me, Stella Russo. Always."

Stella smiled. For the first time in her life, she didn't feel less than. She felt loved, unconditionally, and she loved back with the same ferocity. The rest of her life would sort itself out in good time. She'd already found success.

# CHAPTER FOURTEEN

*Summer...again...*

"ARE YOU SURE about this?"

Stella stared at the terminal sign for a couple beats before smiling at the man on her right. "I need to," she said. "He and I need to talk face-to-face. Dr. Winslow says it's the only way I'll get closure."

"Well, I'm all for closure," Linus replied, "so long as you want it."

"I do."

For the past several weeks, she and her father had been emailing, a conversation begun after Stella sent him a long, soul-baring letter. At first, her father responded with anger, explaining as he always did that he only wanted what was best for her. Little by little, with Linus's support, Stella managed to tell him that she was going to live her own life, and if he didn't find her accomplishments bragworthy enough, that was his problem.

"He's not going to like your decision." He was referring to staying in London and writing a novel. Stella didn't know if being a writer was going to be her lifelong passion, but right now, she was enjoying Agnes's story too much to care.

She managed a shrug. It still hurt, knowing she'd never really have her father's approval, but she was learning to cope. Being loved for yourself made a lot of difference. For the first time in her life, she felt in control. She had a project she enjoyed and a man she adored. Not a day went by that she didn't fall deeper in love with Linus.

"With you by my side, I can handle anything," she told him.

Linus kissed her cheek. "Always, my love. Always."

"Then let's do this." She picked up the cat carrier that was by her feet. "Come on, Toffee. Sooner we get going, the sooner we can get home."

Although in all honesty, she thought, looking at Linus, she was already home.

* * * * *

# THE MARINE'S
# ROAD HOME

## BRENDA HARLEN

This book is dedicated to all members
of the armed forces—and to those who love them.
#NeverForget

## Chapter One

Everyone had a story to tell.

Skylar Gilmore knew it was true, even if a lot of those stories weren't exactly page turners. Still, she was always willing to listen and fascinated by the characters telling the tales at Diggers' Bar & Grill.

From her position behind the polished walnut bar, she heard the accounts of regulars, less frequent customers and even the occasional tourist. To each, she offered a sympathetic ear without censure or judgment. After all, it wasn't her job to counsel—at least not here.

And so it was that she knew Chase Hampton intended to propose to Megan Carmichael before he'd even bought the ring, and that Erica Rainville had decided to leave her husband of twelve years—not because he was having an affair with his secretary but because *she* was, and also that Bobby Tanner and Holly Kowalski had postponed their wedding plans because they were unable to agree on when—or even if—they'd have kids.

Bobby had been in the bar again tonight, lamenting the apparent impasse with his fiancée. Six years older than his bride-to-be, Bobby was eager to start a family. But Holly, the junior deputy in the sheriff's department, wanted to establish herself in her career before she took time off to have a baby. Of course, that led to another argument, as Bobby expected that she would give up her job in order to be a full-time mother to their children.

Sky had to bite her tongue when he told her that. It was the only way to not break her concrete rule about listening without judgment. She didn't disagree that a job in law enforcement could be dangerous. How could she when her sister was an attorney married to the local sheriff? Sky knew only too well that Kate suffered through nights when her husband was called away from home.

But Kate would be the first to say that marriage was a partnership, and though partners might not always agree, they should always support one another. Since Kate and Reid would be celebrating their third wedding anniversary in only a few months, Sky had to trust that her sister was more of an authority on the subject of marriage than she was.

So instead of telling Bobby that he had no right to be making career decisions for the woman he claimed to love, Sky only encouraged him to keep the lines of communication open. He promised to do that, then finished his beer, tipped her generously and headed home to his fiancée.

"Does everyone who sits at the bar spill their guts to you?" Kate had asked one night, after listening to Roger Greenway bemoan the emptiness of his life as he sipped his rum and coke.

Sky couldn't help but empathize with the divorced father who only saw his kids twice a month now that his ex had remarried and moved out of town with them.

"Everyone," she'd confirmed in response to her sister's question.

Because it had seemed true at the time.

Before she'd met the handsome—and mysterious—stranger she referred to as John. In the six years that she'd been pouring drinks at Diggers', he was the lone holdout.

She'd been chatting with Jerry Tate when the newcomer walked into the bar around 9:50 p.m. on a Wednesday night five weeks earlier. But she'd caught a glimpse of him out of the corner of her eye, as he'd paused inside the door and surveyed the room—as if he was looking for someone.

Just over six feet tall, he had broad shoulders that tested the seams of his long-sleeved Henley-style shirt, and muscular legs encased in jeans faded almost white at the stress points. The simple attire did nothing to disguise his strength, and she was helpless to prevent the quiver that reverberated through her system.

And then his eyes had caught and held hers.

She'd started to smile, because she was a friendly person and because it had been a long time since she'd felt such an instantaneous awareness and intense attraction. But he clearly hadn't registered a similar reaction on his end, because he quickly shifted his gaze.

After scanning the room, he squared those wide shoulders and moved resolutely toward the bar. His pace was deliberate, unhurried, and as he drew nearer, Sky noted that his square jaw was unshaven and his eyes were the color of premium whiskey.

Despite the sting of his visual dismissal, Sky curved her lips again as the stranger edged a hip onto a stool at the bar. "Hi there."

His only response was a stiff nod of acknowledgment.

"New to town or just passing through?" she wondered aloud, as he perused the labels on the taps in front of him.

"I'll have a pint of Sam Adams."

A New Englander, she guessed, as she selected a glass mug and tipped it under the spout. There'd been no hint of an accent in his voice, but his chosen beverage might be a clue.

She set the beer on a paper coaster in front of him.

No "please" or "thank you," either, she noted, as he wrapped his hand around the mug.

"Are you from Massachusetts?" she asked.

"Or maybe New York?" she suggested as an alternative when he failed to reply, because New Yorkers had a reputation—deserved or not—for being standoffish and unfriendly.

Still no response.

"Rhode Island?" She grabbed that one out of thin air, hoping the random guess would get some kind of a reaction from him.

He lifted his gaze, and she felt another tug, low in her belly, when those whiskey-colored eyes locked on hers.

"I came in for a beer," he finally said. "Not company or conversation."

She was admittedly shocked by his blunt response.

And maybe a little hurt.

Because while he was certainly under no obligation to want company or conversation, she'd been a bartender long enough to know that people usually came into Diggers' seeking one or the other—or both. Those who only wanted a beer could just as easily crack one open under their own roof. Unless there was a reason they wanted to get away from home for a while, such as a nagging spouse or screaming kids.

The Sam Adams–drinking stranger had no ring on his finger and no tan line indicating that one might have recently been removed. Of course, Sky knew from experience that the lack of a wedding band wasn't necessarily indicative of anything.

Since his remark didn't invite any kind of response, she merely nodded and made her way to the other end of the bar to refill Ellis Hagen's empty glass.

As Sky poured another shot of Jack Daniels over ice, Ellis was happy to chat—even engaging in a little harmless flirting that soothed her inexplicably bruised feelings. And because she refused to let the rudeness of a stranger bring down her mood, Sky allowed herself to flirt back.

Of course, it was easy with Ellis, because they'd dated for a while way back in high school. In fact, she'd lost her virginity in the back seat of his Cavalier after the homecoming dance in her junior year. It had been a mostly forgettable experience for both of them, but he was the first boy she'd ever imagined herself in love with, and she was always happy to see him at the bar and catch up.

Tonight she was grateful, too, as her conversation with Ellis succeeded in taking her mind off the mysterious stranger so that she barely even noticed when he finished his beer and tucked a ten-dollar bill beneath the edge of his glass before walking out again without even a backward glance.

"Who's the new guy?" Courtney Morgan, one of the bar's waitresses, asked Sky.

"I don't know," she admitted, cashing out his tab and dropping his change into the tip jar.

Courtney seemed taken aback by her response. "A quiet one, is he?"

Sky nodded, though she suspected he was more than quiet.

He was a man with secrets—and she wanted to know all of them.

But she pushed him out of her mind, mostly, until the following Wednesday.

The bar was busier than usual that night, because Duke's Diggers—the coed softball team sponsored by the bar's owner—had played a rescheduled game, after which they came into the bar for the free wings that were a perk of playing for Duke.

"We missed you out there tonight," Caleb said to Sky.

He was the team's left fielder—and also the younger of her two brothers, married to his high school sweetheart and now father to an adorable two-week-old baby boy.

"You should have thought about that before you scheduled the game for a Wednesday night," she said, tipping a second pitcher beneath the tap. "How badly did we lose?"

"It wasn't bad at all," he said. "Only two runs. And they never would have got those two runs if you'd been on third."

"I appreciate your confidence, but it's a team sport," she reminded him.

"And the whole team—even Doug, who filled in at third—wished you could have been there."

She turned the pitchers of beer so that the handles were facing him. "Go drown your sorrows."

He shook his head even as he picked up the pitchers. "I promised Brie I'd head straight home after one beer."

"Look at you—a responsible husband and father," she remarked teasingly.

"I'm trying," he said. "It would be a lot easier if Colton would sleep more than three hours at a time."

"No one ever said parenthood was easy." But she could see the fatigue in the shadows under his eyes and felt a stirring of sympathy. "You want me to put in a separate order of wings to go for you?"

He nodded. "Honey hot."

Though not a flavor listed on the menu, Caleb liked his wings hot and Brielle liked honey garlic, so they compromised by getting them tossed in both sauces.

"You gonna share those pitchers of beer, Gilmore?" Chase Hampton called out from the round table in the corner.

"That's my cue," he said and headed off to join his teammates.

Sky had just sent the wing request through to the kitchen when the mysterious drinker of Sam Adams walked into the bar.

And damn, if he wasn't even better looking than she'd remembered.

She glanced at the clock—9:48 p.m.—and wondered if the timing of his appearance was a coincidence or if it was going to become a habit. And while she told herself she wasn't the least bit interested, she couldn't deny that she was curious.

He took the same seat at the bar, gave the row of taps a similar perusal. "I'll have a pint of Sam Adams," he said.

She poured the beer and set it in front of him.

Raucous laughter broke out at the table in the corner and his hand tightened around the mug, gripping it so hard his knuckles went white.

"That's our softball team," she told him, not sure why she was bothering to explain. "Tuesdays and Saturdays are the usual game days, but the rain last week forced the reschedule tonight."

He didn't respond.

Of course not, because he only wanted a beer, not company or conversation.

So she made her way down the bar, clearing away empty glasses and wiping the counter. The stranger finished his beer, put ten dollars beneath his empty glass and walked out again.

For three weeks after that, his routine was the same.

Every Wednesday night, just before ten o'clock, he came into the bar. Sometimes he was a few minutes earlier, sometimes a few minutes later, but it was always and only on Wednesdays.

He ordered one beer, drank the beer, left a ten-dollar bill on the bar and walked out again.

His routine was always the same.

He never came in with anyone.

He never left with anyone.

He never talked to anyone.

And after five weeks, Sky still didn't even know his name.

Sure, there were other ways she might have uncovered some information about him. Haven was a small enough town that she felt confident somebody knew something about the handsome stranger. But she wasn't interested in gossip and she didn't want secondhand information. She wanted *him* to tell her the secrets she sensed he'd buried deep inside—more important, she wanted him to *want* to open up to her.

But she'd settle for his name to start.

A few years earlier, after yet another failed relationship, Sky had decided that she was done with dating. Since then, she hadn't met a single man who tempted her to change her mind—until *he* walked into Diggers' on that Wednesday night.

She glanced at the vintage beer clock on the wall as she poured a couple of pints for Carter Ford and Kevin Dawson.

9:52 p.m.

*And here come the butterflies.*

Jake Kelly slid behind the wheel of his truck, turned the key in the ignition and shifted into gear. Even as he turned onto Main Street, he wondered, *what the hell am I doing?*

For the past two years, he'd focused his efforts on putting the past behind him and moving on with his life. He wasn't trying to forget—he didn't ever want to forget—but he knew that if he couldn't slay his demons, he had to find a way to coexist with them.

"You can't live like a hermit forever," Luke had said, when he visited Haven a few weeks back.

"No one lives forever," Jake had pointed out.

He'd thought the response might make his brother

crack a smile. Instead, the furrow between Luke's brows had only deepened, and he'd spent the next hour trying to get Jake to open up about his emotions, as if talking—especially to a man who couldn't possibly understand feelings of inadequacy and failure—was going to make anything better.

But Jake did promise that he'd make an effort to get out of the house more, to engage in social interaction and meet people. Which was how he'd ended up at Diggers' Bar & Grill that first Wednesday night in early May.

It had been a test, and though he wasn't entirely sure when he left the bar again whether he'd passed or failed, he'd at least had the satisfaction of knowing that he'd completed it. The next week, it was a little bit easier. And the week after that, easier still.

By the fifth week, he was thinking that he might be ready for a bigger challenge—and when he left the community center, he'd intended to head straight home. Yet for some inexplicable reason, he found himself driving toward Diggers' instead.

Or maybe the reason wasn't so inexplicable.

Maybe the reason was as simple—and complicated—as the incredibly appealing woman who worked behind the bar.

Her name was Skylar Gilmore, but most of the regulars referred to her simply as Sky. She had long dark hair that she usually wore tied back in a loose ponytail and eyes that were a unique mix of gray and blue, not unlike a stormy sky, outlined by a sweep of ridiculously long lashes. Her brows were delicately arched, her cheekbones high and sharp and her mouth looked as if it was meant to be kissed.

The unwelcome observation made him scowl.

She was about average height, but there was absolutely nothing average about her curves, shown to advantage by the scoop-necked white T-shirt that hugged the swell of her breasts and the slim-fitting black jeans that molded to her sweetly rounded bottom and long, shapely legs.

The first time he saw her, he'd felt a stir of something low in his belly. It wasn't a familiar or comfortable feeling. But maybe that was because, for the better part of two years, he'd focused on tamping down his emotions so that he wouldn't have to feel pain or loss or longing.

So yes, it had taken Jake a moment to recognize the feeling as attraction, and less than that to dismiss it. Not only because it was uncomfortable and unfamiliar, but because he wasn't foolish enough to let the attraction lead to anything else. He had no intention of making a move on the pretty bartender, because he knew no woman would want to deal with the issues that he was only beginning to deal with himself. And anyway, he had no wish to open himself up to rejection again.

But Sky greeted him tonight, as she always did, with an easy smile.

He didn't smile back.

He had no reason or desire to encourage her.

"Pint of Sam Adams?" she prompted, when he remained silent, scowling at the taps.

He only had to nod, and the beer would be poured and set in front of him. Instead, he heard himself say, "Actually, I think I'll try a pint of Wild Horse tonight."

She moved the mug to the appropriate tap and tilted it under the spout. "Eleven whole words," she remarked. "I think that's a new record, John."

He lifted his gaze to hers, saw the teasing light in her eyes, and felt that uncomfortable tug again. "My name's not John."

"But as you haven't told me what it is, I can only guess," she said.

"So you decided on John…as in John Doe?" he surmised.

She nodded. "And because it rolls off the tongue more easily than the-sullen-stranger-who-drinks-Sam-Adams, or, after tonight, the-sullen-stranger-who-usually-drinks-Sam-Adams-but-one-time-ordered-a-Wild-Horse." She set the mug on a paper coaster in front of him. "And I think that's a smile tugging at the lips of the sullen stranger."

"I was just thinking that next time I'll order a Ruby Mountain Angel Creek Amber Ale," Jake said.

"Careful," she cautioned, with a playful wink. "This exchange of words is starting to resemble an actual conversation."

He lifted the mug to his mouth and Sky moved down the bar to serve a couple of newcomers, leaving him alone with his beer.

Which was what he wanted…and yet, when she

came back again, he heard himself say, "My name's Jake."

The sweet curve of her lips warmed something deep inside him. "You got a last name, Jake?"

"Let's not rush into anything," he said. "We only just met."

She chuckled at that. "Maybe you'll tell me next week?"

"How do you know I'll be here next week?"

"Wild guess," she said.

"You really don't know my last name?"

"I didn't know your first name until a few seconds ago," she pointed out to him.

"And I thought there weren't any secrets in small towns."

"They are few and far between," she said. "But, in the interest of full disclosure, I will tell you that I know you're staying at Ross and Anna Ferguson's house."

"How do you know that?"

"The *G* in Circle G is for Gilmore," she said, naming the ranch property that was situated behind his uncle's land. "Which makes us neighbors."

He considered that as he tipped his glass to his lips and swallowed the last mouthful of beer.

"Well, maybe I will see you next week, neighbor," he decided aloud, as he took a ten-dollar bill out of his wallet and tucked it under the mug. "But right now, I need to get home. Molly's waiting for me."

## Chapter Two

*Who the heck was Molly?*

Of course, Jake didn't stick around long enough for Sky to ask. And so the question continued to prod at the back of her mind throughout the following week.

The context of his remark suggested that Molly was his girlfriend. Or maybe even his wife. A possibility that sat uneasily with Sky—not just because she'd flirted with the man, but because he'd flirted back!

Or maybe she'd read too much into their brief conversation. Maybe the fact that his icy reserve had thawed enough to allow the exchange of a few words had been nothing more than that. In any event, she needed to get over her preoccupation with the man, because he was obviously involved with somebody else and she would never make a move on a guy who was taken.

"You're not going to get many tips with a scowl on your face," a familiar voice remarked teasingly.

Although Sky didn't keep any portion of the tips that were collected at the bar, she deliberately smoothed her brow and curved her lips for her brother-in-law.

"You're out late, Sheriff," she remarked.

"My wife decided that she had to have a spicy chicken wrap and curly fries."

Sky glanced pointedly at the clock. "At nine o'clock on a Wednesday night?"

He shrugged. "I've learned not to ask."

She keyed the order into the computer and sent it through to the kitchen. "Anything else?"

He shook his head. "I had pizza while I was finishing up some paperwork at the office."

"How about a beer while you're waiting?"

Now he nodded. "Yeah, that sounds good."

Sky poured a pint of Icky.

"So…how far along is she?" she asked, setting the mug in front of him.

Reid looked at her blankly. "Far along with what?"

"Maybe I'm wrong," she said. "But when was the last time Kate sent you out on an errand to satisfy her cravings?"

The blank expression on his face slowly gave way to realization. "When she was pregnant with Tessa."

Sky nodded.

"I don't… I can't…" he said, because apparently the possibility had inhibited his ability to form a complete sentence. "Do you really think…she might be pregnant?"

"You'd know the chances of that better than me," she said dryly.

He nodded, acknowledging the point, and lifted the mug of beer to his lips. "We haven't really been trying," he confided now. "I mean, we've been talking about it, but—"

"If you've only been talking, then I'm probably wrong," Sky teased.

Reid chuckled at that, though he still looked a little stunned by the possibility that his wife might be pregnant again. "As an only child, I often wished for a brother or sister," he admitted. "And since Tessa's first birthday, I've been dropping subtle hints about giving her a sibling."

"You only *think* your hints were subtle," she told him.

"And now… I can't believe it…it's finally going to happen."

"You might want to check with your wife before you start passing out cigars," Sky cautioned her brother-in-law. "I was only speculating about the possibility, based on her dinner request."

But now that she'd put the idea in the sheriff's head, he obviously wasn't ready to let it go. "You're right," he said. "I'm sure you're right. Katelyn's dinner order was a clue—and I didn't even pick up on it."

"Or maybe she's just messing with your mind," she suggested as an alternative.

"She wouldn't do that," Reid said.

"Instead of driving yourself crazy wondering, you could just ask her," she said.

He nodded. "I'll do that."

"And if she *is* pregnant, please don't tell her that I ruined the surprise."

"This conversation never happened," he promised. "So long as *you* tell *me* why you keep looking at the clock."

"Just counting the hours until the end of my shift," she said.

Now Reid shook his head. "You're waiting for someone."

"You should put your investigative talents to work in the sheriff's office—except that those in law enforcement generally require actual evidence before arriving at conclusions."

"Lucky for you, being a smart-ass isn't against the law."

She grinned. "And it's a lot better than being a dumbass."

Reid swallowed another mouthful of beer. "I heard Ross Ferguson's nephew has become something of a regular here," he remarked casually.

She wondered if he was changing the subject or if he'd somehow figured out that she was watching the clock in anticipation of Jake's arrival. Either way, she kept her response vague. "Did you?"

"Come on, Sky. Don't make me drag you down to the station for an interrogation."

"The bar isn't quite as sacred as the confessional, but there is an understanding between a bartender and her customers."

"Would you tell me if you'd had any trouble with him?"

"If it was the kind I didn't think I could handle on my own, yes," she said. "But Jake hasn't caused any problems at all."

Reid nodded then, accepting her response.

"Is there any reason you would suspect he might cause trouble?" she asked.

"No," the sheriff admitted. "It's just that he's been in town for a few months now and no one seems to know much about the guy."

"I didn't think that keeping to oneself was a crime in this town, either," she remarked.

"It's not a crime, but it is an anomaly." His cell phone vibrated against the bar and he turned it over to glance at the screen, his brow furrowing.

"Problem?" she asked.

"Another complaint about motorcycles driving recklessly on the highway," he said. "It's the third this month."

"You haven't made any arrests?"

"No one's been able to get even a partial license plate number," he confided. "And the descriptions of the alleged riders and their bikes have been anything but consistent."

"But you know who it is, don't you?"

"I have some suspicions, but without anything more than that—" He shrugged. "I just hope I get some proof before someone ends up seriously hurt... or worse."

Courtney brought a takeout bag from the kitchen and set it on the bar beside the sheriff. "Spicy chicken wrap and curly fries."

"Thanks."

The waitress smiled. "Give Katelyn my best."

"Will do," he promised.

As Reid pulled out his wallet, Sky glanced at the clock again.

9:53 p.m.

"It's Kelly," Jake said, after he'd taken his usual seat at the bar.

Sky wondered if he was picking up where their conversation had left off and, if so, she was a little confused because she'd been certain that "Molly" was the name he'd mentioned the previous week.

"My last name," he clarified, in response to her quizzical look.

"Jake Kelly," she said, trying it out. It was a strong name and suited the man. "So what can I get for you tonight, Jake Kelly?"

"That Wild Horse I had last week wasn't bad," he said.

"You should aspire to something a little better than not bad." She tapped a finger against the green label with the image of reptile bones. "There's a reason Icky is our most popular seller."

He shook his head. "I can't get my head around the idea of drinking a beer that goes by that name."

"It's named after Nevada's official state fossil," she told him.

"It's also the word my three-year-old niece uses to describe brussels sprouts."

"I share your niece's aversion to brussels sprouts," Sky said, tipping a glass beneath the tap to pour a sample. "And I promise you, Icky doesn't taste anything like green vegetables."

"I actually don't mind brussels sprouts," he said, but he still looked skeptical about the beer as he studied the light copper-colored liquid.

"Try it," Sky urged.

With a shrug, he lifted the glass to his lips.

"Well?" she prompted.

"Much better than the sprouts," he decided.

She selected a clean mug from the shelf and poured him a pint.

He reached for the glass before she'd pulled away, and his fingertips brushed over the back of her hand. She knew the contact was inadvertent—even before he yanked his hand away again—but that knowledge did nothing to alleviate the tingles that danced up her arm. And when she glanced at him, she could tell that he'd felt something, too, and that he was none too pleased about the fact.

Of course he wouldn't be, because there was another woman—though she still didn't know precisely what his relationship was with the mysterious Molly—waiting for him at home. And it really sucked for Sky that the first guy she'd experienced any chemistry with in a very long time was involved with somebody else.

"We also have a decent menu," Sky said, "if you ever wanted a bite along with your beer. Or if you wanted to bring Molly in to enjoy a meal."

"Molly?" he echoed blankly.

She hesitated, wondering if she'd made a mistake in mentioning the woman's name. Was he the type of guy who had a different girlfriend every week? Had he already moved on to someone new?

But since he was obviously waiting for an explanation of her remark, she said, "The woman you said you had to get home to last week."

"Oh, right." The hint of a smile tugged at one side of his mouth as he glanced around. "This really isn't her kind of place."

Sky wasn't offended by his remark. Though Diggers' did a good business as both a restaurant and a bar, she knew that the roadhouse-style establishment wasn't to everyone's liking and that its popularity had as much to do with the limited options in town as its menu offerings.

"We do a fair amount of takeout business, too," she said, offering him another option.

"I'll keep that in mind," he said.

She nodded and moved down the bar to serve another customer.

Because she wasn't the type of woman to make a move on another woman's man—but no other man had ever tempted her like Jake Kelly did.

\* \* \*

Twelve weeks after he'd picked up the key from his uncle's lawyer, Jake was still adjusting to life in Haven, Nevada. Molly, on the other hand, had immediately and fully embraced the freedom of the countryside, and he suspected she would be less than thrilled when it was time to go back to San Diego.

Because they *would* have to go back, but not yet.

Not until he'd figured out what he was going to do with the rest of his life now that his military career was over.

It was a question he'd always known he would face one day. He'd just never expected that day to come before his thirtieth birthday. And now, two years later, he was no closer to finding the answer than he'd been when he got his discharge papers along with his purple heart.

"Molly!"

There was no response to his call, so Jake put his fingers in his mouth and whistled. He scanned the yard, looking for any sign of his canine companion, then whistled again.

Finally she appeared, bounding over the fence and racing toward him.

He sighed as she came to an abrupt halt in front of him, her tongue lolling out of her mouth, her big dark eyes shining with happiness.

"You've been trespassing again, haven't you? And probably chasing squirrels, too," he surmised.

Her attention deficit was probably the reason she'd flunked out of training to be certified as an emotional support animal, but the trainer's loss was Jake's gain. Molly had been his closest friend and confidante for more than two years now, and during that time, he'd never awakened from a nightmare alone. She might not always come right away when she was called, but she didn't need a certificate to know when someone was hurting.

"If the neighbors complain, I'm going to have to put up a real fence—or keep you on a leash," he warned her now.

Molly's tail waved in the air.

"And who's this?" Jake asked, as another creature emerged from under the lowest fence rail, apparently having followed Molly home. He dropped to his haunches and held out a hand for the miniature ball of fluff. "Hey there, little guy."

The pup sniffed his hand, then gave his finger a tentative lick, its little tail wagging its whole back end when Jake gently stroked the underside of its chin.

"She's a girl."

Jake glanced up to see another girl—this one of the human variety—climb over the fence.

Not a child but a teenager, he guessed. Maybe thirteen or fourteen, with blond hair tied back in a ponytail. She wore a Foo Fighters T-shirt over a pair of faded denim cutoffs with thong-style sandals on her feet to show off toenails that were each painted a different color.

"And—" the human girl continued, wagging her finger at the pup "—Rey is a very bad girl." Then she looked up at Jake again, offering a shrug and a smile. "We're still working on heel and stay. By the way, I'm Ashley Gilmore."

"Jake Kelly," he told her.

"You're Mr. Ferguson's nephew right? From California? I heard you'd moved in, but I haven't seen you around town," she continued, without giving him a chance to respond. "What do you think of Haven so far?"

"I haven't seen too much of it," he admitted.

She rolled her eyes. "There's not much to see."

He couldn't help but smile at that.

"What's your dog's name?" she asked now.

"Molly."

"She's a Lab?"

"Mostly."

"How old is she?" Ashley wanted to know.

"Almost three years."

"Rey's only three months."

He frowned. "I thought you said your dog was a girl."

"Not *R-A-Y* but *R-E-Y*, like the main character in the latest Star Wars trilogy," she explained. "I'm not a huge fan of the movies, but Rey had her name before I got her. Princess, her mom, was a pregnant stray who snuck into the horse stable at the Silver Star—that's my cousin Patrick's dude ranch—but she had trouble delivering her babies, so Patrick rushed her to the vet clinic in town and Brooke did an emergency C-section and her son Brendan named all the puppies after Star Wars characters and now

Patrick and Brooke are engaged. They haven't set a date for the wedding yet, but it probably won't be before Caleb and Brielle's wedding reception."

And then, before he could ask—or even decide if he wanted to know—she continued, "Caleb is my brother—well, my half brother, because we have the same dad but different moms. And Brielle is his wife, but she's also my cousin. They got married at the end of high school, but then Gramps literally had a coronary when he found out that his granddaughter had married a Gilmore."

"Do you mean literally in its true sense or are you using the new definition of the word?"

"I mean literally in its true sense," she assured him. "He almost died and had to have a triple bypass."

"So what was the big deal about—wait, didn't you say your name was Gilmore?"

She nodded. "It is now, but back then I was a Blake and Gramps had no idea that David Gilmore was my father. Probably because my mom knew that if she told him, her father would have a heart attack."

He was still trying to put together the pieces of information she'd revealed about her family.

"So are you related to Sky Gilmore?"

Ashley nodded. "Skylar's my sister. Half sister," she clarified again. Then her gaze narrowed. "How do you know Sky?"

"I don't really," he said. "But I've been into Diggers' a few times when she's been working behind the bar."

"Our dad hates that she works there."

"Why?"

"Because he didn't pay for a fancy college degree so that she could pour beer at the local watering hole," Ashley said.

He was curious to know what course of study had resulted in her fancy degree, but he didn't ask. He didn't want to appear to be taking too much of an interest in his uninvited visitor's sister.

"Anyway," the girl continued, "Brie blamed herself for Gramps ending up in the hospital, so she filed for divorce and moved to New York City to go to college but Caleb never signed the papers and now they're together again and they just had a baby a few weeks ago. His name is Colton and he's absolutely adorable."

"So your cousin's son is also your nephew," he said.

Her head bobbed again.

"It really is a small town, isn't it?" he mused.

"You have no idea," she told him, with such heartfelt emotion he had to fight against the smile that wanted to curve his lips. "I thought it was bad when me and my mom lived in town, but since we moved out to the ranch, it's even worse. I think they finally gave in and let me get a puppy because there is no one to hang out with and *nothing* to do."

"A dog can be good company," he agreed, certain that he wouldn't have made it through the past two-and-a-half years without Molly by his side.

"The instructor at obedience school said puppies should have the chance to play with other dogs, too, to learn social skills," she said. "And Rey really seems to like Molly."

He could hardly deny it. Not when Molly was sprawled on the grass and letting the puppy crawl over her.

"Is this her ball?" Ashley asked, picking up a tattered tennis ball.

"One of many," he admitted.

"Does she fetch?"

"She would fetch all day if someone was willing to throw for her."

"Maybe she could teach Rey how to fetch." Ashley drew back her arm and let the ball sail through the air.

Molly immediately took off after the projectile and Rey, startled by her canine pal's sudden abandonment, chased after her.

"You've got a pretty good arm," Jake noted.

"I'm gonna play on Diggers' softball team with my brother and sister someday," she said. "But I've gotta be eighteen before I can try out." Her wistful expression lifted when she saw Molly trotting back toward her.

The dog dropped the ball at Ashley's feet and sat, waiting patiently for the girl to throw it again.

Jake knew he should nudge his visitor along. He didn't want to gain a reputation for welcoming uninvited guests. But she was just a bored kid, happy to throw a ball for his dog, and since Molly was obviously happy, too, Jake saw no reason not to let Ashley stay a while longer.

Rey quickly tired out chasing after the bigger dog. When the tiny fluff ball collapsed by Jake's feet, he couldn't resist scooping her up. She snuggled contentedly in the crook of his arm, exhaled a weary sigh and promptly fell asleep.

Ashley glanced at the oversize face of her Apple Watch as Molly dropped the ball at her feet. "I have to go," she said, sounding sincerely regretful. "Exams start next week and my friend Chloe's coming over to study with me."

Jake nodded and exchanged the pup he held for the slobbery ball in Ashley's hand.

Molly looked at him expectantly, obviously wanting him to take over the game her new friend had abandoned.

"Done," he said firmly.

The dog looked at Ashley.

"Done," she echoed.

Resigned to the fact that playtime was over, Molly stretched out on the ground.

"Maybe I could bring Rey over to play with Molly again sometime?" Ashley suggested hopefully.

Jake sincerely doubted that he could stop her, and yet he felt compelled to caution. "I don't know that your parents would approve of you hanging out here."

"They won't mind, so long as they know where I am."

He wasn't entirely sure that was true, but he wasn't going to argue the point with her.

"So...can I?" she pressed.

"If you come by and Molly's in the backyard, I don't think she'd mind playing with Rey," he decided.

Ashley rewarded him with a radiant smile. "You know, socialization is important for people, too."

Though he didn't want to hurt her feelings, he felt he needed to be honest with her. "I'm not sure how long I'm going to be in town, but I wasn't planning on making friends while I was here."

The girl shrugged philosophically. "I've learned that sometimes the best things in life come along when we're not looking for them."

## Chapter Three

On Saturday, Sky headed into town to Diggers' again. But this time, instead of work, she was there for lunch with Alyssa Channing.

The high school math and science teacher had moonlighted as a bartender a couple of years earlier, before falling in love with and marrying Jason Channing. Though Sky had only worked with her for a short while, they'd remained friends, even if Sky's various jobs and Alyssa's new roles as wife and mother made it challenging for them to get together.

After placing their orders, Sky scooped her friend's seven-month-old daughter out of her carrier and cuddled her close. "I can't believe how much Lucy's grown since I last saw her."

"You haven't seen her in almost three months," Alyssa pointed out. "And babies grow fast."

"Why do you sound sad?" Sky wondered.

"Because as fast as she's growing, she's still just a baby... I can't bear the thought of leaving her in the care of a stranger when I go back to work in September," her friend confided.

"It was hard for my sister, too," Sky told her. "There were several times, in the first few months, that Kate went to court with the baby strapped to her body."

Alyssa chuckled. "Unfortunately, I can't imagine my principal allowing that—especially not in the chemistry lab."

"I would guess not," Sky agreed, as her cell phone chimed with a message. She glanced at the screen, more out of habit than interest, because she had no intention of letting anything distract her from catching up with a friend she hadn't seen in far too long.

But worry dropped like a lead weight into the pit of her stomach when she recognized the number and read the brief words.

Can we talk?

"I'm sorry," she apologized to Alyssa. "I have to make a quick call."

"Of course," her friend immediately agreed, understanding the nature of Sky's job as a counselor required her to be available when her clients needed her—and that wasn't often during regular office hours.

Sky returned Lucy to her mama's arms and slipped away from the table, ducking into the alcove by the restrooms where it was a little quieter and she could give her full attention to the conversation with Jodie Dressler.

It had always been Sky's plan to work with kids struggling with grief, to help them cope. But to specialize in such a narrow field would have required her to move away from Haven to a much larger city. Maybe it was the loss of her own mother at a young age, exacerbated by the fear of losing her father, too, when he'd suffered a heart attack eighteen months earlier, that made her cling to the family she had left. Whatever the reason, she'd opted to stay in Haven and use her education and training to help wherever she could. Currently that entailed working a couple of days a week as a teen counselor at the local high school and being on call to counsel victims of abuse at a nearby women's shelter.

Sky had met Jodie at the local high school, where she had office hours two days a week. For the past few months, she'd been teaching the teen positive conflict resolution strategies to help with tension at home. And Jodie had been making good progress, until her mom decided to get back together with an old boyfriend, introducing a whole new source of friction into their already contentious relationship.

"What's going on?" she asked when Jodie answered the call.

Jodie's muffled sobs told Sky that the teen was sincerely distressed, and she struggled to piece together the few words that she could decipher through the girl's tears.

"Where are you now, Jodie?" she asked gently.

"I'm at the p-park...with Mason."

"The park by your house?"

"Uh-huh." She sniffled. "I d-didn't know where else to g-go."

But she'd gotten out of the house, away from her mother's boyfriend, Leon Franks, who was suddenly paying more attention to Jodie than her mom.

"Stay where you are," Sky instructed. "I'm on my way."

"Th-thank you."

Sky disconnected the call and returned to the table where she'd left her friend. "I'm sorry," she said again.

"Don't be. I already asked Deanna for a take-out container." Alyssa gestured to the compostable clamshell on the table beside the plated burger and fries. "When it wasn't a quick call, I figured you might have to go."

"You figured right," Sky said, reaching into her purse for her wallet.

Alyssa waved her away. "Go. I've got this."

"Next time it's on me," Sky promised, giving her friend a quick hug and dropping a kiss on top of Lucy's head.

After almost three years spent working with teenagers, Sky had mostly learned to distinguish between what was real and what was imagined. That wasn't to say that she didn't make mistakes or take missteps, but when she erred, it was always on the side of protecting a child.

She'd just pulled onto the highway when her low-fuel indicator dinged. She glanced at the display: 35 miles to empty.

Muttering a curse under her breath, she quickly calculated the length of her journey. She was headed in the opposite direction of the gas station, but it was less than fifteen miles to Jodie's house, and only a quarter mile more to the park where the girl had said she'd be waiting. She had more than enough gas to make it there and back again.

Of course, she hadn't anticipated that Jodie's mom's boyfriend might come looking for her, prompting the girl to leave the park with her boyfriend. Or that they'd drive to a local fast-food place another five miles away. They met there to figure out a plan of action and, after Mason left for his part-time job, Sky drove Jodie to her aunt's house, where she would spend the night. Though Leon Franks hadn't yet crossed any lines that warranted reporting, Jodie's discomfort around him was enough of a red flag for Sky that she decided to nudge her brother-in-law the sheriff to look into the man's background.

After the teen was settled, Sky finally turned back toward her own home. She eyed the low-fuel light warily but, based on her rough estimate, figured she still had enough left in her tank to get to the Pump & Go.

Eight miles from the gas station, Sky discovered that she was wrong.

Molly loved to ride in the truck, but she didn't love having to stay in the truck when Jake ran errands, so he usually left his canine companion at home when he went to do his weekly grocery shopping. Of course, she heard him swipe his keys off the counter and immediately lifted her head, a hopeful look in her big brown eyes.

"Didn't you have enough excitement making friends with Rey and playing fetch with Ashley today?"

Her ears perked up in response to the word *fetch*, but she didn't get too excited because she could see that he didn't have a ball in his hand.

"All right," he relented. "I should be quick today, so you can come along if you want."

Molly's tail thumped against the ground, more tentative than enthusiastic.

Chuckling to himself, he spoke the words he knew she'd understand. "Do you wanna go for a ride?"

She immediately sprang to her feet and made a beeline to the back door.

"I'll take that as a yes," he said.

Molly raced ahead of him to the truck.

When he opened the door, the dog immediately leaped onto the seat and took up her favorite position by the passenger window, her nose against the glass, her tail wagging.

Jake slid behind the wheel for the trip to Battle Mountain, lowering the passenger side window several inches for Molly.

There was a grocery store in Haven, of course, and he'd stopped in at The Trading Post a couple of times when he'd only needed to pick up one or two items. What he'd learned from those brief visits to the store was that that staff were overly friendly and chatty—not unlike Diggers' sexy bartender, though no one behind the deli counter or at the cash registers had stirred his interest the way Sky Gilmore did. In any event, those visits had cemented his resolve to get his supplies in Battle Mountain, where nobody knew his name or even cared who he was.

He'd just turned onto the highway when he spotted an SUV off to the side of the road with its hood up.

Actually, Molly had spotted the vehicle first and barked to draw his attention to it. She was always excited by the opportunity to meet new people.

Jake didn't want to stop. Besides, Haven being the kind of town where neighbors looked out for one another, he was fairly certain that if he continued on by, the next vehicle to come along would stop to offer assistance to the stranded driver. The battle between his desire not to get involved and his instinct to help someone in trouble was a short one.

"We've got groceries to buy," he reminded the dog, but his foot was already moving from the accelerator to the brake pedal. "And your favorite kibble is one of the items on my list."

Molly barked again—*at him* this time.

"You're supposed to be man's best friend, not my conscience," he grumbled, even as he pulled onto the gravel shoulder.

As he did so, the owner of the stalled Jeep Renegade stepped into view, and he realized it was none other than Sky Gilmore.

She wasn't dressed in her usual uniform of T-shirt and jeans today. Instead she was wearing a cropped sweater with a flowy skirt and chunky-heeled ankle boots, and he couldn't help but take notice of the long, shapely legs beneath the short hem and the sexily windblown hair that tumbled over her shoulders.

Wishing he could have ignored the dog and his own conscience, he nevertheless pushed the door open and, with a terse command to Molly to stay, stepped out onto the gravel.

Recognition widened Sky's eyes even as her lips curved. "Well, hello, neighbor."

Her slow, sexy smile took his breath away. Every. Single. Time. That unwelcome awareness churned in his belly, spread through his veins.

He shifted his gaze even as he took a few steps closer, to peer under the hood. "Engine trouble?" he asked.

"No," she admitted, a little sheepishly. "I ran out of gas."

"You think the gas tank is under the hood?"

She rolled her eyes. "A lot of people will drive by

a vehicle parked by the side of the road, but the hood up is a clear sign of trouble."

And running out of gas was a clear sign of carelessness, he thought, though he refrained from saying so aloud.

"Your SUV doesn't have a fuel gauge?" he asked instead.

"Of course it does."

"But no visible or audible indicators that your fuel is low?"

"Those, too," she admitted, a hint of color staining her pale cheeks.

"So how is it that your tank is empty?"

"I had enough gas to get me where I was going," she said, a little defensively. "But I had to make an unexpected detour, and then didn't have enough to get back again."

"And there were no service stations wherever you went?"

"If your only reason for stopping was to make snide comments, you can go," she said. "I was just about to call my brother to bring me a can of gas."

"I can't in good conscience leave you stranded on the side of the road," he said, turning back to his truck.

"I won't be here long," she assured him.

"And I'm just supposed to take your word for that?"

"You're not supposed to do anything," she said. "You were under no obligation to stop and you're under no obligation to stay."

Whether because she recognized the word *stay* or just wanted to meet his new friend, Molly barked, drawing Sky's attention.

"Quiet, Molly," he said.

The surprise on Sky's face shifted to curiosity as she turned to look toward his truck, where the retriever had her front paws curled over the edge of the lowered glass.

"So Molly's a dog," she mused.

"I never said any different," he said, perhaps a little defensively.

"No," she acknowledged. "But you had to know that I'd think otherwise."

"I can't control what people think," he said, all too aware that he'd been the subject of much speculation since his arrival in town.

"When a man mentions that a named female is waiting for him, it's reasonable to assume he's referring to a woman." She offered her hand for the dog to sniff. "A girlfriend or maybe even a wife." She rubbed the soft fur under the dog's throat, and chuckled when Molly closed her eyes and sighed blissfully.

"If I ever meet a woman as loyal as my dog, I might want to rush home to her," he remarked.

"Sounds like there's a story there."

He shrugged. "Only the same sad tale that's been told a thousand times before."

"Every story is unique," Sky insisted.

Even if that was true, Jake had no intention of sharing any details of his.

"Would I be correct then in assuming that you don't have a girlfriend or wife?"

"No girlfriend or wife," he confirmed. "But lucky for you, I do have a can of gas."

"Thank you," she said, when he retrieved the gas can from the bed of his truck. "I would have called one of my brothers—or even my father, but I'm sincerely grateful that I won't have to, because I'd never hear the end of it."

"No worries," Jake said, uncapping her gas tank and inserting the nozzle. "Though I should warn you, this might not solve your problem."

"What do you mean?"

"Fuel injectors can fail from overheating if they've been allowed to go dry, so putting gas into your tank might not be enough to get your vehicle started again."

"Of course not," she muttered under her breath. "Because no good deed goes unpunished."

The cryptic remark piqued his curiosity, but Jake didn't ask for an explanation. Instead, he focused on his task so they could both continue on their separate ways.

He tipped the gas can, his ears straining to identify a sound in the distance...

*A trickle of sweat snaked down his spine, between his shoulder blades.*

*After six months in Afghanistan, he should be used to sweating by now. But this wasn't his body's futile effort to regulate its internal temperature when it was a hundred and twenty-five degrees outside. This was his body taking cues from his brain, telling him to be alert. To be ready.*

*Because anyone—from the twelve-year-old boy supposedly en route to visit his grandparents in the neighboring village to the seventy-year-old grand-mother on her way to the open-air market—could be friend or foe. It wasn't just the twenty-something-year-old men with hard eyes who could be carrying weapons or wearing explosive devices.*

*And anyone who let down his guard, for even a second, could end up dead.*

*He focused on the sound, attempting to determine the direction of the bike's approach. Not a bike but* bikes, *he realized. At least two—maybe three. He scanned the horizon, looking for the telltale cloud of sand kicked up by churning tires.*

*There—he could see them now. Barely visible in the distance, but moving in their direction.*

"Am I good to go now?"

It was Sky's voice—the distinctly feminine and familiar cadence—more than the question that drew Jake back.

He blinked, and the hazy, barren landscape faded away.

*Not real.*

He exhaled a long, slow breath.

But the motorcycles *were* real, because he could still hear the roar of the engines, approaching fast.

Not terrorists or insurgents, though. He didn't have to worry about ISIS or the Taliban in northern

Nevada. There was nothing to worry about here but his own overactive imagination.

"Jake?" Sky prompted.

"Yeah," he finally responded to her question as he recapped the gas can. "You're good to go."

She smiled then, and he felt that tug again. A distinctly sexual—and decidedly unwelcome—attraction.

"Thanks," she said.

He just nodded.

"Well—" she gave his dog one last affectionate scratch behind the ears "—it was nice to meet you, Molly."

The Lab dropped her chin to rest on the rolled down window as Sky turned away.

Jake felt a bead of sweat begin to snake down his spine for real as the sound of the engines grew louder.

Definitely more than one.

Not terrorists or insurgents, he reminded himself.

Probably just idiot kids racing.

His suspicion was confirmed when the first bike came into view around the bend with two more in close pursuit. All three took the curve wide, crossing to the wrong side of the center line, and going too fast to be able to correct their position.

"Look out!"

The urgency in Jake's tone had Sky's head whipping around.

She sucked in a breath as she spotted the trio of

motorcycles racing toward her. She had to get out of the way, to get off the road, but her feet were frozen, unable to move, even as the bikes drew closer.

Then Jake grabbed her arm and yanked her back, body-slamming her against the bed of his truck. The shock of the impact knocked the air out of her lungs. Her heart was racing; her head was spinning.

The bikes had seemed to appear from out of nowhere, and if Jake hadn't been there to warn her...

No, he hadn't just warned her, he'd saved her.

Or maybe that was a little melodramatic.

She didn't think any of them had passed too close to the spot where she'd been standing, but he'd immediately anticipated the danger and taken action. And she'd be lying to herself if she didn't admit that it was an incredible turn on.

Or maybe it was the press of his hard body against hers that was responsible for waking up her hormones. Because wrapped in his arms, how could she not be aware of him? The heat of his body? The scent of his skin?

And that awareness had her long-dormant hormones doing backflips, celebrating the fact that she wasn't just alive but cradled in the embrace of a strong, sexy man.

"Sky? Are you okay?" Jake loosened his hold and took half a step back, his gaze skimming over her as if assessing her for injury.

She licked her suddenly dry lips. "Yeah."

"You're shaking," he noted, rubbing his hands gently up and down her arms.

She nodded, because it was true. From the top of her head to the soles of her feet, her entire body was trembling. Not with fear, as he suspected, but with awareness and arousal.

"I'm okay," she said again.

While her brain warned her to push him away, her body was encouraging her to take a different tack. Urging her to lift herself onto her toes and press her mouth to his.

But her knees were still feeling a little wobbly, so she settled for leaning forward and pressing her lips to the strong column of his throat.

He jerked back, swallowed.

"Sky…"

She heard the warning in his voice—and the wanting.

And she saw both in the depths of those whiskey-colored eyes as they met and held her own.

"Jake," she answered softly.

A muscle in his jaw flexed, but he gave her no indication of anything he was thinking or feeling. No hint of anything at all before he said, "I knew you were going to be trouble the first minute I saw you."

But even those words were hardly more than a whisper from his lips before they captured hers.

## Chapter Four

She'd fantasized about kissing Jake.

Maybe not by the side of the highway, but the setting didn't matter.

It only mattered that he was kissing her.

True, she didn't know much about him, but there was something between them. It had been there from the beginning, an unexpected spark that quickly ignited a flame. From the beginning, she'd wanted him. And now that the mystery of Molly's identity had been solved, there was no reason to deny what she wanted. What they both wanted.

Because the way Jake was kissing her, she no longer had any doubt that he wanted her, too.

So what if he wasn't a great conversationalist?

He *was* a great kisser.

His tongue swept along the seam of her lips, then slipped inside when she opened for him. Willingly. Eagerly. She pressed herself against him, welcoming the deeper intimacy. Wanting more.

As his mouth moved over hers, hot flames of desire spread through her veins, heating her body, melting her bones. She lifted her hands to his shoulders, needing something solid and steady to hold on to as the earth tilted beneath her feet and the world spun around her.

There were probably a dozen reasons that this was a bad idea. Not the least of which was that she hardly knew anything about him. It had taken weeks for Jake to even tell her his name, but despite his reticence, he wasn't self-absorbed. While their subsequent conversations had been brief, they'd nevertheless given her glimpses of his intelligence and humor. And though he'd only once mentioned a niece, he'd spoken of the child with affection.

Maybe the details that she knew about him were slim, but they were enough for Sky—especially in combination with the powerful chemistry between them. And she decided that kissing Jake couldn't possibly be a bad idea when it felt so incredibly good.

He slid his hands beneath the hem of her sweater, then over the bare skin of her abdomen, making her shiver. His palms were wide and callused, but his touch was gentle, raising goose bumps on her flesh.

It had been a long time since she'd had a man's hands on her, and she gloried in the feel of Jake's touch now. When his thumbs brushed the undersides of her breasts through the whisper-thin satin of her bra, she felt her nipples draw into tight points, begging to be noticed, touched, tasted. And she knew that she wouldn't have protested if he'd lowered his mouth to her breast right there at the side of the road.

Instead, he pulled his hands out from under her top and eased his lips from hers. "Car."

"What?" she said, resisting the urge to whimper in protest of his withdrawal.

"Car," he said again, as a vehicle came around the bend.

Sky recognized the white truck and its driver before he pulled up alongside her Jeep.

"Engine trouble?" Oscar Weston guessed. "Anything I can give you a hand with?"

She smiled to show her appreciation for the mechanic's offer, even as she shook her head. "Already fixed."

A furrow appeared between Oscar's bushy white brows as his gaze slid from Sky to Jake, before shifting back again. "Are you sure there's nothing I can do?"

"I'm sure," Sky said. "It's all good. But thanks."

The man gave a slow nod, sent Jake another hard look, then continued on his way.

"Sorry about that—about Mr. Weston, I mean," she hastened to clarify. "Not about the kiss."

"You don't have to apologize," he said. "But maybe I should."

"Don't you dare," she said.

He seemed taken aback by her vehement response— and maybe just a little bit amused.

"Okay, I won't," he agreed.

She nodded. "Good."

"So are we just going to forget it ever happened?"

Now she shook her head. "I don't want to forget it happened."

Jake's eyes held hers for a long moment before he asked, "What do you want, Sky?"

She replied without hesitation. "You."

His pupils flared even as he took a deliberate step back. "You don't know anything about me."

It wasn't just a statement but a warning, and one that she should probably heed. But for some inexplicable reason, everything she didn't know about Jake didn't matter as much as what she did—that she felt safe in his arms. Desirable. Desired.

For the past few years, she'd tried so hard to be the person everyone else needed that she'd neglected her own needs. Those needs were letting themselves be heard now, loud and clear.

"I know enough," she told him. And then she smiled. "Including where you live."

He swallowed. "Be sure, Sky."

She answered without hesitation. "I am."

He gave a short nod. "I'll follow you—just in case you have any more car trouble."

Sky was trembling still as she slid behind the wheel of her car and turned her key in the ignition, mentally crossing her fingers that her fuel injectors weren't damaged and her car would start. Because now that she'd decided what was going to happen next, she was eager to get there.

The engine coughed and sputtered...then turned over and fired.

Exhaling a grateful sigh, she shifted into drive and headed toward the sprawling log bungalow she'd always known as the Ferguson place.

Ross Ferguson had struggled as a cattle rancher, not because he was unwilling to do the work but because his heart wasn't in it. He'd eventually turned his attention and talent to making furniture from reclaimed wood, creating beautiful pieces and quickly gaining a reputation for himself within the local community.

Unfortunately, there wasn't a lot of demand for his work or a lot of money to be made, and his wife's ongoing battle with Cystic fibrosis meant that there were always medical bills to be paid. So Ross decided to supplement his income by leasing most of his land to the Circle G—an arrangement that was, as far as Sky knew, ongoing to this day.

But she wasn't thinking about Ross Ferguson's legal arrangement with her father as she pulled into the driveway. And at another time she might have stopped to admire the flowers blooming in the beds around the perimeter of the house, perennials that had been planted by Anna Ferguson years earlier. Right now, though, she was more interested in seeing the inside of the house—especially Jake's bedroom.

She stepped out of her Jeep, her heart pounding

with excitement and anticipation, as Jake pulled his truck into the double driveway beside her SUV.

As soon as he opened the door, Molly scrambled out, racing over to greet Sky.

"Yes, hello again," she said, crouching to fuss over the dog. "I came for a visit, if that's all right with you."

"Molly loves when people come to visit. She barks at anyone outside the door, but a guard dog she is not. As soon as they cross the threshold, she's all about making friends."

"Are we going to be friends?" Sky asked the dog.

Molly promptly rolled onto her back, splaying her legs to expose her belly for a rub.

"I'll take that as a yes," she said, indulging the animal's wordless request.

Jake slid a key into the lock of the side door, then held it open for Sky to enter.

A kaleidoscope of butterflies danced and twirled in her belly as she stepped over the threshold and into what was obviously the kitchen. According to her brother-in-law, Jake had been living in Haven for a few months now, but looking around the room, Sky was pretty confident that he hadn't been busy decorating during that time.

The white Shaker cabinets were simple and classic, but the green plastic knobs on the cupboard doors and the faux marble laminate countertop screamed of a bygone era. Several of the green and white checkerboard floor tiles were chipped or cracked and the

Formica table and chairs looked as if they belonged in a fifties diner.

She perched on the edge of one of those chairs to take off her boots, setting them on the mat beside the door. Jake unlaced his—combat rather than cowboy, she noted—and toed them off.

He tucked his hands in the front pockets of his jeans and rocked back on his heels. "Can I get you anything?" he offered. "Are you hungry? Thirsty?"

"I didn't come here for food or drink," she said, moving past him and into what was obviously the living room. The furniture was more modern in here, she noted, the oversize leather pieces and enormous flat screen a stark contrast to the faded floral paper on the walls.

"I know," Jake admitted, following behind her. "But I'm trying to give you a chance to come to your senses."

"I'll be sensible tomorrow," she said. "Right now, I really want you to kiss me again."

"And I really want to kiss you," he said, already dipping his head.

She sighed, a sound of pure pleasure, as his mouth captured hers. He kissed her deeply, hungrily, seducing her with the brush of his lips, the sweep of his tongue. It wasn't just a kiss, it was a promise of so much more, and the realization had excitement coursing through her veins, making her knees weak and her thighs quiver.

Because right here, right now, this was what she wanted.

*He* was what she wanted.

"Take me to bed, Jake."

He responded by scooping her into his arms, making Sky's already-fluttering heart beat faster inside her chest.

Molly, perhaps suspecting that they were playing a game, streaked past them and into the bedroom, leaping onto the bed.

He paused in the doorway and winced. "I, uh, wasn't planning on inviting anyone to come home with me," he said, setting Sky on her feet.

"I invited myself," she reminded him, giving the room a quick perusal.

It was simply and sparsely furnished, with a queen-size bed flanked by matching night tables on one wall and a long chest of drawers opposite.

"Still, if I'd thought there was anything greater than a snowball's chance in hell that I'd bring female company home, I would have put clean sheets on the bed," Jake told her. "And moved that pile of clothes on the chair to the laundry room. And checked the expiration date on the condoms in my toiletry bag."

"I've got some in my purse—condoms, not clean sheets," she clarified.

"Good to know," he said, reaching for the edge of the comforter.

The lump beneath the sheet wiggled.

He pulled it back and pointed to the door. "Out."

Molly lifted her paws to cover her face.

Sky couldn't help it—she giggled.

Jake slanted her a look. "Don't encourage her."

"I'm sorry," she said, not really sorry at all. "She's just too adorable."

"Yeah, she's adorable," he agreed. "But right now, she's also in the way." He turned back to the playful canine. "Molly?"

She dropped one paw, peeking at him with one eye.

"It's not playtime," he said firmly.

The dog let the other paw fall away and tilted her head to look at him imploringly.

"Out," he said, and pointed to the door again.

Molly inched toward the edge of the mattress, moving as slowly as possible, as if to give him a chance to change his mind.

Sky pressed her lips together to hold back another laugh as Jake grabbed the dog's collar and tugged her toward the door, closing it firmly when Molly was on the other side.

Then he looked back at the tangle of sheets again and said, "Do you want to wait in the living room for a few minutes while I sort things out in here?"

"No," Sky said, but tempered her refusal with a smile.

"No?" he echoed.

"There's no point in making the bed now when we're just going to mess it up again."

From the other side of the door came a plaintive whine.

"I have to admit, I feel a little guilty that she's been kicked out of her own room," Sky said, having spotted the dog bed in the corner.

"Molly thinks every room in the house is hers," he said. "In five minutes, she'll be settled on her favorite chair in the living room and forget that she was ever banished from here."

"And what will we be doing in five minutes?" Sky asked, lifting her sweater over her head and carelessly dropping it on the floor.

"Not talking about the dog," he promised, watching as she unzipped her skirt and wiggled it over her hips, leaving her standing before him in only a hot pink satin bra and turquoise lace panties. His eyes were dark as they skimmed over her slowly, approvingly. "I should have guessed you weren't a white cotton kind of girl."

"I like color," she said. "Though I would have matched my underwear if I'd known they were going to be on display."

"I like what you're wearing," he assured her. "But I think I'm going to like you wearing nothing at all even more."

He kissed her deeply then, wrapping his arms around her and pulling her close so their bodies were aligned, breasts to chest, thigh to thigh and all the interesting points in between.

But still it wasn't enough. She wanted skin on skin contact. And he was wearing far too many clothes.

She tugged the hem of his shirt out of his jeans and slid her hands beneath the fabric, exploring the smooth, taut muscles of his abdomen and chest with eager hands. He broke the kiss long enough to pull down the shade over the window, then yank the shirt over his head and toss it aside.

She caught a glimpse of a tattoo on his shoulder—the logo and motto of the USMC in glorious color confirming her suspicion that Jake had served in the military. There was more ink on his other arm, something that almost looked like a list, but it was hard to decipher in the dim light and, truthfully, she was more interested in his muscles than his body art at present. And the man did have spectacular muscles.

Her fingertips skimmed over sculpted abs as they traveled south to unfasten his belt. He helped her there, too, quickly shucking his jeans to reveal a pair of sexy black knit boxers—and an impressive erection. They tumbled together on top of the unmade bed, mouths mating, hands searching, each of them desperate to feel and touch and taste.

She'd only met him a few weeks earlier, so how was it that she felt as if she'd been waiting for him forever? Wanted him forever? As if he might finally be the one to—

*No.*

She firmly shoved that romanticized notion out of her mind. She'd spent far too much time during her teen years trying to fill the emptiness inside her with the attention of boys she wanted to believe actually cared about her. Most of them only cared about scoring—and lied if they didn't.

It was a long time after she'd graduated from high school before she realized that she was responsible for her own happiness, and it took her a few more years after that to find it. But she was happy now. Sure, she had unfulfilled hopes and dreams and three part-time jobs instead of a defined career path, but she was confident that her life was on track to get her where she wanted to go.

Jake wasn't part of her long-term plan, and being here with him now wasn't about anything more than finishing what they'd started with a single earth-tilting kiss on the side of the highway. Because in addition to taking responsibility for herself, Sky had also learned that she didn't need to be ashamed of wanting sex for the sake of sex.

Maybe she wasn't proud of her sometimes less-than-discriminating choices when she was younger, but she was a woman now, with a woman's needs. And it had been far too long since those needs had been satisfied.

But Jake was already on his way to changing that. With every brush of his lips, he communicated his desire. With every stroke of his hands, he stoked the fire that burned inside her. He rained kisses along her jaw, down her throat, then lower still. He nuzzled the hollow between her breasts, his shadowed jaw rasping against her tender skin. Then he found the center clasp of her bra and deftly unfastened it, peeling back the cups to bare her breasts to his avid gaze and eager mouth.

His lips skimmed over the tight bud of one nipple, a fleeting, teasing caress. She bit down on her bottom lip to keep from whimpering, pleading—*More*.

*Please.*—as his mouth shifted to her other breast, another teasing caress.

Deciding that turnabout was fair play, she let her hand brush over the front of his shorts and heard him suck in a breath. She stroked the hard length of him through the soft cotton with a fingertip, up and then down again, the deliberate action eliciting a low groan from deep in his throat. But the teasing caresses weren't enough for either of them, and she started to dip her fingers beneath the waistband of his briefs.

Jake caught her wrist and gently pulled her hand away.

"Give me a sec," he said, before rolling off the bed and disappearing into the adjoining bathroom.

He returned with a square packet in his hand. "I checked the date," he said, as he set the condom on the bedside table.

"We're good?"

One corner of his mouth kicked up in a half smile. "I'm hoping."

Sky smiled, too, as she drew him back down onto the mattress with her. "Well, let's find out," she suggested.

His hands moved boldly over her body, callused palms stroking her skin, sending tingles through her body.

Though he'd drawn the shade, so that only a thin ribbon of light from the late afternoon sun was allowed to squeeze through on either side, she could feel areas of puckered skin beneath her fingertips.

At first, she'd assumed he wanted the shade closed because the window was at ground level, despite the fact that the house was set back from the road and there were unlikely to be any passers-by this far on the outskirts of town. But now she wondered if he'd shut out the light so that she wouldn't see his scars.

Yeah, this wounded warrior definitely had a story to tell. And while Sky couldn't deny a certain curiosity about his military experience, she was more interested in the man himself, and she set about exploring his taut, hard body with her hands and her lips.

He captured her mouth again, his kiss hot and hungry, impatient and demanding, reflecting the same desperate urgency that was building inside her. There was no sweet seduction between them, only heat and passion and need.

"Now, Jake. Please."

He didn't make her ask twice, and she gasped as he thrust inside of her. Her orgasm came hard and fast, crashing over her in wave after wave of pleasure, leaving her stunned and breathless and with a vague thought that the celibacy vow she'd taken almost three years earlier had blown up in spectacular fashion.

Then he began to move inside her, and before she had a chance to draw air into her lungs, the tension started to build again. The glorious friction created by his rhythmic thrusts was almost more than she could bear. And though she wouldn't have thought it was possible to come again while her body was still quivering with the aftershocks of her first orgasm, she was overjoyed to be proven wrong.

*The wind roared in his ears. Tiny grains of sand, whipped into a frenzy, slashed like knives. In the distance, a billowing cloud of dust. Harmless enough in the moment, it would be upon them quickly, reducing visibility to zero, blocking out even the sun.*

Jake felt a hand on his arm. Soft. Gentle.

An unmistakably feminine touch.

No, it wasn't the wind he heard, but the blood pulsing through his veins.

He jolted back to the present and exhaled a long, slow breath as his heart continued to pound like a jackhammer inside his chest.

"Yeah," he decided. "We're good."

Sky chuckled softly. "You're not going to get any argument from me."

Though his body wasn't just sated but spent, he managed to lift his weight off her and roll onto his back.

He hadn't realized how much he'd missed sex until his body was joined together with hers. It was more than just the physical act of mating or the culmination of mutual desire. It was the sense of connection, of becoming a part of something bigger than himself. A connection that he'd been certain he'd lost forever when—

No. He wasn't going to go back there now.

He was just going to let himself be in this moment for the moment.

So resolved, he closed his eyes, a surprising feeling of peace stealing over his body, relaxing his muscles. He actually started to drift off, thinking it might be nice to fall asleep with a warm woman in his arms—and wake with her beside him.

Yeah, it might be nice.

Or it might be a nightmare.

With that sobering thought at the front of his mind, he rolled out of bed and headed to the bathroom to get rid of the condom and get his head on straight—not an easy task when he was feeling so unaccustomedly satisfied and relaxed.

He hadn't planned for this. He wouldn't have dared to even dream it might happen. And just because it had happened—and had been pretty amazing—he knew it would be a mistake to think that the pleasure he'd shared with Sky could ever lead to anything more.

He'd come to Haven because he needed some time and distance to get his life back on track. The absolute last thing he needed was the complication of a woman.

But he couldn't deny that he'd enjoyed being with her.

She was spontaneous and passionate and fun, and while their bodies were intimately linked, she'd made him feel as if he was not just alive but whole and normal.

Unfortunately, he knew that was only an illusion.

But as he recalled the way she'd touched him, her hands stroking every inch of his body, he knew there was no way she'd missed his scars. But she hadn't skipped a beat when she'd encountered the ridges of puckered skin that were an unwanted souvenir of his last tour. Her touch might have gentled as she'd traced the rough edges, but she hadn't recoiled. She hadn't turned away.

And she hadn't asked any questions.

If he was a man capable of opening his heart, he might love her for that alone.

But he wasn't.

Still, he stood there for a moment, looking at her in his bed. The sheet was pulled up high enough to cover the swell of her exquisite breasts, but one of her legs—slim and toned and perfect—was thrown over the top, and her silky dark hair was fanned out over his pillow. She looked so peaceful and contented, as if there was nowhere else she wanted to be, and he felt a tug of something that might have been regret that he had to disturb her.

"Skylar?"

Her eyelids flickered before they lifted, revealing blue-gray eyes that he longed to get lost in. Then her lips curved, and his body—though recently sated—stirred again.

"Mmm?" she murmured.

It was as much an invitation as an acknowledgment—an invitation that he desperately wished he could accept. He wanted to slip between the sheets with her again, spread her legs wide and—

He ruthlessly stomped down on his growing desire and said, "You have to go."

## Chapter Five

Well, that was a new experience, Sky acknowledged, sitting behind the wheel of her Jeep and staring at the closed door of Jake Kelly's house.

Not the sex—although that had exceeded her expectations in the very best way—but what had followed. His summary dismissal of her had been not just surprising but insulting.

Okay, so maybe he liked his own space when he slept. He wouldn't be the first guy who had no interest in cuddling a woman after the deed was done. But instead of rolling over and falling asleep, like a few other guys she'd known, he'd told her to leave.

Bluntly and unapologetically.

And staring at the door he'd closed between them, she couldn't help but feel as if she'd been used.

Which she knew wasn't really fair, because if any using had been done, it had been mutual—and mutually satisfying. And while the logical part of her brain understood that there might be something more going on here, that possibility did nothing to soothe the unexpected ache in the region of her heart.

*You don't know anything about me.*

Yeah, she definitely should have heeded his warning.

Because while she had no doubts that he'd enjoyed the physical act, it was more than apparent to Sky that Jake didn't want anything more.

Of course, if he'd given her the benefit of even five minutes of conversation, she might have been able to reassure him that she wasn't looking for any kind of a relationship right now, either. And that even if she was, she wouldn't set her sights on a moody Marine with obvious intimacy issues.

No matter that they'd had mind-numbing, heart-pounding, body-tingling sex together.

And no matter how much she wanted to experience it again.

She had too much pride and self-respect to chase after any man—especially one who had clearly and unequivocally given her the brush-off.

Of course, she had only herself to blame. He'd told her, the first night he'd sat at Diggers' bar, that he wasn't interested in company or conversation. Obviously he was a man who said what he meant and meant what he said, and she was an idiot for not paying closer attention. Or maybe she was a fool for allowing herself to believe that things had changed over the past few weeks.

Either way, the current situation was no one's fault but her own.

She backed out of the driveway, but she couldn't resist turning her head for one last glance toward Jake's house and saw Molly at the window. Well, at least the dog seemed disappointed to watch her go.

He'd totally blown that.

As Jake stood in the kitchen, staring at the door through which Sky had recently exited, he acknowledged that there were countless other things he could have said or done to communicate his desire for her to leave without resorting to the blunt words he'd used. But when he'd returned to his bedroom after discarding the condom and saw her temptingly naked body sprawled on top of the tangled sheets, he hadn't wanted her to leave at all. What he'd wanted then was to get back into bed with her for an encore performance—Hot, Sweaty Sex, Part Two.

But he was afraid that if he gave in to that desire, he wouldn't want to let her go.

And the one thing he knew for certain was that he couldn't let her stay.

Molly turned away from the living room window and padded into the kitchen. She sat at his feet, looking up at him with big brown eyes filled with sadness.

"I know," he said, acknowledging the truth aloud. "I blew it."

She tilted her head, as if to let him know that she was listening, although her understanding seemed to be limited to the words *walk, run, ride, fetch* and *dinner*.

"Of course, I blew it," he continued. "I'm not ready for a relationship. I barely know how to have a conversation with regular people anymore, never mind interact on a deeper level."

Except that he'd had no difficulty interacting with Sky in his bedroom, and on a very deep level. But he knew he shouldn't feel too proud about that, because the way she'd kept her gaze averted as she gathered up her clothes and dressed, he didn't think he was likely to ever see her naked again.

"It's pretty sad, isn't it, when the most meaningful conversations I have are with my dog?"

Molly tilted her head so far over, he was afraid she was going to end up with a kink in her neck.

"Especially when you're just hanging out with me because you want your dinner," he noted.

Recognizing the word *dinner*, Molly immediately sprang to her feet and danced over to her bowl.

Jake measured out her kibble and dumped it into the bowl.

Then he turned on the oven to heat up a frozen pizza for himself, wishing—for the first time in a long time—that he had someone to share it with.

When Sky got back to the Circle G, she found Ashley at the kitchen table, gluing letters onto a poster board.

It had taken some time for Sky and her siblings to accept that they had a half sister, and longer still for them to acknowledge that their father had real feelings for his youngest daughter's mom. Not just because he'd grieved the death of his first wife so deeply and for so long, but because Valerie was a Blake and the Gilmore-Blake feud was the stuff of legends in Haven, Nevada, with tangled roots that went back five generations.

Now David Gilmore and Valerie Blake were married and Ashley was sleeping in the bedroom across the hall from Sky. And while it had been a surprise to Sky to discover that she had a little sister, she was enjoying getting to know Ashley.

"Homework on a Saturday night?" Sky asked her now.

Ashley nodded. "It's for book fair, and it's worth thirty percent of my final grade."

"How's it going?"

The teen made a face. "Me and Chloe are supposed to be working on it together, but she left."

Sky opened the fridge, took out a can of cola. "Do you need a caffeine boost?"

"Sure, thanks."

She grabbed a second can and carried both to the table.

Ashley popped the tab on her drink, and a furry head popped up from her lap.

"You're not supposed to have the dog at the table," Sky felt compelled to remind her.

"But there's no food at the table," Ashley said, a

point that seemed to remind her: "Although Martina made a plate for you—it's in the oven."

"I guess I missed dinner, didn't I?"

And lunch, she remembered now, thinking of the forgotten takeout container on the backseat of her Jeep. But she wasn't hungry—or she didn't think she was, until her empty stomach rumbled.

"A plate of what?" she asked, even as she opened the oven door to take a peek.

"Meatless meatloaf, mashed potatoes and green beans."

"What did Dad have for dinner?" she wondered aloud, sliding her hand into an oven mitt to remove the hot plate.

Since David Gilmore's heart attack, Martina had been strict about limiting his intake of fatty foods, including red meat—which was a definite bone of contention between the cattle rancher and his longtime cook. And since Ashley and her mom had taken up residence at the Circle G, Martina had embraced the challenge of making occasional meatless meals to accommodate Ashley's vegetarian lifestyle.

"Meatless meatloaf, mashed potatoes and green beans," Ashley said again. "But Martina made his potatoes with skim milk instead of cream and didn't let him have any butter or salt on his beans."

She carried her plate and cutlery to the table. "Did he threaten to fire her?"

Ashley grinned. "Just like he does every day."

Sky picked up her fork and dug into the meatloaf and her sister got back to gluing the cardboard letters that would spell out her project title. But when Sky paused between bites, she noticed Ashley staring at her phone.

"Is everything okay?" she asked.

"What? Oh, yeah." Ashley capped the glue stick and picked up her can of soda, then set it down again without taking a sip. "Actually, I was just thinking about Jodie."

Sky paused with a forkful of mashed potatoes halfway to her mouth. "Who?"

Ashley rolled her eyes. "I know you're not supposed to talk about your clients or patients or whatever they're called, but Chloe told me that her sister's been talking to you about their mom's boyfriend."

"Did she?" Sky said.

Though Jodie had mentioned that she had a sister, she hadn't realized that Jodie's sister was Ashley's best friend because the two girls had different last names.

*"He doesn't pay any attention to my sister,"* Jodie had told Sky, when she'd first reported the uneasiness she felt around her mother's boyfriend.

But Sky knew that opportunity was often a deciding factor in the commission of sexual crimes.

And when she'd met with Jodie that afternoon and asked about her sister's whereabouts, Jodie had assured her that she was safe because she was spending the night at a friend's house. That revelation had alleviated Sky's immediate concerns, because she'd believed that the teen's mother would be home before Jodie's sister returned from her sleepover the following day.

Ashley nodded. "Chloe said Jodie freaked out when their mom told them that Leon would be moving in with them, but she also said that Jodie can be a drama queen at times."

Sky pushed aside her half-eaten plate of food. "What does Chloe think about her mom's boyfriend?"

"She says he's not so bad. He even pretends not to notice when she sneaks one of mom's vodka coolers out of the fridge."

Sky wasn't shocked to learn that her fourteen-year-old sister's best friend was sneaking alcohol, but she was increasingly uneasy with the picture coming together in her mind.

"You said Chloe was here earlier, working on this project with you?"

Ashley nodded.

"Was she supposed to sleep over?"

"Yeah, but then she decided that she'd rather go see a movie."

"Who was she going to the movie with?"

Ashley shrugged. "She didn't say, just that Leon was going to pick her up and we'd finish the poster board another time."

*Leon* had picked her up?

Oh, this was so *not* good.

"You know, it isn't really fair that you're spending your Saturday night working on this project while

Chloe is out having fun," Sky said, aiming for a casual tone.

"I know," Ashley agreed. "But what can I do?"

"You can call Chloe right now and tell her that we're on our way to pick her up so that she can come back here and help finish the project, like she promised."

Sky slept through breakfast the next morning, and after a quick shower, she decided to go into town to grab a bite. On the way there, she decided that she needed some sisterly advice as much as she needed sustenance, so she stopped at Sweet Caroline's before heading over to Katelyn and Reid's house.

"I brought coffee—and donuts," Sky said, holding up the tray of drinks and bag of pastries.

"She looks like my sister, but she's really the devil," Kate remarked, accepting the proffered items.

"You don't have to eat any, if you don't want to," she pointed out.

"The problem is that I want to eat them all."

"Well, at least save one of the jelly-filled for Tessa," Sky suggested, as her niece came running down the hall.

"Auntie 'ky! Auntie 'ky!" The little girl launched herself at her aunt. Sky caught her easily and lifted her for a smacking—and sticky—kiss.

"I think someone already had breakfast," she noted. "I taste maple syrup."

"An' pancakes," Tessa said, already wiggling to be

let down. Since she'd taken her first steps, it seemed to Sky that the little girl never stayed still.

Sure enough, as soon as she set her niece back on the ground, Tessa took off, eager to play.

Ah, the life of a two-and-a-half-year-old, Sky thought, with amusement and affection, as she followed her sister to the dining room.

"Reid took her to the Morning Glory Café so that I could sleep in a little," Kate told her.

"Are you not feeling well?" Sky's tone was deliberately casual as she pried the lid from her cup.

"Just tired," Kate said. "Which isn't as much of a surprise this time around, but still a struggle."

"This time?" Sky grinned. "So he was right? You *are* pregnant?"

Her sister nodded. "But it's still early days, so we're trying to keep the news quiet for a while yet."

She mimed zipping her lips.

"You know the not-so-quiet news making the rounds this morning?" Kate continued. "Leon Franks was arrested last night and charged with supplying alcohol to a minor."

Thanks to her stop at Sweet Caroline's, Sky had already heard the news. "Unfortunately, I don't imagine that will keep him locked up for long." In fact, she wouldn't be surprised to hear that the man had already made bail. But she was keeping her fingers crossed that, whether or not the charges stuck, Leon's arrest would be a wake-up call to Tammy Morningstar to get the man out of her house and out of her life. In the meantime, Sky had at least succeeded in getting an inebriated Chloe out of a potentially dangerous situation the night before—and helped Ashley glue together the pieces of her book fair project.

"Probably not," Kate acknowledged. "But the outstanding warrant from St. Paul, Minnesota on charges of possession of child pornography will."

*That* was news to Sky, and she immediately knew that she had her brother-in-law to thank for following up her request. "I'm not glad that Jodie's instincts were right about this guy, but I'm relieved that he's going to be Minnesota's problem. I assume he'll be extradited to face those charges?"

Kate nodded. "The DA's filling out the paperwork this morning."

"That's a relief," Sky decided.

"Now tell me your news," her sister suggested.

"I don't have any news."

"Are you sure?" Kate pressed. "Because the coffee and donuts suggest otherwise."

"Maybe I did want some advice," she admitted.

"About?"

"Men."

"As a species in general? Or are you referring to someone specific?" Kate asked.

"Jake Kelly."

"Oh?"

Something in her sister's deliberately casual tone tripped her radar. "Do you know him?"

Kate's gaze slid away. "Not really."

"He's a client," she guessed.

"No, but… I guess it's not really a violation of

attorney-client privilege to tell you that Ross Ferguson was. And it's hardly a secret that Jake is the nephew that Ross named as primary beneficiary in his will." Kate looked at her sister then. "But how do you know him?"

"He's been in the bar a few times." Actually, Jake had come into Diggers' six times while Sky was working, but she didn't want her sister to know that she'd been counting.

"And he's a lousy tipper?" Kate guessed.

She managed a smile. "No, he's a decent tipper. But he's a lousy conversationalist."

"So maybe not everyone who sits at the bar is looking for a tête-à-tête with the bartender," her sister suggested.

"But most customers are at least willing to exchange basic pleasantries," Sky said. "It was weeks before Jake even told me his name."

"A man's entitled to his privacy," Kate pointed out.

"I know," she agreed. "But there's something about him—"

"No," her sister interjected firmly.

Sky frowned. "No what?"

"You have enough wounded souls in your life without looking to add another one."

"What makes you think he's a wounded soul?"

Kate pressed her lips together, apparently already having said more than she'd intended to.

"You know that he's former military," Sky guessed.

"That's the rumor around town," her sister conceded.

"And this time, the rumor is actually true. Jake was—or *is*—a Marine."

"Did he tell you that?" Kate asked.

Sky shook her head. "He didn't have to. I saw his US Marine Corps tattoo."

"I've never noticed a tattoo."

"It's on his shoulder, so you wouldn't notice it if he's wearing a shirt."

Her sister's brows winged up. "Are you telling me that you saw him without a shirt on?"

"I saw him with nothing on," Sky confided.

"Oh. My. God." Kate's jaw dropped. "You *slept* with him?"

Her smile slipped, as her sister's question pointedly reminded her that there'd been no sleeping because Jake had kicked her out of his bed as soon as the deed was done. "No, but I did have sex with him."

"But you just told me that you don't know anything about this guy," Kate said, sounding worried.

"How well did you know Reid before you fell into bed with him?" Sky countered.

Her sister's cheeks colored. "Not as well as I should have, or I might have been prepared for him to show up in town a few weeks later wearing the sheriff's badge."

"Then you have no right to judge me," she pointed out.

"I'm not judging, I'm worried."

"Don't be," Sky said. "I know how to look out for myself."

"You were careful?" her sister prompted.

"Always," she promised.

"So was I," Kate reminded her. "Which was all well and good until a condom broke."

She was referring, of course, to the first night she'd spent with her now-husband, Reid Davidson, at a legal conference in Carson City.

"And nine months later, you had a beautiful baby girl," Sky noted.

Kate smiled then. "But that doesn't mean I've forgotten those terrifying moments in the beginning when I was completely overwhelmed and didn't have the first clue what to do."

Sky hadn't forgotten, either—or the guilt she'd felt when her sister told her about the broken condom. Sky had been the one to give Kate the box before her sister went away, to ensure she'd be protected if the opportunity presented itself. Thankfully, everything had worked out for Katelyn and Reid—and Tessa—in the end.

"Well, you don't have to worry," Sky assured her sister now. "There weren't any safety malfunctions when I was with Jake."

"That's good then," Kate said, though she still sounded dubious. "Do you think…are you going to… see him again?"

Sky shrugged, a deliberately casual gesture. "I'm sure our paths will cross."

But the truth was, Sky wasn't sure about anything where Jake Kelly was concerned.

# Chapter Six

In the Marine Corps, Jake had learned the importance of being prepared for any contingency—and that, despite those preparations, it was almost inevitable that things would go FUBAR.

Since moving to Haven, he was trying to embrace routines as a way of feeling more in control of his life. According to the doctor he'd talked to at the VA hospital, routine was supposed to help him cope with change, form healthy habits and reduce his stress levels. Over the past couple of months, part of his routine had been Wednesday night meetings with a veterans' support group at the community center, followed by what he dubbed "immersion therapy" at Diggers'.

Though he had yet to share anything of his own

experiences with the group, he did find some comfort in listening to and empathizing with the experiences of others, proof that he wasn't alone in his struggles to readjust to civilian life. But since that first night when he decided to stop at Diggers' on his way home, his routine had evolved to include a pint of beer at the local bar and grill—and occasionally some casual flirting with the pretty bartender.

Except that now he'd done a lot more than flirt with Sky Gilmore, he found himself in a bit of a dilemma. Should he stick with his usual routine, come directly home after the meeting or opt to stay in for the evening altogether?

He glanced over at his dog, who was stretched out in the sun by the open doors of the converted barn while Jake tidied up what had been his uncle's workspace. When he'd first arrived in Haven and walked into the house where he'd spent a couple of weeks every summer with his aunt and uncle, he'd been assailed by the memories. He could almost see Fred and George—red-haired Irish setters named for the Weasley twins from Harry Potter—jumping and playing in the yard, and could almost smell the scent of cinnamon lingering in the air, as if there was a tray of Aunt Anna's snickerdoodle cookies ready to come out of the oven. But what he remembered most was the love and the laughter, so much so that it seemed to echo in every room.

Yes, Ross had struggled to make a go of it as a rancher, and Anna had battled with health difficulties, but no one who'd spent any time with them would doubt how much they'd loved one another. Though Jake had been taken aback to learn that his uncle had passed within six months of his wife, he realized he shouldn't have been surprised. Ross had often said that Anna was his heart, and without her, there was nothing left to pump life through his veins.

It had been difficult enough for Jake to walk through the front door of their house and know that he wouldn't ever see either of them again. It was even more difficult for him to enter the workshop, where he'd spent so many hours with his uncle during the annual summer visits that were intended to give his parents some time alone together. Even as a kid, Jake had known that he would be a Marine one day, and Ross had never tried to steer him in a different direction. But his uncle had thought it was important for a boy to know how to use some basic tools, and his instructions had been careful, his patience endless and his forgiveness of Jake's mistakes sincere.

*"You can't make an omelet without breaking a few eggs,"* he'd liked to say.

Jake had broken a lot of eggs.

There were bits and pieces of wood scattered around the workshop now, as if his uncle had been sorting through them to find what he wanted for his current project. But there were no plans pinned up on the pegboard, nothing to indicate what, if anything, he had been working on.

Jake's cell phone rang, distracting him from his task, and he set the wood chisel back down on the workbench before picking up the phone. He swiped the screen to connect the call. "Hey, Mom. What's up?"

"I was just thinking about you," Barbara Kelly replied.

When he'd first moved to Haven, she'd "thought about" him several times every day, until he'd threatened to stop answering her numerous calls. Now they talked once a week, on Sunday afternoons. That wasn't to say that she didn't reach out to him otherwise, but she always had a specific purpose for doing so.

"Any particular reason?" he prompted, wondering if he might have forgotten about a special occasion.

Courtesy of the brain injury that was an unwanted souvenir from Iraq, he'd forgotten a lot of things when he first came home. Most of his memories had eventually returned, along with his ability to assimilate and retain new information, but there were still pieces missing.

Was today one of those pieces?

Was it his mom's birthday?

No, that was in November.

"I thought you should know that Margot and Tim are getting married," she said.

The news didn't surprise him. More important, it didn't elicit any kind of emotional response, except relief that it wasn't something he should have known about. Aside from that, he truly didn't care.

"Why are you telling me?" he asked.

"Because I didn't want you to hear it from someone else," she admitted.

"Because you thought it would upset me," he guessed.

"Doesn't it?" she asked gently.

"No."

"You must feel something," she pressed. "It wasn't all that long ago that Margot was wearing your ring."

As if he needed to be reminded.

He'd put the ring on Margot's finger before he went to Iraq the first time, because she'd wanted some kind of tangible reassurance that he was committed to her, to help her through the lonely nights while he was away.

"Our engagement ended more than two years ago, Mom."

"But how do you feel?" she pressed.

Because his mom always wanted him to talk about his feelings, preferring to believe that he was keeping his emotions bottled up rather than that he wasn't capable of feeling anything anymore.

"I feel fine," he said.

Okay, fine was a stretch—or maybe even an outright lie—but as far as his former fiancée's wedding plans were concerned, he really couldn't care less.

"Well, that's good then, because you're going to get an invitation to the wedding."

"How do you know this?"

"Margot called and asked me for your address."

He didn't have to ask if she'd given it. It would never have occurred to his mom to refuse such a request. Instead, he only said, "You should have told her not to waste a stamp."

"You were friends for a long time. You and Margot and Tim," she reminded him gently.

"And then Margot and Tim got *really* friendly when I was in rehab."

"It was a difficult time for everyone."

"Yeah, but only one of us was recovering from a blast injury and enduring hours of daily therapy."

"You're still angry," she noted.

He sighed. "No, Mom. I'm not still angry. I'm just not prepared to celebrate a relationship built on a foundation of deceit and disloyalty."

"Going to the wedding would prove that you're over her."

"I don't have to prove anything to anyone, least of all the girl who screwed around with my former best friend."

"I'm not making excuses for what they did—"

"Good," Jake said, cutting her off.

Barbara's sigh was a reluctant acknowledgment that the topic was closed. "Okay then, tell me when you're going to come home."

"I don't know."

"We miss you," she said.

He knew what she really meant was that *she* missed him, and he missed her, too. But he knew it was best for everyone if he stayed away for a while.

Or maybe forever.

"Well, if you're not planning to come home anytime soon, maybe we could come to Haven to see you," she suggested.

"You'd be bored to death here," he said, offering her an out.

Because the truth was, while his mother might be content enough to revisit the town where she'd grown up and where her brother had remained throughout his adult life, Jake knew she'd never convince his father to come.

As far as Jake could recall, his father had visited Haven exactly once, and had grumbled the whole time that he was there. Major William Robert Kelly had never been a fan of his brother-in-law and he didn't pretend otherwise. In his opinion, Ross was either a quitter or a failure, because after struggling for a lot of years as a cattle rancher, he'd chosen to sell off his stock and lease his land rather than knuckling down and working harder.

"Knuckle down and work harder" was a big thing with the Major. He wasn't entirely unsympathetic to his youngest son, but he continued to espouse the belief that Jake should shake off his moods, get himself back into fighting shape and reenlist. He'd made no effort to hide his displeasure when Jake told him that he was moving to Haven for a while. Then again, he'd always seemed to resent that his youngest son enjoyed hanging out with his maternal uncle, even accusing his brother-in-law of filling Jake's head with sawdust dreams.

Maybe that was why Ross had put Jake's name on the title. According to the date on his will, it had been drafted after Jake had received his medical discharge from the Marine Corps. Maybe Ross understood that his nephew had failed, too, and this was his way of showing that there were always other opportunities in life. If only Jake had the courage to take them.

"I've gotta go, Mom," Jake said. "I've got a meeting tonight."

And then he'd see if he could get a cold beer without a colder shoulder from a certain sexy bartender.

When Wednesday rolled around again, Sky found herself alternately watching the clock—and cursing herself for doing so. Yet she couldn't resist another glance.

9:55 p.m.

And still no sign of Jake.

But why should she have expected anything different?

He certainly wasn't the first guy who'd dropped her like a hot potato as soon as she slept with him. And if she was disappointed, it was in herself as much as Jake, because she'd really thought she was making smarter choices now.

*Next time*, she promised herself.

"Next time what?" Mr. Virga asked her.

She smiled at the retired ophthalmologist. "Next time I'm talking to myself, I'll try to keep both sides of the conversation inside my head."

"They say that talking to—and even arguing with—yourself is okay," the old man said. "It's only when you lose those arguments that you should start to worry."

"Good to know," she said, and smiled as she rang up his bill and took his money.

When she turned back to give Mr. Virga his change, she saw Jake in his usual seat at the bar.

Her heart did a happy little dance inside her chest, but she kept her attention focused on her elderly customer.

"Thanks," she said, when he pushed a tip across the counter to her. "You have a good night now, Mr. Virga."

"I surely will," the old man said, with a wink.

Jake watched the exchange, his expression inscrutable.

"What are you having tonight?" she asked him, playing it cool.

"A pint of Sam Adams."

She grabbed a mug and held it under the tap. "One step forward, two steps back."

"I don't do well with change," he admitted.

"Is that why you're here? Because Wednesday night at Diggers' has become a habit?"

"Partly," he acknowledged.

She set the beer in front of him.

"But mostly because I wanted to see you—to explain."

"You don't owe me any explanations, Jake."

"I kind of feel like I do."

"Neither one of us made any promises. In fact, neither one of us said very much of anything," she remarked.

"I thought we communicated pretty well without words."

"I guess we did," she acknowledged.

His gaze slid to the side, as if to ensure no one was close enough to overhear their conversation. "But this is weird now, isn't it?"

"Does it feel weird?"

"A little," he said.

"Maybe that's because you kicked me out of your bed before I'd even managed to catch my breath after we had sex," she said, her tone deliberately light.

"About that... I'm sorry that I couldn't let you stay."

His remark only raised more questions in her mind, but since this wasn't the time or the place for that conversation, she only said, "Is Molly the jealous type?"

He smiled, apparently relieved that she wasn't pushing for more of an explanation. "More possessive than jealous, I'd say."

She dumped a scoop of ice into a highball glass, squeezed a wedge of lime, poured a shot of gin and added a splash of tonic from the soda gun. "Maybe she just needs to get to know me better," she suggested.

"I think that's a possibility worth exploring," he agreed, as he lifted the mug to his lips.

Sky poured the ingredients for a couple of Nevada cocktails into a shaker, gave it a vigorous shake, then strained the drink into martini glasses for Courtney to deliver. Catching her eye, Adrian Romanos lifted his empty glass. She nodded and tipped a mug beneath the tap to pour him another draft, then made her way down the bar to deliver it.

Adrian was a regular who spent a lot of hours—and more than a few dollars—at the bar, and Sky wasn't going to neglect him just because she'd rather be talking to—and maybe flirting with—Jake. Adrian also worked for the town planning department, and he was chatting with her about the proposed schedule of events for the upcoming Haven Heritage Day celebrations—including the addition of a charity softball game this year—when Jake finished his drink.

Though it would have been out of character for him to hang around after his glass was empty, she was still a little disappointed to watch him pull some money out of his wallet, tuck it under the bottom of his glass and walk out.

Proving to Sky that nothing had changed.

Sure, she'd had the most amazing sex of her life with the man, but he still didn't want her company or conversation.

Good thing she wasn't thin-skinned, or his disappearing act might have hurt her feelings.

Of course, it was her own fault for falling into bed with a man she knew nothing about. She could make excuses for her behavior—and it was true that she'd been feeling lonely and that it had been a very long time since she'd been intimate with a man. But it was also true that neither of those factors was as significant as the attraction she'd felt the first time Jake walked into the bar.

And while she was admittedly a little baffled by his actions, she suspected that Jake's determination to keep everyone at a distance was connected to the scars she'd discovered on his body. Or the invisible ones that he clearly carried inside.

*You don't know anything about me.*

But she wanted to.

The scars, along with military tattoo, suggested that he was a man who'd been through a lot. Though post-traumatic stress disorder wasn't her area of expertise, she was familiar with the basic origins and symptoms. Witnessing or experiencing a traumatic event could result in difficulties in social situations and personal relationships.

She imagined that many people who'd served in the military had witnessed or experienced traumatic events. And she wondered if Jake would ever open up to her enough to tell her about his experiences.

Of course, getting naked with the guy didn't give her any right to poke around in his head. And the fact that she'd been naked with him was a pretty solid reason for her *not* to be the one poking around in his head.

They'd had sex—they didn't have a relationship.

If she was under any illusions otherwise, his exit from the bar without so much as a goodbye had effectively obliterated them.

Sunday through Wednesday, Diggers' closed at midnight. Still, by the time the last lingering customers were gone, the receipts were tallied and the bar was tidied, it was almost 1:00 a.m. Sky exited through the kitchen, as she always did, waving to Marty—who was still up to his elbows in soapy water scrubbing pans—on her way out. The dishwasher usually walked to work, since he lived just down the street, so Sky was surprised to see a truck parked beside her SUV when she stepped outside.

Warning signs immediately flashed in her mind for a split second before recognition set in and she realized it was Jake's vehicle—and the man himself was leaning against the hood of the pickup.

Her heart, ignoring the warnings of her head, started to pound harder and faster.

She took a few steps closer. "What's the matter? Did you run out of gas?"

His lips twitched. "No."

She hadn't realized Molly was in the truck until the dog poked her head out of the open driver's side window.

Unable to resist the animal's imploring gaze, Sky lifted a hand and scratched the soft fur beneath her chin. "What are you doing out so late at night?"

"I told her what you said, about her needing to get to know you better, and she agreed it was a good idea," Jake said.

"And you thought *now* would be a good time for that?"

He shrugged. "I wanted to see you and I thought, even if you were mad at me, you wouldn't be able to resist her."

"I wasn't mad at you."

"You weren't happy with me."

"I'm not entirely sure what I feel," she admitted.

"That makes two of us," he confided.

He came closer, until they were nearly touching.

"I want you, Skylar." The words were barely more than a whisper in the night. "Even though I know I shouldn't, I can't seem to stop wanting you."

"Why do you think you shouldn't?"

"Because my life is seriously screwed up."

"Anything you want to talk about?" she asked him.

He shook his head.

"You just want to go back to your place and get naked together again?"

"It's not a very tempting offer, is it?" he acknowledged ruefully.

"It works for me," she said.

"Really?"

"Yeah. When you left the bar earlier tonight, I was convinced that the best sex of my life was going to be a one-night stand."

"The best sex of your life?" He grinned. "I'm flattered."

"Maybe *life* is an exaggeration," she said. "Prior to Saturday, it had been a really long time for me, so my perception might have been a little skewed."

"Or maybe you just need an encore performance to convince you."

Then he drew her into his arms and lowered his head to cover her lips with his own.

His hands slid up her back, a sensual caress,

then down again, over the curve of her buttocks. She could feel the evidence of his arousal pressed against her belly and thrilled in the knowledge that he was as turned on as she was.

The flood of desire through her veins was as familiar as the flavor of his kiss. She didn't know what it was about this man that made her respond to him so intensely, but she couldn't deny that she did.

And knew that she was in serious trouble.

Tonight, Jake's bed was made with clean sheets, his dirty clothes had been dumped in the hamper and he'd sprayed air freshener to get rid of any lingering doggy odors. He hoped Sky would be impressed, because Molly sure wasn't. His faithful companion had sneezed several times then tossed her head in the air and escaped to another part of the house. But she'd forgiven the indignity to her sensitive nose when he'd scooped up his keys and invited her to go for a ride.

Still, he found himself having second and third thoughts as he followed Sky's taillights through the dark night. Not about what *he* wanted—because he'd known what that was as soon as he'd walked into Diggers' tonight and saw her behind the bar—but about the mixed signals he was sending to her.

He'd tried to be honest about what he was and wasn't offering. And mutual pleasure was likely to be the extent of it. Truthfully, he hadn't been certain he'd be able to give her even that the first time. He'd known the parts were in working order, but he hadn't been intimate with a woman since long before he'd been sent home via medical transport—and even during the brief period after his return when he was still with Margot, neither his mind nor his body had been any condition for sex. But he didn't want to be thinking about that when he should be focused on seduction. And on Sky.

Though he had no doubt that he'd satisfied her the first time, they'd both been in a race to the finish. He was determined to show a little more patience this time—and a lot more finesse.

His determination lasted only until she touched him, the stroke of her soft hands on his hard body snapping the leash of his self-control. What was it about Sky Gilmore that made him want her with an intensity that bordered on desperation?

Was it the way her lips curved whenever she saw him walk into the bar, as if she'd been watching and waiting for him?

Was it the light in her eyes that seemed capable of illuminating the deepest darkness inside him?

Or was it simply the escapism that she offered?

Because when he was touching Sky, there was no room in his head for thoughts of anything else.

No worries. No remorse. No regrets.

There was only the sweet scent of her hair, the silky softness of her skin, the tantalizing seduction of her body.

She was slim and toned and, to his eyes, so absolutely perfect that he knew he—scarred as he was on the inside and out—could never be worthy of her. He wondered that she couldn't see it as clearly as he did, because if she did, whatever this was between them would already be over.

But he was selfish enough not to let that matter right now. He could ignore the fact that they were a real-life beauty and beast for the thrill of having her in his arms for a few more hours.

And he knew their time together was likely limited to that. He wasn't a man a woman made plans with for the future. If it had been true when he was on active duty, it was even more so now. There was so much she didn't know about him, and when she uncovered his secrets, it would change everything.

She'd shown admirable restraint so far, but she would inevitably want to know about his scars. And his tattoos. In fact, he was a little surprised she hadn't asked already. Surprised and grateful. Perhaps she sensed his reticence to talk about his past. Or maybe she was smart enough to have put the pieces together without the need to ask any questions—in which case she was undoubtedly smart enough to put some distance between them.

Right now, it was the intensity of the attraction between them that was getting in the way of her ability to see the situation clearly. And his, too.

But sex was one thing. Intimacy was something entirely different. And as much as he wished he could let her stay, he wasn't ready to fall asleep with her. Because it was in sleep that his guard was down and the dreams came. Dreams that he couldn't bear for her to witness. Not only because he didn't want her to know about the demons that plagued him, but because he worried that letting her stay might put her at risk.

Everyone knew stories about veterans who returned from assignment and lashed out at loved ones—parents or spouses or even children. Because in the midst of a flashback, a soldier, sailor, airman or Marine didn't see that parent or spouse or child, only a threat to be neutralized. Though he'd never woken up with a weapon in his hand, his training had made him a weapon. And that meant anyone close to him could be in danger—as the events of last New Year's Eve had proven all too clearly.

But how to explain that to Sky without admitting how broken he truly was? How could he tell her the truth when he knew that the truth would result in losing her? Because while he wasn't prepared to let himself get too attached to the sexy bartender, he also wasn't ready to let her go just yet.

But this time, when he walked back into the bedroom, she was already halfway dressed.

He was admittedly relieved that he wouldn't have to nudge her on her way—and maybe also just the teensiest bit disappointed.

Still, he felt as if he should say something.

*This was fun?*

*Thanks for coming?*

*Maybe we can do this again sometime?*

While he was trying to figure out what that something might be, her cell phone chimed.

Jake glanced at the clock on his bedside table and frowned.

Despite the lateness of the hour, Sky didn't seem surprised by the communication. And after texting a quick reply, she tucked her phone into the back pocket of those snug-fitting jeans.

"This was fun," she said, combing her fingers through her hair and pulling it back to secure it with a ponytail holder. "But I have to go."

## Chapter Seven

Jake could hardly protest that Sky was rushing off when he needed her to leave, but he was also curious about where she was going, because he was almost certain it wasn't home.

"Do you need me to drive you somewhere?" he asked, as he pulled on his jeans.

She held up her keys. "I've got my car."

"Have you had your engine checked since you ran out of gas?"

She brushed a light kiss on his lips. "Go back to bed, Jake."

Instead, he followed her through the kitchen to the side door. Molly—who'd been banished from the bedroom again—jumped up from the sofa and joined them, her tail wagging.

Sky slid her feet into her low-heeled boots, then crouched to give the dog a scratch behind the ears.

"Will you text me when you get home?" he asked her.

"No."

He frowned. "Why not?"

"Because we don't have that kind of relationship," she pointed out, in a matter-of-fact tone.

"What kind of relationship do we have?" he wondered.

Which, even as the words left his mouth, he realized was exactly the kind of question that would have made him duck and cringe if she'd asked it.

"Is this really a conversation you want to have at—" she turned her wrist to check the time on her watch "—two thirty-seven in the morning?"

*No.*

In fact, it was a conversation he knew they weren't ready to have at all. But once again, his brain and his mouth seemed to be having a communication problem because he said, "It seems as good a time as any."

Sky shook her head. "Good night, Jake."

Then she walked out and closed the door, leaving Jake on the other side, scowling.

As a man who closely guarded his own secrets, he could hardly demand to know all of hers.

It was none of his business who'd been texting her in the middle of the night, and yet, he couldn't deny that he felt a little uneasy not knowing where she was going or who she was meeting.

*Keep your eyes and ears open at all times. Anything can happen, anywhere. If you realize you've let your guard down, it's already too late.*

Except that this wasn't Mosul or Kandahar—this was sleepy little Haven, Nevada in the glorious U S of A and he needed to stop jumping at shadows.

There was no reason for him to worry.

So he went back to bed, but he didn't fall asleep.

What if she ran out of gas again and ended up stranded in the dark?

She'd assured him that she wasn't in the habit of ignoring her car's low-fuel warning, and he had no reason not to believe her. Besides, if she had any kind of trouble, she had her cell phone to call for help— her father or one of her brothers, probably.

She wouldn't call him because, as she'd pointed out, they didn't have that kind of relationship.

And because they'd never exchanged numbers.

Bodily fluids, yes; contact information, no.

He knew where she worked and where she lived, but he didn't know how to get in touch with her if he just wanted to say hi or maybe even ask her to go out sometime.

And yeah, thinking about it now, he realized that he probably should ask her out on a real date sometime.

But where would they go? What would they do?

And how had he jumped from being resigned that they'd never have a relationship to wanting to take the first step toward building one? Especially when just thinking about the possibility made him sweat.

Molly hopped up onto the mattress beside him, nudging his arm with her nose. Because even without a piece of paper, she was capable of reading and responding to his moods. And she added light to his darkest days.

He lifted a hand to stroke her soft fur. "It's okay, girl."

She settled in, resting her chin on his chest.

"What do you think?" he asked her now. "Should I ask Sky to go out with me? Dinner in a restaurant doesn't seem so scary," he decided. "I should be able to handle that, don't you think?"

Molly wagged her tail.

"Do you think she'll say yes? Or do you think she's already figured out that I wasn't exaggerating when I told her my life was seriously screwed up?"

Her tail continued to wave back and forth.

"That's not very helpful, you know," he told her.

She inched further up on the mattress, so that she could swipe at his chin with her tongue.

"Maybe I should just accept the status quo," he continued. "Because you and me have a pretty good thing going here, don't we? Quiet roads for long morning runs, lots of open space for throwing and fetching. We eat when we want, we sleep when we want—or when we can," he acknowledged. "We don't have to worry about anyone's schedule but our own. We don't need to invite a woman into our lives to mess with all that."

And yet, as he finally drifted off to sleep with

Molly beside him, he was starting to think that he wanted one.

But not just anyone.

He wanted Sky.

Sky cranked up the radio and sang along at the top of her lungs as she drove through the darkness of night to the urgent care center on the south side of town. The music kept her focused, so that she didn't drive herself crazy trying to figure out what was going on with Jake—or speculate about what the situation might be when she arrived at her destination.

The message from the supervisor at the women's shelter had been brief, asking only if she was available to visit a patient at the local urgent care clinic. When she'd responded in the affirmative, Deirdre had told her to reach out to Jenny Taft when she got there.

The name sounded vaguely familiar to Sky, but she didn't immediately recognize her former classmate when she walked into the exam room after clearing her visit with the doctor on duty. It wasn't just the bruises and the swelling that distorted the young woman's features, it was the flatness of her blue gaze—a complete absence of life that used to sparkle in the former homecoming queen's eyes when she was Jenny Reashore, before she'd married third-string quarterback Darren Taft.

"Sky," Jenny said, obviously having no similar difficulty recognizing or remembering. "What are you doing here?"

"I'm here to see you," she replied.

"Why?"

She lowered herself into the plastic chair beside the bed. "Because I'm a part-time counselor at April's House, a nearby shelter for abused women and children," she explained, in case the name was unfamiliar to Jenny. "I thought you might want to talk to someone about what happened to you tonight."

The other woman looked away. "I don't think I need to talk to someone about falling down the stairs."

"Okay," Sky said, taking her cue from the patient. "We can talk about anything you want."

"I don't want to talk. I don't even know why I'm still here." Jenny winced as she pushed herself up on the bed. "I need to get dressed. I need to get home."

"I don't think you should go anywhere until the doctors have a chance to review all your test results," Sky cautioned.

"I'm fine," Jenny insisted.

"You're not fine," she said, her tone gentle but firm. "You've got numerous bruises and contusions, three cracked ribs and a probable concussion."

Tears filled Jenny's eyes as she listened to Sky inventory the extent of her injuries. "Darren meant to fix the railing," she said. "He warned me to be careful going downstairs, but I had my arms full of laundry and my foot slipped and…" She started to shrug, then sucked in a pained breath as the movement strained her damaged ribs.

There were all kinds of reasons that women—and men—stayed in abusive relationships. But Sky also knew that sometimes, even when they wanted to leave, they were afraid to take that step, their fear of the unknown even greater than their fear of the abusive partner. Part of her job was to make sure they knew there were options.

But if Jenny wasn't even willing to acknowledge that her husband had hurt her, there wasn't really anything Sky could do to help her. Still, she felt compelled to try one more time. "Are you sure you're telling me everything that happened?"

"I'm sure," Jenny insisted.

"Okay," Sky relented. "And where was Darren when you fell?"

"At work."

"Where does he work?"

"What does that have to do with anything? I slipped and fell down the stairs," she said again.

"Is that what he told you to say?"

Jenny closed her eyes, to hide the tears that welled up again. "Darren loves me."

"Love shouldn't leave bruises—on your body or your spirit," she said.

"I fell. And Dr. Beaudoin had no business suggesting anything different."

"The doctor didn't call April's House," Sky told her.

"Then who did?" Jenny wanted to know.

"Your mom."

This time, when the tears came, Jenny didn't try to hold them back.

\* \* \*

No matter how many times he told himself it was none of his business or concern, Jake couldn't stop wondering about the late-night text message Sky had received. As he went through the usual routines of his day, unanswered questions continued to nag at the back of his mind.

He spent most of the afternoon in the yard with Molly, cutting the grass and raking the clippings. He even pulled weeds from the flowerbeds, all in the hope that Ashley might happen by with Rey, giving him the perfect opening to casually ask the teen how her sister was doing.

But the day faded away with no sign of Ashley or her dog.

As he watched the sun dip in the sky, its light reflecting off the barn windows, he remembered that the caulk around the frames was cracked and peeling. Which meant that he'd have to make a trip to the hardware store soon to get supplies to fix the problem.

Since he was thinking about it now, he might as well go, he decided. And if he was thirsty after he finished running his errand, then it would be perfectly reasonable to stop at Diggers' for a drink before heading home again.

He was feeling quite pleased with himself and the whole scenario he'd planned out—until he walked into the local watering hole and discovered a stranger in Sky's usual place behind the bar.

This bartender was about six feet tall with wide

shoulders and a nose that looked like it had been broken several times. He wore a knit golf shirt with the Diggers' logo and the name Duke stitched beneath.

"What can I get for you?" Duke asked.

Jake hesitated, uncertain of his next move and unwilling to acknowledge his deep disappointment. "Coffee," he decided.

The bartender filled a mug from the carafe on the warmer. Then he grabbed a caddy filled with sugar packets and creamers from beside the coffee maker and set it down beside Jake's cup.

"Thanks."

Duke nodded and moved to the other end of the bar.

"Coffee's a lot better at The Daily Grind," the customer sitting a couple seats over remarked.

Jake had seen him at the bar a couple of times before and thought he remembered Sky calling him Ellis.

"Maybe," Jake allowed.

*Undoubtedly*, he amended, after taking the first sip of coffee that was entirely too strong and a little bit stale.

"But I figured the customers were more likely to mind their own business here."

"Or maybe you came in looking for Sky," the other man suggested.

Jake lifted the mug to his lips, not bothering to respond. He certainly wasn't willing to confide his motives to this stranger.

"She doesn't work here on Thursdays."

The "here" implying to Jake that she had another job somewhere else.

He reluctantly swallowed another mouthful of coffee. "I didn't ask."

"No, you didn't," Ellis acknowledged. "But I thought you might be wondering."

"Nope," he lied. "I was just running errands and wanted a cup of coffee."

The other man shrugged and turned his attention back to his beer.

Jake left some money on the bar beside his cup, still half full.

As he drove toward home, he cursed himself for not even considering the possibility that he might trek all the way into town and she might not be there.

But at least he had the caulk he needed to fix the windows.

*"Christ, it's hot as hell out here," Moore grumbled, sweat dripping down his face as he sprawled on his back under the camouflage cover.*

*"Thanks, Captain Obvious," Lopez drawled.*

*The point man saluted. "My pleasure, Major Sarcasm."*

*"That's because we're in hell," Jake said. "And it's not Captain but Lance Corporal Obvious. Don't be giving him a promotion he hasn't earned or a rank he can't."*

*A couple of the men chuckled. Most were too hot and irritable to manage more than weak smiles.*

*"It's not really hell but purgatory," Baker said.*

*"And heaven is waiting for us all back in the U S of A."*

*"Doesn't mean we're ever gonna get there,"* Lucey pointed out.

*"We'll get there,"* Lopez said, *needing to believe it. "We just have to survive ten more weeks in this godforsaken dust bowl."*

*"Nine weeks and six days,"* Walker corrected.

*"But who's counting?"* Jake asked dryly.

*Of course, they were all counting. Because as proud as they were to serve their country, as deeply as they believed in their mission, no one really wanted to be stuck in the desert, more than seven thousand miles away from their families and friends.*

*Well, no one except maybe Lance Corporal Brian Lucey, who'd enlisted as soon as he turned eighteen, because the possibility of getting his balls blown off by an IED was preferable to the certainty of being pummeled by his father's fists.*

*And while the prospect of seeing real action had seemed exciting when they geared up for their deployment, the reality of it had quickly dimmed the shine of their expectations.*

*But it was the assistant radio officer who spoke up now to say,* "I'm *counting. 'Cause me and Kelli-Lynn are gonna get married when I get back."*

*"Hell, Lopez, why would you go and do something like that?"* Moore wanted to know.

*"'Cause after almost ten months here, marriage doesn't seem quite as terrifying anymore."*

*"You just want to put a ring on her finger before*

*she realizes that she can do a lot better than you,"* Walker said.

*Moore snorted and offered a fist bump to the RO.*

*"I'd rather risk my life than my heart,"* Moore insisted.

*"We do that every day,"* Lopez pointed out. *"And having a wife at home means I'm guaranteed to get laid on homecoming."*

*"You only need a uniform for that,"* Baker told him.

*They were all laughing when—*

Jake jolted awake, his breath coming in short, shallow gasps, his chest tight.

*Just a dream.*

But it felt *so* real.

Even now, he could hear the echo of the blast ringing in his ears. The wailing sirens. The piercing screams.

*"Concentrate on your breathing. Deep breaths. In and out through your mouth.*

*"Let the air fill your chest…hold it there…then slowly let it out again."*

With the doctor's words echoing in his head, Jake silently counted to four as he drew oxygen into his lungs, held it for a count of one, then exhaled to another count of four.

He felt a nudge against his side as he drew in another laboring breath. He lifted his arm and Molly immediately moved in to snuggle close.

Her warm presence immediately soothed him, chasing away the lingering remnants of the dream.

Or had it been a flashback?

He was never entirely sure. Some of the details were indelibly imprinted in his mind, snippets of conversations clearly remembered.

But the blast hadn't happened then. Not like that.

They'd been on their way to a recon post when their Humvee was taken out by an RPG.

Not that he remembered the event or much else about that day. And he wasn't sure if it was a blessing or a curse that the brain trauma he'd suffered had wiped it from his memory.

All he had left were pieces and fragments that his subconscious mind tried to put back together—usually in his dreams.

Molly nudged him again.

"You want to go for a run?"

She leaped off the bed, ready to go.

"All right," he conceded. "But let me put some clothes on first."

By the time he'd pulled on a pair of shorts and a T-shirt and brushed his teeth, she was waiting at the door, quivering with anticipation.

When they'd first moved to Haven, he'd put her on a leash whenever they were out, worried that she might take off after a rabbit or something and not be able to find her way back. But she hated the leash and, after almost tripping him up more than a few times—on purpose, he had no doubt—he'd relented.

And she'd rewarded his trust by never venturing too far from his side.

He opened the front door and she bolted through

it, in case he might doubt how eager she was to get going. But she waited patiently while he locked up and turned the knob to test that it was secure. He was probably the only homeowner in Haven who bothered with such precautions, but most of the other residents had lived there for generations and knew all their neighbors.

Another reason he wasn't sure that country living was for him, though he'd admittedly slept better since he'd made the move three-and-a-half months earlier. It was still rare for him to sleep through to sunrise. If he got four or five hours, he considered that a good night. More important to Jake, the nightmares that had plagued him since everything went to hell in Iraq were less frequent and less intense— this morning's episode notwithstanding.

Of course, that might just be a normal part of the healing process and unrelated to his change of address, he acknowledged, as he jogged toward the road, Molly by his side.

And while it was certainly progress, it wasn't enough.

Almost three years after his discharge from the Marine Corps, he still didn't have a plan for his future.

Without the military, he'd been at a complete loss. Drifting. Unfocused.

He'd started to study communications in college, confident that those skills would be in demand in the private sector if he ever decided to leave the military. But when Luke had deployed to Afghanistan to fight the Taliban, Jake had packed up his books and enlisted, eager to join his brother in the fight for freedom and justice.

He'd thought he might go back to college eventually and finish the degree he'd abandoned. But he hadn't anticipated that the headaches, a less frequent but still lingering side effect of the trauma, would make it difficult for him to stare at a computer screen for long periods of time.

*"What are you going to do with your life now?"*

Major William Robert Kelly asked the same question every time Jake went home.

And his reply to his father's question was always the same: *"I don't know."*

Because what could he do when everything he'd known and wanted had been taken away from him? His career was over and his other job prospects were dim; his fiancée had jilted him for one of his best friends; and he couldn't even be in a crowd of people without starting to sweat.

*"Well, you better figure it out."* Not a suggestion so much as an order. *"You can't sit around for the rest of your life."*

Barbara Kelly would attempt to intercede on her son's behalf, her patient and gentle tone a marked contrast to her husband's brusque demands. *"He just needs some time."*

*"It's been six months,"* the Major would grumble.

And then, six months later, *"It's been a year."*

And another six months after that, *"It's been a year and a half."*

Because eighteen months should have been long enough to put the shattered pieces of his life back together.

But every time they had the same conversation, Jake was reminded again that he was a failure—his medical discharge an unsightly stain on the otherwise pristine fabric of the Major's reputation. Because Jake wasn't already distraught enough about the lack of any kind of direction for his future.

*"You could reenlist,"* the Major would offer as a suggestion. *"There would be waivers required, but I know people who could help move things along."*

As if he was unaware of the process.

As if he hadn't already looked into the possibility.

*"No!"* his mom would immediately protest, her tone no longer so patient or gentle, her eyes filled with tears. *"Dammit, Bill, hasn't he been through enough? He doesn't need you putting those kinds of ideas in his head."*

*"He doesn't seem to have any of his own in there."*

*A frustrating truth that would force an exasperated Jake to confess, "I don't have a lot of anything but ringing in my head these days."*

*"I thought you said the symptoms were going away."* His mother again, immediately concerned.

*"Going away doesn't mean gone."*

And so it went, every time Jake and his father got into a discussion about his life.

But over the past few months, he'd finally stopped feeling bad that he'd disappointed his father.

Mostly.

And while he hated knowing that his mother continued to worry, there was nothing he could do about that. No matter how many times he told her that he was fine, she refused to believe him.

Of course, she'd always had an uncanny ability to know when he was lying.

## Chapter Eight

By the time they hit the mile and a half mark, Jake was feeling a lot better. He signaled to Molly to turn around and head back. As they neared the house, he slowed to a jog, already thinking about breakfast.

The dog had more stamina than he did, and at this point she usually raced ahead to the door, eager for her morning bowl of kibble.

Today she ran past the door and into the backyard.

He stopped and fisted his hands on his hips, gulping air into his lungs. "What do you think you're doing?"

She turned to look at him, obviously wanting him to follow.

"Go on and chase rabbits, if you want," he told her. "But I'm hungry."

She whined, her big brown eyes imploring.

He sighed. "You want to play with Rey, don't you? I'm glad you've made a new friend, but I doubt that Ashley's out with her pup in the morning on a school day."

Molly wagged her tail as she trotted closer to the split-rail fence that bordered the Ferguson property—likely designed to keep the Circle G cattle on their own property more than anything else. It certainly wasn't effective at keeping his dog out.

"If you saw a rabbit, you might as well give up now, because you'll never catch it."

Molly was undeterred, though she paused at the fence, as if waiting for him to catch up. But she didn't wait long before she sidled under the lowest rail and popped up on the other side.

"That's Mr. Gilmore's land and you're trespassing," he told her.

Actually, according to the lawyer, it was his land, but currently subject to a lease agreement with the Circle G.

Molly just wagged her tail.

He turned and started back toward the house, confident that she would fall into step with him. As tempted as she might be by rabbits or squirrels or even the possibility of finding Rey, her first loyalty was to the man who put kibble in her bowl.

But she didn't follow.

Instead, she barked.

He stared her down. "Come."

She didn't come.

"I'm not chasing after you," he said. "I've already run three miles today and I want my breakfast."

Of course, his reasoning did nothing to persuade her.

In obedience classes, he'd been taught to encourage compliance with the command by grabbing her collar and tugging to draw her toward him while repeating the word so that she learned its meaning. But he had to catch her first.

"Molly, come," he said, his tone firm.

She barked again.

Muttering under his breath, Jake marched over to the fence.

"I'm going to call that obedience school and ask for my money back," he grumbled as he climbed over the rail.

Molly, confident that he would follow, headed off through the tall grass.

"I've heard that some ranchers in these parts shoot first and ask questions later," he called out, as he followed her path to a clearing near a copse of trees. "You better hope Mr. Gilmore isn't one of them."

"He's not…usually."

He stopped abruptly when he realized Sky was sitting with her back against one of the trees, her legs stretched out in front of her.

"And my stepmother dragged him off to the antique and craft market today anyway, so no worries on that front today."

He suspected that Molly had somehow known Sky

was there, that she was the reason his dog had been so insistent on breaching the barrier.

And the dog was right now being rewarded for her obstinacy and disobedience with Sky's attention. Of course, Molly was totally lapping it up, sprawled on her back with her legs splayed to afford easy access to her belly for rubbing.

He shook his head. "You are such a slut."

Sky's head tipped back. "Excuse me?"

Luckily she sounded more amused than offended by his remark.

"I didn't mean—I meant—Molly. I was talking to the dog," he said, stumbling through the explanation.

The hint of a smile played at the corners of her mouth. "I can't believe it—you're actually blushing."

He scowled. "I am not."

"I was talking about the dog," she deadpanned.

"So much for man's best friend," he muttered.

Molly basked in the attention of her new friend, unrepentant.

"You've been out running," Sky guessed.

"Oh. Yeah," he admitted, suddenly aware of the sweaty T-shirt stuck to his body. "We were on our way back when Molly decided that she wanted to go exploring rather than go home."

Sky lifted her hand to shield her eyes from the glare as her gaze skimmed over him. "I didn't know you were a runner."

He shrugged. "It's not who I am, it's just something that I do." He dropped onto the grass beside her, so that she didn't have to stare up at the sun. "So...how are you?"

"I'm okay," she said.

"So why are you sitting in the middle of an empty field all by yourself?"

"It's where I come to think sometimes."

"Are you thinking about anything in particular?" he asked.

"Actually, just before you showed up, I was thinking about breakfast."

"Coincidentally, that was my thought, too—before Molly took off," he confided. "Do you want to come over to my place for bacon and eggs?"

"Are you cooking?"

He nodded. "Breakfast is my specialty."

"In that case, yes," she decided.

Molly sat nearby, her focus on Jake at the stove as he pushed strips of bacon around in the pan. Sky was at the table, a cup of coffee in her hands, watching with amusement as the dog watched the man.

"Is there any chance that she's going to get a taste of what you're cooking?" she asked.

"No," Jake said. "But she's an eternal optimist."

"Well, that's at least nicer than what you called her earlier—assuming that you were, in fact, talking about the dog."

"I *was* talking about the dog," he insisted. "Because she'll roll over and spread her legs for anyone in exchange for a belly rub."

"Still, maybe we should talk about what happened with us," she said.

"Why?" he asked warily.

"Because I don't want you to think that I would have gone home with anyone who stopped to fill my gas tank—or waited for me in the parking lot outside Diggers' after work."

"I don't think that," he said.

"But you don't know, do you? Because you really don't know anything about me, despite the fact that anyone in town would be more than happy to fill in the details—real or imagined—if you asked even one question."

"I try to mind my own business."

"Because you don't want other people shoving their noses into yours," she guessed.

He just shrugged.

Not that Sky needed any more of an acknowledgement. And while she was frustrated by his continued reluctance to open up to her, she had to believe that his offer to feed her was at least a step in the right direction.

"Is there anything I can do to help?" she asked him now.

"Cooking bacon and eggs isn't really a two-person job," he told her.

"I could make toast," she offered.

"Except that I didn't get to Battle Mountain this week for groceries, so I don't have any bread," he said.

"You do know there's a grocery store in town, don't you?"

"Yes, I know there's a grocery store in town," he confirmed. "I just prefer to do my shopping in the city."

"The prices are probably a little cheaper at the supermarket," she acknowledged. "But the cost of gas to get there would cancel out any savings." She sipped her coffee. "Or maybe you don't go to Battle Mountain just to save a few bucks."

He didn't respond to that, except to say, "You can check the freezer. There might be a couple of English muffins in there."

She opened the door and discovered the space filled with frozen pizzas and prepackaged microwaveable meals, ice-cream bars and yes, a partial bag of English muffins.

Sky untied the package, took out two muffins, then tied it up again and returned it to the freezer.

"Toaster's in that cupboard," Jake told her, pointing with the spatula.

"Based on the contents of your freezer, I'm guessing that you don't do a lot of cooking, aside from bacon and eggs," she remarked, as she set the appliance on the counter and plugged it in.

"Not a lot," he agreed. "Though I'm a gourmet when it comes to cooking frozen pizza."

"Jamie Oliver better watch his back," she said, tongue in cheek.

"Who?" he asked.

She chuckled softly. "And considering the stack of frozen pizza boxes, I'm going to assume that you have yet to discover Jo's."

"Actually, I've had Jo's pizza a couple of times." He lifted the bacon out of the pan and put it on a paper towel to absorb the grease.

"A couple of times?" she echoed.

He nodded as he cracked eggs over the pan.

"How long have you been in Haven?"

"Almost three months."

"And you know about Jo's but you've only had the best pizza in the known universe, conveniently located on Main Street in this very town, twice?"

"The best pizza in the known universe?" he echoed dubiously.

"You don't agree?"

"It was good," he acknowledged.

"Good?" Her tone was incredulous. "French macarons are good. Swiss cheese is good. Jo's pizza is a culinary masterpiece. If I had to pick only one food to eat for the rest of my life, it would be Jo's pizza."

"It's good pizza," he said again, reaching into the cupboard beside the stove for a couple of plates.

At the same time, the toaster popped, forcing Sky to turn her attention to buttering the muffins.

As Jake plated the bacon and eggs, she found the cutlery drawer and set forks and knives on the table.

"Juice?" he asked, taking a jug from the fridge.

She held up her mug of coffee. "No, this is fine, thanks."

He poured a glass for himself, then joined her at the table.

"How are they?" he asked, after she'd sampled the first bite.

"Really good," she said, lifting another forkful to her mouth.

Jake focused on his own breakfast then. He was mopping up the yolk on his plate with the last bite of English muffin before he said, "I stopped in at Diggers' last night, after a quick trip to the hardware store."

"I'm surprised you didn't go to the hardware store in Battle Mountain," she said, only half teasing.

"So I guess you don't work on Thursdays," he said, pointedly ignoring her cheeky remark.

"Did you go into Diggers' looking for me?" she asked, both surprised and pleased by the possibility.

"I just thought, since I was in town, that I'd say hi."

"Now I'm almost sorry I wasn't there," she said. "But I only work a couple shifts a week."

"So what do you do with the rest of your time?" he wondered.

"Careful," she warned. "Asking questions about my life might lead to a quid pro quo."

"I'm willing to take my chances," he decided.

"Then I'll tell you that the rest of my time is split between my other jobs, spending time with my family and friends and playing coed softball with the Diggers during the summer."

"What's your other job?"

"I think it's my turn to ask a question now," she said and paused, considering. "I'll start with an easy one—are you going to eat that last slice of bacon?"

"What?"

"I'll take that as a no," she said, and snagged it from his plate.

"That was your question?"

She nodded as she bit into the crispy meat. "Your turn again."

"Okay," he said, obviously relieved that she hadn't ventured into personal territory. "Tell me about your other job."

"I'm a youth counselor at the local high school."

"A counselor helps kids pick out their courses and figure out what colleges to apply to, right?"

"That's a guidance counselor," she said. "My job is to give them tools and strategies to deal with stuff like cyberbullying and sexual harassment and drug and alcohol abuse."

"That's heavy stuff," he noted.

She nodded. "And the adolescent years can be particularly challenging ones, so it's crucial that teens know there's someone they can talk to, in confidence, whenever they need to."

"Even if it's two o'clock in the morning?"

"Even if," she agreed.

"Is that why you were in such a hurry to leave here the other night?"

"I was planning to leave, anyway," she pointed out. "But no, the text message was from a nearby women's shelter where I volunteer."

"Apparently you have a much busier schedule than I realized."

"Too busy sometimes," she acknowledged.

"So why don't you cut back on your hours? Or even give up one of the jobs?" he suggested.

She shrugged. "I only have office hours at the high school two days a week, although sometimes I get called in at the request of a student or to address a specific issue. And I usually spend a few hours at April's House on the weekends, but I'll also go in during the week if the shelter is busy."

"And Diggers'?"

"I'm there every Wednesday and Friday and every other Sunday," she said. "The late hours take a toll sometimes, but I really enjoy the interactions with customers. The Daily Grind might be popular for hot coffee and hotter gossip, but Diggers' is the heart of the community. It's where people gather for a drink after work or to grab a bite with friends or to celebrate all the big and little milestones in their lives.

"In three years, I've seen a lot of milestones, though there are still people who don't approve of me working there," she confided.

"Like your father?" he guessed.

She frowned. "How'd you know that?"

"Ashley mentioned it."

"When were you talking to my little sister?"

He shrugged. "She brings Rey over when she's bored."

"Then she must be here a lot," Sky decided. "Because she's *always* bored. And it's going to be even worse when school's out for the summer."

"Because most of her friends live in town," Jake

noted, obviously echoing one of her sister's common complaints.

"It was no different for me when I was growing up," Sky pointed out. "Although I had a sister and two brothers, so I was never really alone—even when I wanted to be."

"Forced proximity makes convenient playmates."

"Sounds like you speak from experience," she said.

"I have a brother," he told her. "Luke. He's four years older than me."

"Where did you grow up?"

"Here and there."

"Military brats, huh? Is your dad a Marine, too?" At his questioning look, she shrugged. "Even in the dark, that tattoo on your shoulder is hard to miss."

"Yeah," he finally said. "My dad's a major in the US Marine Corps."

She didn't know a lot about military structure, but she knew that major was a pretty high rank.

Jake gathered up their plates and pushed away from the table, a clear indication that the topic of conversation was closed.

"Do you want me to give you a ride home?" he asked.

"No, I can walk," she said. "I just didn't expect to be kicked out *before* we had sex this time."

He seemed taken aback by her response.

"I invited you to come over for breakfast because I didn't want you to think that all I wanted from you was sex," he said.

"Are you saying that you don't want to have sex?"

"Men pretty much always want to have sex," he told her.

"And yet, I've been here—" she glanced at the watch on her wrist "—more than an hour, and you haven't even kissed me."

"It's been a concerted effort to keep my hands off you," he promised.

"I like when your hands are on me."

"Good to know, but—" he held them up now and took a step back "—I was actually thinking we might try something different next time."

"What do you mean by different?" she asked, her tone wary.

"I mean like going out for dinner."

"We just had breakfast and you're already thinking about dinner?" she teased.

"I wasn't necessarily suggesting tonight."

Her pretty blue-grey eyes sparkled. "Are you asking me on a date, Jake Kelly?"

"Yes, I'm asking you on a date, Sky Gilmore," he confirmed, parroting her with a smile.

"Then I'm saying yes," she told him. "When? Where?"

He wanted to say tonight but since that might come across as too eager, especially considering her remark about their recent meal, he suggested Tuesday instead.

She gave a slight shake of her head. "I can't do dinner on Tuesday," she said, sounding sincerely regretful. "Tuesdays are game nights."

"Game nights?"

"The coed softball team I mentioned—I play third base," she explained.

"The hot corner," he noted, impressed. "You must be good."

"I am," she said, but it was a matter-of-fact statement rather than a boast.

"Okay, so you have baseball on Tuesday and you work on Wednesday, so how about Thursday?"

"Thursday sounds good to me," she agreed.

"Okay, then," he agreed. "We'll do it on Thursday."

"But dinner first, right?" she teased.

He smiled, appreciating not just her humor but the promise implicit in her words. "Definitely dinner first."

## Chapter Nine

It was Sky's opinion that one of the best things about not having a regular full-time job was that she was often available whenever a friend or family member needed her. And while she wasn't always thrilled to be enlisted to run errands for the ranch, she never hesitated to step up when Katelyn needed someone to watch Tessa for a couple hours or her sister-in-law Macy asked for help with the triplets.

So on Wednesday afternoon, when Kate called to tell her that she was still stuck in a trial that should have been finished two days earlier, Sky happily agreed to take Tessa to her Tadpole lesson at the community center. The swimming class was made up of a small group of toddlers who, along with their parents or caregivers, were taught water safety and foundational skills.

Tessa's favorite part was when she got to be a starfish, spreading her arms and legs wide and floating on top of the water with her aunt's hand supporting her back. She was less enamored of the putting-her-face-in-the-water part.

When the class was finished, Sky and Tessa returned to the locker room to shower—"We hafta wash off the kwoween, Auntie 'ky"—and get dressed. Of course, toweling the little girl's head wasn't good enough for Tessa, who insisted on standing beneath the hand dryer until there wasn't a drop of moisture left in her hair.

"I think I understand now why your mom warned me that a half-hour swim class takes two hours," Sky remarked, as she wrapped the wet swimsuits in their towels before tucking them into Tessa's glittery pink backpack. Of course she didn't really mind, because she'd enjoyed every minute of those two hours she'd spent with her adorable niece.

But they weren't done yet. Because on their way to the exit, they had to go right past the library.

"Books! Books!" Tessa insisted.

And there was no way Sky, a lifelong lover of reading herself, could possibly say no to her.

Another half an hour later, they were finally on their way out of the building, with half a dozen books stuffed in the front pouch of Tessa's backpack, away from the damp towels.

Sky held her niece's hand securely in hers as the

little girl carefully navigated the outside steps. As Tessa reached the bottom, Sky caught a glimpse, out of the corner of her eye, of a truck pulling into the parking lot.

Was that... Jake's truck?

She turned her head for a better look, surprised to realize that it was. And even more surprised when his passenger side door opened and a woman got out.

Sky recognized the stunning, statuesque blonde as Natalya Vasilek, an assistant manager at Adventure Village who occasionally came into Diggers' with her coworkers for a drink and a bite to eat. In addition to working at the family-friendly activity center, Natalya was a former naval aviator who organized weekly support group meetings for other military veterans.

As Nat came around the back of the vehicle, Sky saw that she carried a wide flat box from Sweet Caroline's Sweets. Donuts or some other kind of pastries for the meeting, she guessed.

Jake fell into step with the other woman, obviously continuing whatever conversation they'd been having in the car. In fact, he was so focused on what they were talking about, he was almost at the bottom step before he spotted Sky standing there with Tessa.

He stopped abruptly in mid-stride and his lips started to curve, as if he was happy to see her, but the curve didn't quite reach the point of a smile before his gaze shuttered.

"Hi," Sky said, her greeting encompassing both of them.

"Hey, Sky." The other woman's easy response was accompanied by a real smile, even as her gaze shifted from Jake to Sky and back again, curious and assessing.

Jake's response wasn't quite as easy, and Sky realized he wasn't just startled by this chance encounter but maybe a little uncomfortable, too.

Because he was with Nat?

Or because he didn't want her to know that he was going to a support group?

Nat clearly sensed the subtext between them because she gestured to the box she carried. "I'm going to take this inside," she said, and made her escape.

Jake nodded, though his attention never shifted away from Sky.

"I didn't expect—what are you doing here?" he asked, when Nat was out of earshot.

"My sister was stuck in court, so I brought Tessa to her swimming group today," she said.

"I swimmed," her niece said proudly.

His gaze shifted now to the little girl clinging to Sky, and his expression immediately softened. "Do you like swimming?"

Tessa's head bobbed up and down as she released her aunt's hand to reach both arms up into the air and stretch her legs out. "I a 'tarfiss."

"She means starfish," Sky translated.

He nodded. "I've got an almost-three-year-old niece, so I'm pretty fluent in toddler-speak. Plus, the pose," he acknowledged. "Definitely a starfish."

Tessa beamed at him. "An' I got books."

"At the library?" he guessed.

The little girl responded with more head bobbing.

"Sounds like you've both had a busy day."

"And mine is a long way from over," Sky said. "I need to get Tessa home so that I can go home and get ready for work."

Jake nodded. "I'll see you later then?"

She smiled. "I hope so."

Natalya was almost finished arranging the chairs by the time Jake made his way to the usual meeting room.

"I thought I was here to help you set up," he remarked.

"So did I." But her remark was followed by a smile to assure him that she wasn't bothered by his tardiness.

Still, he felt compelled to say, "You could have waited for me."

"I'm perfectly capable of unstacking chairs, Jake. The main reason I asked you to come into town early was because I needed a ride."

And he knew it hadn't been easy for her to ask for even that small favor. Natalya Vasilek was one of the most fiercely independent people he'd ever met, and he suspected that she would have preferred to walk to the community center from home rather than accept a ride, except that she had to pick up the donuts from Sweet Caroline's.

"How long are you going to be without wheels?" he asked her now.

"Just a couple more days—I hope." She finished with the chairs, then moved into the kitchenette to begin making coffee. "It's just frustrating to be inconvenienced by something that wasn't at all my fault."

She'd given him a quick rundown of the situation on the phone, explaining that someone had backed into her car in the parking lot at Adventure Village. What annoyed her even more was that the driver of the other vehicle took off. Thankfully, there were surveillance cameras on the property that recorded the incident, so her car was now being repaired and the other driver's insurance was paying for it.

"Well, I'm generally around," he said now. "If you need me to play chauffeur again."

"Thanks," she said. "But I only tagged you tonight because we were coming to the same place."

"How are you getting to and from work?"

"I've been hitching a ride with a coworker."

"Is this, by any chance, the coworker that you've sort of been seeing?" he asked.

"It might be," she allowed.

"So…things are going well?" he prompted.

"They might be."

He caught the hint of a smile on her face. "Good for you, Nat."

"What's going on with you?" she asked.

It was the same question she asked him every Wednesday, and every Wednesday he gave her the same answer: "Nothing much."

But somehow, over the past several weeks, they'd

become friends. And tonight he actually had something to tell her. Something he wanted—maybe even needed—to talk about. "I've got a date tomorrow night."

"A date," Nat echoed. "That sounds promising."

"Does it? Because I'm already thinking it was a mistake to ask."

"I'd suggest that we save the talking about your feelings and concerns part for the meeting, except that you seem to clam up whenever there are more than three people in the room."

While he wouldn't say that he clammed up, it was true that he didn't share personal insights or anecdotes with the group. He went to the meetings because his doctor had suggested that interacting with others who had similar experiences might help him feel less alone. It did that, and it got him out of the house at least once a week.

"So tell me why you're thinking it was a mistake," Nat suggested now.

"It just seems like a really big step, and I'm not sure that I'm ready."

"So why did you ask her out?"

"Because I want to be ready," he admitted.

"You really like her," she noted.

He nodded. "I really do. But she has no idea how completely screwed up I am."

"So tell her," Nat urged. "Honesty and communication are at the core of any good relationship."

"I've tried to tell her."

"Have you?"

"Well, I started to…but then… I didn't really know what to say. Or maybe I just didn't want to talk about it. I know she has a right to know what she's getting herself into…except that I'm not sure whatever is happening between us is anything. And I'm pretty sure that if she did know, she'd run away—far and fast."

"I don't think you're giving her enough credit. I'd bet that Sky Gilmore can handle whatever you throw at her."

He frowned. "How did you know I was talking about Sky?"

"Please," she said. "I nearly got singed from the heat between the two of you, even standing several feet away."

"Is that all you're going to say about it?"

She flipped the switch to start the coffee brewing. "Are you asking for my approval?"

"How about your opinion?"

"I've always liked Sky," Nat told him.

"You don't think I'm aiming too high?"

"Of course I think you're aiming too high. Sky isn't just beautiful and smart, she's kind and compassionate. She's always ready and able to volunteer for anything that will help the community and happy to give of her time and expertise without expecting anything in return. She is an amazing woman who could no doubt do a lot better than a grumpy old vet like you."

He frowned at that, and Nat smiled before continuing, "I also think she just might be a woman who's capable of understanding and appreciating you, and you deserve no less."

That night, Jake wasn't waiting for Sky when she left the restaurant. But they'd exchanged contact information over the weekend, and she saw now that he'd sent her a text message.

You want to stop by after work?

The time stamp of that message was 12:37.
Then, at 12:41, it was followed up with:

If you're not too tired.

Just the thought of seeing Jake again seemed to magically lift away the weariness of the long day.
*Definitely not too tired.*
She tapped a quick reply:

On my way.
If it's not too late.

His reply was immediate:

Definitely not too late :)

The smiley face emoji made her smile as she exited the parking lot.

Both Jake and Molly were waiting for her at the door when she arrived. But this time, instead of leaving a trail of clothes on the way to the bedroom, Jake took her hand and led her into the living room.

"Are we trying something different again?" Sky teased.

"As a matter of fact." He lowered himself onto the sofa, then drew Sky down on his lap, and settled his mouth over hers.

His kiss was different this time. A leisurely exploration rather than a means to an end. And if Sky was a little surprised by his restraint, she was more entranced by his technique. As his lips teased and tempted her own, desire raced through her veins like a drug, making her heart race and her blood pound.

*Was it possible to become addicted to a man's kisses?*

She thought maybe it was, as the more kisses they shared, the more she wanted.

She shifted in his lap, so that her knees were bracketing his hips. So that she could lift her arms to his shoulders, linking her hands behind his head. His arms banded around her, pulling her closer until her breasts were pressed against the firm wall of his chest. Her nipples immediately tightened to hard aching points. Between her thighs, she could feel solid evidence of his arousal, proof that he wanted her, too.

She slid her hands beneath the hem of his shirt, her fingers gliding over his warm, taut skin, instinctively gentling as they skimmed the jagged scar that ran from just above his hip almost to his armpit.

Jake caught her wrists and pulled her hands away.

"It's hard to remember that I'm trying to take things slow when you're touching me," he told her.

She was glad to hear his breathing was labored, because she needed a moment to catch her own breath before she could respond. "Isn't it a little late to start taking things slow?"

"I know this seems a bit backward," he acknowledged. "But I want to get to know you—and for you to know me, so that you know what you're getting into."

She narrowed her gaze. "It sounds like you're dumping me."

"No!"

Sky was somewhat appeased by his quick and vehement denial.

"Though truthfully, I didn't expect that you'd want to have anything more to do with me after that first day," he confided to her now.

"You're referring to the day you told me to get out after we'd mated like bunnies?" she teased.

"I didn't say 'get out,'" he denied. "But yes, when you were willing to give me another chance after that, I knew you were truly unlike any other woman I've ever known."

"Good," she said. "I hate to be predictable."

"Does that mean you're not going to barrage me with questions?" he asked, sounding both skeptical and relieved.

"I'll try to limit my inquiries to a trickle," she promised. "But questions about what exactly?"

"Why I was at the community center with Natalya."

"Oh. I assumed that you were both there for the veterans' support group meeting."

He frowned at that.

"Was I wrong?" she asked.

"No," he admitted.

"So why do I get the impression that you're disappointed by my response?"

"I'm not disappointed, I'm just…surprised," he realized. "Margot would sulk if I so much as smiled at another woman."

"Now I have a barrage of questions," Sky said, leaning back a little to better see his face. "Starting with—who's Margot?"

He winced. "You're so easy to talk to that sometimes I forget to filter the words that come out of my mouth."

"And yet you're not answering the question," she noted.

"Margot was…my fiancée."

"Oh." She took a moment to consider this revelation. "I didn't realize you'd been engaged."

He shrugged. "It feels like it was a lifetime ago."

"How long ago was it really?" she pressed.

"She gave back the ring about two years ago."

"How long did she wear it?"

His brows drew together, as if he was trying to remember. "Almost five years?"

"That's a pretty lengthy engagement," she noted.

"Yeah," he agreed.

"Did you have a date set for a wedding?"

He shook his head. "During those five years, I was gone more than I was home. It was hard enough to commit to a night out with friends, forget planning the kind of wedding she wanted."

"But you did want to marry her." It was a statement more than a question, as Sky tried to wrap her head around the fact that this taciturn man had been planning a happily-ever-after.

"Sure," he said. "I mean, my focus was on the Marine Corps, but I looked forward to coming home from a deployment and seeing her face in the crowd. To know that there was someone there for me. My parents always came to the homecomings, too, but everyone's parents were always there. Having a pretty girl waiting was something special."

She didn't miss that he'd said "a pretty girl" rather than use his fiancée's name, making Sky wonder if he'd truly been in love with the woman who'd worn his ring or if he'd just wanted to feel connected to someone back home. Or maybe she was reading too much into his word choice, because she didn't want to think that the man she was starting to fall for had fallen for someone else, even if that relationship was long over.

"So what went wrong?" she asked him now.

"It turned out that she loved the idea of being with a man in uniform more than she loved me. And when I no longer wore the uniform, she found someone else. Actually…she found him before I got my discharge papers."

"Hence your comment about Molly being more loyal than any woman you've ever known," she realized, aware that it couldn't have been an easy admission for him to make, and glad he felt comfortable enough with her to share the whole truth of his failed relationship.

"Yeah. I guess I'm having a little trouble forgiving Margot for that," he acknowledged.

"Do you think you should forgive her?"

He shrugged. "I don't think it's okay that she cheated, but I understand that I was no longer the man she'd fallen in love with."

"Love endures all things," Sky said.

"If you're such an expert on the subject, what are you doing here with me?" he wondered.

"I'm only an expert at looking for love in all the wrong places," she confided.

"That would explain it," he said.

"You don't have to worry," she assured him. "I'm not looking for anything more than what we've found between us."

"It's good, isn't it?" he asked, the hint of a smile curving his lips.

"Very good," she agreed, and kissed him again.

Sky couldn't remember the last time she'd been out on a date. Hanging out with a group of friends that included males, sure. But a one-on-one date with a guy she really liked? It had been ages.

"Why are all your clothes on your bed?" Ashley asked, hovering in the doorway of Sky's room.

Looking at the pile of discarded clothes, Sky had to sigh. "Because I can't decide what to wear."

"For what?"

"I've got a date," she confessed.

"I thought you were on a dating hiatus," Ashley said, remembering what Sky had told her when she'd asked why she didn't have a boyfriend. Or girlfriend, she'd been quick to present as another option, to assure her sister that she wouldn't judge.

"I was, but now I'm not."

"So who are you going out with? Is it Jake?"

"Why would you think it was Jake?" Sky asked her.

"Because you've known everyone else in this town forever, so if you wanted to go out with any of them, it would have happened before now," Ashley said.

And probably had, she acknowledged, though she didn't share that with her sister.

"You're right," she said instead. "I'm going out with Jake."

"Where are you going?"

"Just for dinner."

"A casual restaurant or fancy restaurant?"

"I have no idea," she admitted.

"No wonder you can't figure out what to wear," her sister sympathized. "You want to wear something nice, because it's a date, but you don't want to overdress and have him think you're making a bigger deal of the event than it is."

"Insightful commentary from someone who isn't allowed to date yet," Sky remarked.

"Don't remind me," Ashley said, sounding pained. "But I'll be prepared when Dad finally gives the thumbs-up."

Sky held a skirt and top in front of her. "What do you think?"

"I love the skirt." Ashley rifled through a pile of tops on the bed. "But with this top."

Sky swapped the pink one in her hand for the blue from her sister and turned to face her reflection in the mirror. "Hmm…you're right. This one's better."

"So maybe you'll let me borrow this one—" Ashley, still holding the discarded pink top, looked hopeful "—to wear to the movies tonight?"

"Do you have a date?" Sky asked.

Her sister rolled her eyes. "I'm not allowed to date—remember?"

Yeah, Sky remembered.

She also remembered that, when she was Ashley's age, being told she couldn't do something rarely stopped her from doing it.

"So who are you going to the movies with?" she asked.

"Chloe."

"Then you don't need this," Sky said, tugging the shirt out of her sister's hand. "Because Chloe won't care what you're wearing."

"There might be some other people there tonight," Ashley admitted. "I mean, the movie theater's a public place, right?"

"Uh-huh," Sky agreed.

"So if we happen to run into some other people that we know and decide to sit together, there's nothing wrong with that. And even if Chloe specifically invited other people who might be boys, it's still not technically a date, right?"

"Are you asking me or telling me?"

Ashley sighed. "I really didn't care who else was going—I just wanted to see the movie. But then Chloe decided to invite her boyfriend, and then he invited his friend, and now I'm really nervous about going because his friend is really cute and whenever I think about sitting next to him in the theater, I get this quivery feeling in my stomach."

"I agree with Dad that you're kind of young to be dating," she said, handing the pink top back to her sister. "But going to the movies with a few friends shouldn't be taboo."

Ashley rewarded her with a radiant smile. "Thanks. For the top, I mean."

Sky nodded. "Just be smart and be safe—and don't let anyone put their hands under that top."

Her sister looked horrified by the very thought. "I wouldn't… Never," she promised.

Though she was skeptical about the "never" part, Sky felt confident that her sister had established limits for her night at the movies.

"But what if…" Ashley chewed on her bottom lip. "What if he wants…to kiss me?"

"That's entirely up to you," Sky said. "No one else."

"Chloe French kisses her boyfriend," the teen confided now. "She says it's a real turn on, but it sounds pretty gross to me."

"I think you're starting to realize that Chloe does a lot of things you're not comfortable doing, and that's okay. You need to set and respect your own boundaries."

"Do you let Jake put his tongue in your mouth?" Ashley's cheeks turned pink as she asked the question.

Not just his tongue, Sky mused, but she was definitely not going *there* with her little sister.

"I can appreciate that you're curious about some things, and that's perfectly normal and natural," Sky said instead. "But I'm going to keep the details of my private relationships private."

"Have you had sex with him?" Ashley asked, her eyes widening.

"Refer to previous answer."

Her sister huffed out a breath. "Well, it's not like I can talk to mom about this stuff."

Sky perched on the edge of the mattress beside Ashley. "Actually, I bet your mom would be glad to answer your questions—so long as they aren't about the details of what goes on in her bedroom."

"You're right," the teen acknowledged. "It's just that talking to your mom about this stuff is awkward, you know?" Then her eyes went wide and her cheeks colored again as she suddenly realized that her sister didn't know, because Sky's mom had died when she was only seven. "Ohmygod, Sky… I'm *so* sorry."

"It's okay, Ash," she said. "And actually I *do* know, because Grandma tried to have those talks with me—when I got my first period, bought my first bra, went to my first high-school dance. So yes, I understand awkward."

She also remembered that when there was something she really wanted to talk about, in the absence of her mother, she'd naturally turned to her big sister. So maybe she shouldn't have been surprised that Ashley had come to her, even if their relationship was a recent revelation for both of them.

## Chapter Ten

Jake was waiting outside when Sky arrived.

"Am I late?" she asked.

"No."

He brushed her lips with a soft, lingering kiss that made her belly quiver in the same way her sister had described.

"I just didn't know what you'd be wearing and I didn't want Molly jumping and messing you up."

She did a quick twirl. "Do I look okay?"

"Better than okay. You look amazing."

"You clean up pretty good yourself," she said, appreciating how handsome he looked in a chambray shirt and khaki pants. "And not a dog hair in sight."

"I would have been happy to pick you up at your place," he said.

"This is easier."

"Because you don't want me to meet your father?" he guessed.

"We're neighbors in a small town—I'd assumed you'd already met my father."

"But not as your date," he remarked.

"And that's what I was trying to save you from," she said. "The interrogation that goes along with that title."

"I know how to handle an interrogation—name, rank and serial number."

She smiled, pleased that he no longer seemed to be keeping his military service a secret—at least not from her.

"Well, I have a question for you," she said. "Where are we going tonight?"

"The Chophouse."

"In Battle Mountain?" she guessed.

He nodded and opened the passenger-side door of his truck for her to climb in.

"There are restaurants in Haven," she reminded him, when he was settled behind the wheel.

"That I can count on the fingers of one hand without using my thumb," he noted. "And of those four, you work at one, your brother owns another, and while the Sunnyside Diner does a great all-day breakfast, I think we've eaten enough eggs together."

"And for some inexplicable reason, you're not a fan of Jo's pizza," she remembered.

"I like it just fine."

"And yet your freezer is full of the frozen kind."

"Maybe because I don't want to go into town every time I'm in the mood for a pizza."

"Definitely worth the trip," Sky argued.

"The first time I had it, I thought the same thing," he agreed.

"And the second?" she prompted.

He sighed. "I walked into the restaurant and before I could even give my name at the takeout counter, the woman working the register—who I assumed to be Jo—said, 'Your medium sausage and peppers is just coming out of the oven now.'"

"It was the wrong order?" Sky guessed.

"No, it was the right order. But I don't need everyone in town knowing what I eat on my pizza."

"And since then you've deprived yourself of Jo's pizza because you'd rather be anonymous than well-fed?"

"It sounds ridiculous when you say it like that," he acknowledged.

"It is ridiculous," she said. "I'll be the first to admit that it's sometimes annoying that everyone seems to know everyone else's business. When you live in a town like Haven, you forfeit your anonymity, but what you get in return is a sense of belonging to the community.

"But I'm willing to make you a deal," she said, as he pulled into the parking lot adjacent to the restaurant.

"What kind of deal?" he asked warily.

"If this date thing goes well enough tonight that

we decide we want to do it again, we'll eat at your place next time—and I'll pick up the pizza from Jo's."

"That sounds good to me," he agreed.

"This is really nice," Sky said, after they'd been seated. The décor had a masculine bent, with lots of stone, wood and leather, with subdued overhead lighting supplemented by candles on the tables. But it was the scent of grilled meat that really appealed to her empty stomach.

"I hoped you'd like it," he said.

"Have you been here before?"

He shook his head. "No, but it had good reviews online."

"What did we do before the internet?" she mused.

"I'm pretty sure we didn't take pictures of our every meal to share with the world."

She chuckled. "I take it you're not a fan of Instagram?"

"I'm not a fan of social media in general," he admitted.

"I'm not surprised," she said, tongue in cheek. "Considering it's got the word *social* in it."

Jake narrowed his gaze, but whatever his intended reply, he bit it back when the waitress appeared beside their table.

"Can I get you something to drink while you're looking at the menu?" she asked. "We have a selection of red and white wines, available by the glass or bottle, a variety of craft beers and an extensive cocktail list."

"Sky?" Jake said, deferring to her.

"I wouldn't mind a glass of wine," she said, skimming the list of options at the front of the menu. "The Stoneridge Estates pinot noir."

The waitress nodded.

"And you, sir?" she asked Jake.

"I'll have a Coke," he said.

Sky continued to peruse the menu offerings, mentally debating between the striploin and ribeye because she didn't believe in going to a steak house and ordering anything but steak. She glanced up to ask Jake what he was going to have, and found his gaze was on her rather than the menu in his own hand.

"You're staring at me," she said.

"I can't help it—you look particularly beautiful tonight."

"I think it's the candlelight," she said.

"No." He shook his head. "It's you."

"And you haven't even been drinking," she said lightly.

"I'm surprised," he said. "You don't strike me as the type of woman who'd have trouble accepting a sincere compliment."

"I don't," she said. "But I grew up with a sister who's truly beautiful. If you'd met Katelyn, you'd understand."

"I have met her. She was my uncle's lawyer."

Sky nodded. "Then you should understand."

"She's very attractive," he acknowledged. "But when I walked into her office, I didn't feel the same kind of awareness I felt when I walked into Diggers' and saw you."

"Lucky for you, considering that Kate's married to the sheriff," she remarked.

When the waitress returned with their drinks and a basket of warm bread, Sky ordered the striploin with a fully loaded baked potato and the seasonal vegetables—broccoli and carrots. Jake opted for the T-bone with the same sides.

"So tell me," Sky said as she buttered a slice of bread, "why a man who, by his own admission, prefers anonymity, would move to a town like Haven."

"I wanted to get out of San Diego and, when I found out that my uncle had put my name on the title before he passed away, it seemed like my best option. Maybe my only option."

"Were you surprised to learn that he'd left this place to you?"

"More than," he confided.

"He never talked to you about it?"

He shook his head. "Although, to be honest, the last time I was here was the summer before I went away to college. No, it was the Christmas holidays during my first year of college. Fifteen years ago." He shifted his gaze to the window. "I didn't even make it back for Anna's funeral because I was…out of the country."

"You mean deployed?"

He nodded.

"Why do you do that?"

"What did I do?"

"Avoid referencing your military service."

He lifted a shoulder. "It's just not something I'm comfortable talking about."

"Do you talk about it in your Wednesday night support group?"

"No," he admitted.

She wished he would talk to her, but she knew this wasn't the time or place to push him for answers to her questions. Instead she asked, "You were close to Ross and Anna?"

He nodded again. "My brother and I used to spend a couple weeks with them every summer when we were kids."

"And yet our paths never crossed back then," she mused.

"I'm glad they crossed now."

"Me, too." Sky smiled, even as she saw the situation developing out of the corner of her eye. The young waiter—his eyes on a pretty girl dining with her family—turning abruptly, directly into the path of a busboy, knocking the bin of glasses that he carried out of his hands.

She had a split second to brace herself, but she didn't think to warn Jake—and didn't know if it would have mattered anyway.

There was a loud crash…

*The pressure wave from the blast sent Jake stumbling even before he registered the sound of the boom some distance away. Flying shards of blown-*

*out glass flew in every direction, not just dangerous but potentially lethal—*

"Jake."

*He blinked, trying to focus through the cloud of dust that filled the room.*

"Jake."

Sky reached across the table and touched a hand to his arm. "Are you okay?"

He blinked. His nostrils were flared, his breathing shallow.

"Yeah." He swallowed. "I just… Can you give me a minute?"

"Sure," she said.

He pushed away from the table and walked out of the restaurant.

Jake couldn't remember the last time he'd been on a first date with a woman. And as he focused on inhaling and exhaling to help ward off the impending panic attack, he acknowledged that his first real date with Sky Gilmore was also likely to be his last.

*"Triggers can be sights, sounds or scents that remind you of the trauma. They can happen anytime, anywhere. Quite often they will happen at inopportune times and inconvenient places. You need to learn to recognize the signs and utilize your coping mechanisms."*

Well, at least he hadn't tackled his date, upended the table or reached for a weapon that he wasn't carrying.

Was that progress? Should he be proud?

He scrubbed his hands over his face.

What had he been thinking, asking her to go out with him?

The problem was, when he was with Sky, he sometimes had trouble thinking. Or at least remembering all the reasons that he didn't do the things that most normal people did. Because when he was with her, he felt normal. No, he felt invincible, as if he could take on the world with her by his side.

He'd been looking forward to this opportunity for them to spend more time together and get to know one another a little better outside of the bedroom. Because when they were naked and horizontal together, they didn't tend to do a lot of talking. And being with Sky made him want to open up, perhaps for the first time in years. So much so that he'd thought he might be able to tell her things that he'd never told anyone else outside of a doctor's office.

"Jake?"

He heard the tentativeness in her tone. Or maybe it was fear. He could hardly blame her for being scared. Some days he scared himself.

He turned slowly to face her, though she was mostly in shadow.

But she stepped closer now, into the light, and he saw that she wasn't scared but worried.

About him.

"Are you okay?" she asked.

"Yeah," he lied. "Sorry about that."

"There's no reason for you to apologize."

He appreciated the sentiment, but he didn't share it.

"I just need another minute and then I'll meet you back inside."

"Why don't you give me your keys instead?" she suggested.

"Why?"

"So that I can drive us home."

"But…we haven't had dinner yet," he said inanely.

As if there was any chance she'd want to share a meal with him now.

"We'll have it at your place," she said, holding up the takeout bag he hadn't realized she was carrying.

He felt as if a ninety-pound pack had been lifted off his back. The tension in his neck immediately lessened, the tightness in his chest eased.

"Keys?" she prompted.

He dug them out of his pocket and put them into her outstretched hand.

She didn't say anything as she pulled out of the parking lot and turned back toward Haven, and he didn't know what to say.

When they got back to his place, Molly made a big fuss over him, as if he'd been gone for days rather than a couple of hours. Or maybe she knew how much he needed her unwavering love and support, because even when Sky walked in with the doggy bag containing their steaks, Molly didn't move from his side.

"Go into the living room and relax," Sky said. "I'll heat up the food and let you know when it's ready."

"You don't have to do that," Jake said. "I'm sure you'd rather—"

"Go," she said again, pointing toward the living room.

So he went, too exhausted to argue any more.

But he did feel compelled to apologize once more, when their dinner had been reheated and he was seated across from her at the kitchen table.

"I'm sorry. I should have realized it was a bad idea—I did realize it was a bad idea." He stabbed his fork into a broccoli spear. "I picked up the phone to cancel at least half a dozen times."

"But you didn't," she noted, slicing into her steak.

"Because I wanted to prove myself wrong. I wanted to prove that I could at least take a pretty girl to a restaurant and fake being normal for a few hours. Guess that didn't work out so well, did it?"

"How long have you been having panic attacks?"

"A couple of years."

"Have you talked to anyone about what causes them?"

"You mean a shrink?" he guessed.

"I mean a qualified professional," she clarified.

"Aren't you a qualified professional?"

"PTSD isn't my area of expertise," she told him. "Not to mention that sleeping with a patient violates all kinds of rules that would result in my license being revoked. But if there's anything you want to talk about, I'm more than willing to listen."

"I don't know what to say, how to explain something I don't understand, though there were plenty of doctors who made me try."

"Can you tell me what kinds of things trigger a response?" she prompted, her tone encouraging.

He sighed. "Anything. And yet nothing consistently," he admitted, obviously frustrated by the fact. "Sudden noises. Flashes of light."

"I don't imagine the Fourth of July is a lot of fun for you," she said lightly.

"Fireworks are a definite trigger," he confirmed. "As I found out this past New Year's Eve."

"What happened then?"

"I didn't even want to celebrate," he confided. "But it was the first time in several years that both me and my brother were home for the holidays, and my mom insisted that the whole family should be together.

"Luke and his wife Raina offered to host dinner. I was a little uneasy all night—because me and my dad can't be in the same room for too long without butting heads over something, usually the lack of a plan for my future," he acknowledged. "But it was a really nice evening. Raina's not only a fabulous cook, she managed to keep the conversation focused on mostly neutral topics.

"Everything was great until the kids next door lit a handful of cherry bombs. Just kids being kids, right?"

Jake looked off in the distance, his expression bleak.

Sky reached across the table to squeeze his hand, a silent gesture of support.

She didn't need him to tell her the rest of the story. She could see the direction it was going clearly enough to figure out the end for herself. But if Jake was finally ready to talk, she wanted to listen and support him.

To reassure him that he wasn't alone.

"But those pops sounded like gunfire to me," he continued. "And I reacted without thinking. Because in a combat zone, if you think, you're dead, so you learn pretty quickly to take action.

"Benjamin, my nine-year-old nephew, was closest to me, and I threw him to the ground, covering his body with my own." His Adam's apple bobbed as he swallowed. "I thought I was protecting him."

He closed his eyes, but not before she caught a glimpse of both guilt and regret in his anguished gaze.

"Instead, I knocked the wind out of him, scared him half to death—and did a pretty good job of freaking out everyone else, too."

"You thought you were protecting him," she reminded Jake.

"The next day, I went to see my sister-in-law, to apologize for traumatizing her son. I was prepared for her to tell me to stay the hell away from her family—that seemed the most reasonable response to me," he acknowledged. "Instead, she invited me in for coffee and spent the next hour trying to make me feel better."

"Sounds like she's quite a woman."

"She really is," he agreed. "My brother lucked out when he fell in love with Raina. She's been nothing but supportive of his career, despite the fact that she's raising their kids on her own when he's deployed.

"But despite Raina's assurances that no harm had been done, the incident scared the hell out of me. I couldn't risk something like that happening again and really hurting someone, so I decided to leave San Diego for a while, until I got my life back on track.

"Of course, she brought Benjamin to see me before I left. And he apologized to me." Jake shook his head, as if marveling over the fact. "He said he was sorry that he'd cried and he understood I was trying to protect him, because I was a Marine, just like his dad."

He looked away, a muscle in his jaw flexing, and Sky knew he was grappling to maintain control of his emotions.

Just listening to him recount the story had Sky feeling a little teary-eyed herself.

"But I'm nothing like his dad. Luke has done close to a dozen tours in fifteen years, moving steadily up the ranks. He's a gunnery sergeant now, and no doubt he'll probably be a major someday, like our dad."

"Is that what he wants?" she asked.

"It's what we both wanted. Only I couldn't cut it."

She took his hand again, linked their fingers together.

"Obviously I don't know the details of what you saw or did during your time in the Marine Corps, but I think maybe you need to cut yourself a break," she told him. "Everyone's experiences in combat are different, and even those who share the same experiences may process them differently. Anyone can end up with PTSD and it's estimated that between ten and twenty percent of veterans who served in the Middle East do."

"Someone's been doing some research," he noted.

"I spent six years in college," she said. "Old habits are hard to break, but I apologize if I overstepped."

He shook his head. "You didn't."

"So you said that Benjamin's nine, but you'd previously mentioned a three-year-old niece," she said, attempting to maneuver the conversation to a less difficult topic.

"Christina," he said. "And between Ben and Christina is Nate. He's six. Thankfully, he and his little sister were both tucked into bed by the time the kids next door brought out the firecrackers."

"You miss them a lot," she said. "I can hear it in your voice when you talk about them."

"Yeah, I guess I do," he said. "I got to spend a fair bit of time with them over the past couple of years. Kids give you a whole different perspective on life. Maybe it's naïve or idealistic, but they make me believe there's some hope for the future of this screwed-up world."

She nodded, understanding. "I've got two nieces and three nephews, and my sister Kate is expecting another child early in the new year. But I wasn't supposed to say anything about that just yet," she suddenly remembered. "Because they aren't ready for the news to be public knowledge."

"I don't know how I'll resist telling all my friends in town," he remarked dryly.

She smiled then. "You must be feeling better—your smart-ass attitude is back."

"I am feeling better," he said. "Thanks."

But she could see in his eyes the toll that the whole evening had taken on him, so she pushed away from the table and carried their plates to the sink.

"Stop," he said, when she started to run the water.

"What?"

He took the bottle of soap from her hands. "You're not washing the dishes."

"I don't mind."

"I do," he said. "You didn't get the dinner out that you were promised—I am absolutely *not* letting you tidy up the kitchen."

"I used half those dishes," she pointed out.

He picked up the tea towel and dried her hands.

She didn't bother to protest. Instead, she asked, "Do you have any plans for next Thursday night?"

"No."

"I'll bring the pizza then."

"I thought the deal was only valid if tonight went well."

"You didn't have a good time tonight?"

"I had a panic attack in the restaurant."

"Just a little one," she said. "And then we came back here and enjoyed our excellent steaks and loaded baked potatoes."

"I'd say the steaks were more overcooked than excellent."

"Maybe a little, because I reheated them in the microwave," she acknowledged. "But do you know why I said yes when you invited me to go out with you tonight?

"I'll give you a hint," she said, before he had a chance to respond. "It had nothing to do with wine or candlelight."

"Am I supposed to guess now?" he asked.

She shook her head.

"I said yes because I wanted to be with you."

"You really need to set the bar higher," he told her.

"Thursday night," she said again. "I'll bring the pizza."

"Aren't you going to ask what toppings I like?"

"Sausage and peppers," she said, proving that she'd been paying attention when he told her about his second visit to Jo's. Then she brushed her mouth against his. "I'll see you around six."

## Chapter Eleven

"Do you really think we're going to eat two pizzas?" Jake asked, when he greeted Sky at the door the following Thursday night.

"Considering that I haven't eaten all day, yes," she told him, reaching down with her free hand to scratch behind Molly's ears. The greeting had the dog's whole back end wagging.

"But if we don't, you can put the leftovers in the freezer," she said, as she toed off her shoes. "Because even reheated, Jo's pizza is better than anything from the frozen foods section in the grocery store."

"Why haven't you eaten all day?" he asked, apparently stuck on that part of her response.

"I was busy."

"Too busy to grab a bite?" His tone was dubious.

"Yeah," she said. "I had a meeting with the guidance department at the high school early this morning about an honor roll student who's suddenly skipping classes and failing tests, then I went to court to provide moral support for a client who was testifying in a custody hearing that will decide whether or not her abusive soon-to-be ex-husband gets unsupervised visitation with their kids. When court broke for lunch, I went back to the high school to talk to the student who was the subject of the morning meeting, scheduled a follow-up with him for tomorrow, then returned to the courthouse for the afternoon session. After the hearing was finally adjourned for the day, I called Jo's to order the pizza, then I picked it up and brought it here."

"And you told me you didn't have a full-time job," he remarked.

"If I did, I'd probably work fewer hours," she acknowledged. Then her gaze snagged on the bottle on the counter. "Is that wine?"

"Yeah. I don't have a clue about grapes or vintages, so I called the restaurant we didn't eat at last week to ask about the reds on their wine list and this one sounded familiar."

"It's one of my favorites," she said, absurdly touched by his effort. "And I would really enjoy a glass of it right now."

"I'll open it," he promised, retrieving a corkscrew from the drawer of utensils. "But I think you should have a slice of pizza first."

"I'm not going to get drunk from one glass of

wine on an empty stomach," she promised, setting the boxes on the table so that she could wash her hands.

"Let's not test that theory," he advised.

"All right." After drying her hands on the towel that hung on the handle of the oven, she reached into the cupboard to retrieve plates for their meal.

"I've got plates in the living room," he said, as he pulled the cork out of the bottle. "I thought we'd eat in there tonight."

"Okay," she agreed, guessing that there was a game that he wanted to watch on the big screen.

She picked up the pizza boxes again and followed him into the living room, stopping short when she saw that he'd draped a cloth over the coffee table and set it with what she guessed had been his aunt's good china, real silver and linen napkins.

She placed the pizza boxes in the center of the table. "What is all this?"

"A feeble attempt to make up for the fact that you didn't get your fancy candlelight dinner the other night. And *damn*—" he finished pouring the wine into her glass, then reached into his pocket for a book of matches "—I forgot to light the candles."

She sipped her pinot noir as he struck a match and held the flame to the wick of the first candle, then the second.

"This is really sweet," she said. "But really not necessary."

He opened the lid of the pizza box and, using an

intricately embossed cake server, lifted a slice of pizza out and set it on her plate.

"Does eating off of good china mean we need to use a knife and fork?" she asked, wondering about the purpose of the cutlery.

"Of course not," he assured her with a shake of his head. "I only put the silverware out because the table setting looked unfinished without it."

"Thank goodness," she said, picking up her slice and biting into it. The flavors of gooey cheese, tangy sauce and spicy sausage exploded on her tongue. "Mmm...*sooo* good."

"And suddenly, I'm feeling unnecessary," Jake remarked dryly.

"Why?" she asked, already bringing the pizza to her mouth again for another bite.

"Because you're making the same sounds over that pizza as you make in the bedroom."

"I am not," she denied.

"Trust me," he said. "I'm intimately familiar with your sighs and moans."

"Well, I've had a very satisfying relationship with Jo's pizza for a lot of years," she told him. "And it looks like Molly wants to get acquainted with it, too."

"No," Jake said to the dog, who was inching ever closer to the coffee table, her nose twitching.

"Do you ever let her have treats from the table?"

"No," he said again, responding to Sky's question this time. "Not only because people food isn't good for dogs but because it gives her gas like you wouldn't believe."

"And how do you know that if you don't give her treats?"

"I learned that lesson the hard way," he admitted. "I used to let her have the occasional piece of cheese or last bite of a burger. And then I realized that those treats had a very specific and undesirable effect."

"Maybe Ashley's been sneaking treats to Rey," she mused. "That little dog makes a really big stink sometimes."

She looked at Molly, who had wriggled close enough that her nose was pressed against Sky's leg.

"Sorry," she said. "But Jake says you're not allowed to have this."

Molly looked at her pleadingly.

"It's not me, it's him," she said, pointing.

The dog actually sighed, making Sky smile.

"How did you two end up together?" she asked Jake now.

"My sister-in-law got her for me from a friend who trains service dogs."

"She's a service dog?"

He chuckled at that. "No. She totally flunked the test to qualify for training."

"And yet, just having a pet can be therapeutic," Sky noted. "Dogs, in particular, can be very intuitive, even without special training."

"She's certainly been good company," Jake said. "And she's always there when I wake up from a nightmare. Sometimes she even manages to wake me, before things get really bad." Then, before she could comment or ask about the nightmares, he continued, "Plus taking her out for exercise ensures that I get exercise, too."

Sky took her cue from him and let the subject of his nightmares drop—for now. "I'm not disciplined enough to exercise every day," she confided.

"It sounds like you spend a lot of time running from job to job every day," he noted.

"That's not the same thing. And between the running today, I spent a lot of hours just sitting on my butt at the courthouse."

"Is that why you're wearing those fancy clothes? Because you were in court today?"

She glanced at her attire, amused by his description. "A jacket and pants are fancy clothes?"

"Comparatively," he said. "Because I'm accustomed to seeing you in jeans and a T-shirt behind the bar at Diggers'. Although the outfit you had on last Thursday was nice, too. And then there was that very memorable day that you were stranded on the roadside wearing a snug little sweater, short skirt and chunky-heeled boots."

"You remember what I was wearing?"

"Oh yeah," he said, nodding. "It was the day I discovered that you've got really spectacular legs."

"Thank you?" she said dubiously.

"Of course, my recollection of what you were wearing under that sweater and skirt is even more vivid." He grinned. "You've got spectacular underwear, too."

"And you haven't even seen what I've got on today," she teased.

"Are you going to let me take those fancy clothes off of you so that I can?"

"I'd be disappointed if you didn't," she told him.

"I won't let you leave here disappointed tonight," he promised.

And proceeded to prove that he was a man of his word.

Jake was hovering in that state of postcoital bliss halfway between asleep and awake when Sky's voice cut through the silence.

"I should be heading home," she said. "It's late."

"Will you be grounded if you miss curfew?"

"I don't have a curfew, but I have a little sister who does and I'm trying to set a good example."

"She does look up to you," he noted.

"How would you know?"

"She talks about you all the time. Or maybe she just talks all the time. Honestly, I sometimes want to tell her to pause and take a breath."

Sky chuckled softly at that, then her expression grew serious. "Do you mind her hanging out here? Does she get in your way?"

"Nah, she's mostly harmless. And Molly loves when she's here, because Ashley will throw the ball forever."

"Rey still prefers to play keep-away," Sky said, sliding to the edge of the mattress to reach for her discarded clothes. "She fetches the ball, but then refuses to let go of it."

"Yeah, we've been working on that a little." He

shifted closer to peer at a blue mark on Sky's skin. "What's this?"

She had to twist her head to see the back of her arm. "Oh. I guess I must have hit the ground harder than I thought."

"Hit the ground?"

She nodded. "When I dove to catch Connor Neal's line drive Tuesday night."

"You got this bruise playing baseball?"

"Making the final out," she clarified. "Which ensured that we won the game."

"Competitive much?" he asked, sounding amused.

"Baseball is more of a passion than a pastime in this town."

"Still, you should be more careful."

"I should be more careful?" she challenged, skimming her fingers gently down his side, over a ridge of puckered skin.

"Yeah, well, that isn't from anything I did on purpose."

"What's it from?"

It was the first time she'd asked. The first time she'd made any reference to his scars, though he knew there was no way she could have missed them when they were naked together.

"I crashed into a market cart…after being thrown through the air when our Humvee was hit by an RPG."

"Afghanistan?" she guessed.

"I did a tour in Afghanistan," he told her. "But that was the last one, in Iraq."

"Is it okay that I asked?" she wondered, sounding worried.

"Yeah. Truthfully, I'm surprised it took you this long."

"I figured if you wanted me to know, you'd tell me. But then…well, you know the thing about the cat and curiosity."

"And now you know," he said.

Which wasn't really true, and he braced himself for the follow-up questions he felt certain would come after his admission.

But Sky surprised him again, only saying, "What I don't know is why you're making a fuss over a little bruise."

"Because I don't like to think about you being hurt."

"It doesn't hurt. Not really. And the bruise will be gone in a few days," she assured him.

"You really dove for a line drive?" he asked, not just to keep the topic focused on her injury rather than his own, but because he really wanted to know.

"I really did," she confirmed.

"I think I'd enjoy watching you play softball," he said.

"Games are at Prospect Park every Tuesday night at seven and the occasional Saturday afternoon at two."

"I'll keep that in mind."

"But I should probably warn you, there isn't a lot in the way of entertainment in this town—"

"Shocking," he said.

"—so we draw pretty big crowds," she continued, pointedly ignoring his interjection.

"What's a pretty big crowd?"

"There are usually thirty to forty spectators at most of our games."

"I'm surprised you don't have law enforcement at the park for crowd control."

"Connor Neal is the deputy sheriff."

"The hitter of the line drive you snagged?"

She nodded.

"You're lucky you didn't get taken in for grand larceny."

"I didn't get a chance to ask you last week about your big date," Natalya said, when Jake showed up at the community center the following Wednesday night.

"I was glad you didn't," he confided. "So that I didn't have to tell you that it was a disaster."

She winced sympathetically. "That bad?"

He nodded and, because it was Nat and he knew she'd understand, briefly summarized what had happened at the restaurant.

"It sounds like Sky handled the situation," she remarked when he'd finished the story.

A lot better than he would have anticipated.

Of course, if he'd anticipated any of it, he would never have asked her to go out with him.

"She did," he agreed. "But she shouldn't have had to."

"Have you seen her since then?"

"Yeah. We had pizza at my place last week."

"And how did that go?" she asked.

"That was good." But it was thinking about what had come after the pizza that made him smile. "Really good."

"So maybe your big date wasn't such a disaster," Nat suggested. "Maybe Sky needed to see your response to a situation like that to know how you'd react—and how she would, too."

"I still don't know that I'm ready for a relationship," he confided.

"Regardless, it looks like you've got one."

"I don't even know how long I'm going to be in Haven."

Nat smiled then. "That's what I said, too—five years ago."

But Jake knew he couldn't stay in Haven.

This was only a temporary detour in his life, and he'd get back on track as soon as he found the track again.

But as he settled in his usual seat for the meeting, he found himself wondering if he was really even looking. And as he listened to others talk, not about the traumas they'd endured but the struggles that came after, he wished that he could do the same.

It wasn't that he didn't want to talk about his experience, but that he couldn't. Every time he thought he was ready to say something, his throat would close up so that he couldn't even speak.

Tonight, after Doug Holland—who'd survived friendly-fire in Syria—finished talking about his ongoing struggle with anger management, Jake decided it was his turn. He was ready to open the gates and let the demons out.

*My name is Jake Kelly...*

The words were there, but they wouldn't come out.

Apparently he wasn't ready to open the gates after all—or maybe they were rusted shut.

*He'd enlisted because he wanted to serve and defend his country. To not just defeat the bad guys but seriously kick their asses and return home a bona fide hero.*

*By the time Jake was halfway through his first tour, he was no longer concerned about being hailed a hero—he just wanted to make it home alive.*

*He was proud to wear the uniform. To be a Marine like his dad and his brother. But life in a war zone was a special kind of hell, particularly when the bad guys weren't readily identifiable. The enemy was nowhere and everywhere, and if a man let his guard down for half a second, he could end up dead...*

*Ask Jonesy, the radio operator who'd gone outside the wire to retrieve an errant football. Except that no one could ask Jonesy anything anymore, because he'd been taken out by sniper fire.*

*Jake's recon team had a new radio operator now. Corporal Anderson Walker was a third-generation Marine, earning him the nickname Trey. He didn't play football and he sure as hell didn't venture out-*

*side the wire without a combat helmet and body armor.*

*But he was a good man.*

*All the men on his recon team were good men.*

Molly nudged his shoulder, waking him before the memory-slash-dream could turn into something darker.

He drew in a deep breath and pushed himself up in bed.

"You want to go for a walk?" he asked.

She waited patiently while he pulled on some clothes.

The night was dark, the sky full of stars, the moon a crescent of silver. The stillness of the countryside had taken some getting used to after living back in San Diego for the past few years. Just as he knew the faster pace of San Diego would take some getting used to after living in Haven for several months.

*If* he went back to San Diego.

He frowned at that thought.

Of course he was going back. He never intended to stay in Haven permanently—just until he got his life on track, however long that might be.

Later that day, Jake was again in the converted barn, taking inventory of the equipment and supplies and wondering what the heck he was going to do with everything, when Molly barked and left her usual post by the open doors. There weren't many things that drew her from his side, unless they were rabbits, squirrels or Ashley and Rey. So he wasn't surprised when his young neighbor stepped inside the workshop.

"What's going on with you and Sky?" she asked without preamble.

"What makes you think there's anything going on?"

"I'm very intuitive," she said.

"Isn't that just a fancy word for nosey?"

"I've been called that a few times, too," she admitted. "But most people cut me some slack because I didn't have a father for the first twelve years of my life."

"Lots of kids grow up in single-parent homes. How is that an excuse to butt into other people's business?"

"In this case, one of those other people is my sister," Ashley pointed out. "So that kinda makes it my business."

"I don't think Sky would agree with you on that."

"Probably not," the kid acknowledged. "But I can't help but worry about her."

"Why's that?"

"Because she's always so busy taking care of other people that she sometimes forgets to take care of herself."

"Maybe you are intuitive," he noted. "But that doesn't mean you're not nosey."

"I saw her Jeep in your driveway when my mom brought me home from Chloe's the other night."

"And?"

"And then she didn't come home until three o'clock in the morning," Ashley said.

Though he'd teased Sky about having a curfew, he hadn't realized she'd stayed so late—or that she apparently had reason to be concerned about the example she was setting for her sister.

And if he no longer rushed Sky out the door as soon as they finished making love, she seemed to accept that he wasn't yet ready to let her stay overnight. That he wasn't yet ready to let her know all his demons. That his freak out at the restaurant was only the tip of the iceberg.

"But you don't know for certain that she didn't go somewhere else between the time that you saw her Jeep in my driveway and when she got home," Jake pointed out.

"No," she acknowledged. "But she was smiling when she came up the stairs, and she's not usually in a good mood when she comes home after dealing with some kind of crisis."

He was pleased by this confirmation that Sky had left his bed obviously satisfied, but it was the latter part of Ashley's comment that prompted him to ask, "Does she ever talk to you about those crises?"

Ashley immediately shook her head. "She would never violate a client's confidentiality. But I know that Mrs. Morningstar's boyfriend had naked pictures of Jodie because Jodie is Chloe's sister and Chloe's my best friend."

"How old is Jodie?" he wondered.

"Sixteen."

"And she let her mom's boyfriend take naked pictures of her?" His stomach roiled at the thought.

"Oh, no," Ashley was quick to assure him. "She didn't know he'd put a nanny cam in one of her teddy bears."

"I hope he's in prison now."

She nodded. "In Minnesota. He was extra—" She wrinkled her nose, as if thinking hard to remember the word.

"Extradited?" he guessed.

"That's it," she confirmed.

Jake had known that Sky had to deal with some weighty issues as both a youth counselor and volunteer at the women's shelter, but he suspected the situation Ashley was talking about had hit particularly close to home for her because of her sister's connection to the family. Of course, having lived her whole life in Haven, Sky probably dealt with personal connections more often than not.

"So what are you doing in here?" Ashley asked, clearly ready to move on to another topic of conversation.

"Not a whole helluva lot of anything at the moment," he told her.

She made her way around the room, examining the tools and materials.

"Don't touch anything," he cautioned, as she reached toward the miter gauge of a table saw. "I don't want to have to mop up the blood if you chop off a body part."

She immediate snatched her hand away. "Eww."

He held back a smile.

"What is all this stuff?" she asked.

"Mostly tools for making furniture," he told her.

"Is that what you do?"

He shook his head. "No. My uncle was the carpenter."

"I know. He made the table and chairs in our dining room, and the fancy cabinet where my mom keeps her best dishes."

"He made a lot of stuff for other people," Jake said.

Good, quality furniture that would last for generations, and yet a lot of the furnishings in his own home looked like garage sale markdowns. Of course, good furniture cost money, which was in short supply for Ross and Anna Ferguson. So while his uncle had been capable of making heirloom pieces, he couldn't afford to keep them.

"What's this?" Ashley asked, pointing to a tool on one of the workbenches.

"That's a pocket hole jig."

"What does it do?"

"It helps you drill pocket holes so that screws can be inserted at an angle, along the grain of the wood rather than through it. It makes the joint stronger and more stable."

He perched on the edge of a sawhorse, watching as she made her way around the room, pretending to be interested in items whose names and purposes eluded her.

"What are you really doing here, Ashley?" he asked her.

"I'm bored," she admitted.

"Why don't you go hang out at the mall?"

"Haven doesn't have a mall. And I don't have a driver's license, which means I'm stuck out here in the middle of nowhere with nothing to do and no one to talk to."

"Some of us enjoy being in the middle of nowhere *with no one to talk to*," he said, deliberately emphasizing the last part.

She didn't take the hint.

"Maybe you could show me how to make something," she suggested.

"I'm not sure I remember how half these tools work," he told her.

"Oh," she said, sounding disappointed.

"But maybe we could spend some time teaching Rey to drop the ball after she fetches it," he suggested.

The girl immediately brightened. "Okay. But I should warn you, she's not a very quick learner."

More than an hour later, after Ashley and Rey had gone, Jake returned to the workshop and picked up a board from the top of the stack. Though he had forgotten most of what his uncle had taught him so many years before, he had an idea in his mind and nothing else to do at the moment.

Ross had enjoyed working with reclaimed wood. He said the old weathered boards reminded him of himself: one part of his life—his struggles as a cattle rancher—finished and another just beginning. The nicks and scars in the wood were proof of its experience and ensured the finished product would have unique character.

Remembering his uncle's words now, Jake realized that the same analogy could be applied to his own life.

What he'd been, the career he'd had, was no more.

If he wanted to move forward, he needed to reinvent himself.

And maybe he could start right here.

## Chapter Twelve

Sky just wanted to go home.

It had been a really crappy day, and now she wanted nothing more than to crawl into bed and pull the covers over her head until morning.

Or maybe next week.

She didn't know what impulse made her turn into Jake's driveway before she reached the Circle G. In fact, she was about to shift into reverse to pull out again when Molly came around from the back of the house, her tail wagging so happily that Sky couldn't bear to disappoint the dog by leaving again without at least saying hi.

So she parked, climbed out of her Jeep and crouched to greet the Lab.

"Hey," Jake said, his lips curving into an easy

smile when he saw her. "I wasn't expecting to see you tonight."

She straightened up, suddenly uncertain again. "Is it okay that I stopped by?"

"Anytime," he replied without hesitation.

Inexplicably, her eyes filled with tears.

"Hey," he said again, tipping her chin up. "What's going on?"

"I just had a really crappy day," she confided.

"You want to talk about it?"

She shook her head. "Could you just—never mind," she decided, already turning back toward her car. "This was a bad idea. I shouldn't have come here. I don't know what I was thinking."

He caught her hand before she could find the handle. "Maybe you were thinking that you needed a friend," he suggested.

"Are we friends, Jake?"

"At the very least," he assured her. "And maybe working toward something more."

She managed a smile, though it wobbled at the edges.

"You want to come in for a cup of coffee?" he invited.

"Yeah, that sounds good, thanks."

Sky sat at the table while Jake moved around the kitchen, filling the reservoir with water, measuring grounds into the filter.

"How about food?" he asked.

"What?"

"Did you have dinner, Sky?"

"Oh." She shook her head. "No."

"I could heat up some leftover pasta for you."

"Thanks, but I'm not hungry."

He retrieved two mugs from the cupboard.

"Want to tell me about your day?"

"I want to, but I can't," she said.

"So what can I do?" he asked.

"Nothing," she said.

"Let's try something anyway," he suggested, tugging on her hands to draw her out of the chair.

She wasn't really in the mood for sex, but maybe that was why she'd come here. Maybe, subconsciously, she'd known that getting naked and sweaty with Jake would push everything else out of her mind—at least for a while.

But instead of starting to unbutton her blouse or even lowering his head to kiss her, he simply put his arms around her and held her close so that she could hear his heart beating, steady and strong, beneath her cheek.

And it was that gesture—the simplicity and sweetness of it—that broke the barrier and the tears that she'd mostly managed to hold in check could be held back no longer. She cried and cried, until there were no tears left, and all the while, Jake continued to hold her.

"I'm sorry," she said, when she finally managed to pull herself together.

"There's no reason to be."

"I soaked your shirt."

He glanced down at the damp fabric. "It needed to be washed anyway."

She tried to smile, but now that the storm of emotion had passed, her head was pounding.

"Do you have any Tylenol?"

"Headache?" he guessed.

She nodded. "I always get one when I cry too much."

"How often is that?"

"Not very," she assured him. "I'm usually pretty good at holding it together, but today was just…" She left the sentence unfinished, but he got the message.

He retrieved a bottle of pills from the cabinet and poured her a glass of water.

"Thanks."

"Why don't you go to my room and lie down?" he suggested, after she'd downed the pills.

The prospect of falling into bed right now was almost too tempting. "Because I should get home."

"You're always looking after everyone else," he said. "Why don't you let someone else take care of you for a little while?"

"You already have," she said. "And I'm grateful."

"You shouldn't get behind the wheel with your head hurting. And you'll feel better after a quick nap."

"Are you sure you don't mind?"

He responded by turning her toward the exit from the kitchen. "Go."

So she went.

Molly followed, then jumped up onto the bed to stretch out beside her.

"I'm going to assume you're allowed up here because I don't want to send you away," Sky said.

The dog settled in, and Sky fell asleep on top of the covers and stayed that way until morning.

Whey Sky woke up, it took her a moment to orient herself to her surroundings and realize where she was.

Jake's bedroom.

She reached over to touch the other pillow, but there was no evidence that he'd been there with her. There were, however, more than a few yellow hairs visible on her pant leg, confirming that Molly had snuggled with her for a while.

She ducked into the bathroom to splash some water on her face, wipe away the smears of mascara under her eyes with a tissue and rinse with the mouthwash on the counter. Then she made her way to the kitchen, where Jake was measuring coffee grounds into a filter.

"Déjà vu," she said.

He hit the button to start the machine brewing, then turned to greet her with a smile. "Good morning."

"When I stopped by last night, I didn't plan to crash," she told him.

"It wasn't a problem."

"Still, you should have woken me up and sent me home."

"I liked watching you sleep in my bed."

"You watched me sleep?"

"Not all night," he assured her. "But I did check on you a few times. Though I needn't have bothered, because Molly stuck pretty close to your side the whole time."

Sky lifted a hand and ruffled the dog's fur, hoping to convey both her affection and appreciation.

"Where did you sleep?" she asked Jake.

"On the sofa."

"That couldn't have been very comfortable," she said, trying to imagine his six-foot frame folded onto a five-foot couch.

His smile was wry. "I've slept in a lot worse places."

"Oh. Right." Afghanistan and Iraq, she remembered now. And possibly other countries that he hadn't mentioned. "In that case, I won't feel too guilty about stealing your bed."

"You shouldn't feel guilty at all. If I didn't want you here, I wouldn't have asked you to stay."

"As I recall, you invited me to stay for a nap."

"And didn't you nap?"

She chuckled. "Sure, we'll go with that."

He set a frying pan on top of the stove and drizzled some oil in it. "I've got bread today, but I'm short on eggs," he told her. "French toast okay?"

"Are you offering to cook for me again?"

"You have to fuel up," he said. "It's a game day and breakfast is supposedly the most important meal."

"It *is* a game day," she said. "But I didn't expect you to remember that."

"I not only remembered, I stopped by the park last week to watch a few innings," he said, as he scrambled the eggs he'd cracked.

"I thought I caught a glimpse of you and Molly by the bleachers at Diamond Two."

"That was us," he confirmed.

"Why didn't you come to the dugout to say hi?"

He shrugged as he dipped a slice of bread into the egg mixture. "You mentioned it was mostly parents or spouses who come out to the games."

"And we don't have that kind of relationship," she said, echoing the words she'd spoken once before. Then she followed up with the question he'd asked her: "So what kind of relationship do we have?"

"I thought we established yesterday that we were friends—and maybe more."

Since he was busy at the stove, she retrieved two mugs from the cupboard and filled them from the coffeepot. "Are you going to come out to the game today?" she asked him.

"I might stop by for a few innings."

"It's a long way into town for just a few innings," she pointed out.

"But totally worth it to see you in those snug-fitting pants," he assured her.

"Maybe I could come over later tonight and you could see me out of them," she suggested.

"Even better."

\* \* \*

Not long after Sky had gone, Ashley and Rey showed up again.

"I didn't expect to see you today," Jake said.

"I wanted to say thanks for texting me last night to let me know that Sky was crashing here."

"I didn't want you to worry—or wait up all night waiting for her to come home."

"I don't know that I would have stayed up *all* night, but I might have worried," she allowed.

"And you did say thanks when you replied to my message," he pointed out.

"I also wanted Rey to get some exercise because she has to be on a leash when we're at the ballpark."

"Right, it's a game day today, isn't it?" he said, as if he didn't already know.

Ashley nodded. "Are you gonna come?"

"Maybe. I've started something in the workshop, so we'll have to see what progress I make."

"I thought you said you weren't a carpenter."

"I'm not. I'm just messing around."

"Are you in the military?" she asked him.

"Not anymore."

"What branch were you in?"

"Marines."

"Once a Marine, always a Marine."

He looked up, both surprised and amused by her response.

"My mom's a big fan of NCIS, and I watch it with her sometimes," she told him.

"I thought kids your age only watched YouTube videos," he remarked.

"I'm not a kid," she said.

"Right. Sorry."

"Why aren't you in the military anymore? Is it because of your PTSD?" she guessed.

"You really do just blurt out whatever's on your mind, don't you?"

She shrugged. "I heard it mentioned when my mom and Sky were talking the other day."

His scowl deepened.

"Sky didn't say that you had PTSD," Ashley hastened to explain. "In fact, she argued that my mom shouldn't speculate about the condition of a man she's never even met, but my mom worries that Sky isn't seeing the situation clearly because of her feelings for you."

"Did you take notes while you were eavesdropping on their conversation?"

"My teachers say I pay close attention to detail."

But Jake could tell it was more than that, and he suspected the girl was worried about the conflict between her mother and half sister. That maybe, despite her outward bravado, she wasn't entirely confident of her place in the world—or even within her new family.

"And I thought you'd be more interested in Sky's response than my listening skills."

"I'm not going to ask what your sister said," he assured her.

Ashley smiled like a cat with a mouthful of feathers. "But you want to know, don't you?"

Yeah, he wanted to know, but he wasn't going to ask—not without knowing for sure that he was prepared to hear the answer.

Prospect Park did double duty as a neighborhood park, complete with swings, seesaws and a climbing structure, and a sports facility, with soccer pitches, baseball diamonds, basketball courts and even a designated area for lawn bowling. In the ballpark area, there were sets of stadium seats behind each of the home and visitor dugouts—if a players' bench behind a length of chain link fence could be called a dugout—and a small concrete-block building with food services at the front and restroom facilities at the back.

The concession offerings were limited to hot dogs, nachos, peanuts, popcorn, candy bars and hot and cold drinks, but there were a handful of picnic tables nearby and several were occupied when Jake arrived.

As he surveyed the scene, he noted that there weren't a lot of empty seats on the bleachers, and most of the spectators proudly displayed their team loyalty with baseball caps or T-shirts that matched the logos of one team or the other. Duke's Diggers wore grey pants with dark blue T-shirts emblazoned with a cartoon depiction of a grizzled prospector holding a pickax in one hand and a gold nugget in the other. The opposing team—the Haven Hawks, sponsored by Jo's—was in red and white.

Jake spotted Ashley, seated in a folding lawn chair behind the backstop, the scorebook in her lap. Rey's leash was tied to the leg of her chair, and the pup was curled up on the grass beside her.

Molly must have spotted them at the same time, because she tensed at his side, eager to take off and visit her friend as soon as he gave her the okay.

Jake didn't give the okay.

"Sorry, girl," he said instead. "Not today."

It was the same thing he'd said to her the last time they were at the park.

And the time before that.

But they stayed until the end of the game today, when the Diggers ran off the field after making the final out, whooping and hollering in celebration of their victory. Sky smiled as one of her teammates tugged on the ponytail threaded through the hole in the back of her hat.

Glad to know that she was having a much better day than the one before, he turned away. "Let's go home, Molly."

Sky glanced around, a seemingly casual survey, as the spectators began to gather up their stadium cushions and concession garbage at the end of the game. She didn't see Jake anywhere, although she'd been certain she'd caught a glimpse of him earlier. And if she was disappointed that he hadn't stuck around, she was pleased to know that he'd been there.

"You had a successful day at the bat," Caleb noted as she packed her bat and glove into her equipment bag.

"Thanks." She tugged on the zipper.

"Two for three with four RBIs," he continued.

"Are you the official league statistician now?" Sky asked.

"Nah. But I was thinking that you've earned yourself a beer," he said. "You coming to Diggers'?"

"Not today."

"Why not?"

"Because I want to get home and shower," she said. "Plus, I promised to drop Ashley off at Chloe's." She had some reservations about her little sister hanging out at Chloe's house since the incident with Leon Franks and learning that Chloe had a taste for vodka coolers, but she understood the importance of the friendship to both girls. More important, she trusted that Ashley had a good head on her shoulders and wouldn't hesitate to reach out if she found herself in a situation that was at all uncomfortable for her.

"No other plans?" he prompted.

"What do you really want to know, Caleb?"

"If there's any truth to the rumors I've heard about you being involved with Ross Ferguson's nephew."

"His name is Jake Kelly," she said. "And since when do you pay any attention to gossip?"

"Since it comes from a trustworthy source."

Sky frowned. "What's your trustworthy source?"

"Our sister."

"Kate?" Sky didn't believe it. There was no way her by-the-book attorney sister would divulge any information that had been shared with her in confidence, even if in the comfort of her own home over coffee and donuts.

Caleb shook his head. "Sorry, I should have said our *little* sister."

"Ashley," she realized.

He nodded. "She said she saw your car in his driveway the other night and then heard you sneaking into the house at three a.m."

"She should have been sleeping at three a.m."

"So it's true?" he asked.

"I'm twenty-five years old," she reminded him. "I don't have to sneak anywhere."

"So it's true," he decided.

"What it is, is none of your business."

"I'm your brother—"

"My brother not my keeper," she interjected.

"I'm worried about you, Sky."

"You don't need to be."

"It's hardly a secret that you have a lousy track record with men," Caleb said, not unkindly.

"No, it's not," she acknowledged. "But thanks for the reminder, anyway."

Her brother sighed. "Come on, Sky. Don't be mad."

"I'm not mad."

"I just don't want to see you get hurt again, and no one really seems to know much about this guy."

"Jake," she said again. "And I know him."

"Do you?" he challenged.

Before Sky could respond to that, Ashley came over to join them. "Are we going to go sometime today? Chloe's texted me five times in the last five minutes."

"We're going right now," Sky promised, shouldering her bag and starting toward the parking lot.

Caleb fell into step beside her. "Just…be careful," he urged.

"I always am." She unlocked the car and Ashley climbed into the back seat with her dog.

"I love you, sis."

And with those words, Sky's irritation melted. Because she knew they were true. She might not appreciate Caleb's interference in her personal life, but she knew that his concern was motivated by affection.

"I love you, too, PITA," she said, using the acronym for *pain in the ass*.

He grinned, relieved to know that he was forgiven.

Sky tossed her bag into the back of her SUV and climbed behind the wheel.

As she drove toward Chloe's house, she couldn't help but reflect on her brother's remarks. Because Caleb was right. She did have a lousy track record with men.

Everyone that she'd loved—or thought she'd been in love with—had left her.

Maybe she shouldn't include Peter Jarrett on that list, because it was probably inevitable that their relationship wouldn't have survived them going to different colleges in different states. But he'd promised her that they'd make it work because he loved her. And she'd wanted to believe him because she loved him, too. Then he'd dumped her before Thanksgiving that first year.

She'd held off falling in love again until her third year at UNLV. But Xavier Leroux had been in his final year, and when he graduated, he moved on to bigger and better things—and another woman.

Archie Collins had been one of her faculty advisors when she was working on her master's thesis—an ill-advised relationship that had probably lasted longer than it should have. But right or wrong, she'd loved him, too. And although technically she'd left him when she moved back to Haven, the end result was the same.

In the end, she was alone.

And she knew that if she fell for Jake, he'd be no different.

He'd already told her that he didn't intend to stay in Haven for the long-term. It was just a temporary stop—a convenient place for him to get his life together.

Staying in this small town had never been part of his future plans.

Except that he didn't really have a plan.

So maybe he would change his mind. Maybe, if he could find the peace here that had so far eluded him everywhere else, he would stay in Haven.

Maybe he'd stay with her.

## *Chapter Thirteen*

Sky didn't make it back to Jake's house later that night.

After driving Ashley to Chloe's house, she took Rey back to the Circle G and left the pup in the care of her father and stepmother so that she could shower off the dirt and grime from the game. She'd just stepped out of the enclosure and wrapped herself in a towel when her cell phone chimed with a text message.

An hour later, Sky was back in town, sitting across from Jenny Taft at the kitchen table in her mother's house.

"I wasn't sure you'd come," the former cheerleader said, sounding both surprised and relieved. "I wasn't very nice the last time I saw you."

"As I recall, you weren't having a very good day."

The other woman managed a smile, then immediately lifted a hand to cover her mouth—and hide the tooth that hadn't been chipped the last time they'd talked.

"So why did you want to see me?" Sky asked.

"When you came to the clinic, you said that there were options…for people in…" She seemed to struggle to say it, to acknowledge the truth.

Sky waited, not wanting to put words in Jenny's mouth.

"Abusive relationships," the other woman finally continued.

"There are always options," Sky assured her.

"He wasn't always…mean," Jenny said. "In the beginning, Darren was really sweet. Even now, sometimes he brings me flowers, or just kisses me softly, and I know he loves me." She dropped her gaze to her hands, folded neatly in her lap. "But those times aren't very often anymore. Not compared to the times that he's mean."

"Can you give me examples of what he does when he's mean?" Sky asked gently.

"He yells. A lot. Almost all the time now." She swallowed. "I know he's unhappy. When we were in high school, he thought for sure he was going to get a football scholarship, but that never came through and he had to go work in the mines, just like his father."

"It's always hard to let go of a dream," Sky acknowledged. "But I bet you had dreams, too, didn't you, Jenny?"

"Not big ones."

"Tell me about them," she urged.

"There was a time that I wanted to be a teacher," she confided. "I always thought it would be nice to have a decent job, go on vacation once a year, maybe to Disneyland with the kids—" her smile was wistful "—after we had kids."

"And now?" Sky prompted.

"Now I know I won't ever have any of those things with Darren."

"Because he yells?"

Jenny nodded. "And sometimes…" She looked at Sky now, her expression stricken. "Sometimes he hits me."

Sky knew the admission wasn't just a crucial first step in moving forward for victims of abuse, but often the hardest one to take. And she credited Jenny's mother for helping her to take that step now.

"I don't want to be hit anymore," Jenny said, her eyes filling with tears.

Sky waited, sensing there was more the other woman wanted to tell her. After another minute, Jenny continued.

"I was pregnant once…about six months ago." She swiped at the tears that spilled onto her cheeks. "I lost the baby. It wasn't Darren's fault—and I'm not making excuses this time. Even the doctor said that sometimes these things just happen."

Sky nodded.

"I cried for a long time afterward. I cried and cried, and Darren got mad at me for mourning a baby that was hardly the size of a pea when I lost it. And I was sad that I'd lost the baby, but I think I was relieved, too. Because I knew that if I had Darren's baby, I'd never get away from him.

"So I went to my doctor and I asked to go back on birth control pills." She wiped away more tears. "The day that you came to see me at the clinic…that was the day he found my pills. He was so mad. I don't think he wanted a baby any more than I did at that point, but he was mad that I'd made a decision about birth control without consulting him."

"What did he do?"

She closed her eyes. "He grabbed me by the hair and shoved me against the wall. He punched me. And he kicked me."

"Are you telling me now that you didn't fall down the stairs that day?" Sky asked.

Jenny shook her head. "I didn't fall down the stairs," she confirmed. "He pushed me."

Though Sky wouldn't have said that she and Jake had settled into any kind of a routine, she was nonetheless surprised when he walked into the bar on Friday night.

"Sam Adams?" she asked, already reaching for a glass.

Jake shook his head. "Give me a shot of Jack Daniels."

Sky set the mug back on the shelf. "Straight up or on the rocks?"

"Straight up."

She reached for a glass and poured a shot of whiskey.

"What's the occasion?" she asked, as she set the drink in front of him.

Jake's only response was to lift the glass to his lips and toss back the alcohol.

"Another one," he said, pushing the empty glass toward her.

Sky frowned but acquiesced to his request. "Are you going to tell me what's going on with you?"

"I'm not here for company or conversation," he said, echoing the words he'd spoken ten weeks earlier.

"That's obvious," she noted dryly. "But I thought we were already friends."

He lifted his gaze to hers then. "You might want to reconsider. Most of my friends don't fare too well."

And there, she knew, was the heart of the story he had yet to tell her. Because the bits and pieces he'd shared about his life before coming to Haven were nothing more than that. But she hadn't pushed, suspecting that if she did, he'd just withdraw further. Instead, she'd waited, confident that he would open up when he was ready.

She hadn't anticipated that he might be ready on a Friday night when she was working in a packed bar. So she poured and mixed, filling orders and keeping an eye on Jake as best she could.

"Another one," he said, nudging the glass toward her again.

She tipped the bottle over the glass. "That's a lot

of whiskey for a guy who usually limits himself to a single draft beer," she remarked.

He tossed back the third shot.

She finished an order for Courtney, then called out to Rowan, who was working the other end of the bar. "Can you hold down the fort for two minutes?"

Her bartending partner nodded as he mixed drinks. "A quick two minutes," he agreed. "That looks like a bachelorette party just coming in."

Sky glanced toward the door and noted the group of women decked out in sparkling tiaras and satin sashes identifying them as bridesmaid, maid of honor or bride.

"I have no doubt you can deflect amorous advances and mix cosmopolitans at the same time," she said lightly.

"Of course, I can," Rowan agreed with a wink. "But your two minutes are ticking."

She ducked away from the bar and into the kitchen, relieved to see that Duke was still there. The owner of Diggers' usually stopped by most nights to check on his business and chat with his customers—and sample whatever was on special from the kitchen that day.

"I'm glad I caught you," Sky said, as her boss carried his empty plate and cutlery to the sink. "I need a favor."

Jake didn't protest when Sky took his arm and guided him through the kitchen and out the back door of the restaurant. In fact, he didn't say anything at all until she opened the passenger door of her Jeep and nudged him in that direction.

"Where are we going?"

"I'm taking you home," she told him.

He shook his head. "I don't want to go home. I want another drink."

She held up the bottle of JD from the bar. "You can have another drink at home."

That seemed to satisfy Jake, as he got into the SUV without further protest.

Molly was, as always, happy to see her master return. And though she let Sky fuss over her, too, she stayed close to Jake's side. The dog might have flunked training, but there was no doubt that she was sensitive to Jake's moods and protective of him.

After walking through the door, Jake immediately went to the cupboard to retrieve two glasses, then reached for the bottle in Sky's hand.

"Don't pour one for me," she said. "Jack Daniels and I broke up a long time ago."

"I don't see much of him anymore, either," he said. "But we still get together once a year."

"Why tonight?"

"Why not?" he countered, and tossed back another mouthful of whiskey.

She moved past him and into the living room, because she sensed it was going to be a long night and preferred not to spend it on a hard chair in the kitchen.

Jake—and, of course, Molly—followed.

He set the bottle and glass on the coffee table before dropping onto the sofa. Frowning, he reached into his back pocket and pulled out his cell phone, then tossed it on the table, too.

"Are you going to tell me what's going on?" she asked.

"Why do you think something's going on? Can't a guy stop by the bar to have a few drinks without an interrogation?" he challenged.

"I'm not interrogating you," she denied, keeping her tone level. "I'm wondering why a man who usually doesn't drink anything more than a single pint of beer when he comes into the bar is suddenly knocking back shots of hard liquor."

Jake knocked back another before replying. "I used to drink a lot. Probably too much and for too long." He stared at the amber liquid in the bottle for a long moment, then shook his head, his expression bleak. "But no amount of alcohol could make me forget."

"How long has it been?" she asked gently.

"Since what?"

"I'm guessing today is the anniversary of whatever happened that led to the end of your military career."

"Not much gets past you, does it?"

"I'm not asking you to share anything you don't want to," she said, ignoring the bitterness in his tone. "I just want you to know that I'm here if you want to share."

"People always want to hear the war stories," he said, pouring another shot. "Like drivers slowing by the scene of a car wreck on the side of the road. There's a morbid fascination…a need to know what went wrong…and a sense of relief that it happened to someone else and not you.

"When they meet someone who's seen action, they want to know all the details of battles fought and won. It's like we're actors playing at war on a movie screen and not real people who wake up every morning wondering if it might be our last.

"And they don't seem to know—or maybe don't care—that most of us don't want to talk about it. Most of us just want all the noise in our heads to go away. Just for a day. Or even an hour." His tone was as anguished as his expression. "And then we feel guilty for wishing that we could forget. Because if we don't remember those who didn't make it back— if *I* don't remember my team—who will?"

"Can you tell me about them?" she asked.

He seemed surprised by her request. "You want me to tell you about my recon team?"

"Actually…can you start by telling me what a recon team is?"

"You don't know much about the military?" he guessed.

"I can give you chapter and verse on breeding cattle, but the divisions and ranks of the armed forces are a mystery to me."

"You learn fast when your boots are on the ground." He poured another drink. "But in answer to your question, Marine Division Recon are the reconnaissance assets of the MAGTAF. Marine Air-

Ground Task Force," he explained in response to her blank look.

She nodded, encouraging him to continue.

"It was our job to observe and report on enemy activity and anything else that might be significant to military operations, such as surveying routes, examining bridges and buildings, assessing LZs and DZs—landing zones and drop zones," he clarified before she could ask.

"How many soldiers are on a team?"

He shook his head. "On a USMC recon team, none. A soldier serves in the army."

"Okay, how many *Marines* are on a USMC recon team?"

"Usually six," he told her. "The team leader, assistant team leader, point man, radio operator, assistant radio operator and slack man."

"You were the team leader?" she guessed.

He saluted sharply. "Staff Sergeant Jake Robert Kelly at your service."

"And the rest of your team?"

"Sergeant Ken Baker was the assistant team leader and one of the toughest guys I've ever known—unless he was talking about his wife or any one of his three daughters, then he was a complete marshmallow. We called him Tex, because he was from El Paso and you could hear hints of his hometown in his voice.

"Our point man was Lance Corporal Calvin Moore, otherwise known as Big Red because he stood six-feet-five-inches tall with a mop of ginger hair. No one was surprised to learn that he'd played on the basketball team in high school, but he'd also played trumpet in the marching band and liked to sing in the shower. Especially AC/DC tunes," Jake said, and smiled a little at the memory.

"Our radio operator was Corporal Anderson Walker. When Tex found out that he was a third generation Marine, he dubbed the RO Trey. Trey was a hardcore video gamer who could kick anyone's ass at *Call of Duty*, but he hated having to fire a real weapon. He didn't hesitate, when the need arose, but he never found any pleasure in it."

It wasn't the names and roles he recited but the personal details that made Sky realize these men had been more than just Marines under Jake's command. They'd been his brothers in arms, his family. And her heart ached for him, because she'd guessed what was coming.

"Corporal Mario Lopez was our ARO," he continued, "nicknamed Merlin because he was nothing less than a wizard when it came to fixing problems with the communications equipment. And there were frequently problems with the communications equipment. He was a quiet guy, totally smitten with his high school sweetheart and counting the days until he could marry her when he got back home.

"And then there was Lance Corporal Brian Lucey, our slack man. He was another one from Texas—San Antonio, I think—but because the name Tex was already taken, he got Ditto. He enlisted as soon as he turned eighteen, desperate to get away from his abusive father. Or maybe he joined the Marine Corps to toughen him up so he could hit back. He had such a chip on his shoulder in the beginning, but he quickly became an integral part of the team."

"How many of them did you lose?" she asked gently.

"Four. Three almost right away, because of their proximity to the blast. Merlin somehow held on for almost seventy-two hours, but he never regained consciousness. Trey was the only other survivor, but he lost the use of both of his legs. I was the lucky one," he said, his tone bleak.

"Merlin recognized Salah-al-din Hajjar walking down the street as we made our way through a remote village near Dohuk. He'd worked with us as an interpreter on an earlier mission and we wanted to get his take on some recent intel, so me and Trey jumped out of the truck to flag him down, just before the RPG hit.

"The force of the blast threw us about twenty feet—or so I was told. I don't remember any of it. And the not knowing is almost as bad...or maybe even worse...than remembering."

She'd seen the ink on his upper arm, of course, and realized it was a list of names:

Sgt Ken Baker.

Cpl Mario Lopez.

LCpl Calvin Moore.

LCpl Brian Lucey.

Now she understood why.

"Theirs are the names tattooed on your arm," she said.

He nodded. "I wasn't there for the funeral. I'd been airlifted back to the US because of the head trauma, and I wanted—needed—in some way, to honor them. To ensure that I don't ever forget—even if I can't remember what happened.

"The doctors say it's not unusual after a brain injury, but I can't help thinking that if I could only remember, there might have been something I could have done …something that might have ensured they all came home."

"You can't hold yourself responsible for what happened," she told him.

"But I am responsible. It was *my* team. They were *my* men." He scrubbed his hands over his face to wipe away the tears that had spilled onto his cheeks. "Tex had a wife and three kids. Merlin was planning to get married. They were good men. They didn't deserve to die. And there was no reason for me to live, except that I jumped out of the truck to try to catch up with Hajjar."

She knew there were no words that could possibly make him feel any better. Sure, she could tell him that it wasn't his fault, but no doubt he'd already been told the same thing by countless people before her. It didn't matter that it was probably even true. The only thing that mattered was the grief and the guilt that obviously weighed heavy in his heart.

"We want to believe that we'd more easily accept the tragic events that happen if only we could understand why," she said. "As if there could possibly be some reason or higher purpose that would help it all make sense. But even if that were true, it doesn't really change anything. Knowing the how or why certainly can't bring back the lives of those we've lost."

He nodded and lifted his glass to his lips, then put it down again to look at her more closely. "Who did you lose?"

"My mom," she confided.

"How?"

"She died in a riding accident when I was seven. I'm not trying to equate her death with the loss of your men," she hastened to assure him. "I only wanted you to know that I understand how the what-ifs can haunt you."

"You were seven—what could you have done any differently?" he wondered.

"Had oatmeal for breakfast."

He looked at the nearly empty bottle of JD. "Either I've had too much of this or not enough, because that didn't make any sense to me."

"My mom loved to ride," Sky explained. "Every morning after we'd all had breakfast, she'd saddle up Honey and go for a ride.

"The morning of the accident, I overslept a little, and everyone else had finished eating by the time I sat at the table. She had a bowl of oatmeal waiting for me, but I wanted toast with Grandma's homemade strawberry jam."

*"Make your own stupid toast," Katelyn had said. Because Mom had invited Katelyn to go riding*

*with her that morning, and Sky's sister was eager to get started.*

*"I want Mom to make it," she'd insisted.*

"Maybe if I hadn't insisted on having toast that morning, my mom would have started out on her ride five minutes earlier. And maybe when she got to the ridge, whatever spooked her horse wouldn't have been there yet and she wouldn't have fallen. She wouldn't have died."

And Kate wouldn't have had to watch it all unfold.

"It's hard not to wonder," Jake acknowledged.

She nodded, because she knew Kate still wondered, too. If she'd called 9-1-1 using their mom's cell phone instead of riding back to the house for help, could the paramedics have got there in time to save her?

Jake offered his glass to Sky. "Are you sure you don't want some of this?"

"I'm sure," she said, taking the now-empty bottle from his other hand.

He'd undoubtedly overindulged and would pay the price tomorrow, but he hadn't drunk as much as he probably thought because the bottle she'd brought from the bar had been more than half empty before she'd even poured his first shot at Diggers'. She returned from the kitchen, only a couple of minutes later, with a glass of water and the bottle of Tylenol to find Jake asleep on the sofa.

Sky didn't worry about trying to get him to the bedroom. As he'd pointed out to her once before, he'd slept in worse places than the sofa in his living room.

She did worry about the nightmares he'd mentioned and the likelihood that they would plague him tonight. But as reluctant as she was to leave him alone to battle those demons, she sensed that he wouldn't want her to stay. Maybe they were gradually working their way toward a real relationship, and maybe they'd taken a few steps closer tonight, but they weren't quite there yet.

So she put the glass and the pills on the end table, plugged his phone into the charging cable there, and gave the Lab a scratch behind her ears.

"Take care of him, Molly."

The dog lifted her head, as if to acknowledge the request, but she didn't move from Jake's side.

So Sky pulled a blanket up over both of them and headed back to her own home. Once there, she sat outside on the porch steps for a while, leaning against a support post to look up at the stars and pray to the heavens that her wounded warrior would find peace.

## Chapter Fourteen

Jake felt the press of something cold and wet against his cheek. "Go away," he muttered.

Molly nudged him again.

He sighed wearily. "I really need to put in a doggy door."

And while that was probably a good plan for the future, the idea was absolutely no help to him now.

Molly whined.

He pushed himself into a seated position and opened bleary eyes just as his phone began to blast *Reveille*—the ringtone he'd assigned to his brother's number. It had seemed funny at the time. This morning, not so much.

He grabbed for the phone—not because he wanted to talk to Luke so much as he wanted the damn music to stop.

"'Lo," he said, wondering if the hoarse syllable was his own voice. His mouth felt as if it was stuffed with cotton, his head felt as if jackhammers were trying to break through his skull and his whole body ached.

"Jake?"

He cleared his throat. "Yeah."

He kicked off the blanket that was tangled around his legs and rose to his feet. Molly raced to the door.

"I've been going out of my mind with worry. Why didn't you return my calls?"

"You called?" He opened the door, squinting against the bright morning sun as the dog streaked past him.

"I left four, maybe five, voicemail messages yesterday," Luke said impatiently.

"I didn't get any—oh." As the fog that surrounded his brain began to clear, memories of the night before slowly came into focus. "The battery on my cell phone died when I was out."

"You sound like hell," his brother said bluntly. "Are you drunk?"

"Nah." He measured kibble into Molly's bowl, wincing as even the sound of the dry food dropping into the metal container hurt his head. "Just hung over."

His brother let out a heavy sigh. "I should have been with you yesterday. You shouldn't have been alone."

"I don't need a babysitter. And... I wasn't alone," he admitted.

"Getting up close and personal with Jack Daniels doesn't really count as having company."

"Ha ha," he said. But then, because he understood that his brother was sincerely worried, he added, "A real live person was with me last night, along with JD."

"Have you been making friends out there in the middle of Nowhere, Nevada?"

"I've gotten to know some people," he said vaguely, opening the door again to let Molly in. She raced over to her bowl, skidded to a stop and plopped her butt down, waiting for his signal.

He gestured a wave and she immediately dug in.

"Well, that's good then," Luke said, though his tone was dubious. "Any idea when you're coming home?"

"No."

"Benjamin's been asking about you."

"Me or Molly?"

The dog lifted her head up momentarily, then resumed eating.

"Well, the two of you are a package deal," Luke said.

Jake managed a chuckle. "Tell him I'll bring her for a visit soon."

"It's Dad's birthday next month. Why don't you come home then?"

"Because the last family get-together didn't end so well," he reminded his brother.

"That wasn't your fault," Luke said.

"No one else freaked out over the sound of fire-crackers."

"Maybe you just have faster reflexes than me and Dad."

"Yeah, that's it," Jake said dryly.

"Well, if you don't have any plans to come home in the near future, maybe I'll come out to see you," his brother suggested.

"That's really not necessary, Luke."

"I know it's not necessary, but I want to come."

"Why?" Jake asked, equal parts curious and wary.

"Because you're my brother and I haven't seen you in a long while."

"I'm fine," he said.

"You don't sound fine."

"I overindulged a little last night," Jake acknowledged. "It's something I do once a year."

"It's been three years."

"I know how long it's been," he snapped back.

"Of course, you do," Luke agreed. "I'm sorry."

He sighed. "No, I'm sorry. I'm hungover and short-tempered."

"How about the weekend after next?" his brother suggested.

"Would it matter if I said no?"

"Not likely."

After he'd disconnected the call, Jake wandered back to the living room and dropped down onto the sofa.

He noticed the glass of water on the side table then, and a bottle of Tylenol beside it.

Sky, of course. Always taking care of other people.

He wrestled with the childproof cap, swallowed a couple of pills, then stumbled to the kitchen again to put on a pot of coffee.

While the coffee was brewing, he let the hot water of the shower pound on his shoulders as memories of the previous evening slowly came together in his mind.

Mostly he remembered Sky. She'd been there and taken care of him. He'd bared his soul to her, sharing all of his deepest and darkest secrets. And he'd cried. And while she hadn't run screaming into the night, he had to wonder if—in the light of day—it would prove to be too much for her.

After he was showered and dressed and starting to feel at least a little bit better, he carried his cell phone with him into the kitchen. She hadn't called or texted yet, but he didn't want to miss it when she did.

*If* she did.

Molly was dancing by the door when he opened the cupboard for a mug to pour his first desperately needed cup of coffee. "You already went outside and I'm going to need a couple more hours and gallons of coffee before I even think about going for a *R-U-N*," he said, just as a soft knock sounded.

"You were telling me that we had company," he realized, as he opened the door to Sky.

"Did I knock too loudly?" she asked in lieu of a more traditional greeting. "I didn't want to make too much noise, in case your head was hurting this morning."

He stepped back to allow her entry. "In case?"

She winced in sympathy. "How bad's the hangover?"

"I've had worse."

"Maybe this will help." She handed him a travel mug.

"I've got coffee on in the kitchen."

"It's not coffee," she said. "It's the tried-and-true Gilmore secret hangover cure."

He looked wary. "What's in it?"

"It's a *secret* hangover cure," she said again.

He looked dubious as he lifted the lid to examine and sniff the contents. "It doesn't smell too bad," he allowed.

"Try it," she urged.

He took a tentative sip, then another.

She set a grocery bag on the counter, then picked up the mug of coffee he'd poured and lifted it to her lips.

"That was my coffee," he said.

"Coffee's a diuretic and you need to hydrate," she pointed out.

"Still taking care of me, huh?"

"Hangover Basics One-Oh-One."

"Thanks. And for everything you did last night, too."

"I didn't really do anything," she denied.

"You were here for me."

"I didn't want you to be alone. And the fact that you came into Diggers' instead of buying a bottle and bringing it back here suggested to me that you didn't really want to be alone, either," she said.

"I don't keep alcohol in the house," he confided, as she began to unpack the grocery bag. "What's all that?"

"I wasn't sure what you had in your fridge, so I brought a few things over to make breakfast—unless you've eaten already."

He shook his head and eyed the ingredients: eggs, ham, ricotta, red pepper, spinach.

"Are you going to make omelets?"

"A frittata."

He narrowed his gaze. "Isn't that just another word for quiche?"

"No, a quiche has a crust." She set a pan on the stove and began prepping the ingredients. "You don't have to give up your 'real man' card today."

"Didn't I forfeit that last night?"

"No." She met and held his gaze. "Real men aren't afraid to show emotion."

"Speaking of," he said, though it wasn't a very smooth segue, "my brother called this morning. He's planning to come to Haven for a visit."

"You don't sound happy about that," she noted.

"I'd be happy to see him if he didn't have an agenda," Jake told her.

"What's his agenda?" she asked curiously.

"To check up on me."

"That's not an agenda—it's the job of big brothers," she said, as she dumped the spinach and peppers into the pan. "When is he coming?"

"The weekend after next, apparently." He finished the secret hangover cure and grabbed another mug from the cupboard.

"Two more glasses of water before coffee."

"Anyone ever tell you that you're bossy?"

"All the time," she said unapologetically.

He reached for a glass and filled it with water. "*Anyway*, I was wondering if I could ask a favor."

"Of course," she replied without hesitation.

"Would you…when Luke is here…would you… pretend to be my girlfriend?"

*Pretend?*

It required a concerted effort for Sky to keep the smile on her face so that Jake wouldn't know how much his offhand request had both disappointed and hurt her. Because although they hadn't defined their relationship—beyond a vague "friends…and maybe working toward something more"—she'd started to think that hanging out and having off-the-charts sex together meant that she actually *was* his girlfriend, no pretending required.

Obviously that was her mistake.

She poured the egg-and-cheese mixture into the pan. "Why do you think you need a pretend girlfriend?"

"So he'll stop worrying that I'm isolated and alone in the middle of Nowhere, Nevada."

"He's your brother—why can't you just tell him the truth?"

"And what do you think the truth is?" Jake wondered.

"That you're making progress toward getting your life back on track," she said.

"Is that really how you see it?" he asked her.

"Of course it is. And I would think, if anyone could understand what you've been through, it would be your brother, who's spent fifteen years in the military," she pointed out.

"That's exactly why I can't tell him," he said.

"I don't understand," she admitted.

"Luke is doing what we were both supposed to do—but he's a success and... I'm a failure."

She immediately shook her head. "You're not a failure. You're a hero."

He scoffed at the notion. "My brother has a wife and three kids, and I'm afraid to even let you spend the night in my bed."

"You're just afraid that I'll steal the covers," she teased.

He managed a smile at that, but it quickly faded. "I'm broken, Sky."

"That happens sometimes when people have to endure too much," she acknowledged. "And then sometimes they need some help putting the pieces back together."

"What if the pieces won't fit back together?" he wondered aloud.

"They might not fit in quite the same way, but they're all part of the whole. Although, if you're really concerned, you might want to look into something more focused than a once-a-week meeting at the community center," she ventured. "There are residential PTSD treatment programs available at private facilities in Nevada and California and lots of other places."

"You've been doing research again," he guessed.

"I'm trying to help."

"I already told you how you can help when Luke comes to town."

Despite the pang of disappointment in her heart, she couldn't refuse his request—or resist the opportunity. "Okay, I'll pretend to be your girlfriend when your brother comes to visit *if* you agree to be my date for my brother's wedding next weekend." She made the offer hopeful that the outing would help Jake realize that though he'd always carry the scars of his former life, he'd already started to make a new one in Haven—with her.

"How many brothers do you have?" he asked.

"Two."

"Aren't they both married already?"

"They are," she confirmed. "But Caleb and Brielle eloped in Vegas eight years ago, with no one there to celebrate with them, so they're having a belated reception next Saturday."

He hesitated.

"I promise I won't leave your side for a single minute."

"You know I'm not good with crowds," he said. "I barely managed to stay at the bar the night the baseball team was there."

"But since then, you've actually been out to watch some of the games."

He didn't sit on the bleachers, with the other spectators, but she knew that his willingness to even venture into the park was a step in the right direction.

"That's just because I like the way you look in the uniform," he told her.

"Apparently you like the way I look in short skirts, too," she reminded him.

"Will you be wearing a short skirt to this wedding?"

"Is your willingness to accept the invitation contingent on the length of my hem?"

"Maybe." He grinned. "I do like your legs."

"And I did buy a new dress for the occasion when I was shopping with Ashley the other day, and the skirt falls to about here—" She touched her thigh, a couple of inches above her knee.

"Then my answer is yes," he said. "I just hope you don't regret asking."

*"How much longer are we gonna be stuck in this godforsaken dust bowl?" Tex asked.*

*"Nine weeks and six days," Merlin told him.*

*"But who's counting?" Jake asked dryly.*

*"Merlin's counting the days to his wedding." Ditto followed up the remark by humming a few bars of Mendelssohn's* Wedding March—*horribly off-key.*

*"More like his funeral," Big Red said.*

*Because ribbing one another was how they passed the time, and joking about death helped lighten the mood when they were living and working in hostile territory.*

*Jake tuned them out, mostly, and let his thoughts drift.*

*Nine weeks and six days.*

*That didn't seem so long now. Not after almost ten months had already passed.*

*He could understand why Merlin was eager to get home and celebrate with a wedding. They missed so much when they were gone. Not just important dates and special occasions, but everyday stuff, too.*

*Maybe he'd talk to Margot about setting a date for their wedding. They'd been together for less than six months before his first deployment, but even then he'd known that he wanted to spend his life with her. So when she'd hinted that a ring on her finger would reassure her that he loved her as much as she loved him, he hadn't hesitated to put one there.*

*She'd been happy enough with the ring that she hadn't pressed him to set a date. The subject did come up every once in a while, but their timelines were always vague... "sometime in the next couple of years" or "maybe next summer."*

*He knew he was lucky to have her. It wasn't easy for a woman to stick with a man who could be gone for months at a time, maybe even longer, and she always seemed happy enough to talk to him when he was able to call. She didn't nag at him or get all weepy like he'd heard other guys grumble that their girlfriends, fiancées, wives or lovers did. Margot was always proud and supportive, thrilled to be able to tell everyone she met that her fiancé was a Marine.*

*Maybe it was time to change that status to hus-*

*band and start the rest of their lives together, Jake mused.*

*Maybe—*

*He was flying through the air even before he heard the boom of the explosion.*

*Did his life flash in front of his eyes?*

*He didn't think so, though there had been flashes of moments and memories as he seemed to fall in slow motion—right up until he slammed into the ground.*

He woke up in a cold sweat, trembling from head to toe, his hip throbbing, his ribs burning. He scrubbed a hand down his side to reassure himself there was nothing broken, no blood spilling onto the packed earth.

*"Deep breaths. In and out through your mouth."*

He wasn't on the ground. He was in his bed.

He wasn't in Iraq. He was in Haven, Nevada.

*"Let the air fill your chest...hold it there...then slowly let it out again."*

Molly pressed closer to his side, her chin propped on his chest, her presence calming him as nothing else could.

He lifted a shaky hand to stroke it down her back.

*"Deep breaths. In and out through your mouth."*

He closed his eyes and concentrated on his breathing, though he knew he wouldn't get any more sleep that night.

Another Wednesday. Another meeting.

Tonight Bill Seward was telling the group about

his most recent communication with Lan Nguyen, a woman he'd known back in Vietnam and with whom he'd recently reconnected through social media. She'd invited him to come for a visit and Bill was intrigued by the idea of seeing her again, but he wasn't sure he was ready to face all the memories that a return to the country would inevitably dredge up.

The group wasn't much help. Some were encouraging him to take the trip, to take a chance, others were cautioning him against making any hasty decisions, and a few—like Jake—were keeping their thoughts and opinions to themselves.

"Let us know what you decide to do," Nat said, ready to move on.

"I will," Bill promised.

"Anyone else want to share anything?" she asked, her gaze moving around the circle.

Jake was sweating through his shirt, but his throat was as dry as the desert. He shifted in his chair, the movement causing one of the metal legs to scrape against the floor.

Nat looked at him, silently encouraging.

"My name is Jake Kelly," he began, then had to pause to clear his throat. "I was a staff sergeant in the Marine Corps before I was sent home with my brain scrambled...

*He didn't talk for very long. He wasn't ready to tell this group of not-quite-strangers his deepest and darkest secrets, but it was a start. An important start, he acknowledged to himself. And hopefully the beginning of some real healing.*

When the meeting was finally over, he was more than ready to head to Diggers' for a drink—and to see Sky.

"Jake—"

He paused at the door when Nat called out to him.

"—can you hang on for just a sec?"

"Sure," he agreed, remaining where he was until she'd finished chatting with Geena Perrault.

"Do you need a ride home?" he asked when the other woman had gone, guessing that was why Nat had asked him to wait.

"Thanks, but Kevin's coming to get me." She glanced at her watch. "Very soon, in fact, so I'll make this quick."

He held out his hand, palm open and facing up.

She lifted a brow.

"I'm not going to get a gold star for speaking up in class tonight?"

"If I'm not mistaken, you already got a purple heart."

He narrowed his gaze. "How is it that you know things people don't tell you?"

"Because I know other people," she said. "And I ask the right questions."

"Well, since you apparently don't need a ride and I'm not getting a star, what did you want to talk to me about?"

"A partnership opportunity."

"I'm listening," he said, more wary than curious.

"I have a friend, Connie, who trains emotional support animals in Indiana—at least, she has for the past twelve years," Nat explained. "But now she and her husband are moving to Battle Mountain, so she's looking for a place to board and train the animals locally as well as someone to help her out. Since you have a fair amount of space at your ranch and time on your hands, I thought of you."

His immediate instinct was to say no without any questions asked, because a partnership sounded too much like a commitment and Jake wasn't ready to make a commitment to anyone or anything. But while he'd been telling himself that Haven was merely a detour on the map of his life, he'd been struggling for months—years—to find his own path again. And now he had to wonder...could this be it?

"I appreciate the thought," he said instead, perhaps a little surprised to realize it was true. "But I still don't know how long I'm going to stay in Haven."

"That's what you keep saying," she acknowledged. "In any event, you don't have to be here to rent your barn and yard to Connie."

"I'll think about it."

"But if you decide to stay," Nat continued, "you might actually enjoy working with her."

"Training dogs?" he said dubiously.

"You've done a decent job with Molly."

"Molly failed her training as a service dog. Actually, she didn't even get that far. She failed the test to get into training."

"The standards for service animals are much higher, the requirements much stricter," she pointed out. "Emotional support animals are companions that provide support and comfort."

Exactly what Molly did for him.

And the more he thought about it, the more intrigued he was by the idea of helping others in similar situations find pets that could help them.

"When is your friend moving to Nevada?"

"Not until September. But she's going to be in Battle Mountain next weekend, house hunting with her husband, if you want to meet her."

"I'll think about it," he said again.

Nat's smile was just a little bit smug. "I know you will."

## Chapter Fifteen

"Is this First Date, Take Two or Second Date, Take One?" Jake wondered aloud, as he tucked his shirt into his pants.

Molly didn't even lift her head off her paws, a sure sign that she was pouting. Obviously she'd figured out that he had plans for the evening that didn't include her.

"I'm leaning toward Second Date, Take One," he said. "And leaving the disaster that was First Date on the cutting room floor."

He turned away from the mirror to face the dog. "Stop sulking." But he did feel a little guilty that he was abandoning her to another night home alone. "You'll always be my best girl, but Sky looks much better in a dress."

Molly was unmoved by his platitudes.

"And maybe, if I don't freak out during Second Date, Take One, then Sky will come back here later. You'd like Sky to come for a visit, wouldn't you?"

That got a half-hearted tail wag.

Jake scratched behind her ears. "I'll try not to be too late," he promised.

Molly still didn't seem happy, but she rose to her feet and followed him to the door.

Tonight, Jake was picking Sky up at the Circle G. If she had any residual concerns about him meeting her family, she'd pretty much tossed them out the window by inviting him to be her date for a family wedding.

He pulled up close to the house and got out of his truck, inexplicably nervous. Sky opened the door before he could knock. Obviously she'd been watching for him, probably because she wasn't convinced that he'd actually show up. Truthfully, he'd had some moments of doubt himself, but not only was he there, he was on time and—

*Wow!*

Jake didn't know much about women's fashions, but he knew what looked good—and Sky looked *really good*.

She was wearing a halter dress made of some kind of flowy material in a deep blue color that brought out the blue in her eyes. The strappy silver sandals on her feet added several inches to her height, so that her mouth—shiny with pink gloss—was almost level with his. Her hair was up—no doubt in deference to the heat—and glittery blue stones dangled from her ears.

"You told me about the length of the skirt," he acknowledged. "But you didn't warn me that my heart would go into palpitations when I saw you wearing it."

"Then I guess it's lucky for you that I know CPR," she told him.

"Maybe you could start with some mouth-to-mouth," he suggested.

"Like this?" she said, and brushed her lips lightly over his.

"That's a good start," he agreed, drawing her into his embrace.

His hand skimmed upward, over the silky fabric—and even silkier skin bared by the low back of her dress—to cup her head, adjusting the angle and deepening the kiss. Her lips parted willingly, her tongue dancing and dallying with his. Her scent, something soft and floral, teased his nostrils and clouded his mind.

"I think your heart is just fine," Sky said, when she'd finally pulled back and taken a moment to draw air into her lungs. "And if we don't get going, we're going to be late."

"You really want to go to this thing?" he asked, more resigned than enthused about their plans.

"Considering that 'this thing' is my brother's wedding, yeah," she said. "Plus, we had a deal."

"I know," he admitted. "But now that I see you in that dress, I really want to get you out of it."

She brushed another quick kiss on his lips. "Later."

He knew that word was as good as a promise.

Because even after five weeks, the passion between them had yet to dim. He wasn't convinced that it could last, and he was certain there would come a time when really great sex wouldn't be enough, when she would want more. And Jake wasn't sure that he was capable of giving her any more—no matter how much he might want to.

He pushed those uneasy thoughts aside for now and turned his truck in the direction of the Silver Star. "Is it true that Caleb and Brielle split up shortly after their wedding, eight years ago, because your grandfather had a heart attack when he found out?"

"Not my grandfather, Brielle's grandfather—who's also Ashley's grandfather," she noted.

"That's right. She told me that part of the story," he remembered. "So is the grandfather going to be there today?"

"Not only will he be there, he's hosting and paying for the whole thing," Sky told him.

"Really?"

She nodded. "I think he feels guilty for driving a wedge between them all those years ago and this is his way of trying to make up for it." She gestured to a laneway ahead. "That's the Silver Star."

Jake put his indicator on and made the turn into the long drive.

He understood that this formal reception acknowledging the marriage of Brielle Channing and

Caleb Gilmore was a big deal because of the acrimonious history between the families. He hadn't realized that it was going to be such a big event. Based on the quantity of vehicles that lined either side of the laneway and the number of people milling about, he would guess that half the town was in attendance.

Sky must have been taken aback by the size of the gathering, too, because she said, "We don't have to stay all night."

He nodded. And while he appreciated her willingness to accommodate his limitations, this was something he wanted to do for her. Because it was important to her and she was important to him.

As they made their way through the crowd, Jake was surprised to realize that he'd already been introduced to a fair number of the guests in attendance.

Sky's sister, Katelyn, was actually the first person he'd met in town, as her office had been his first stop to get the keys to his uncle's house when he arrived. He hadn't known then that the attorney was married to the sheriff, or that they had a daughter—the little girl who'd shown him her starfish pose at the community center.

Liam was the next oldest, after Kate. Sky had mentioned that Liam and his wife Macy had three kids. She hadn't mentioned that they were triplets. As if chasing after three toddlers didn't keep the couple busy enough, he learned that Macy also managed the day-to-day operations of the Stagecoach Inn while

Liam helped his father and brother keep everything running smoothly at the Circle G.

After Liam was Sky, then Caleb. He'd been the youngest of Dave Gilmore's offspring for a long time, until they'd discovered that Valerie Blake's daughter, Ashley, was their half sister.

In addition to her siblings and their spouses and kids, Jake was introduced to Sky's father and stepmother, her grandparents and various aunts, uncles and cousins, some having come from fair distances to share in the celebration.

"I can't believe how completely they managed to transform a horse paddock into the perfect venue for a wedding reception," Sky remarked to him.

As it was his first visit to the Silver Star, Jake couldn't remark on the transformation, but he had to admit the setting was nice. Everywhere he looked, there were buckets overflowing with greenery and white blooms. Fence rails had been draped with evergreen boughs decorated with more white flowers and bows. Bistro lights were strung overhead to illuminate the temporary dance floor when it got dark, and nearby was the food tent, reputed to contain long tables with an abundance of hot and cold foods, layered trays of sweets and cookies, a champagne fountain, kegs of beer and coolers filled with sodas and juice pouches.

But before Jake and Sky could get close enough to check it out, they were cut off by Ashley.

"Hurry," she urged, directing them toward rows

of chairs set up facing a gazebo. "The ceremony's about to start."

"Ceremony?" Sky echoed.

Her sister rolled her eyes. "This is a wedding, you know."

The bride wore a floor-length vintage lace wedding dress with cap sleeves, a wreath of flowers on her head and cowboy boots on her feet. Her groom was in a Western tux complete with cowboy hat and boots. And as Brielle Channing and Caleb Gilmore renewed their vows in front of their families and friends—including their infant son, Colton, who watched from the arms of his maternal great-grandfather—there was no doubt that love had finally triumphed over the feud between their families.

"I'm sorry," Sky whispered. "I really thought this was just supposed to be a party in celebration of their marriage, not an actual exchange of vows."

"I'm not freaking out," Jake assured her. "Well, not because your brother and his bride are making promises about forever, anyway."

Sky linked their fingers together and squeezed his hand. "Everyone will spread out after the ceremony. Well, they'll make a beeline for the food, and then they'll spread out."

They were part of that beeline when the *I do*'s were finally done. After they'd filled their plates, they found an empty table tucked in the corner, but their solitude didn't last for long.

Liam wanted to dance with his wife, so he dumped

the triplets on "Auntie 'ky"—as Jake had heard Tessa call her. Thankfully, Ashley came over to help with Ava, Max and Sam, followed by Kate and Tessa, then Regan Neal, sister of the bride and wife of the deputy sheriff, joined them, adding two more babies— her twin daughters, Piper and Poppy—to the mix.

Jake pushed his chair back from the table, ostensibly to make room for the newcomers but also to give himself room to breathe.

"Everything okay?" Sky asked, perhaps concerned that he was going to bolt.

He nodded. "I'm just going to check out the desserts."

"Oh, you have to try the brownies," Regan told him.

"And the cheesecake bites," Kate said.

"Can you bring me a pineapple square?" Sky asked hopefully.

"If there are any left," Ashley said. "Grandma's pineapple squares never last long."

"I'll do my best," Jake promised, and made his escape.

Of course, checking out the desserts had been an excuse to get away from the table, but now that he had a mission, he was determined to track down a pineapple square for Sky.

Looking around the gathering, he had to wonder why she'd invited him to come. She certainly didn't need him there to keep her company, surrounded as she was by family.

And kids.

There were a lot of kids running around.

A lot of babies being cuddled and kissed.

Watching her with her nieces and nephews, it was readily apparent that they adored her as much as she adored them.

It was equally obvious to Jake that she was the type of woman who was meant to have a family of her own.

The idea shouldn't have made his chest feel tight. He didn't have to worry that she had expectations of a future or a family with him. They both knew that whatever this thing was between them, it was only temporary.

Except that it didn't feel temporary when he was with her.

Dalton Butler, another regular at the Wednesday night veterans' group, had talked about the difficulties of going home after being deployed, the challenges of trying to fit into a life that no longer fit him after everything he'd seen and done.

Jake could relate to what he'd said. He'd felt the same way in San Diego.

But here it was different. In Haven, he felt as if he could start again with a clean slate.

And when he was with Sky, there was nowhere else that he wanted to be.

Sky was alone with Colton when Jake finally returned, not just with one pineapple square but a whole plate of them.

"They were restocking the tray when I got there," he told her.

"And since everyone else is gone, I don't have to share," she said, gleefully reaching toward the plate.

"How about sharing with the guy who battled back hordes of salivating wedding guests to bring them to you?" he suggested.

"I guess I could share with him," she agreed, holding a square close to his mouth.

He bit into the pastry, his lips closing around her fingertips, suckling on them gently.

"Don't you go getting me all stirred up when I'm sitting here with a baby in my arms," she said.

He grinned, unrepentant. "Do you stir up so easily?"

"All you have to do is look at me," she confided.

"I want to do more than look—I want to dance with you."

"Really?"

"Really."

"In that case, let's polish off our dessert, find another babysitter for Colton and hit the dance floor."

Valerie scooped Colton out of her arms before Sky could even ask if her stepmother wanted to look after the baby for a while. Sky knew that her father's wife had been disappointed that she'd only ever had one child of her own—and she was overjoyed that her marriage to David Gilmore had given her lots of grandchildren to love and spoil.

While Sky was talking to her dad and his wife,

she noticed that Jake was in conversation with Reid by the bar. On her way to meet up with her date, she stopped to chat briefly with her cousin Haylee, visiting from California, and when she turned around again, she saw that her date had been waylaid by the groom. With a shrug, she headed for the bar to get a glass of wine—and have a little chat with her brother-in-law, who was standing on the periphery of the crowd, sipping his beer.

"I saw you talking to Jake a little while ago," she noted. "What was that about?"

"I wasn't giving your date a hard time," he promised. "I just wanted to let him know that we'd arrested the motorcyclists who'd been racing on the highway."

"You were able to identify them?"

"Thanks to Jake."

"What did he have to do with it?" she asked curiously.

"He's the one who gave us a description of the drivers, their bikes and partial plate numbers."

Obviously he was more observant than she, because Sky had only seen a blur when she'd been pressed up against Jake's truck. Or maybe it was the presence of the man that had made it difficult for her to focus on anything else.

"That's good then," Sky remarked.

"What isn't good is that you didn't tell me about your close encounter with the reckless trio," Reid said.

"I didn't see the point when there was nothing I could add. Everything happened so fast."

"Regardless, I don't want you to ever hold out on me again," he admonished sternly.

"Or what?" she couldn't resist challenging.

Her brother-in-law didn't hesitate to bring out the big guns. "Or I'll tell your sister."

"No more holding out," she promised.

"One more thing," he began.

She eyed him warily over the rim of her glass as she sipped her wine. "What's that?"

"She likes him."

"Who likes whom?"

"Katelyn likes Jake," he clarified. "And she's generally a good judge of character."

Sky smiled then and kissed her brother-in-law's cheek. "Good to know, because I like him, too."

"I didn't think I was ever going to get you alone," Jake said, as he moved with Sky on the dance floor.

"You haven't had a horrible time tonight, have you?"

"It hasn't been horrible at all," he assured her.

"Good."

"But this part is definitely my favorite. I like the way you feel in my arms."

She tipped her head back to smile at him. "That's convenient, because I like being in your arms."

"Of course, naked in my arms would be even better."

"Hold on to that thought for just a little while longer."

"I've been holding onto it all night. It's the only reason I'm still here."

"I know this isn't easy for you," she said. "And I hope you know that I'm grateful you agreed to come with me today."

"I'm not sure your father approves of me being here."

"Did he say something to you?"

"No words are needed when I can see him glowering from clear across the paddock."

"That's not personal," she assured him, as the last bars of the song they'd been dancing to faded into the night.

The tempo of the music immediately changed, and the dance floor was suddenly packed with bodies twisting and gyrating.

Jake backed away from the crowd and closed his eyes.

*"Let the air fill your chest..."*

"Jake?"

*"...hold it there..."*

Sky slid her hand down his arm, uncurled his fingers to link them with her own.

*"...then slowly let it out again."*

"Are you okay?"

He managed to nod.

He was okay, it was just a lot of noise and a lot of people.

But he needed to get out of here.

There was too much noise.

Too many people.

He needed to be alone.

Sky squeezed his hand gently, reminding him of her presence.

And when he looked at her, everything and everyone else faded away, making him realize that he didn't really want to be alone—he wanted to be alone *with her*.

"Are you ready to go?" she asked.

He nodded. "I'm sorry, I just—"

She lifted her free hand and touched her fingers to his lips, silencing his explanation. "I'm ready to go, too."

Sky didn't worry about saying goodbye, even to the bride and groom. After all, they were celebrating the beginning of their happily-ever-after and she was still looking for hers.

Was she foolish to think that she might find it with Jake? To believe that he might finally be the man who could love her enough to want to stay with her?

She knew it was too soon to be making declarations or dreaming of a future for them, especially when he wasn't even ready to call her his girlfriend. But she felt as if they'd made definite progress tonight.

And the night wasn't close to being done.

Of course, they first had to spend some time fussing over Molly when they got back to his place. But Sky didn't mind one bit. Over the past several weeks, she'd fallen in love with the dog right along with the man.

*Too soon*, she reminded herself sternly.

When they finally made it to his bedroom, Sky unhooked the fastening of her halter and wiggled out of the dress so that she was standing in front of him wearing only a teeny tiny bra and even tinier panties in matching ice-blue lace.

"I'm having those heart palpitations again," he warned.

"You better lie down—" she pushed him back, so that he fell on top of the bed "—and let me take care of you."

He shifted up on the mattress and she straddled his hips with her knees.

"Did I ever tell you how glad I was that you ran out of gas that day?"

She chuckled as she unfastened the buttons that ran down the front of his shirt. "You think I ended up in your bed because you played Good Samaritan?"

"That role seemed to appeal to you more than that of sullen stranger," he noted.

"You only think so," she told him, opening his shirt to run her hands over the rippling muscles of his chest and stomach. "The truth is, the first time that sullen stranger walked into Diggers', I knew that I wanted him."

"The first time?" he said skeptically.

She nodded. "Oh, yeah. The moment our eyes locked, my heart started to pound inside my chest and I thought, he's the one who will finally end my extended period of celibacy."

"When I saw you, I thought, 'This woman is going to be trouble.'"

She paused with her hand on his belt. "You said something along those lines before you kissed me the first time," she recalled.

"What I didn't know then was that you'd be worth every minute of it."

"As long as you know it now," she said, and lowered her head to kiss him.

He let her be in control for about two minutes, then he flipped her onto her back, quickly discarded the rest of his clothes and lowered himself over her.

Now *he* kissed *her*, and it was long and slow and deep. Then he skimmed his mouth over her jaw… down her throat…and lower to nuzzle the hollow between her breasts.

His shadowed jaw rasped against her tender flesh, making her shiver. Then his lips found her nipple, and the shocking contrast of his hot mouth on her cool skin made her gasp, made her yearn.

As his mouth continued to taste and tease her breasts, his thumbs hooked the sides of her panties, tugging them over her hips and down her legs. He nudged her thighs apart and his thumbs glided over the slick flesh at her core, parting the folds, seeking and finding the center of her feminine pleasure.

She was quivering with want, with need, when he finally reached for the square packet on the bedside table to sheath himself before burying himself deep inside her.

From the beginning, there had been passion between them. But now, in addition to that passion, there was tenderness and affection. He held her hands above her head, their fingers entwined, as their bodies moved together in a sensual rhythm as old as time, pushing them ever closer to the pinnacle of pleasure—and over the edge. And he captured her mouth again as he found his release.

If she'd been thinking clearly—if she'd been able to think *at all*—she wouldn't have said it. She would have clenched her jaw tight and pressed her lips together to hold back the words. But her brain was pleasantly fuzzy in the aftermath of passion and her heart was so full that the words just slipped out, a whisper against his lips: "I love you, Jake."

The words filled Jake with equal parts joy and terror.

And while he couldn't deny that he'd developed strong feelings for Sky during the time that they'd been together, he was still reluctant to trust that what they had together was real. Afraid that he would somehow end up hurting her without ever intending to. And even more afraid that Sky might wake up one morning and discover that he wasn't really what she wanted or needed—and that he never would be.

So he didn't respond to her announcement except to ask, "Will you stay with me tonight?"

## Chapter Sixteen

Sky hadn't expected a reciprocal declaration. Well, maybe there was a tiny part of her that had *hoped* Jake might have come to the realization over the past five weeks that he was in love with her, too. But she understood that he was wary of getting involved and his heart was still healing. Not just from the loss of the men who had been like brothers to him—although that scar was undoubtedly the deepest, but also the abandonment by his fiancée and the lack of support from his father, who she thought should have been his staunchest ally.

But his family was his to figure out. She just hoped he knew that she had his back. Wherever. Whenever.

And maybe he did know, because when he awoke in the night, sweaty and shaking, he reached for her.

Of course, he had to reach over Molly, who'd jumped up onto the mattress as soon as Jake started muttering and thrashing. Sky didn't object to the Lab's presence because she knew Molly was looking out for her master, and the dog retreated to her own bed again as soon as she knew he was okay.

And then Sky used her hands and lips and body to show him the truth and depth of the feelings in her heart.

When Jake awoke in the morning with Sky in his arms, he had the strangest sensation inside his chest. A sense of belonging, as if he was exactly where he needed to be. That with Sky, he hadn't just found home but peace.

Except that it was crazy to be planning a future with a woman just because he'd managed to sleep through the night with her in his bed.

*I love you, Jake.*

The words she'd whispered to him echoed in his head, tempting him with possibilities and promises.

But he'd heard those words before.

He'd even let himself believe them.

Sky wasn't Margot—he knew that. And he couldn't help but wonder how things might be different now if he'd met her first. If he'd known her before his life had fallen apart.

*She* wouldn't have stopped loving him.

He knew her well enough now to be certain of

that. Sky was smart and strong, sexy and fun, loving and compassionate and fiercely loyal.

She was everything any man could ever want in a woman.

But he wasn't worthy of her love.

Not now.

Maybe not ever.

Jake was already up and cooking breakfast when Sky made her way to the kitchen.

"I could get used to waking up to this," she said.

Right away, she realized her mistake.

The stiff smile that curved Jake's lips turned into something that more closely resembled a grimace before he turned away to fill a mug with coffee for her.

"Thanks," she said.

He nodded.

"You look like you were out running already this morning," she said, searching for a neutral topic of conversation.

"Yeah. Now that the warmer weather's here, it gets too hot for Molly later in the day," he said. "And we're usually up early, anyway." He gestured toward the table with the spatula in his hand. "Have a seat. This is just about ready."

She sat, and he put a plate of sausages and eggs in front of her.

"So is it confirmed that your brother's coming to town next weekend?" she asked, as she picked up her fork and poked at her eggs.

Jake nodded as he settled across from her.

"I'm scheduled to talk to the seventh and eighth graders about online safety at the elementary school on Friday, but other than that, I'm available whenever you want me to meet him."

"Actually, I've been thinking about what you said, and I've decided that you're probably right."

"Words I always like to hear," she said lightly. "But maybe you could be a little more specific."

"I should be honest with Luke."

She nodded slowly. "I did say that."

"And you were right. It's past time to stop pretending and own up to what my life really is."

"Your life is nothing to be ashamed of, Jake."

"It's nothing to be particularly proud of, either."

"I guess we'll have to agree to disagree about that," she said. "Because I truly believe you should be proud of not just who you are and what you've done in the past, but everything you're doing now."

"I'm not really doing anything now."

"No? Because it looks to me like your uncle's workshop is undergoing another transformation."

"A friend of Nat's is looking for a place to board and train emotional support animals," he acknowledged. "I'm just trying to see if the space would be suitable for her needs."

"Oh," she said, feeling not just deflated but annoyed with herself for getting her hopes up.

Jake cut off a bite of sausage and popped it into his mouth.

Sky pushed her eggs around some more. "So...

when am I going to get to meet your brother?" she finally asked.

"I don't know what Luke's plans are for his visit. We might not be able to coordinate schedules."

"Now I get it," she said. "This sudden urge to be honest with him is a way of cutting me right out of the picture."

He didn't even deny it. "I'm trying to do what's best for you, Sky. And if we keep doing this...if we continue spending time together..."

"Spending time together?" she echoed, stunned. "Is that all this has been to you?"

"You have to know that I care about you, but—"

"I *love* you, Jake. Maybe I didn't intend to let those words slip out last night, but I'm not sorry they did. I'm tired of trying to deny what's in my heart and hiding the truth of my feelings so I don't scare you away."

"I *am* scared," he admitted. "Mostly of the possibility that I'll end up hurting you."

"Newsflash, Jake—if you didn't want to hurt me, you wouldn't be dumping me without giving our relationship a real chance."

"I'd only end up hurting you more if I tried to be the man you want and need."

"You *are* the man I want and need," she insisted.

He shook his head. "I told you from the beginning that I was a bad bet."

"I didn't believe it then and I don't believe it now," she said.

But it was obvious to Sky that *he* believed it, and she knew that no one but Jake could change that.

She pushed her chair away from the table and carried her plate to the sink.

"Please, Sky…"

"What?" she demanded, when he faltered. "Please, Sky, *what*?"

He only shook his head.

Molly, sensing the tension between her two favorite people, whined plaintively.

The sound squeezed Sky's already bruised heart.

"That's the problem," she said. "You don't know what you want. Or maybe you do know but you're afraid to admit it. Afraid to take a chance on everything I'm offering."

She slid her feet into her sandals and grabbed her purse.

"When you figure it out, you know where to find me."

Sky hated being a fool.

But it wasn't the first time and, considering her track record with men, it probably wouldn't be the last. And while it sucked that she couldn't seem to make a romantic relationship succeed, she had a good life. She had her friends and her family and work that she enjoyed—and maybe it was time to reconnect with some of those friends.

Alyssa Channing was first on the list. They'd chatted briefly at the wedding about rescheduling their aborted lunch from several weeks back, but now they actually did so.

"It's so good to finally be able to sit down and catch up with you," Alyssa said, after the waitress had delivered their meals to the table the following Saturday afternoon.

"It's been a crazy busy summer."

And so much had happened since the last time she was here with Alyssa—the same day that she'd run out of gas on her way home after meeting with Jodie. The same day Jake had come to her rescue and she'd ended up back at his house. In his bed.

Had it only been six weeks?

Had she really fallen in love so quickly?

"Tell me all about it," Alyssa urged. "And don't spare any of the sexy details about your military man."

"Actually, that's old news," she said. "I'm not seeing Jake anymore."

Her friend winced. "I'm sorry."

Sky waved a hand dismissively. "Let's not waste our time talking about it."

"Your call," Alyssa assured her. "But I should warn you that he just walked into the restaurant."

Of course, Sky had to look.

And as her gaze met Jake's across the room, she silently berated herself for not considering the possibility that their paths might cross this weekend. Jake didn't venture into town very often, but she should have expected that he'd take his brother out for a meal while Luke was in town. And since dining options in Haven were limited, she should have anticipated that they'd end up at Diggers'.

"Do you want me to ask Geena for takeout containers?" Alyssa said. "It's a nice day for a picnic in the park."

Sky shook her head. "No, this is good," she lied. "But it is a nice day, so we could take Lucy to the park for a walk after lunch."

"And maybe stop at Scoops for ice cream on the way?" her friend suggested hopefully.

"Definitely."

And if Sheila Enbridge, the proprietor, wanted to speculate that Sky Gilmore was soothing her broken heart with three scoops of chocolate fudge brownie supreme, she really didn't care.


Jake couldn't finish his lunch and get out of Diggers' fast enough.

The whole time he was eating food he didn't remember ordering and couldn't taste, he cursed himself for not foreseeing that he might run into Sky at the restaurant where she worked.

True, she worked on the bar side and she hadn't actually been working, but he should have anticipated the possibility.

*If you realize you've let your guard down, it's already too late.*

"For someone who's been here almost five months, you haven't really made yourself at home," Luke remarked when they were back at the house.

"Why do you say that?"

His brother gestured to the kitchen walls. "If this was my place, those flowers would have been the first thing to go."

"I thought about it," Jake said. "But I wasn't sure how long I was going to stay and I didn't want to start any major renovation projects that I wasn't going to stick around to finish."

"And now?" Luke asked.

He shrugged. "I'm still not sure how long I'm going to stay."

He only wished he had somewhere else to go.

Somewhere he wouldn't be assailed by thoughts and memories of Sky every way he turned.

"Well, at least Uncle Ross finally updated some of the furnishings." Luke ran a hand over the smooth wood surface of the kitchen table. "He did really good work, didn't he?"

"Actually, I made that table," Jake told him.

His brother's brows lifted. "Guess you were paying attention when he was showing us how to use all those fancy tools."

"I didn't remember much," Jake said. "The table's a pretty basic design."

"Basic or not, it looks great." Luke put both palms flat on the top and pushed forward and back, then grinned at his brother. "Just checking to see if it's level."

"Might be that both the table and the floor aren't," Jake said.

His brother chuckled. "I'm going to be honest, when Mom first told me that you were going to be staying here awhile, I didn't think it was a good idea. But maybe I was wrong. Maybe this is the right place for you right now."

"I thought maybe it was, too. But now I'm not so sure."

"Your doubts have anything to do with the attractive brunette you kept stealing glances at during lunch?" his brother guessed.

"Yeah," he admitted.

"So why didn't you introduce me to her?"

"Because I screwed up—just like I always do."

"I would have liked to meet her, but not making an introduction is hardly a screwup."

"No, I meant that I *screwed up*," he said again, with emphasis this time.

Understanding flashed across his brother's expression. "Ah. Now I get it. But maybe you could fill in some details for me?"

Jake shook his head. "You're only here for a couple of days, and it would take longer than that to explain."

"So buy her some flowers and tell her you're sorry," Luke suggested.

"Does that work with Raina?" he wondered.

"Sometimes," his brother said.

"What do you do the other times?"

Luke grinned. "R-rated stuff in the bedroom."

Jake winced. "TMI."

"You asked."

"My mistake."

"So start with flowers," his brother urged.

"She deserves someone better than me."

"I'm probably a little biased," Luke admitted. "But I don't know anyone better than you."

"A former Marine with PTSD and no career prospects?"

"A decorated veteran who's steering his life in a new direction."

"That's a good spin," Jake acknowledged.

"I don't know how I'd cope if I didn't have Raina and the kids to go home to, and I've never had to deal with anything as up close and personal as you did," his brother said. "What happened to your team would have messed up anyone, and sometimes even having family to ground you isn't enough."

Then Luke slid a business card across the table.

"What's this?" Jake asked.

"It's the number for a residential treatment facility specializing in PTSD."

"You've been asking around for help for your crazy brother?"

"No." Luke held his gaze. "I asked my therapist if she knew of any good programs in this area."

Jake frowned at that. "Since when do you have a therapist?"

"Since about six years ago," Luke said.

"For real?"

His brother nodded.

"How did I not know this?"

"Because it's not the type of thing we talk about."

Jake wasn't sure if the "we" was intended to refer

to their family or veterans, but he could acknowledge that both interpretations were equally applicable.

"It was Raina's idea," Luke told him now. "When I came back from my third—or maybe it was my fourth—deployment, she suggested that talking to someone about my experiences might help me transition back to civilian life."

"Did it?"

His brother shrugged. "It doesn't hurt."

"Six years?" Jake looked at his brother again for confirmation. *"Really?"*

Luke nodded. "I talk to her about once a month, if I'm in town. More often if necessary. And Raina and I go together a couple times a year."

"Why didn't you ever tell me?"

"Because I didn't want you to know. I didn't want anyone to know. But I've realized that pretending everything is okay doesn't make it so, and healing is an ongoing process.

"No one expects that a thirty-day program is going to miraculously stop the nightmares and flashbacks or make you let go of your guilt and grief. But it just might help you learn to live with it and move on with your own life. Maybe even with the brunette from the restaurant."

Jake shook his head, refusing to be tempted by the prospect. "She deserves someone who doesn't have to deal with that kind of stuff."

"Maybe she does," Luke agreed. "But from where I was sitting, I'd guess the woman wants *you*."

* * *

Jake's brother left Haven on Sunday.

Sky was aware of his departure because she saw his truck in Jake's driveway when she drove past on her way to the Trading Post just after lunch, but it was gone when she returned home a short while later.

Jake's truck had been missing, too, though she'd let herself believe he was only running an errand. But when she passed his house again the following day, she realized he was gone—and she suspected that he wasn't coming back.

It wasn't just that the driveway was empty, it was that his house looked closed up. Abandoned. Lonely.

That was kind of how she felt, too.

"Why do I always put my faith in the wrong people?" Sky asked her sister, over coffee and donuts the following Sunday morning.

"Are we talking about any wrong people in particular?" Kate asked.

She nodded. "Jake Kelly."

Her sister seemed surprised. "Watching the two of you together at Caleb and Brielle's wedding reception, it looked like things were going well."

"I thought so, too," Sky said.

"What happened?"

"I don't know." Then she sighed. "Or maybe I do know."

"If you want me to commiserate and empathize, I'm going to need a little more information than that," Kate said.

"We had a great time that night. Actually, we had a lot of great times over the past few weeks, but now..." she blinked back the tears that stung her eyes "...now he's gone."

"Where'd he go?"

Sky shook her head. "I don't know."

"He didn't tell you?"

"He didn't even say goodbye."

Her sister responded to that with a single word that questioned Jake's parentage.

"Ba-turd," Tessa echoed.

Kate winced. "Oh, that one's going to come back to bite me."

"Ba-turd," the little girl said again, confirming her mother's prediction.

"Come here, Tessa." Sky patted her knee.

Her niece climbed up and immediately reached for the cell phone Sky had pulled out of her pocket. She pointed to the screen.

"This is bat turd," she said, enunciating carefully. "In some places, it's used as a fertilizer to make flowers grow pretty."

"I 'ike fwowers."

"Do you think you could maybe draw me a picture of a flower?"

"O-kay," Tessa said, scrambling down from her aunt's knee to search for her crayons.

"You are a marvel," her sister said to Sky. "And he obviously has no idea what he walked away from."

"I feel so lost, Kate. Lost and sad and confused and so many other emotions. All those times I cried over broken relationships… I don't think my heart has ever really been broken before. Not like this."

"Maybe because you were never all the way in love before," Kate suggested.

"What does it say about me that when I finally did fall, I picked a guy who couldn't love me back?"

"I wouldn't be so sure that he doesn't love you."

"He left," she said again. "Without a word."

"And for that he's flower fertilizer," her sister agreed, making Sky smile through her tears. "But without knowing why he left, you can't claim to know what's in his heart."

"That doesn't make me feel any better."

"I don't know if there's anything that will," Kate admitted. "And I can't think of anything to say that doesn't sound patronizing or cliché."

"Give me something," Sky pleaded.

"It will get better," her sister said. "Each day, it will be a little bit easier to get out of bed, to go on with your life without him."

"I know I can live without him," Sky said. "I just wish he'd given me the chance to show him how much better both our lives could be together."

"Do you want me to have Reid track him down and arrest him?"

"On what grounds?"

"Breaking and entering your heart?" Kate suggested.

Sky managed another smile. "A tempting thought, but no. Right now, I think the only thing worse than living with a broken heart would be for Jake to know that he broke my heart."

"Are you sure he's gone for good?"

"I'm not sure of anything," she admitted. "All I know is, one day he was here, the next day he was gone."

"And maybe tomorrow he'll be back."

But Sky wasn't going to let herself count on it.

"How are you doing?" Sky asked when she met Jenny at the courthouse the following Thursday morning.

"I'm scared," the other woman said. "Not of Darren as much as everything else that's going to happen."

"That's understandable," she said. "But I'm going to be here with you. If you have any questions about anything, ask."

"I feel like such an idiot."

"You're not an idiot," Sky said firmly.

"But I let him do it for so long… Do you think the judge will believe I liked being hit?"

"No, I don't think the possibility will even cross the judge's mind."

"He—Darren—" Jenny clarified "—said that if I ever told, people would think that I liked it."

"He only said that because he didn't want you to tell," Sky reminded her.

Jenny nodded. "I wish I had a lawyer. I know you said I should get one, but Darren closed out all the accounts, so I have no money. My parents offered to help, but they don't have a lot of money, either, and they're already doing so much for me."

"You do have a lawyer," Sky said, watching her sister walk into the courtroom. "In fact, here she is now."

Jenny followed the direction of Sky's gaze, but she still looked confused when the introductions were made.

"I appreciate you being here," she said to Kate. "But I can't afford a lawyer."

"I'm taking your case pro bono," the attorney said. "That means you don't have to pay for my legal services."

"But why would you do that?" Jenny wondered.

"I have a full-service practice with a lot of clients who can pay, and that allows me to help other clients who can't."

"I don't know how to thank you," Jenny said. Then her gaze shifted to Sky. "Either of you."

"There is one thing you can do for me," Sky said.

"What's that?"

"Go back to school and get that teaching certificate you always wanted."

"You don't think I'm too old?" Jenny asked, half skeptical and half hopeful.

"It's never too late to follow your dreams," Sky told her.

"That's good advice," Kate said, looking at her sister. "For all of us."

## Chapter Seventeen

"Get your head in the game, Gilmore."

Caleb's sharp rebuke snapped Sky back to the present.

"What?"

Her brother shook his head. "You're on deck."

"Oh." She swapped her baseball cap for a batting helmet and jumped up from the bench to head toward the on-deck circle, grabbing her favorite bat on the way. She took her position and gave a practice swing.

Joel Rosenthal hit a line drive straight into the second baseman's mitt for the third out of the inning.

Sky leaned her bat against the fence and caught the glove that her brother tossed to her. She traded the batting helmet for her ball cap again and jogged out to her usual position on third base.

"Head in the game," Caleb reminded her, as he moved past her to left field.

She pushed her preoccupation aside and focused her attention on the batter stepping up to the plate.

A walk-off two-run homer resulted in a 5–4 loss for Diggers' in their second game of the round-robin tournament leading up to the Heritage Day Slo-Pitch Charity Championship. It was their first loss—and not Sky's fault in any way—but she knew that, depending on the scores of the other games, it might be enough to jeopardize their appearance in the championship.

"Everything okay with you?" Caleb asked as they were packing up after the game.

"Sure," she replied, not looking at him. "Why do you ask?"

"You seemed a little distracted tonight."

"I've just got a lot on my mind."

"Anything you want to talk about?"

She shook her head.

"Work stuff?" he guessed.

It was a believable excuse—and certainly easier than acknowledging the truth—so she nodded. Because she didn't want to admit to her brother, or even herself, that she couldn't stop thinking about Jake. Wondering where he was and what he was doing. Because it was pathetic to want a man who didn't want her, and the fact that he'd left town was a pretty clear indication that Jake didn't want her.

She impulsively hugged her brother.

"What was that for?" Caleb asked warily.

"For being you."

"The most amazing brother in the world, you mean?"

"And because I'm grateful to know that you'll always be in my corner, no matter what."

"Always," he confirmed.

The championship game of the Heritage Day Slo-Pitch Charity Championship was at three o'clock the following Saturday afternoon. Despite their earlier loss in the round-robin, Duke's Diggers advanced to the final against Sweet Caroline's Sweethearts—a group that was anything but a bunch of cream puffs.

It seemed to Sky as if the whole town had turned out to watch the big game, packed onto the bleachers or huddled along the sidelines in folding lawn chairs, their feet propped up on coolers.

The Gilmores were out en masse. Katelyn and Reid and Tessa; Liam and Macy with Ava, Max and Sam; Caleb's wife Brielle with baby Colton; her dad and Valerie; and Sky's grandparents. Duke was there, too, not only to cheer on his team but add coaching assistance at third base. In addition, she recognized several of the bar's regular customers: librarian Lara Reashore, theater owner Thomas Mann, and even Jo had entrusted her staff to watch over the pizza ovens so that she could take in at least part of the game.

It was a closely contested event—at least in the beginning. But the Diggers rallied for six runs in the bottom of the sixth, which put them ahead by five. And yet, Sky couldn't help but notice that Ashley didn't seem as excited by the prospect of victory as everyone else on their side of the diamond. Even when they held onto the lead until the final out, the scorekeeper's cheers were uncharacteristically subdued.

After the players had shaken hands and the championship trophy was presented, the field quickly emptied of players and spectators.

"What's wrong?" Sky asked, when most of her teammates had gone, leaving her alone in the dugout with her sister.

Ashley shook her head. "Nothing."

"I thought we had a deal, that you wouldn't say nothing when it's obviously something."

"It's my own fault, for expecting too much of people," her sister said unhappily.

"Anyone in particular?" Sky pressed.

Ashley started to shake her head again, then stopped. "Yes," she admitted. "But I don't want to talk about him."

"Ah," Sky said. "This is about a boy."

"No," her sister immediately denied. "Well, yes. But it's not who you think."

"We're not talking about Chloe's boyfriend's friend, the one you met at the movies?"

"No. It's… Jake."

"Jake?"

Her sister nodded. "I texted to tell him about the game today. I thought maybe he'd had enough time to realize how much he missed you and he'd come to watch and then you'd get back together."

Sky had to swallow around the lump that had risen in her throat. "Oh, Ashley."

"He didn't even reply to my message."

"I'm sorry."

"Why are *you* sorry? You didn't do anything wrong."

"I'm not sure Jake did anything wrong, either."

"How can you say that?" her sister demanded. "He left without even saying goodbye."

To Ashley, too, Sky realized now.

"I can say that because I know he's dealing with a lot of stuff right now—stuff that no one should have to deal with," she said gently.

"It doesn't matter," Ashley decided, but her tone told Sky that it mattered a lot.

"Okay," she agreed. "Just remember that I'm here if you ever want to talk."

"I know," her sister said. And then, more hesitantly, she added, "I'm here for you, too, if you ever want to talk. I know you probably think I'm just a kid, but I'm a pretty good listener."

"You are a pretty good listener," Sky said. "And a really great sister."

Ashley smiled at that.

Sky put her arm around her sister's shoulders. "Come on," she said. "Let's go celebrate our victory with a root beer."

The championship trophy was three feet of polished plastic, as gaudy as it was tall, but it came with bragging rights—at least until the season ended, when a new champion might potentially be crowned. The victors passed it around with the same reverence afforded the World Series trophy, and after all the players had had the opportunity for a photo with the Champions Cup, Duke took it back to the bar to put on display.

"What do you think?" the boss asked, as he pushed the liquor bottles on the top shelf to the sides, making space in the middle for the award.

"It looks good," Sky said approvingly from the other side of the counter. She glanced questioningly at Ashley, who nodded as she sipped her root beer.

"It sure looks a helluva lot better than you do," her boss remarked.

Sky lifted a hand to her swollen cheek. "Those leg guards that catchers wear are hard."

"We were up by five runs at that point," Duke pointed out as he wrapped some ice in a towel. "Why you felt the need to slide head-first into home plate instead of staying put on third—*like I told you*—is a mystery to me."

"I was safe at home," she reminded him.

"Yeah, you were safe," he grudgingly acknowledged, handing the towel across the bar to her.

She applied the ice to her cheek as Geena set two plates of burgers and fries in front of them. "Thanks."

"Are you girls going back to the park for the fireworks later?" Geena asked as Sky nibbled on a fry.

She shook her head. "After this, I'm going home to soak my weary muscles in the hot tub."

"But it's Heritage Day," Geena reminded them.

"A time to celebrate with friends and family and pyrotechnics in the sky."

Sky appreciated the sentiment, but she didn't really feel up to celebrating—especially when the one person she'd planned to *not* celebrate with was gone.

*Each day, it will be a little bit easier*, Katelyn had promised.

And, after three weeks, Sky was finally starting to think it might be true.

She still missed Jake. Every morning when she woke up, he was the first thought on her mind, and every night when she went to bed, he was the last. Wherever he was, she hoped he was doing okay, and that Molly was close by, watching over him.

It figured that just when Sky had finally stopped hoping Jake would walk through the door, he did so.

More than five weeks after he'd left town, on a Wednesday night at just about 9:55 p.m., he came into Diggers', took his usual seat at the bar and—casually, as if nothing had ever happened between them and he hadn't been gone for more than a month—ordered a draft beer.

Not a Sam Adams, though.

This time, he asked for a pint of Icky.

There were so many emotions warring inside her that Sky didn't know what she was feeling. Joy. Anger. Relief. Frustration. Love.

Taking her cue from him, Sky went through the motions, as if she was pouring a beer for any other customer on any other night. As if she hadn't given him her heart—and had her offering summarily rejected.

She shut off the tap and set the mug of beer on a paper coaster in front of him, pleased to note that her hands were steady though her insides were shaking like leaves in a hurricane-force gale. She had so many questions, about where he'd been—and about why he'd come back—but she didn't let herself ask them. She didn't let herself give him any hint of how much she'd missed him, though there was no denying that she had.

Jake didn't say anything, either, but he looked at her over the rim of the mug as he lifted it to his lips, and his gaze held hers for an endlessly long moment. She wished she could read his expression, but she'd never been able to guess what he was thinking and she didn't dare let herself speculate.

But she kept an eye on him while she continued to serve and chat with other customers at the bar. She didn't want to look away, for fear that if she let him out of her sight for a second, he'd disappear again.

Wherever he'd been and whatever he'd been doing for the past five weeks, he looked good. Really good.

Almost as if he'd been on vacation.

And maybe he had.

Maybe while she'd been miserably unhappy without him, he'd been frolicking in the sand on a tropical island with Molly.

Except that she didn't really think he was the frolicking type.

When he'd swallowed the last mouthful of beer,

Jake pulled his wallet out of his back pocket and set a ten-dollar bill on the bar beside the empty mug.

Her stomach tightened into painful knots as she braced herself to watch him push away from the bar and walk out the door.

She wanted to say something, but her throat was tight.

Her heart aching.

Was this really how it was going to be?

As if they were strangers all over again?

Courtney set her tray on the corner of the bar and read off her order pad: "I need a pint of Icky, a pitcher of Wild Horse with three glasses, a vodka martini, dirty, with two olives, and a Coke."

Sky busied herself getting the drinks.

She didn't look at the stool where Jake had been sitting, because she didn't want to watch him leave. Because she knew that it would rip her heart out of her chest again.

When Courtney's tray was loaded, she glanced down to the other end of the bar, to see if any of her other customers needed a refill.

Jake was still there.

Watching her.

She took a couple of steps in his direction, even as she cursed herself for being unable to stay away. When she was standing in front of him again, he placed a square velvet box on top of the money.

Sky just stared at it, her pulse racing.

She made no move to reach for the box, so Jake

opened the lid to reveal a square sapphire surrounded by diamonds and set on a platinum band.

The murmur of voices faded as the bar's other patrons abandoned their own conversations in favor of eavesdropping on the scene that was playing out before them.

Sky swallowed and tucked her hands into the front pockets of her jeans, resisting the urge to reach for the ring. "That's a heck of a tip."

"It's not a tip," Jake told her. "It's a proposal."

She looked at him then. "Is it?"

He nodded. "I know diamonds are traditional, but I thought the sapphire would suit you better."

"A proposal usually includes a question," Ellis Hagen pointed out from the other end of the bar.

"Sky knows I'm not good with words," Jake said.

And maybe she should snatch up the ring and the man, but after five weeks, she wanted more. She needed more. She needed to know that she mattered enough for him to make the effort.

"I think I deserve the words," she said to him now.

He nodded again. "You're right. You do. So how about if I start by telling you that I love you?"

She felt her throat tighten. "That's a pretty good start."

"A slow start, I'd say, if this is the first time you're saying the words," Gavin Virga chimed in.

Jake looked at Sky, his expression chagrined. "I obviously didn't think this through," he acknowledged. "Or I might have chosen a less public venue."

"But you're here now," Sky said, mentally crossing her fingers that he wouldn't walk out. "And the next round's on me if everyone else can shut up for five minutes and at least pretend to mind their own business."

"But this is so much more interesting," Doug Holland said.

Sky shot him a withering glance.

"Shutting up," he promised.

She turned back to Jake.

"It's true," he said to her now. "I love you. I don't know when or how it happened, but the more time I spent with you, the more I couldn't imagine my life without you. I didn't want to imagine a life without you in it.

"But I needed some time to get my life together before I could ask you to share it—because more than anything, what I want is to share my life with you. Because I love you, Sky, and I hope you still love me, too."

"I do," she confessed softly. "But I thought I'd freaked you out by telling you how I felt."

"What freaked me out was knowing how *I* felt," he confided. "Because I watched you with your family at the wedding, and I saw the closeness between you and your siblings, the way you dote on your nieces and nephews. And I knew you needed to be with someone who could give you a family of your own."

"What I need is to be with someone who loves me. And if, at some point down the road, we can work kids into that arrangement, that would be great. But if not, at least we'd be together."

"I want to give you everything you want," he said. "Everything you deserve. That's why I left."

"I'm confused," she admitted.

"You're not the only one," Jerry Tate remarked.

But Jake's gaze didn't shift from Sky's face. "I completed a thirty-day residential PTSD treatment program in Reno," he said, ignoring the other man's remark. "I needed to know that I could tackle my issues, to be worthy of you."

"You don't ever have to tackle anything on your own," Sky told him, coming around from behind the counter to take a seat beside him, wanting to ensure that this part of their conversation couldn't be overheard.

Though she would have liked to know where he was and what he was doing, she understood now why he'd kept that information to himself. That he'd probably had doubts, not just about the effectiveness of the program but his ability to stick with it.

And the realization that he'd not only sought treatment but completed a program brought on a whole new wave of emotions. Surprise. Gratitude. Happiness. Pride.

"How was it?" she asked gently.

"Brutal. Intense." He lifted his gaze to hers. "Life-changing."

"In a good way?" she asked cautiously.

"Yeah." He leaned closer and brushed his lips over hers in a gentle kiss. "In a very good way."

She smiled. "I'm glad."

"But I'm still a work in progress," he warned.

She knew that was true. She knew that he would likely battle the demons that haunted him for the rest of his life. But hopefully now he knew that he didn't have to battle alone. That if he let her, she'd gladly take up a sword and fight by his side—for Jake and their future together.

"I understand that you might not want to rush into setting a date or anything like that," he continued. "But I hope you'll at least agree to wear my ring on your finger, so you can look at it every day and know how much I love you even if I'm not always good at telling or showing you."

"You're doing just fine so far," she said, and held out her left hand.

"Is that a yes?"

"That's a very emphatic yes."

He removed the ring from the box and slid it on her third finger—to the accompaniment of cheers and applause around the room.

"Now kiss her," Ellis urged.

"Like you mean it this time," Gavin said.

Jake heeded their advice.

"What if I do want to rush into setting a date?" she asked, when he'd finally eased his lips from hers.

"You'd make me the happiest man in the world," he assured her.

"That's good," she said. "Because I don't want to wait to start the rest of my life with you. But there is one thing you might have to do first."

"Ask your father's permission?" he guessed.

"More like my sister's forgiveness," she said.

"I've already spoken to both of them," he told her.

Her brows lifted. "Before you came to see me?"

"I needed them in my corner in case I had to go to Plan B."

"What was Plan B?"

"Begging you to give me a second chance."

"I don't want you to beg," she said. "I just want you to love me."

"And I always will," he promised.

\* \* \* \* \*

# COMING SOON!

We really hope you enjoyed reading this book.
If you're looking for more romance, be sure to
head to the shops when new books are
available on

## Thursday 20th August

To see which titles are coming soon, please visit

**millsandboon.co.uk/nextmonth**

# MILLS & BOON

## Coming next month

### A WILL, A WISH, A WEDDING
#### Kate Hardy

'Miss Grey changed her will three months ago,' the solicitor confirmed, 'and she was of sound mind when she made her will.'

You could still be inveigled into doing something when you were of sound mind, Hugo thought. And Rosemary liked to make people happy. What kind of sob story had this woman spun to make his great-aunt give her the house?

'There are conditions to the bequest,' the solicitor continued. 'Dr Walters, you must undertake to finish the butterfly project, turn the house into an education centre — of which she would like you to assume the position of director, should you choose — and re-wild the garden.'

The garden re-wilding, Hugo could understand, because he knew how important his great-aunt's garden had been to her. And maybe the education centre; he'd always thought that Rosemary would've made a brilliant teacher. But, if Rosemary had left the house to his father, as her previous will had instructed, surely she knew that her family would've made absolutely sure her wishes were carried out? Why had his great-aunt left everything to a stranger instead? And he didn't understand the first condition. 'What project?'

'I'm editing the journals and co-writing the biography of Viola Ferrers,' Dr Walters said.

It was the first time he'd heard her speak. Her voice was quiet, and there was a bit of an accent that he couldn't quite place, except it was definitely Northern; and there was a lot of a challenge in her grey eyes.

Did she really think he didn't know who Viola Ferrers was?

'My great-great-great-grandmother,' he said crisply.

Her eyes widened, so he knew the barb had gone home. This was *his* family and *his* heritage. What right did this stranger have to muscle in on it?

'Miss Grey also specified that a butterfly house should be built,' the solicitor continued.

Rosemary had talked about that, three years ago; but Hugo had assumed that it was her way of distracting him, giving him something to think about other than the gaping hole Emma's death had left in his life. They'd never taken it further than an idea and a sketch or two.

'And said butterfly house,' the solicitor said, 'must be designed and built by you, Mr Grey.'

*Continue reading*
A WILL, A WISH, A WEDDING
Kate Hardy

*Available next month*
www.millsandboon.co.uk

# MILLS & BOON

## THE HEART OF ROMANCE

---

## A ROMANCE FOR EVERY KIND OF READER

---

**MODERN**

Prepare to be swept off your feet by sophisticated, sexy and seductive heroes, in some of the world's most glamourous and romantic locations, where power and passion collide.
**8 stories per month.**

**HISTORICAL**

Escape with historical heroes from time gone by. Whether your passion is for wicked Regency Rakes, muscled Vikings or rugged Highlanders, awaken the romance of the past.
**6 stories per month.**

**MEDICAL**

Set your pulse racing with dedicated, delectable doctors in the high-pressure world of medicine, where emotions run high and passion, comfort and love are the best medicine.
**6 stories per month.**

**True Love**

Celebrate true love with tender stories of heartfelt romance, from the rush of falling in love to the joy a new baby can bring, and a focus on the emotional heart of a relationship.
**8 stories per month.**

**Desire**

Indulge in secrets and scandal, intense drama and plenty of sizzling hot action with powerful and passionate heroes who have it all: wealth, status, good looks…everything but the right woman.
**6 stories per month.**

**HEROES**

Experience all the excitement of a gripping thriller, with an intense romance at its heart. Resourceful, true-to-life women and strong, fearless men face danger and desire - a killer combination!
**8 stories per month.**

**DARE**

Sensual love stories featuring smart, sassy heroines you'd want as a best friend, and compelling intense heroes who are worthy of them.
**4 stories per month.**

---

To see which titles are coming soon, please visit

**millsandboon.co.uk/nextmonth**

# MILLS & BOON
## MEDICAL
### *Pulse-Racing Passion*

Set your pulse racing with dedicated, delectable doctors in the high-pressure world of medicine, where emotions run high and passion, comfort and love are the best medicine.